DRAGON KNIGHT CHRONICLES

AWAKENING
THE

—— BOOK 1 ——

BLOOD CALLS

—— BOOK 2 ——

HUNTED
THE

—— BOOK 3 ——

SEARCH
THE

—— BOOK 4 ——

ANDREW WICHLAND

ACKNOWLEDGMENTS

Thanks go to
Lily of Partners In Crime for Editing and
Mara of Covered by the Rose for making the title pages

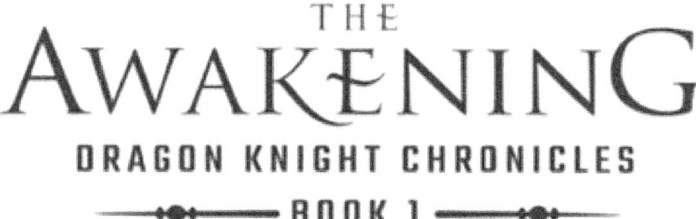

THE AWAKENING

DRAGON KNIGHT CHRONICLES

BOOK 1

Frail Hope

EIRIAN FLEW THROUGH the night as fast as her large wings would allow. As often as she could, she looked over her shoulder. In the moonlight behind her horned tail, she saw two figures flying after her. Even though they were still miles away, they were slowly catching up.

She turned her head back around, placed one of paws against her lower abdomen, and thought about her unborn children. Her wings were beginning to strain. As she flew above a sea of trees, a sharp pain raked through her lower abdomen.

"No, not now, it's too early; just a little longer, my children," she pleaded with them. However, the pain increased, and she faltered a little in her flight and ducked behind a hill.

Relieved to spot her destination, she began her descent into a clearing. She landed awkwardly on three paws, because the fourth paw clutched a box. Folding her wings, she surveyed the area. Trees of monstrous size surrounded her. A stone gateway was set about forty feet behind a smooth crystal, which was nearly ten feet in diameter. Along the edge of the crystal, lines of runes ran along the side. At the top, sides and the bottom four lines of runes crossed to meet at a circle in the middle.

Eirian quickly hopped forward to the crystal, arched her neck, and brought her head down. When she opened her mouth, fire shot from it, enveloping the crystal. Then she closed her mouth, stopped the bombardment of fire, and hopped back. Now the runes were shining like the moon. Five beams of light shot from the crystal to the stone gateway and ran along the inner frame. After a moment, the beams met at the center, and the gateway formed a light that flowed like water.

"We're almost out, my children; just a little longer," she said.

A fresh wave of pain ran through her body, and as fast as she could, she hopped forward on three legs and passed through the gateway. She emerged on a small mountainside on a different planet.

For the rest of the known Galaxy, the planet she was now on was known as Ta Jar. But like all planets that housed a non-magical settlement, it now had a different name. To all free people it was known as Amal.

Once again, trees filled the area, but she saw a small town in front of her. It appeared to be less than a mile away.

She collapsed onto her side and hummed a tune as her body began to change. Her forelegs and paws turned into arms and hands, while her hind legs and paws became legs and feet. Her spikes shrank into her body, and her horns disappeared into her skull, where light-brown hair flowed out. Her tail pulled into her spine, while her snout shrank and formed into a nose. Her scales turned into white skin, and her wings surrounded her and became a light-blue, flowing robe.

All the while, her body shrank in size until she was almost five times shorter in length and almost twelve times thinner than her true body. However, two things remained the same. Her swollen belly and her eyes were still as violet as her scales had been.

When the transformation was complete, Eirian stood up on her bare feet and looked down at the village. Holding onto her belly, and still clutching the gold-embroidered, wooden box, she started her descent.

How can humans stand just having two legs? she thought as she stumbled through the streets of the village. The moon was still out, and some of the villagers stared at her as she walked through the night.

Ignoring their looks, she quickly got out of the streets as hover cars went by. She stopped at a small, single-story, shingle-roofed house. The front of the house stood on stilts, and a small flight of steps led up to the porch. She stumbled up the steps and banged on the door. After several long moments, a light turned on inside, and a shadow moved under the door.

The door finally opened, revealing a woman who was struggling to pull on her bathrobe. She appeared to be of Asian descent, and Eirian guessed she was in her late twenties or early thirties. She wore a kind smile despite the fact she had clearly been woken in the middle of the night.

"May I help you?" the woman asked as she tied the sash. Seconds later, a man joined her at the door. He wore a pair of pajama pants, but his broad, muscular chest and arms were bare. He was also of Asian descent and was a head taller than the woman at his side.

"Chikako, who is it? It's almost one," said the man, but he stopped when he saw Eirian and his eyes went wide. "Eirian?" he muttered. The woman at his side looked at him.

"Jun, my old friend, I need your help," Eirian said. Then she fell, and Jun caught her before she hit the ground as another contraction went through her body.

The man brought her inside the house. He led her into the bedroom and helped her get settled on a sleeping mat.

"Who is this woman, Jun?" Chikako said.

"She's an old friend, Chikako. Now go wake the doctor. She's in labor," Jun said.

Eirian reached out and grabbed his arm tightly. "No . . . doctor . . . you . . . must . . . do . . . it . . ." she said through gritted teeth. Then she threw her head back in pain.

Jun looked at Eirian for a moment as she writhed on his bed. Then he turned to Chikako.

"Honey, get me a bowl of water, some string, scissors, clean washcloths, and soft blankets. Hurry!"

Chikako quickly left the room, and he turned back to Eirian. She gripped his hand tightly, and he said, "It'll be alright," but as another wave of pain engulfed her, she wasn't sure if his words were intended to reassure her or himself.

Almost four hours later, Eirian was drenched in sweat, and the lower part of her robe was soaked in both sweat and blood. Weakly, she leaned back on her elbows and then slowly reached out for her two sons and her daughter, whom Chikako wrapped in soft blankets. As she held them in her arms, tears ran down her face. She took a deep breath and then looked from her three children to her friend Jun and his wife, Chikako.

"They're beautiful, aren't they?" she asked them as she gazed at the babies.

"Just like their mother," Jun said, and Chikako nodded, smiling broadly.

"Jun, there is a particular reason I came to you and your wife," Eirian said. She tried to hide the desperation in her voice. "I must ask you something."

"What?" Jun asked. His expression showed he dreaded what she was going to say.

Trying to smile, she laid down her youngest two children and held out her first-born. "Raise my first-born as you would your own."

Before he could reply, she added, "My other son and daughter must be separated, too. Give my second- and third-born to trusted families in another village and give those friends the same instructions I will give you now. Don't tell any of the children they're one of three until they're ready to know."

She reached beside her for the wooden box and opened it. Inside were eight bracelets, each with a different colored crystal in the center. The sides of each bracelet had a different design and little raised engravings of weapons.

She showed her friends the bracelets. "You'll know when the time is right when they receive their bracelets. Make sure they grow big and strong, and don't tell them about me until they're ready," she said. Then she broke into sobs.

Chikako and Jun reached out and took the children from her. Immediately, she covered her mouth and started humming a tune. When she drew her hand away, she held three teeth in her palm. Unlike human teeth, these were an inch long, curved back, and sharp: dragon teeth.

"Along with other things, these will protect them and help them find each other," she said.

Holding the dragon teeth as if they were made of glass, she slipped one into each of the children's blankets. Gingerly, Eirian climbed to her feet, took a few wobbling steps forward, and looked down at her two sons and daughter. Tears overflowed down her face as she bent down and kissed her children.

She then looked up at the couple. "Thank you for doing this for me. Five others will be chosen besides my sons and daughter. I must go now." She headed for the door.

"Eirian, you just gave birth. You should rest," Chikako said, stepping forward to stop her.

As Eirian reached the door, she stopped, but she didn't even look back. "If they find me here, it won't take them long to find my children. I must go in order to protect my children and the village from them. I pray I'll see the children again." Then she left the house.

At first, she walked down the street, but soon she ran, tears flowing like a river down her cheeks. When she reached a safe distance from the village, she began to sing the same song she'd hummed after entering the planet. A few moments later, she spread her wings, once more a dragon, and flew back to the gateway.

As she approached the area, she took a deep breath and released a ball of fire at the crystal, which opened the gateway. She flew through the gateway and back where she came from, back into the night sky. As she soared over the trees, she spotted her pursuers coming her way.

Now it's time to fight, she thought. Anger replaced her sense of loss at giving up her children, and she sped toward them.

Just before the two dragons reached her, they broke formation, one heading left, the other right. In response, she banked to the side. Swinging her tail forward, she nailed one dragon in the head with her horned tail. As he fell to the ground, his head caved in, she turned sharply and fell in behind the other dragon.

The two weaved all over the sky as the remaining dragon tried to get her off his tail. When she got close enough, she arched her neck a little, took a deep breath, and aimed her head forward, fire racing from her mouth. Before the fire reached him, however, he peeled and shot up. Then he twisted back down, connecting hard with her back and buckling her wings.

As they plummeted to the earth, the battle continued. She tried to get her jaws around his neck, and he aimed for hers.

"Don't mess with this mom!" Eirian growled. Using her wings, she forced her opponent to the ground and kicked off with her hind legs.

His back hit the ground first, knocking down a few trees with a series of loud crashes and a single loud crack.

Muscles straining, she spread her wings with a snap like thunder. She sailed forward a little before crashing hard onto the ground. Her wings brushed against the trees, and dirt and debris flew everywhere. When the dust, branches, and leaves finally settled, she gingerly climbed to her paws. She tested her wings and flinched in pain.

At least my sons and daughter are safe from the Black Dragon, she thought. Still, he won't be happy when he learns his two goons failed to capture me. And if he finds out I gave birth, he'll start looking for all of them, not just me.

She folded her wings and galloped away as fast as she could.

✱✱✱

In the house on stilts, Chikako comforted the fitful baby in her arms. "What should we call him? Eirian didn't name him."

Jun reached for the baby. As he held his new adopted son, the baby opened his eyes.

"I name you Alac—Alac-Ryuu," he said, and Alac cooed.

Chikako picked up the other newborns. She said, "Jun, they're all lovely children. Do we really have to separate them?"

Jun looked at her and nodded. "Yes, unfortunately, we do. I'll send the younger boy to a friend of mine, and the girl will go to a friend of yours. If they stay together, the Black Dragon will find them quickly."

"Who was that woman? And what makes these children so important?" Chikako pulled up a chair and sat across from Jun at their table.

"I can't explain it now, but trust me, they're important. In fact, they're more important than either of us can imagine," he said.

He rose from the table and carefully placed each child gently on the mat. Then he returned to the table, took the box, and opened the lid.

Chikako peered inside. "What are they, anyway?"

Jun closed the box carefully. "The keys to their future."

Alac-Ryuu Jun Yamamoto

Twelve years, three hundred sixty-four days later...

THE SUN ROSE over the little house on stilts. Inside the house were signs of happiness. On the mantelpiece over the fireplace, a brigade of photos showed bits and pieces of this family's life together: a little boy in a hover stroller posing with his parents, taking his first step, playing with his father, dancing on his mother's shoes.

The sun's light crept into one of the rooms and fell onto the closed eyes of a twelve-year-old boy. When he was in school, his teachers and family called him Alac or Alac-Ryuu, but to his closest friends he was just Ryuu or Robin. He turned over on his mat, trying to get more sleep, and then heard a knock on his door.

"Alac! Time to get up, honey! Breakfast is almost ready."

It was his mother. Alac groaned and pulled the blankets over his head.

"Alac-Ryuu Jun Yamamoto, get your butt out of bed now and come to breakfast!" Her voice was kind despite the command. Then he heard her walk away.

He smiled and climbed out of bed. As he gazed briefly in the small bedroom mirror, he saw the curved tooth, which hung from a necklace, shone white on his well-toned chest. His body was muscular from years of training and hard labor. A short while later, he climbed out of the shower wrapping a towel around his waist, hair wet from the water.

8

After wiping some steam from the mirror to brush his teeth. His eyes drifted down to the counter. Where his light dampening contacts and white noise plugs were.

For a second, he eyed them before shaking his head and leaving the bathroom. Back in his room, he grabbed some clothes from the closet and started to get dressed.

Walking down the hall, he stopped in front of a larger mirror to adjust his dark hair, which went down to his shoulders. He pulled out a strip of leather and tied his hair back. His face had a savage type of beauty. His features were sharp and angled, particularly around his eyes and ears, which were slightly pointed at the top, middle, and bottom, giving them a backwards stroking angle. Sometimes when he looked in the mirror, the intenseness of his features startled him, but the thing he liked most about his appearance was his hazel eyes. They were a mix of different colors that seemed to shift at random. He looked in the mirror often to see what colors he could get out of them. Nevertheless, he didn't place all of his focus on his good looks. In school, he' already jumped twelve grades ahead. Now he attended his father's school, which was hidden high in the mountains. He did pretty well in his classes, but sometimes the others made fun of him for his age, for being the head teacher's son, and for the unusual shape of his ears.

As he finished tying his hair back, he paused and lowered his gaze, thinking back to when he'd first started at the academy. He'd been only five, but even then he was as tall as a teenager and six times stronger than a man. As much as his rapid development had scared most of the village, it had frightened him more.

He remembered walking into the academy as a new student. The older students constantly stared at him, though some showed more curiosity than derision. Now, eight years later, at the verge of thirteen, he already had the body of an eighteen-year-old but had only gotten stronger and a diamond-sharp mind. Still, instead of gaining more acceptance at the school, in some ways things got worse.

Shrugging off the memory, he continued down the hall, pulling on his jacket. When he entered the kitchen, his mother was serving pancakes to his dad. Jun was now in his late thirties. Like Ryuu, he was muscular in body, although Ryuu knew he had far to go before he would ever catch up to his father's experience.

His mother had long hair, which she also tied back in a ponytail. She was beautiful, with a slim body. Ryuu knew, however, that her willowy appearance was misleading, because it distracted observers from her broad shoulders and the rolling muscles under her honey skin. In truth, she was just as strong as her husband. She also served as one of Ryuu's teachers, although she preferred to work with him at home, avoiding any possible encounters with the drifters, smugglers, and pirates who frequently landed on their planet to give and take food and supplies.

"Morning, Dad," Ryuu said, sitting at the table opposite his father.

"Morning, Alac. It's good to see you out of bed."

His mother put the plate of pancakes on the table. Ryuu served himself a few and reached for the maple syrup. Then he looked up at his parents and grinned.

"Soooo, you guys doing anything later?" Ryuu asked them.

His father shook his head. "Apart from your exam tonight—which you should be getting ready for—nothing much." He turned his attention back to his pancakes.

"What about tomorrow?" Ryuu asked. He picked up his fork and took a bite.

His mother said, "Well, I promised the neighbor I'd help her redesign her kitchen tomorrow. I'll be out all day."

His father tapped his fork against the table. Then he smacked his hand to his forehead. "Wait—tomorrow is a special day!" he said.

His mother stared at them, a look of shock on her face slowly appearing.

Ryuu smiled. It's about time, he thought.

Then his mother snapped her fingers and pointed at Jun. "Yeah, it's someone's birthday tomorrow, isn't it? I hope she doesn't think we've forgotten!" She took a bite of her pancakes.

"Ah, that's . . . err . . . she?" Ryuu said, smile fading.

His father nodded. "It's an instructor's birthday tomorrow." He turned to Chikako. "Don't worry; I bought her a fruit basket."

"Remind me to give it to her."

Ryuu looked down at his food, disappointed. They forgot.

***

Soon after, Ryuu grabbed his sky surfer. Based on vintage photos from history books, he had concluded that, when open, it looked like an old-fashioned surfboard without the rudder, but in its collapsed position, it looked like a small, box-shaped plate about a foot wide and tall. Most important, it had the ability to fly. It was not as powerful as a sky rider, which was for racing and transport, but it was enough for recreation.

"Don't forget. You need to be ready for the exam by nine this evening," his father called out to him as he raced for the door.

"You got it, Dad!" Ryuu said. He bolted down the stairs, jumping the last few.

"And I want you back here at least two hours before that," his mother called. "Seven p.m. Okay?" She handed him a bag. "I've packed you a lunch. Maybe you and your friends can have a picnic."

"Thanks, Mom." He stuffed it into his backpack. Then he headed down the stairs, and the door swung shut.

He knew he would have to carry the sky surfer until he reached the village gates. Outside his house, he met up with one of his best friends, Bryan. Bryan was almost a head taller than him, with lighter skin that rippled with bulging, toned muscles. He had dark red hair and brown eyes.

"Hey, Ryuu!" he said, and they grasped hands.

"Hey, LJ!" he said. "Ready to go meet the others?"

"Ryuu, you are not Robin Hood, and I am not Little John!" Bryan said. He smiled and added, "You read those books way too much. Just because you're the best shot and swordsman in the class and I'm the best staff man doesn't mean we should change our names."

They began to run, dodging a few people on the street. When one shouted after them, Ryuu stopped running and turned to his friend.

"I'm serious, LJ. Books and movies like Robin Hood give people hope. They remind them that folks can rise from the ashes of their loss. These heroes have one goal: to help save the oppressed and innocent from those who would do them harm. These are men of honor who have lost everything. But instead of seeking revenge, they've devoted themselves to saving lives from tyrants like the Black Dragon and his Sentinels target." He shifted his weight and continued. "That's why I read those books; they give me hope for a bright future where we don't have to be afraid—where we don't have to look over our shoulders for an enemy who could be anyone we know."

Ryuu knew Bryan suffered more than any of his other friends. His entire family had been slaughtered by the Black Dragon's Sentinels when their caravan was attacked. Bryan had escaped only because of his parents' courage and faith to launch him out of the last escape pod. Now he lived with one of the many foster families in town.

Like so many refugees calling Amal home.

"You're right, Ryuu," Bryan said. "I understand. And I was just teasing. You can call me LJ whenever you want." Then he grinned and the mood lightened. "Now come on, Robin, we've got to meet the others. Allison says her brother has upgrades for the sky riders."

They raced each other down the center street, dodging hover cars and bikes as they went, showing off a few of the skills they had learned in school. In synchronized motion, Ryuu and Bryan flipped onto the hood of a hover car, ran along it, leapt forward, rolled along the ground, and continued running. The pair then darted for the sidewalk. People leaped out of their way, with some frowning at them while others emitted bursts of laughter.

Soon they exited the village gates, pressed a button, and threw their sky surfers ahead of them. The units extended automatically, with the front curved and the thrusters behind. The sky surfers hovered in the air as the boys, still running, leapt forward onto them.

As Ryuu landed, with his legs bent and his back heel pressed on the starter, his feet were bound down. Then, as the jets fired, the boys rocketed forward. They cheered as they soared up and above the trees, weaving left and right. They soon came to the stone arch in the woods that stood next to the crystal embedded in the ground.

Standing next to the crystal and leaning against the arch were the rest of their friends, and Ryuu seized this second opportunity to show off. He leaned back on his board and shot higher into the air at a vertical angle at breakneck speed. Then, at the height of his climb, he pressed the button again with his foot, and the engine died.

Ryuu closed his eyes a dreamy expression moving over his face as he tumbled back to the ground. He twisted, flipped, and spun as he dropped faster and faster from the sky to the ground. Finally, he grabbed the nose of the board and spun a circle, increasing in speed even more.

At the last second, as he approached the tree line, he slammed his heel onto the button, and the sky surfer dipped below the trees. Ryuu weaved left and right, avoiding the trees and branches as he sped forward through the forest. He broke out of the trees by zooming between two tightly spaced branches and out into the clearing, where he whizzed through the gateway, his friends cheering. He circled the clearing once and then landed with the board hovering about a foot in the air.

His friend Allison was as tall as him. She had short, dark brown hair, which shifted over her Elven ears, and a muscular body which rippled under her ebony skin and grace that almost matched Ryuu's. Her beautiful face, which included dark-blue eyes, usually caught the attention of the boys in school, but most wouldn't dare approach her for a date. In fact, she broke the finger of the last guy who tried.

She was one of the top students in school, but her progress was sometimes halted by her temper, which was on a shorter fuse than Ryuu's. In class, she tended to be the first to volunteer answers without thinking, and outside class she was known for barreling into reckless decisions with hardly ever thinking about them.

The two grasped hands. "Ryuu, you're one gutsy guy. I like that; it reminds me of me." They laughed.

"Now I know I'm in trouble," Ryuu said.

Allison's twin brother, Eric, came up and joined them. While Eric had more muscles and the broad chest of a young man, he generally matched his twin's appearance right down to the last hair on his head.

Allison, quick to fight, often stepped up to the plate while Eric puzzled things out from an intellectual point of view. He and Ryuu were top of the class in schoolwork. As well, Eric was a martial arts champion who was second to none with tonfa sticks.

Ryuu looked at the last friend of the group: Aiolos. Known as the class clown, he was still quick-witted and did well in school even though the teachers needed to bring his attention back to the lesson every five minutes or so. Aiolos was a free-spirited blonde, whose carefree approach to life managed to clash enough with Allison's reckless one that sometimes the two friends were at odds. Ryuu always appreciated his friend's good nature, particularly during tough times. Now he and Aiolos grasped hands and pulled into a back-slapping hug.

Aiolos stepped back, looked at Ryuu, and smiled widely. "Ryuu, your success with that nose grab spin was positively inspiring," he said. The others looked at them and nodded.

Ryuu said, "Thanks, man." Then he turned to Eric. "What kind of upgrades do you have for the sky riders?"

Eric smiled at this and walked over to a set of sky riders hovering in the air in a straight line. They looked like various sports motorcycles with no wheels front and back, and each had a small but powerful jet propulsion system where the taillights would have been.

He patted the seat on a bright-yellow one. "Last night I initiated an overwrite of essential system programming. Also, I removed nonessential equipment from the primary source so the velocity should be doubled," Eric said.

Allison looked at Ryuu. "You speak Geek, so please, I beg you: translate for the rest of us."

Then she looked at Eric and added, "No offense, bro."

He shrugged.

Ryuu laughed, shook his head, and tried to explain. "He said he's stripped them of excess body fat. And he overwrote the thruster protocols, which means we can now accelerate beyond the original, restricted speeds. In other words, he's given us some sweet rides."

The group cheered and Eric gave a bow.

They immediately decided to test out the modifications Eric had made. However, before Ryuu put his helmet on, he grabbed Eric by the elbow and said, "You did put them at a speed where the thrusters won't have a meltdown, right? The thrusters were set at those speeds by the manufacturer for that reason. So you didn't exceed the heat buildup, did you?"

Eric smiled. "Why do you think I removed the extra weight?" Then he placed a half ring around his neck and pressed a button on the side.

Blue-colored metal plates with flames began to slide up and along the sides of his head, but they left a gap around the top half of his face. When the plates reached the ring around his neck and connected, an inflating sound occurred, and padding expanded from the inside. On the side of the head, a panel slid back, revealing three buttons one on top of the other.

Eric pressed the middle one, a black-shaded visor lowered into place, and he hopped onto the blue bike.

Ryuu sighed as he climbed onto his red bike and activated his own helmet, which was red with a gold dragon design. *One of the main ways people can tell they're related, but that's half-elves for you,* he thought.

He pressed the ignition button, and the engine roared to life. Ryuu closed his eyes and smiled at the powerful noise of the engine. He twisted the gas. The engine roared louder, and his smile got wider with the sound of it.

"Ryuu!" It was Allison's voice. He opened his eyes, and there on his visor was a 3-D image of her face.

She gave him a sly smile. "Hey, first one around the mountain is the winner, eh?"

He smiled back. "You got it, Ace. Let's race. The rest of you guys in?" he asked, and images of his other friends popped up on his visor.

"You know it."

"Affirmative."

"You'd have to beat me away with a stick."

"Okay," he said. "One, two, three, GO!" Then he gunned the engine and took off like a flash.

He sped above the forest. After a few seconds, he looked behind him and saw them catching up on their sky riders, with Allison on green, Bryan on yellow, Aiolos on white, and Eric on blue. Soon they were neck and neck, and as they sped on their way, the ground turned into a multicolored blur of endless motion. Ryuu gunned the engine and shot forward. He had no doubt his friends were still in close pursuit.

Ryuu rolled to the right and went into a light dive when they reached a ravine on the side of the mountain. Alongside his friends, he sped down the ravine at a breakneck pace, dodging the rocks that jetted out at odd angles and formation. They became neck and neck again after Ryuu put his sky rider into a spin and flew through a tight rock hole.

For the next several moments, they raced down the ravine in a tight formation, with each one fighting for the lead. Finally, as Ryuu ducked under a rock formation stretching from both sides, the end of the ravine came into view. They raced on, gunning their engines. The rock wall got closer and they began to run out of space.

At the last second, with Allison in the lead and Ryuu in a close second, they were up and out of the ravine. A few mountain goats being herded by some the villagers were spooked as the friends roared overhead, and the villagers shouted after them. Ryuu laughed with joy as they rocketed into the trees, out of sight of the villagers on the ground.

Now they weaved left and right as they zoomed through the maze of towering mountain trees. Moments later, they burst from the tree line and zoomed upward.

Ryuu lowered his head, then looked ahead again. The group rounded the corner, and once again, they were all neck and neck.

Soon the gateway was in sight. He leaned forward and floored it, shooting forward.

Seconds later, Ryuu and Allison fought for supremacy. He was in the lead; she was in the lead. At the last second, Ryuu banked up, rolled around Allison, pulled ahead of her, and shot between the two stones a second before her. He thrust his fist into the air, cheering his victory.

He came to a skidding stop and hovered in midair as the rest of the group ground to a halt behind him. Then they formed a circle, facing each other. Ryuu pressed the middle button, and his visor shot up into the helmet. Grinning, he looked at everyone.

"It's okay! You can say it!" He leaned on his bike.

They each raised their visors. Allison rolled her eyes and said, "There goes his ego!" Then she smiled.

Aiolos removed his helmet and grinned.

"Yeah, his helmet is readjusting to fit his newly inflated head!" The sneering voice came over their coms.

Before Ryuu could respond, he heard the rumble of sky riders coming up from the village toward them. He recognized their bikes and turned quickly to his friends.

"Here comes trouble."

Team Locksley

THE RIDERS SPED towards Ryuu's group, halted their bikes, and faced them. The teenager on the rider in front of Ryuu quickly pushed the button of his helmet, which retracted to reveal the short blond hair and handsome face of one of the most popular students in his father's school: Dulglad. One by one, Dulglad's friends followed suit. Most of them were big, strong muscular boys who, despite their bulging muscles, were stupid. The last person in line, facing Allison, was the only girl. She had long blonde hair.

By name, they were Babieca, Bamber, Kade, and Melinda, and none of their smiles looked genuine.

The two groups stared at each other for a few minutes. Finally, Dulglad leaned on his bike and broke the silence.

"So. I see you and your friends still being inflated showoffs, eh, Alac?"

Ryuu smiled. "It's not our fault you and your friends can't fly, Dulglad. Besides, it's not being a showoff if you can bring it." Aiolos, who was next to Allison on Ryuu's left, nodded.

At this, Dulglad's expression turned to fury, and he sat up straight. "We can take you any time. Just name the time," he declared. His friends nodded.

Smiling, Ryuu looked at his friends. He knew they got his idea when they each nodded, replaced their helmet, and zoomed away.

Dulglad and his friends were clearly curious. In fact, the larger boys looked dumbfounded as they watched Ryuu's friends go.

Ryuu leaned more onto his rider. "They'll be back in twenty minutes. How about when they get back, we play sky hockey, you against us. First team to reach ten wins."

Dulglad grinned. "Fine, you're on. See you in twenty." Then he pressed the button on his helmet ring, the visor replaced itself, and the group zoomed away.

Sighing, Ryuu brought his rider to a rest about a foot above the ground by the gateway. He dismounted and looked back at the village, wondering if Allison would lose her temper or keep it in check. He smiled as he recalled Bamber had been the recipient of the broken finger. Aiolos would probably be their strongest player. He tended to show a lot of his free spirit during a game, and the insults and banter usually flew out with rapid speed due to his quick tongue and wit.

Soon his vision shifted from the village. He settled back onto the seat of his bike and looked up at the clear blue sky. His thoughts moved on to his mother and the reason why she'd left him when he was born.

He closed his eyes, and a small tear ran down his cheek as he recalled the day when he found out Jun and Chikako weren't his birth parents. About a year ago, they had sat him down in the living room and explained the events of that fateful day. The shock had hit him pretty hard. Up until that point, he'd felt like the villagers looked down on him. In fact, one of the main reasons he always worked extra hard at school was to prove his merit. However, some of the teachers frequently accused him of cheating, and he never felt accepted by anyone but his small circle of friends. Before he got his friends, contacts, and earplugs, his peers would suddenly toss loud noisemakers, blow dog whistles, cause sudden flashes of light, and stink bombs near him, and put miniscule sour things in his food and drink. Then laugh as he writhed on the floor protecting his ears, stumble around blinded, cover his nose with whatever was on hand as he ran from the stink, and spit out whatever was in his mouth, but he never knew why. Finally, he knew.

During the days that followed, he questioned if he really belonged in the village and the clan. He even made plans to leave, but when he had tried to sneak away in the middle of the night, he discovered a small group of supporters was waiting for him. That night, his parents and friends persuaded him to stay, and when he had finally agreed, the entire group smiled. Some friends had even cheered.

He brushed aside the tear. Still, even to this day, he wasn't certain his parents told him everything about that night. However, they hadn't been willing to answer any more questions, and he didn't want to appear ungrateful.

As he delved deeper into his memory, he thought back to when he first met his friends.

***

It was after one of the mandatory pilot classes where they all had to qualify. As per usual, he picked it up fast—and he spent most of the class getting snide remarks from both his teacher and his classmates.

When the class finished, his mind was still on the lesson. As he walked down the hall, he planned how he could improve in the next one. Then somebody shoved him from behind, knocking him down. He whipped his gaze around, teeth bared. Dulglad and his friends laughed as he attempted to get back off the ground.

That's how he first met Bryan, who came to his defense, offered him a hand, to haul him to his feet. Then, as the others hung back to watch, Ryuu launched himself at Dulglad, knocking him to the ground.

This was how his father found him: surrounded by teachers trying to break up the fight as some students cheered it on. At that point, Ryuu was in the middle, holding Dulglad over his head like a rag doll.

Ten minutes later, he sat outside his father's office, with Dulglad hunched on the seat across from him dabbing at a bloody nose. Bryan was in the office, and Dulglad's father had also been summoned. Neither Dulglad nor Ryuu talked to one another, although they did exchange an occasional glare. Ryuu did his best to ignore the voices that seeped out through the closed door.

"... is a menace! I told you he was too dangerous to be around the other children! He nearly killed my son!" It was Dulglad's father. "It's bad enough you allow those half elves — but we don't even know what he is!"

"Master Iga, that's not exactly how it happened." This was Bryan's voice.

"Mr. Hunson!" snapped Dulglad's father. "I do not recall asking for you to speak!"

"And yet it's why he is here in the first place," came his father's voice. "And on that note, from what Mr. Hunson and others told me, it was your son who started this skirmish. So maybe you should use this incident to teach your son not to provoke a fight."

His father's voice continued. "Furthermore, you know Allison and Eric lost their mother and father to the Black Dragon's forces. Fighting in the resistance, they died as heroes so others would live. As I have reminded you, it is not up to you to select the students we admit to this school for training. Further, considering the evidence against your son, you know he could be facing suspension for his actions in provoking Alac-Ryuu. However, I will be talking to Alac-Ryuu next. He will also have to face consequences for his actions."

There was silence for a few moments, followed by angry footsteps, and the door was thrown open. Standing there was Master Iga, who shot Ryuu a dirty look. Then he motioned for Dulglad to follow him, and the pair swept away.

"Alac-Ryuu, would you come in here?" his father said.

Sighing, Ryuu climbed to his feet and walked inside.

Before him, his father sat at his ornate desk with his elbows resting on top and his fingers interlaced. His gaze was downcast, and his head was leaning against his fingers.

"Close the door behind you, Alac-Ryuu."

After doing what he was told, he walked forward to sit before his father. For a few moments, nothing but silence filled the room.

Then his father finally raised his gaze to look at Ryuu.

"Well, I see you certainly are making an impression, Alac-Ryuu," he finally said.

"But Dad, I didn't—"

"I know you didn't start the fight," his father interrupted, "but the way you handled it is inexcusable." He sat back in his chair. "I know you're only five, Alac-Ryuu, but you need to remember how powerful you are compared to your classmates. You could have seriously hurt Dulglad, if not killed him."

His father let the statement settle for a moment. Ryuu lowered his gaze in shame at the disappointment in his father's voice.

Then his father continued. "I have something for you." He indicated the holo book lying on his desk before him. "I first set it aside because I thought you might enjoy it. Now I hope it will inspire you to become better than you are."

Then he turned to Bryan. "Mr. Hunson, I am hoping you will help my son learn to control his temper. Would you and your friends please look after him and find better ways to . . . vent it out?"

For a second Bryan was silent as he looked from Jun to Ryuu. Then he nodded. "Yes, Grandmaster Yamato."

Smiling, his father waved his hand. "Thank you. Both of you are dismissed."

After standing and picking up the book, Ryuu left with Bryan. They walked down the hall in silence. Then Bryan finally asked, "So . . . what's the book?"

After glancing at him, Ryuu held it up and turned on the cover.

Robin Hood.

***

He was so engrossed in his thoughts he didn't realize the others returned until he was poked hard on his shoulder. He jumped, fell off his rider, and looked up at Allison's smiling face as he lay on the ground.

"Ryuu, this is space command," said Aiolos. He leaned over and placed his hand over his mouth, giving his voice an echoing sound. "We're calling your head back to your body."

Ryuu laughed as he climbed to his feet and looked around at the rest of his friends. Each was carrying a bag with equipment for sky hockey. Bryan had also brought a bag for Ryuu, which he opened immediately. Inside his bag were two sets of medium and large rings; a single, larger ring; what looked like a small metal rod; and a pair of boots with red buttons on the inside of the heels.

Ryuu slipped the medium-sized rings onto his arms right on top of his biceps. The larger rings he pulled onto his legs, and they stopped just above his knees. He slipped on the largest ring, which went up to his waist. Seconds later, everything automatically shrank to fit snugly. Finally, he slipped on another half ring around his neck and replaced his shoes with the boots. Then he turned at the sound of approaching engines. Dulglad and his friends were coming at them at top speed on their bikes.

Ryuu turned to look at his friends. He nodded. Each pressed the buttons on the rings, which expanded into full gear.

On Ryuu's arms, the rings expanded down past his elbow and encased his entire hands, including his fingers. The rings on his legs expanded up and down, but stopped just above his ankles and below the ring around his waist. Then they melded with the boots and the waist ring. The one around his waist expanded up his chest. Then it encased his shoulders and the top sections of his arms. Like before, the ring on his neck expanded up his neck, but it stopped at his hairline and chin. Finally, there was a flash of light as the force field mask activated.

When the plates were finished expanding, the friends looked like they were partly encased by some sort of armor. All the suits turned scarlet, but because Eric was the goalie, his armor, which was thicker, included a blue rectangular shield on one arm and a large goalie glove in the other. As the friends waited, their opponents dressed in a similar fashion; their gear turned a deep green.

Slowly, the two groups gathered and faced each other.

"Ready to lose?" Dulglad asked, a cocky smile on his face.

Ryuu smiled. "You wish," he said.

Dulglad's smile turned into a deep frown. Then he stepped away and gathered his team around him.

Ryuu gathered his own team, and as they formed a circle, he placed his hand in the center. One by one, his friends placed their hands on top of his. Pumping their hands, they called out their team name as one: "LOCKSLEY!" Then they clicked their heels together.

Their boots hummed as they shot into the air, hovering about twenty feet up. Then they started to set up for the game. Eric took some balls from his glove and tossed them to either side of him; they stopped about six feet apart. They hovered for a moment, then emitted beams of light that connected, forming a goal.

Allison and Aiolos tossed a couple more balls toward him, and they hovered about another twelve feet on either side of Eric. They emitted two beams of light that connected behind Eric's goal and connected to the balls Dulglad's friends had set up on the other end, forming the playing field. The lines appeared with multiple flashes of light as force fields formed below them and made the walls. When the arena was set, Allison, Ryuu, and Aiolos moved up to the centerline with Melinda, Dulglad, and Bamber.

When the six of them met, they all held the short sticks in their hands and activated them. The sticks lengthened, forming hockey sticks that each player gripped with both hands, except for Eric and Kade, who had goalie sticks. Allison and Aiolos took their positions as Ryuu's left and right wings as they faced off against Melinda and Bambar.

Bending his legs, Ryuu faced off against Dulglad and the two waited, eyes locked on each other, every now and then swatting each other's sticks. From above fell a puck, which came down between Ryuu's and Dulglad's sticks. On the rebound of the puck, which hit the field, Dulglad checked Ryuu hard, taking the puck.

Ryuu slid down the field a bit then rolled back onto his feet. I should have known they'd play dirty, he thought as he skated after his opponent.

Bryan skated up to intercept Dulglad, but he was hooked from behind by Melinda, and Dulglad whipped past him. Eric skated out, challenging him, but he was checked hard by Bamber. Then Melinda knocked the goal a foot to the right, and Dulglad scored. Ryuu gritted his teeth in frustration as beams of light where the puck had dropped from counted the score.

As the puck soared up to where the score was displayed, the rest of Ryuu's team took their starting positions on the field. Dulglad's team continued to pull off just about every dirty trick in the book, but without a referee, they weren't called for it or forced to play fair. Soon it was 0–9.

After Dulglad scored another goal, Ryuu rolled back onto his feet, and his team gathered around him. Ryuu raised his visor and looked at his friends. They were as angry as he was about the dirty way Dulglad's team was playing.

"This isn't sky hockey; it's a demolition derby," Eric said behind him.

"I say we give these guys some major payback," Allison said. She brandished a fist in the air.

Ryuu pointed at her. "I'm with you, Allison, but we're doing it by the book. Agreed?" All of his teammates nodded.

Dulglad and Ryuu faced off again, and this time when the puck dropped, Ryuu won the face-off. Allison checked Melinda and took the puck. She darted up the field, then drop-passed the puck to Ryuu, who skated behind her. Switching positions, he dodged Babieca, skated behind their goal and then passed the puck to Aiolos.

"HONEY, I'M HOME!" he shouted. Then he fired a slap shot and scored above Kade's raised glove.

Cheering, they reformed the lines, and an agitated Dulglad faced off against Ryuu, who was grinning. Dulglad won the faceoff this time, and

Ryuu stole the puck by skating up and over him on the side of the boards, with Bryan in front of him skating up the field.

Over Bryan's shoulder, Ryuu spied Melinda, Bambar, and Babieca coming at them, and Melina shouted, "He can't check all three of us!"

As they collided, Bryan did check all three of them at once, and they slid in three different directions. Ryuu's and Bryan's sticks fell in perfect sync with each other as they shot for the goal. They stopped right in front of it, and Kade stared at Bryan. Then Ryuu scored right between Bryan's and Kade's legs.

After taking their positions, again Ryuu won the face-off by knocking the puck between Dulglad's legs. He skated around him, passed to Allison, flipped over Babieca, and then swerved over and checked Melinda into the force field wall. After Ryuu received the puck, he juggled it into the air, fired a shot, and scored.

Team Locksley scored four more times in a matter of four minutes, and Dulglad's team was clearly willing to resort to any means to try to stop them. As Ryuu skated up the field, dribbling the puck around his stick, he fired a slap shot just as he dodged around Melinda, who spun around, bent over, and flip-checked him onto his back. He heard cries of outrage as he landed hard on his back. Quickly, he raised his head to see his shot score. Curling up, he leapt to his feet and turned to face Melinda.

Bryan skated up and placed a hand on his shoulder.

"Alac—" Bryan started, but when Ryuu glared at him, he backed off.

Ryuu pushed off toward her, and she looked him dead in the eye.

"Go ahead," she muttered at him.

He glared at her, then leaned forward. "Nine," he muttered. Then he skated around her and took his position.

Dulglad took his position in front of Ryuu, a grin on his face. "Chicken," he muttered, and Ryuu cocked a grin.

Ryuu won the face-off, but he sent the puck hurtling back toward Bryan, who got it. Allison, Aiolos, and Ryuu darted back. The four of them skated back around Eric and the goal before returning to make a formation, skating up the field. They passed the puck between each other to keep Dulglad's team guessing. When Ryuu got the puck, the other three retreated and checked whoever was in his way.

It was just Ryuu and Kade now. Kade skated forward, challenging Ryuu as he progressed. Ryuu skated forward and faked a shot to Kade's left. While Kade did a wall block, Ryuu back-handed at his right. The seconds seemed to last for hours as the puck sailed forward toward the goal and Kade's glove raised. The puck missed the glove by millimeters. It sailed into the goal, and the buzzer sounded, ending the game.

Ryuu cheered, raising his hands into the air as the scoreboard flashed the score: 9–10. The rest of his team rushed forward, and they started skating in a tight circle, placing the heels of their sticks in the center.

"GOOOO LOCKLSLEY!" they shouted as one, bringing their sticks up and interlocking them as they slipped into a group hug.

When they broke apart, Ryuu turned to see the field had dissolved after the balls fell to the earth. Dulglad glared at him briefly. Then he and his friends deactivated their sticks, jumped onto their bikes, and sped off.

Ryuu shook his head, knowing this latest round of the long line of clashes between the groups was far from over. In a few hours, they would all meet again at the Academy to take their final exam.

Samurai

AFTER A QUICK picnic lunch, Ryuu and his friends sat near the gateway for hours, talking about what happened in the game and their dramatic comeback. Ryuu and Allison were re-enacting his final shot when Ryuu caught sight of her watch. He grabbed her wrist and turned it so he could see it better.

"Oh, man, my mom is going to kill me!" Ryuu darted to his rider and grabbed his surfer. "Sorry, guys, I've got to get home."

He tossed the board forward and jumped on.

"Good luck!" Ryuu heard them call in the distance. He leaned as low as he could on his surfer, and the ground turned into one big, blurred mass.

Ryuu squinted his eyes, which stung from the rushing air blowing into his face. He slowed down when he soared over the village, and less than a second later, he spotted his home. Looking down, he could see his mother in the backyard, sitting on her knees with a teapot over a fire in front of her and a circle of cutting mats standing erect behind her. He zoomed above their front yard, deactivated the board, slipped off, and fell twenty feet to the ground, landing on bended knee.

The board folded up, and Ryuu lifted his hand and caught it. Then he darted up the stairs and into the house. His father wasn't home. He must have left for school to prepare for tonight's exam, Ryuu thought. Then he darted into his room, stripped off his shirt, and put on the clothes he would need for the test with his mother, which would be next.

As soon as he was dressed in his loose, baggy, traditional Hakama pants and his traditional Keikogi overlapping jacket, Ryuu rushed to the back door, slid it open, and walked out onto the lawn toward his mother. He sat on his knees next to her, with the teapot in front of them.

She was dressed like him, with her hair tied back. She had a Katana sword on her hip, and her eyes were closed.

She said, "Right on time, Alac-Ryuu, although I thought I heard you in a little rush in the house."

Ryuu smiled at her, lowering his gaze down to the sash that was folded neatly at his knees and the Katana at his right side.

"You know what to do," she said.

First, he placed his hands on the sash and bowed to her. As he sat up, he picked up the sash with the same movement. Then he unfolded it and tied it over his eyes.

Next, he picked up the sword. He lifted it with both hands while he bowed his head, then he tucked it into the sash around his waist and waited.

After a moment, the water in the kettle began to whistle, and Ryuu lifted it from its holder and placed it gently on a clay coaster. He then took two cups and went through a traditional tea ceremony with his eyes covered. When he was finished, he handed one cup to his mother, picked up his own, and waved a hand over it. Then he drank.

When they were finished with their tea, Ryuu put the cup down, and his hand shot up and caught her shuto knife hand before it could connect with his face.

"Good. Move onto the next stage," she said.

Ryuu leaned forward and put his toes under him. Then he pushed himself onto his feet and walked around the small fire. He stopped after a few steps and turned around on his heel, facing the way he'd come. He took a deep breath, then gripped his sword and drew it slowly.

Next, he gripped the sword with both hands and slashed the air at ten different spots around him. Each of his attacks he struck differently, using an upward, side, or downward slash. Before he faced the way he came, he sheathed his sword and stood straight as an arrow, waiting.

Without warning, he drew his sword, and there was a clash of steel on steel as his mother began her attack. He brought his sword down in a wide arch, and as he stepped back, keeping low, he listened to what was around him with his ears and with his feet. He turned slightly and parried another blow.

They exchanged a few more blows with each other. As he turned lightly to the left, he brandished his sword so fast he knew it must look like nothing more than a blur. After ducking and quickly turning, he spun around and parried another blow. Then he ran the blunt edge up to elbow level and pressed it against something. He twisted it a little to persuade his attacker to stop.

After a moment, he withdrew his sword, sheathed it, and stood straight, one hand on the sheath. He then felt his mother stand in front of him, and they bowed to each other. He stood straight as he felt and heard her move away from him. A moment later, he drew his sword in a flash and felt something impact on the blade. He shifted the sword and blocked again and again, each something impacted his sword blade.

After the last blow, he sheathed his sword and waited. Soon he felt her coming. She grabbed him around the neck, and he was forced to bend over. He grabbed her ankles and stood straight, which made her fall back against the ground, knocking the wind out of her. Still holding onto her, Ryuu twisted around, sat on her, and placed her leg in a lock until she patted the ground three times.

He rolled off her and stood straight, with one hand on his sword. He waited for her to make her move. When she came at him again from behind, he rammed his elbow into her gut. Then he grabbed her wrist with one hand, grasped her under her armpit with the other, threw her over his shoulder, and twisted her arm around into a lock. Once more, she patted the ground, and he rolled off her again, rose to his feet, and waited.

He suddenly felt her come at him again from behind. This time she managed to put him a blood choke. He got low on his knees and gripped her arm, knowing he didn't have long before he was out. He got down on one knee, threw his hips forward, and flipped her over his shoulder hard onto the ground. Then he stood straight, waiting for her to make a move again.

This time she came at him from the front, and he grabbed her hand. She twisted his arm around as she stepped behind him. Locking out her wrist, he brought her back, flipped her onto her side, and punched down a centimeter from her face. He stood straight and waited for her next attack.

This time it came from his front, and as she grabbed his collar, he grabbed hers, and she threw him into the air, twisting around. He grabbed her neck with his legs and brought her down hard. As he held onto her arm, she landed on her back, and he held her wrist in an arm bar. He twisted wrist, and put her in a double lock. She patted the ground again, and he rolled back onto his feet.

"Remove the blindfold, Alac-Ryuu," said his mother.

He slipped it off and looked at her in front of him, then at the cutting mats around the two of them. They were all now six inches shorter than they had been before. Some of them had been cut at various angles, with shattered arrows around them. He couldn't help but smile as he looked back at her. Then they walked back to the fire.

They knelt across from each other again.

"Recite the seven virtues and their meaning," his mother commanded.

Ryuu breathed deeply.

"One, Gi: the right decision, taken with equanimity; the right attitude; the truth. When we must die, we must die. Rectitude.

"Two, Yu: bravery tinged with heroism.

"Three, Jin: universal love; benevolence toward humanity and compassion.

"Four, Rei: right action—a most essential quality; courtesy.

"Five, Makoto: utter sincerity; truthfulness.

31

"Six, Melyo: honor and glory.

"Seven, Chugo: devotion; loyalty."

His mother held her stern gaze on him for a long moment, and then she smiled from ear to ear. "Well done, Alac-Ryuu, very well done. When we started, you were my student to my family's style. Now you've earned the right to call yourself Samurai." She bowed to him.

Ryuu smiled back at her. "Thank you, my mother." He bowed to her.

***

A half hour later, Ryuu was sitting at the coffee table dressed in black. In front of him were weapons and tools he would need for the test with his father that night. He looked at the clock every few seconds, taking deep breaths. His mother soon came out of the kitchen, another cup of tea in her hand. He was far too nervous to eat dinner, and he was glad to see she understood.

She placed the tea in front of him, and he picked it up and drank deeply.

"Relax, honey," she said. "If you perform like you did earlier, you'll be fine."

He put the cup back down and looked at her. "You wouldn't be singing the same tune if you were in my place, Mom." He looked at the clock again. "It's time."

One by one, he picked up the weapons and tools from the table and slipped them into their proper place. He picked up the remaining pieces of his uniform, pulled the balaclava over his head, and tucked it under his jacket. The last piece, a long strip of cloth, he tied over the spot where his mouth would have shown, and when he was finished, the only part of his body that showed was his eyes.

His weapons were a Kumai knife carrier, which was strapped to his upper right leg, and a shuriken, a star-shaped weapon with projecting blades, which was contained in a carrier strapped to his other leg. He slipped the three-pronged, bladed-edged Sais to their sheaths, which were connected to the Kumai knives and, shuriken carrier, and buckled them in.

He then slipped the chucks into the antigravity belt around his waist, which the carriers were strapped to.

The last weapons he picked up were his sword, quiver, and bow. He quickly tied the three to his back. Feeling like his limbs had turned to lead, he faced his mother and smiled behind his mask as best he could. Then he left through the back door as silent as the dead, and after sprinting across the lawn, he leapt into the trees.

A ways in, Ryuu stashed some of his weapons away in a tree hollow. Then he leapt away, memorizing the area so he could find them again.

For the next few minutes, Ryuu leapt from tree to tree. He was so quiet; the animals gave no warning of his presence, even when Ryuu landed next to an owl. Ryuu looked at creature as it turned his head. Then it gave a small hoot and flew off.

Ryuu traced the owl's path as it moved across the clear night sky. The moon was full, and the stars were bright. He thought, it has begun.

Ninja

RYUU CREPT THROUGH the forest in the late hours of the night, keeping his knees bent and cross walking with his hands out for balance. As he walked, he kept looking left and right. He saw only trees, but he knew more was out there. After taking a few more steps, he froze and dropped lower. In the moonlight, he ran a finger along a wire that was almost invisible in the gloom.

Making up his mind, he took a few steps back, and from his carrier he drew a four-pointed star shuriken. He stepped behind a tree. After a moment, he whipped around and threw the star, which cut the wire. A log swung down lengthwise and past him, and he exhaled deeply, relieved he'd not been standing in front of it.

He leapt up and wall-jumped up to a tree branch. Then he ducked down, keeping a sharp watch on his surroundings. Quick as a flash, he drew his sword when a black-clad figure approached. Then he spun around, and blocked his opponent's sword, which was aimed at his head. As he pushed the sword away, he fell off the tree, flipped around, and landed on his feet. When he looked up, this opponent was gone.

He stated moving away, as quiet as the dead, hunting what he couldn't see or hear. Suddenly, he stopped. His eyes darted to his right. He leapt up on a tree branch and reached into his carrier. He whipped around and flung a four-pointed metal star. It sailed about twenty feet away, where one of the blades became embedded in a tree right in front of another black-clad figure. This figure, who had a staff across his back, stopped dead in his tracks and stared at the star as he was coming around the tree.

Quietly running along the branch until he reached the end, Ryuu leapt from it, throwing a flying sidekick. The other figure looked at him and then ducked under the kick, which put a foot-shaped hole in the tree. Before the staffed figure could retaliate, Ryuu spun around in the air and threw a sidekick to his head.

Ryuu flipped backwards back onto his feet. They landed and assumed fighting stances. When they circled each other, the staff bearer pulled out his staff and twirled it above his head and behind him, one hand extended outwards. Ryuu recognized it and took a closer look at the clad figure in front of him.

"I'm a warrior chosen by a creature that's connected to all four elements of life," Ryuu said.

The staff bearer got out of his fighting stance. "I'm a warrior bound by a code to protect the weak, abused, and the innocent," he said. It was Bryan.

Bryan put his staff away, and the two grasped hands. Then he pointed at his friend. "Remind me to kick your butt later, Ryuu," he said.

Ryuu patted him on the shoulder.

"Fat chance, Bryan, my friend. Now let's finish this examination," he said, and the two headed out together.

After traveling for almost ten minutes, they stopped and examined their surroundings.

"You take cover down here. I'll take the trees, LJ," Ryuu said.

Even in the dark, Ryuu could see his friend roll his eyes. "Sure thing, Robin. Good luck," he said. Then he moved off.

Ryuu watched him go. Then he leapt up into the trees started following Bryan by jumping from branch to branch. He made a brief stop on an oak with a large hole, and, reaching in, he pulled out a quiver full of arrows and an unstrung bow in a strapped leather tube. He placed both items over his shoulder and continued to follow Bryan as the two looked for their target.

They traveled like that for another ten minutes. Then Bryan was attacked by their target. As he started to fight back, Ryuu leapt from his hiding spot and double-kicked the attacker in the chest. Using the momentum of the kick, the figure flipped back, pressed a button on his belt, and then dived directly into the ground.

Ryuu and Bryan stood back-to-back, looking down at the ground, with weapons drawn at the ready.

"We've got a mole on our hands," Bryan said.

"Well, you know what they say, bro. Fight fire with fire."

They looked at each other and nodded. Then they quickly pressed the buttons on their own belts and sank into the ground, following their target.

A few seconds later, the three figures burst back to the surface with an ear-splitting sound that reverberated through the forest like a train crash. Their target pressed another button on its belt and started running through the air. Seeing this, Ryuu and Bryan mimicked his moves and followed him as fast as they could.

As they were catching up, there was a faint buzzing sound like a bee, and the figure dodged onto a tree branch, barely escaping a pair of Sais. Ryuu couldn't tell who had launched them until Allison and Aiolos leapt into view onto a branch to the side of their target. As Allison passed by, she retrieved her Sai swords and twirled them in her hands. Then she got into a fighting stance, with one Sai reversed.

Aiolos drew a pair of numchucks, and they quickly turned into a blur of motion like the prop of an antique plane: left, right, up, and down. Next he grasped both ends in his hands, ready for what was to come. Ryuu drew his bow, fitted an arrow to it, and placed their target in his sights.

Their target looked at the two groups—one in front and one to the side of him—and he took a step back.

"I wouldn't keep moving if I were you," a fifth person told him.

Ryuu recognized the voice. It was Eric.

Their target whipped around and stared at Eric, who was standing on a branch, bow in hand, with an arrow sighted at the target. The figure looked from Eric to Aiolos to Allison to Bryan to Ryuu. Before anything else could happen, Ryuu heard a faint rustling, and his nostrils were filled with a pungent odor when the wind changed.

He turned his eyes up just in time to see a small orb- like object drop between them. Then went off. He doubled over, eyes shut in agonizing pain, as a blinding flash of light and a deafening sound filled his head.

He twisted and turned as his ears rang with the blast of noise. While it felt like his eyes were being stung by white hot needles

Then he felt a rush of air. Before he could right himself, his side slammed against something hard that sent him spinning. Twice more he collided with hard objects—first in the back and then in the head. Finally he came to a hard stop on the unforgiving ground.

As his body rang with pain, he curled up into a fetal position. ears and eyes still covered as best he could.

He couldn't tell how much had passed, but when he finally was able to open his eyes, he saw nothing but blackness. Suddenly he realized rough, gloved hands shaking him hard.

"RYUU! RYUU!" someone was screaming. "RYUU ANSWER US!"

"Stop shouting! My ears hurt enough as it is," he whimpered.

"Oh, thank the gods." Bryan's voice was filled with relief.

"Anything else we should know?" came Allison's voice.

"I can't see," Ryuu answered. "And my head feels like a starship landed on it. What was that?"

He heard Aiolos speak next. "That's not surprising, considering the blow to the head you took falling. And to answer that question, it was a flash bang. Our target booked it when you fell."

"Eric, help me to sit him up," Allison said gently putting him into position. "Ryuu, I'm shining a light in your eye. Do you see it?"

Ryuu just stared ahead. The blackness seemed never ending. "Nothing," he answered.

"Gods above!" Allison cursed. "I wish we took more than basic first aid. But from what I can tell from your pupils, you might have a slight concussion."

"You guys wait here. I'll get help." Brian said.

"NO!"

Ryuu heard everyone turn toward him.

"Ryuu you need—" Allison started.

"I know who did it." They fell silent. "I smelled him. It was Dulglad."

"Bastard!" Brian barked. "His father must have told him our grid, and they set this up to ensure we fail!"

"Not you, me!" Ryuu growled. He climbed to his feet. "And I'm not going to quit! They are not going to stop me from graduating!"

"But Ryuu, you can't see," Eric said. "How are you going to continue?"

"I can hear, and I can smell!" he hissed. Then he followed a scent to a tree and felt for a branch. "You guys will be my eyes. We all used flash bangs in training; we know this is temporary..." He turned, holding the branch to keep himself steady.

"Ryuu, that was in daylight, and it took half an hour for your sight to return," Brian said. "And that isn't counting—"

"I can do this!" Ryuu snapped. "Our target is still in the area! Get me up high enough and I can help you find him! You know we need every advantage we can get!"

For the next few seconds, Ryuu could almost hear the silent argument between them.

Then he heard Allison step forward. She wrapped her arm around his waist and put his arm over her shoulder. "Hang on," she muttered, and with her help, they climbed higher and higher into the trees.

When they reached a suitable spot, Allison settled him on a branch. She helped him kneel, gripping the branch in his hand.

Focusing on what his mother had taught him, he turned his head left and right to catch every sound around him while his ears slowly began to stop ringing. He took several deep sniffs, and the smells of the forest flooded him.

For the next ten minutes, he remained like that, going through the same movements. His aim was to pull that one particular scent and sound to help his friends.

As the minutes ticked by, the urgency to find their target grew rapidly, along with his rising panic he would not be able to stop his friends from being dragged down with him.

Just as the tension reached a boiling point, he froze. After taking two more sniffs, he whipped out a kunai knife. Spinning in a new direction, he hissed, "That way!"

Ryuu heard the others move forward. Carefully drawing back against the trunk of the tree. Ryuu raised his gaze upward as he focused on the return of his senses.

Moments later, he faintly heard, "You learned to work as a team; now it's time to work alone." Then he heard the breaking of glass, and he knew the target was gone.

When his friends returned, they cheered their success in the first part of this final test of their training.

"Eric, you're a genius!" Allison said.

"About time you admitted it, Allison."

"Did you see the look in his eyes when he realized we had herded him?"

"Hey," Bryan interjected, "me and Ryuu should get the credit for that! I did the herding, and Ryuu sniffed him out!"

"True," Ryuu said, "but this isn't over yet. We now have to accomplish that alone. We can't rely on each other as a team anymore. From here on out, it's one on one."

The group's sense of jubilation was quickly replaced with an air of nervousness.

"You really know how to kill a mood there, Ryuu," Bryan said.

Ryuu shrugged. "I'm just saying how it is. I don't mean to sound negative. Now let's head up the mountain to the Academy and finish what we started tonight. That is—after my sight returns."

Journey to the Academy

IT TOOK NEARLY an hour for his sight to return. When it did, the group spent the next thirty minutes jumping from branch to branch, moving further up the mountain. Ryuu felt like his legs were made of lead. Eventually, he stopped and looked up a ridge that was covered by the forest's oldest trees at the mountain's highest points. A waterfall flowed out of the ridge, into a pool in front of them.

Ryuu and his friends dropped down to the ground. All around them, the blades of grass swayed in the night air.

He looked at his friends and nodded. "Okay, let's do it."

They darted along the edge of the water until they reached the side of the waterfall. After a quick look around, Ryuu pressed on a medium-sized rock. Suddenly they were standing on the edge of the mountain, higher up still, in the forest region of a location only Ryuu's father, the grandmaster, knew. In front of them was the Gold Dragon Academy, which was built in the Japanese castle style with pillars and sloping roofs that didn't rise above the cover of the trees.

The Academy, founded centuries ago, was now run by Ryuu's father, who was dedicated to training a new generation of warriors. For centuries, the Black Dragon had failed to find it, and now the Academy also stood as a symbol of hope, especially for members of the Resistance, which many of the students joined after the completion of their training.

Ryuu and his friends stood there for a moment, just looking at it.

Aiolos folded his arms and said, "And to think that after tonight some of us may never see this place again."

Ryuu nodded and turned to his friends. "What are your plans for after tonight?"

Allison said, "Straight to the Resistance for me." Then she added, "That's after I take care of a few things here."

Eric said, "I follow my sister."

"Same here," Bryan agreed.

That left Aiolos. "Me, too. What about you, Ryuu?"

At first, he remained silent. "I don't know," he finally said. "My father has been asked to start training his replacement. I may stay and work to take his place here. Or else I... just might strike out on my own."

"What?" Allison demanded. "Why?"

Sighing, Ryuu looked away. "Look, I've been here for my whole life, and I'm still having trouble fitting in." He turned back to them. "Do you really think that—beyond you guys—I'd find more acceptance among their ranks? Or the same derision?"

After a few beats of silence, Allison put a hand on his shoulder. "We'll miss you, bro," she said. "No matter what you decide. We'll always be there for each other."

He smiled at them. "Well, you'll know where to find me, hopefully. Let's go!"

Once again, Ryuu took the lead, and they ran through the woods toward the Academy as fast as they could. He kept his hands back for balance as he leaned forward. They soon reached a narrow stone path, which had stone walls on either side that stood about ten feet high. They twisted and turned with the passage and leapt or flipped over obstacles as they darted along.

Eventually they approached a pit in the ground and leapt over it. One by one they grabbed a pole, which was embedded into the solid stone, and flipped over the pole a couple times before launching forward onto a platform set into a stone wall. Darting around the corner, they came to a wall and wall-jumped up to another platform. Then they darted forward again down the passage toward a series of ropes.

They each took out a four-pointed shuriken and hurled it to the side. The ropes started to shoot up, and they leapt up after them, hands outstretched. When they grabbed the ropes, they shot up like rockets through the stone tunnel.

At the top of the tunnel, where the pulley system ended, they released the ropes. One by one, they were launched into the air. Ryuu tucked his legs close as he shot into the sky over the same wide ravine where they had raced their sky riders earlier. The ravine separated the two woods on either side and the Academy. He pressed the buttons on his anti-grav belt as he soared through the air. Then he flipped around as they started to come down in the courtyard of the school, and his descent slowed.

At the end of the flip, he grabbed the branch of a tree on the edge of the ravine, swung under it, and flipped off it. He landed on one knee in the middle of a stone path in front of the main wooden gates and remained in that position, scanning the area with his eyes.

The courtyard was almost full.

His friends landed beside him.

"Looks like we're almost the last ones here," Allison muttered.

"Are you that surprised?" Eric asked her.

"No, not really."

"We're just too good," Aiolos said. "Despite almost being sabotaged."

"Aiolos, don't get overconfident."

"Oh, come on, Bryan, don't kill the mood."

"Aiolos, be serious."

"Ryuu, even you have to admit we're the best in the school."

"Yes, but it doesn't mean we should boast, especially since half the teachers here think I cheated my way to the top," Ryuu said. Then the group fell silent.

For half an hour, they remained that way, down on one knee and hand, waiting for more teams who'd passed to arrive. Eventually, fifteen more teams arrived just inside the time frame. Ryuu looked over at Dulglad's group and noted with some satisfaction his group looked beaten up. When all the teams were assembled, he heard grinding metal, and the giant wooden doors began to open.

Bit by bit the doors opened, and standing inside the doors was Ryuu's father, the grandmaster. He was wearing the traditional red grandmaster kimono with the lotus symbol of the clan on both of his shoulders. When the doors were all the way open, he stepped forward and surveyed the students as he walked down the line, looking each team member in the face.

The last team he checked was Ryuu's. He started with Aiolos and worked his way down until he finally reached Ryuu. Unable to resist, Ryuu glanced at his father, and the two looked each other in the eye for a split second before Ryuu dropped his gaze to the ground.

Jun smiled, walked back to the entrance, and looked at the students. He spread his arms wide and said, "I congratulate each one of you on a job well done on this part of the exams. Out of all the teams, only one failed to pass this part of your final examination. But for those who have passed, I would like to say I'm proud of each one of you for your notable effort. Now it's time for the second—and most important—part of your final examination. This will test all your personal knowledge as a ninja, and the passing of this test will bring an end to your training here. For some of you who have reached the age of eighteen, the completion of this test will mean not only the end of your lives here at the Academy but also the end of your lives here on this planet as you journey forth into the unknown."

Ryuu briefly looked at his friends. He would miss each one of them.

Then his father continued.

"I'll call you forward one at a time, and you'll proceed inside for the examination. Take this warning seriously. Be careful which path you choose. I wish you all luck, and let the second part of the examination begin!"

He stepped back into the shadows and vanished completely.

The Final Exam

ONE BY ONE, their names were called.

"Allison Cromnae."

Allison stood in a flash. She glanced at her friends, darted into the Academy, and soon was out of sight. For a little more than an hour, the others remained where they were, waiting for her to pass or fail while the moon and stars slowly crept their way across the sky. Then
. . .

"Eric Cromnae."

Over the course of several hours, the students in the courtyard lessened one by one until only Ryuu remained. Then, at long last, . . .

"Alac-Ryuu Jun Yamamoto."

Ryuu shot to his feet, stepped inside, and whipped around when he heard the gates start to close behind him. When they were completely closed, he was encased in darkness. After his eyes adjusted, he looked around through the gloom. Ahead of him were three tall, open doors.

He took a breath and quickly decided to try the middle door. As he approached the frame, a thick stone wall slammed down. He jumped back a little, surprised, then looked at the door to the left.

You'd think after almost thirteen years I'd be used to this, he thought. Dad said we were supposed to pick which way we wanted to go. He was about to enter through the doorway when he heard a loud crack above him.

He quickly turned back and leapt. Then he rolled back as another wall shot down and hit home where he'd been standing just a second ago. Breathing hard, he turned to look at the only unblocked passage.

Why this way? Probably the hardest of the three and the most dangerous. The teachers are probably trying to get me to quit or to prove that I cheated, he thought, and walked toward it.

He took a step over the threshold then jerked back, looking up, but nothing came down. He then took a deep breath and moved forward. When he was about twenty feet in, he stopped and looked back. The wall still hadn't fallen. Then he looked forward toward the pitch-black hall.

"I'm not going to quit," he muttered and started down it.

He walked down the hall in the darkness, his back to the wall with his hands hovering about an inch or two from it. Approaching the end, he peeked around the corner, eyes darting left and right, hearing and seeing nothing.

Something's not right. This doesn't feel like a test, he thought, but he had little choice other than to continue down the hall.

Through the darkness, he took a couple of steps forward. Suddenly, he leapt forward as, one right after other, sharp pointed rods shot out of the wall and into the opposite wall. He wall-jumped, flipped, rolled, and did everything in between to avoid being impaled by the poles.

He breathed hard, then ducked and rolled forward as a foot slammed into the wall where his head had just been. He whipped around as someone dressed like him stepped out of a concealed room and looked at him for a second, then crouched. Ryuu mimicked his movements in a flash.

Less than a second later, Ryuu threw a kick behind him, and it connected to another attacker, who was coming from the rear, followed by others. Ryuu then threw a front kick to the opponent in front of him, knocking the attacker back a couple steps. Next, he spun around, blocking a blow with his knee. He then jumped and used his leg to nail the attacker with a kick to the head. As he spun to the ground, Ryuu grabbed the attacker around the neck with a one-arm chokehold. His opponent's face turned down and he gave it a quick jerk.

Ryuu heard a snapping sound from the neck. He released him, and he fell to the floor, twitching. Ryuu then dropped down and swept the legs out from under the opponent beside him. Next, as the attacker was sitting up, Ryuu's leg swung forward in a blur of motion, nailing him across the face and sending him face-first into the floor. Ryuu rolled over him, pulled his head back, and struck him hard in the base of the neck with a shuto.

Ryuu then rolled forward and turned to face the last attacker, who climbed to his feet and stared at him. The two crouched in fighting stances, and Ryuu's attacker fired a hook kick to the head. Ryuu ducked under it, then blocked a roundhouse from the other leg, and his attacker took a step back after blocking a roundhouse from Ryuu.

For another long moment, they faced each other. Without warning, Ryuu's attacker hopped forward and threw a roundhouse. Ryuu blocked it, and his attacker threw a turning sidekick, which Ryuu blocked before throwing his own. His attacker blocked the kick and then threw a roundhouse, followed by another hook kick, which Ryuu blocked. Ryuu leapt up, nailing his attacker with a crescent kick to the head.

His opponent was knocked to the ground, but he rolled back onto his feet, and they faced off again. Ryuu threw a roundhouse, which his attacker blocked. When his opponent brought his foot down, Ryuu threw a punch, which his attacker sidestepped, driving his elbow into Ryuu's gut. To Ryuu's dismay, his attacker got a few more punches in before he could back off.

His attacker came after him again, throwing punches that Ryuu blocked. Ryuu nailed his opponent with a palm strike to the face. After this move, he whipped around, nailing the attacker with a backhand and knocking him off his feet. Seconds later, his attacker rolled back onto his feet and threw a front kick, which Ryuu grabbed. He then lifted his opponent off his feet, slamming him back onto the ground.

The next time his attacker was back on his feet, they circled each other. His opponent threw a punch at Ryuu's head. Ryuu blocked it, took hold of it, spun around, and flipped his foe onto his back. In a flash, his assailant was back on his feet. He spun around and kicked Ryuu's lower leg.

Ryuu gritted his teeth behind his mask as he struggled to stay standing, and his attacker threw a second kick. Ryuu blocked it, and as his enemy threw a third kick, he countered with a sidekick to his attacker's other knee. His attacker went down hard but was back on his feet in a flash.

His opponent tried to nail Ryuu with a high sidekick to the head, but Ryuu dropped down and nailed a second sidekick to the same knee. His attacker went back down, and Ryuu was back on his feet as his enemy got back up again. They stared at each other for half a second. Then Ryuu's attacker threw another punch.

Ryuu blocked it, caught it, and nailed his attacker with a backhand across the face before driving his gut into his rising knee. Ryuu forced his face up and nailed it with a palm strike to the face, immediately followed by a second one, driving him back before jumping up and nailing a second jumping crescent kick. His attacker hurtled to the ground before slowly climbing to his feet.

This time his attacker threw another punch, which Ryuu spun around, driving his elbow into his attacker's back. Ryuu nailed him with a second elbow to the gut before putting him in a one-arm chokehold. His attacker struggled a little, but Ryuu turned on the spot so they stood back-to-back Ryuu still held onto his attacker's head on his shoulder with both hands.

Ryuu felt his foe's feet dangle against his calves as he struggled to free himself from Ryuu's grasp. Then Ryuu jerked his attacker's head back, heard a snap, and let him go. He felt his attacker slide down his back onto the floor, where he didn't move.

Ryuu turned and looked down at the three assailants at his feet. Then he bent down and removed the masks from the two who were not moving. Beneath each mask was a black piece of dark metal, and Ryuu recognized it was where a holographic face would have been displayed before he had snapped each neck, cutting the power.

"Combat Bots," Ryuu muttered, before he moved on to the one who was still twitching.

He pulled back the mask and was glad to see the holographic human face. Then he lifted its right arm up with no resistance. He pulled its sleeve back and opened one of its access command ports. As soon as it was all the way up, the screen lit up, and Ryuu frowned at the red words printed on it.

KILL ALAC-RYUU

He pressed a button. A data strip popped out near the programming port, and he slipped it into his gauntlet before darting down the hall. At the next corner, he flattened himself against the wall and waited. Suddenly he threw a ridge hand, nailing a Combat Bot in the throat.

Before the Combat Bot could get its bearings, Ryuu grabbed it around its head and flipped it onto its back. Before the Bot could make a counterattack, Ryuu, quick as a flash, dropped down and grabbed it by the head. He twisted it hard to the side. He heard it snap, and when it didn't move after that, he continued.

He now knew this was planned to be more than a final test of his skill. This was a hunt, and he was the prize buck of the herd.

Well, this is one head that won't be mounted over their fireplace, he thought. Then he continued to move silently.

After the third corner he passed without any incident, he started to get a little edgy, so he stopped and looked around. He drew one of his Kunai knives from his leg sheath, twirled it around his finger by the ring at the end, and slashed a big X on the wall. He then continued onward. Ten minutes later, he stopped again, looked around, and slammed his fist into the wall.

As he stared at the giant X, he realized he was standing exactly where he'd been ten minutes ago. He looked around the bend, drew some of his Tonki metal balls from a pocket on his belt, and tossed them down the hallway. He watched the hallway for a few seconds, but nothing happened. Then he drew a couple more and tossed them behind him. Still nothing.

A second later, he heard a small sound no louder than a mouse scurrying across the floor. Without much surprise, he watched as the opposite corner at the end of the hall began to turn. A few seconds later, it opened a hall headed in a completely different direction.

Ryuu waited a moment. Then, confident, he stepped out into the middle of the hall but froze at the threshold. Why do I have the feeling everything is completely safe? he thought.

Unable to shake the feeling, he reached inside another belt pocket, pulled out a handful of powder, and held it close to his mouth. After taking a deep breath, he blew the power down the hall, and his eyes went wide with what he saw. From the ceiling to the floor—and every other angle in between—were lines of tightly grouped lasers.

There's no pattern to them, and they're too close together to slip by them, he thought. He was even more worried about what they might trigger.

Ryuu darted forward at full speed, and a second later, right behind him, lasers started firing from one wall to the other. He raced ahead of the laser fire as he rounded the corner. After running almost flat out for almost twenty minutes, dodging around corners and doing everything he could to keep ahead of the laser fire, he saw something that almost brought him to a stop.

Ahead, a section of the ceiling and floor rose up and down, sealing him in. He ran as fast as his legs would carry him, and when the two walls were about a foot apart, he dived forward, hands thrust out in front of him, and sailed between them, his feet barely clearing the gap just before it slammed closed. He rolled on the ground, whipped around, and looked at the solid wall behind him, breathing hard in relief.

"That, I doubt, is part of the testing," he muttered. Then he stood straight and continued on his way at a brisk run.

At the next turn, he flattened himself against the wall and pulled out a star shuriken. Using one of the blades as a mirror, he checked the hall before dashing down it. After the next turn, he finally relaxed. There was a sliding

Japanese door at the end of the hall. He slipped out a shuriken, hurled it halfway down the hallway, and watched as it planted itself into the stone floor.

A split second later, what looked like an axe swung out of the wall and planted itself in the opposite wall.

Ryuu shook his head. "This is getting kind of freaky," he said aloud. Then he walked forward and picked up the shuriken.

He stepped around the axe, slid back the door, and stepped into an area that resembled an old-fashioned, Dojo-decked room. One of his teachers sat on his knees, a sheathed Katana on the floor at his side, facing the opposite wall. Even from the back, he was recognizable.

As Ryuu slid the door closed behind him, the man shifted.

"I see you've made it this far. Impressive for a cheat," he said.

The man stood up, picking up the katana, and turned to face Ryuu with his usual sneer. Ryuu said nothing but unslung his bow and slipped a couple of arrows from the quiver. Ahead, his teacher, in a ring of steel, drew his sword and dropped the sheath at his side.

"Tonight you'll be exposed as the cheat you are," he said. The man got into a fighting stance and charged forward.

As Ryuu fired all the arrows, which were blocked by his teacher's sword, his teacher closed the distance between them. Ryuu ducked when the man reached out with his sword to swipe Ryuu's neck. As soon as the sword cleared, quicker than a flash, Ryuu hooked him around the neck with the string of the bow. His teacher turned to face him as the momentum pulled the bowstring.

Ryuu looked him in the eye for half a second before letting the bow go, and it slammed into his teacher's face, knocking him off his feet.

"Cheat that," Ryuu mocked, standing over him.

Ryuu looked at his teacher, who now had a massive bump on his forehead and a bloody, broken nose. He then picked up his bow and started to leave. Stopping in mid-step, he looked back at his teacher. Quickly making up his mind, he returned to his teacher's side and drew one of his kunai knives.

He used it to cut a section from his teacher's clothes. He folded up the cloth, dabbed the blood from the man's nose, then took some herbs from a secret pocket. He crushed the juices out of them, poured them onto the cloth, and placed it on his teacher's forehead before silently leaving the room through the sliding door on the opposite wall.

Ryuu looked down the hall and smiled when he saw the night sky light the opening at the end. Then he heard a loud, grinding sound. He darted forward as fast as he could as the walls began closing in on him. He knew if he didn't make it out in time, he would be crushed like a grape between two fingers. He felt his heart beating under his ribs as he ran flat out. The walls continued to get closer and closer, threatening to turn him into a pancake.

His muscles burned from the constant usage, and he could almost hear them screaming at him to stop. He silently gave himself a pep talk.

Come on, Alac-Ryuu Jun Yamamoto. You're almost through this! You can rest all you want when this is over, but right now, you've got to run or be killed!

The gap became smaller and smaller, but somehow he went faster.

When he was barely a few yards from the exit, with his pumping elbows scraping the walls, he leapt forward, spinning hands and arms outstretched. His fingertips were clear . . . his elbows were clear . . . the walls were inches from his face . . . his head was clear . . . his chest and stomach were clear . . . he felt the walls barely scraping his knees. The walls slammed home just as the tips of his toes cleared; he was out, and he rolled onto his back, completely out of breath.

He lay there for a moment, looking up at the night sky. Then, uncontrollably, he started to laugh, unable to stop even as he heard running footsteps coming his way. He was still laughing when several masked faces appeared in his vision, peering down at him.

"What's up with him?" Allison said.

"He seems to be showing a loss of motor control," Eric answered.

"What?" Bryan said.

"He's lost it."

"No he's just . . . giddy," Aiolos said.

"Hey, Aiolos." Ryuu reached up and grabbed Aiolos's arm, still laughing.

"What?"

"Have you ever seen such a beautiful night?" His laughing increased.

Aiolos looked at Eric and said, "No, you're right on the button, Eric. He's definitely lost it."

This only made Ryuu laugh even louder.

The Dragon Knights

RYUU WAS STILL laughing when they helped him sit up, and he saw his father examining the wall he'd just run out of. When Ryuu was finally able to calm himself down, he stood and his father came over. Jun glanced at Ryuu for a second, then back at the wall, then at Ryuu again.

Jun then jabbed a thumb back at the wall. "Did you just come from there?" he demanded.

Ryuu nodded, and his father took a couple steps back in shocked surprise.

"Alac-Ryuu Jun Yamamoto, what possessed you to go that way?" he snapped. "That was the course I took when I was tested for the position of grandmaster!"

Everyone stared as he continued, "And for that matter, who the heck left it open? It was supposed to be closed for the testers tonight!"

Ryuu shrugged and removed his mask. "I didn't have much of a choice in the matter. I was going to go for the opening in the middle when a solid stone wall stopped me. It almost crushed me, too."

"Damn," Aiolos muttered. "First it was that flash bang, and now this."

"FLASH BANG!" his father barked, whipping around, and Ryuu shot Aiolos a hard look. "Would one of you tell me exactly what is going on tonight?"

During the next five minutes, Ryuu explained everything that had happened. When he was finished, his father stared at him.

54

"Incredible. That's never happened before. And I never imagined that Shuji would go to such lengths!"

Then he asked to see the data strip Ryuu had taken from the Combat Bot.

Ryuu bent his right wrist back, and with two fingers from his left hand, he pulled the strip from under his gauntlet. His father took the strip and then bowed to him. Alac returned the gesture and then his father walked away, the strip clenched in his fist.

After Jun left the area, Ryuu's friends put their hands on his shoulders and back. They each congratulated him on getting through the course in one piece.

"Man, I can see why that's only for Grandmaster Status testing," Eric said. "No safety features, no chance of stealth entry, and you always have to be on the move, with an outcome of pass or die."

Ryuu nodded. "You don't have to tell me. What'd you guys do?"

Allison glanced at him as they walked in the same direction his father had taken. "We took the middle passage. It was pretty much a snatch-and-grab mission, whereas yours sounds more like an assassination," she said.

Ryuu nodded. "Yeah, and the only way to get in and out was being a one-man army and a tight squeeze."

Ryuu slipped his mask back on as the rest of the class came into view. They were lined up in two rows. All the teams were sitting back on their heels, facing a low stage about ten feet from the first row of students. Across the opening, banners with Japanese lettering hung from the pillars.

They stepped inside the walled courtyard, and Ryuu's eyes traveled over the brightly colored banners that had been put up for the graduation ceremony.

They made their way to the front of the group, sat on their knees, and waited. After a couple of minutes, they heard the teachers walk down the lane and onto the stage. Once on the stage the teachers began to assemble in a line in front of their students, and Ryuu noticed one had an ice pack strapped to his head and a bandage around his nose. He averted his gaze.

He'll be feeling that in the morning, he thought, as he heard Aiolos give a small cough. He looked at his friend and shook his head slightly. He didn't want to aggravate the tense situation any further.

When all the teachers were assembled, there was a puff of smoke, and when it cleared, Ryuu's father stood before them in his grandmaster kimono. Jun briefly glanced at the teacher with the ice pack, but then returned his gaze to his students, and he smiled and spread his arms wide.

"Congratulations, all, on a job well done in tonight's final examination. Well done, well done indeed," he said.

When Jun lifted one of his arms, revealing an oriental box, Ryuu sucked in his breath. Beside him, he heard his teammates do the same. He watched as his father opened the lid, exposing small black-and-white medallions that bore the clan and school crest.

When the lid was completely open, Ryuu's father faced his students again.

"When I call your name, come forward and receive your master status. Allison Cromnae!"

Allison jumped to her feet, walked onto the stage, and smiled at Ryuu's father. Jun picked up a medallion and held it in front of her.

"Allison Cromnae, from this moment forward until forever, you shall be known as Red Bear because you're strong, fierce, and unstoppable until you achieve your goal." She bowed forward, and Jun slipped the medallion around her neck.

She bowed to him again and retook her seat.

"Eric Cromnae," the grandmaster said, and he picked up another medallion.

"Eric Cromnae, quick-witted, cunning, strong, and yet with a kind heart. You shall be known as Silver Ape," he said.

Eric bowed, and Jun smiled. Then he slipped the medallion around Eric's neck. After another bow, Eric retook his position.

"Bryan Hunson," Jun called, and Bryan moved forward. The grandmaster picked up another medallion.

"A team player, a will of iron, loyal to a fault to your friends, to your family, to your cause, and to yourself. You shall be known as Iron Wolf," Ryuu's father said.

After more bowing, Bryan moved back to his friends.

"Aiolos Hudson." Aiolos quickly moved to the stage. Ryuu's father picked up another medallion and faced him.

"Quick witted, fast, reckless at times, boisterous, humorous, but with a will as free as the wind itself. You shall be known as White Falcon."

Ryuu's legs felt like lead as he anticipated his turn. Then his father looked in his direction and called out, "Dulglad Iga."

Ryuu frowned as Dulglad stepped forward, got his name and medallion, and retook his seat. One by one, the other students went forward and received their names and medallions. After the last one walked back to retake his seat, Ryuu saw that there were no more medallions left for him.

He lowered his gaze. I failed, he thought. He seemed to feel Dulglad's nasty smile burning an imprint into his back, and a couple teachers chuckled.

Then Jun continued. "There is one student here whose name I didn't call yet. Tonight he was forced into a test that called upon skills above and beyond the requirements of his graduation. He faced great peril if he failed, which would have meant the loss of his own life. He has prospered in combat, evasion, gathering information, and cunning. He finished his mission, setting a new record for the course, and at the end he even helped his fallen foe.

"He is to be honored tonight for his impeccable bravery in the face of mortal danger and the unknown. So it's my great pleasure to call my son, Alac-Ryuu Jun Yamamoto," he said.

Ryuu looked up at his father and felt all eyes turn on him. After a moment, Allison gave him a small push, and he climbed to his feet. He walked onto the stage and stood before his father. His eyes darted to the teachers for a split second. Some looked unhappy, while others refused to meet his gaze.

His father smiled at him. Then, from his own neck, he unclasped his medallion and held it in his hands. "Alac-Ryuu Yamamoto, brave as a tiger, wise, cunning, kind at heart, righteous, comrade, a will of fire with a temper to match, and loyal to all who stand by you. You shall be known as Dragon's Fire, and it's my honor to make you, this day, Grandmaster," he said. He clasped the medallion around his son's neck.

Overcome with joy, Ryuu struggled to maintain his composure as he bowed to his father, who bowed back. Then he returned to his seat. He could barely contain his enthusiasm as his father addressed the assembled students.

"Again, well done to you all. It's been my deepest honor to have known and taught you. Whatever journey awaits you beyond the walls of this school, always remember the family that was forged here. And now, go forth, my brothers and sisters, and whatever path you choose, may you face it with your hearts open and your heads held high!"

As one, the students leapt to their feet, cheering.

Immediately, Ryuu was bombarded by his friends, who nearly tackled him to the ground.

"GRANDMASTER RYUU! HA! HA!" Bryan called out, shoving Ryuu's fist into the air.

"Positively spectacular!" Eric shouted, slapping Ryuu on the back.

"Everyone make way for Grandmaster Dragon's Fire!" declared Aiolos in a loud, formal voice.

Ryuu looked at everyone as he slipped off his mask. "Come on, guys, I'm not the only one who graduated tonight," he said, but inside, he wanted to jump for joy.

"Yeah, but none of us graduated as a grandmaster! Now, what are you made of? Make some noise!" Allison took his shoulders and shook him.

Ryuu finally gave in to his desires and jumped up and down, rejoicing as loudly as he could.

After almost an hour of celebrating, the students began to file out of the school and make their way home.

"I don't know about the rest of you, but I could eat a rhino," Eric said, as the group came out of the woods and Ryuu looked out at the rising sun.

"Come on; my house is closest," Ryuu said, leading the way.

The house was dark and quiet as they entered the kitchen. They moved silently, not wanting to wake his mother, and paused at the fridge. Before he could press the door release button to open the fridge, he paused. On the front of the unit, a light flashed. When Ryuu pressed it, a holographic note appeared.

Alac-Ryuu,

Went next door to help a neighbor. Be back soon.

Pizza in the fridge.

Mom

PS: Your father called and told me.

I'm so proud of you.

"At least we get the place to ourselves," Aiolos said.

Ryuu looked at him. "Well, don't get any ideas. Your last one got me grounded for a month."

Despite his recent victory, he was still disappointed no one had remembered his birthday. "I guess we've got pizza for my birthday," he said gloomily. Then he pressed the release button, and the fridge door slid into itself.

As he took out the pizza, he heard his friends moan and groan behind him.

"Darn," Allison said. "That's today?"

"Not you guys, too!" he groaned, turning back to them.

"Oh, come on, Alac, give us a break," Bryan said regretfully, running his hand down his face. "The finals drove it out of our minds," he finished and Ryuu looked over at him.

Not trusting himself to speak, Ryuu took a bite of cold pizza and turned to walk into the living room, sliding back the door. As he reached for the light button on the wall beside the door, the lights flicked themselves on.

At once, a strong sense of flight or fight bombarded Ryuu as he was instantly blinded and deafened by a variety of sights and sounds.

"SURPRISE!" the small crowd shouted.

Ryuu blinked at them, pizza dangling from his mouth.

An uncontrolled smile spread across his face as he read the signs on the walls. The first said, HAPPY BIRTHDAY! Below it, what looked like a hastily scrawled sign added, GRANDMASTER ALAC-RYUU JUN YAMAMATO!

"Oh, I hate you guys!" he barked. But he was laughing as his parents came over, and they formed a group hug.

"Happy birthday, my boy," his father said, slapping his shoulder.

"I can't believe you thought we would forget!" his mother said. "And you should have seen the look on your face when the light went on!" She gave him a peck on the cheek.

He tried not to think about his expression. Instead, he muttered, "Don't talk to me right now. I hate you!" His parents laughed along with him as friends and neighbors came forward to offer their birthday greetings.

"Well, don't give us all the blame," his father said. "This wasn't completely our idea." Out of the corner of his eye, he saw his friends edging toward the back door.

The crowd parted a little, laughing, as Ryuu took off after his friends. As they barreled outside, he threw himself lengthwise, tackling them, and for a couple of minutes the friends wrestled across the ground, bits of grass and dust swirling in the air from their mock fight. Eventually they ended in a tangled heap. Catching his breath, looked back at the house, where the rest of the party guests were laughing and shaking their heads from the open door.

Ryuu quickly changed his clothes, and thirty minutes later they were all laughing, eating pizza, chips, and other party snacks, dancing, and playing games. The party lasted well through the day, although some of Ryuu's friends took quick naps to recover from the night's events. Through it all, despite his surprise at being successfully tricked, he couldn't help enjoying the double celebration.

As the sun began to set and the lights dimmed a little, his mother brought him a birthday cake with lit candles. The guests all sang "Happy Birthday," and Alac closed his eyes and made the same wish he made every year: to be reunited with his birth mother, wherever she was.

Smiling, he blew out the candles. The party guests applauded and brought forth gifts as his parents handed out the cake. He opened each present with eager hands and a glint in his eye. He was admiring a new sky surfer when some of the guests parted to allow one of the oldest members of the community to come forward. Ryuu lowered his head in respect.

"Mr. Orleaus," he muttered.

Mr. Orleaus smiled at him. "Well, happy birthday, Mr. Yamamoto, and congratulations on becoming grandmaster." He bowed back.

Then a sneering voice from the doorway added, "Out of sheer dumb luck."

Ryuu and the others turned to see Dulglad, who leaned against a doorframe. He was surrounded by his friends, who all wore the same hard looks on their faces.

"Oh, is that what your father said?" Ryuu asked. He heard a couple of his friend's snicker.

Dulglad's face hardened at once. Mr. Orleaus ignored the tension and continued.

"The gift that I bring to you this special day is not like one you've received yet, for it's a story. A story that's a part of us, of a time that's long since been over. A time when we didn't have to hide on backwater planets. A time when fear didn't ruin our lives, and we lived in peace and harmony in the age of technology of Humans, of magic, and of Dragons. The age of the Dragon Knights." A couple people looked at each other, muttering.

"And you would condemn us by telling this story? You stupid old man!" Dulglad snapped. He stalked forward, and Ryuu stepped in his way.

He and Dulglad stared daggers at each other. Finally, Ryuu broke the silence and said, "It's my birthday, and a gift to me. I'll hear it. Anyone who doesn't want to hear it and prefers to forget our past, when we lived in peace, may leave." Then he added, "Besides, you forget we're already condemned. If the Black Dragon's forces ever find us, we will all be captured and sold as slaves. Or annihilated."

He glanced at the people around him. Some were muttering, but no one moved to leave. Ryuu looked back at Dulglad and his friends. "And you?" he asked.

One by one, Dulglad and his friends stepped back, but they didn't leave. Ryuu, struggling to keep his breathing calm, finally returned his attention to Mr. Orleaus. Their eyes locked for a moment, and Ryuu motioned for the man to continue.

Mr. Orleaus bowed again, moving to the center of the living room. Then he cleared his throat and turned to face them, arms wide. "Listen well, for the tale I tell is a part of everyone in this room.

"We are each controlled by our past, and unless we learn from it, we have no chance of a better future.

"Ages upon ages ago, after centuries of hiding, people and creatures of magic revealed themselves to the non-magical beings. For a long period after that, they worked happily together and reached for the stars. They even found and restored dead planets, including the one we now stand on.

"Unfortunately, prejudice and mistrust began to grow between the magical and the non-magical races. One day the tension rose so high, both parties seemed to snap. No one knows who started the fighting, but it grew to such an intensity both sides realized if they continued, they would destroy each other.

"Therefore, one day, emissaries from both sides called for a cease-fire. For an uncounted time, they negotiated, until they finally decided to find a way to link the races, binding their fates together as one, for the sake of peace for all. Ultimately, so conflict could never rise between the nations again, they decided to create a band of immortal warriors to keep the peace and bring justice to the stars.

"These warriors would not be a part of one of the nations, but both. This would ensure no warrior would ever be biased to the other party. Rather, they would honor and respect a perfect blend of magic and technology. Through this agreement, the emissaries planted the seeds that founded one of the greatest and bravest groups of men and women in all the ages: The Dragon Knights.

"For years, the non-magical beings pooled all their knowledge of technology together, a knowledge that surpasses ours even today. Then seven members of the most powerful magical race, the Dragons, poured their magic into that greatest technology, and thus they forged the armors of the Dragon Knights. With the armors completed, the Dragon Knights chartered a star ship dubbed the Sherwood to reach out to all the people of the stars. And for millennia, peace reigned throughout the nations, and under the protection of the Dragon Knights led by the brave and just Avalor, all people and creatures flourished."

Mr. Orleaus paused as Ryuu glanced around, wondering how many had Avalor as their hero. Looking back, he saw Mr. Orleaus and shook his head sadly. He said, "If only it could have lasted."

Then he sighed deeply and continued, "From within the ranks of the Magical and Non-Magical Council whose members included the representatives of all races, a mighty Black Dragon considered the pact between the magical and the non-magical to be a joke. His objections grew so much that one of the leaders of the council, the Gold Dragon, who was the strongest of all the magical beings, forced him to leave. For a few more years, peace continued, and the Black Dragon's words were forgotten.

"Then one day, on an agricultural planet, a shadow fell as the Black Dragon and his army descended upon the people, enslaving the non-magical beings. At first, the Gold Dragon sent emissaries to the Black Dragon, but all messages were ignored, and many messengers were killed. Soon the Black Dragon's forces spread like an evil wave. Then the cold day came when war was declared, and the Knights were called in to lead the forces of the nations.

"As powerful as the armies and navies were, they were no match against the power of the Black Dragon. The only one who could match his might was the Gold Dragon, and when the two finally met in combat, a battle waged like never before. The lives of all free people hung in the balance.

"For days, the two dragons battled for supremacy over the other. When the battle finally settled, the Gold Dragon was slain, and the Black Dragon proclaimed himself ruler over all. Over the years, hope faded as one by one the Knights were hunted down and killed, their armors seized.

"And from the day of the last Dragon Knight's death and the disappearance of the Sherwood nearly a century ago, enslavement and fear have met the masses of the people of both nations, forcing ours into hiding. No one knows what happened to the Sherwood, and the only clue to its location was a message transmitted from the last Knight, saying that it is 'within the eye of the god of the gods.' But from these ashes was born the Resistance, whose leader is shrouded in shadow and mystery. Now fighters both magical and non-magical gather to await the next generation of Dragon Knights, and with them the birth of the next Gold Dragon," Mr. Orleaus concluded.

The room was silent as the story ended. Some people exchanged uneasy looks, and Ryuu saw his father put a comforting hand on his mother's shoulder. After a couple minutes, people started muttering. Taking a breath, Ryuu wiped his eyes and looked out at the setting sun.

Clearing his throat, he thanked Mr. Orleaus, picked up a drink, and walked to the middle of the room. When he was sure he had everyone's attention, he said, "Well, I want to thank everyone for this party, though some of you, whom I won't name, are now on my hit list." A couple people laughed, and he smiled at his friends. Then he continued, "But again, thank you for coming, even if it's for someone as boring as me . . ."

A few more people laughed, while others just shook their heads.

". . . and for all the gifts and everything. I know it's starting to get late, so I'll conclude with this." He raised his drink. "To the return of the Knights!" he declared.

Around him, people froze in their tracks and stared. For a long moment, he stood there with a raised drink as only silence met him.

Then Bryan, Allison, Eric, and Aiolos raised their drinks. Bryan said, "To the return of the Knights!"

"Dragon Knights unite!" Allison offered.

"To the Knights!" Eric chimed in. "And the downfall of the Black Dragon!"

"Dragon Knights kick butt!"

Everyone looked at Aiolos for a second. Then all the guests raised their drinks, and soon the room was filled with a milder version of that toast. And, as Ryuu smiled, they all drank.

The Right Thinking

AS ALAC WAS in the kitchen saying goodbye to a few of his neighbors, his friends came up, and Allison slapped him on his shoulder.

"Now you definitely remind me of me, because the speech was nice and short, and that toast took a lot of guts!" she said and handed him another drink.

"Thanks." He smiled. "You guys do realize I'm going to get you back for this, right?"

Aiolos said, "Oh, come on, man, you know you loved it."

Ryuu laughed in spite of himself and nodded. Then, as they moved back toward the living room, he froze. He could hear Dulglad's loud voice coming from outside.

"That freak is going to get us all killed one day!"

Ryuu's face hardened, and his friends frowned. When Ryuu glanced out the window, he saw Dulglad talking to his friends.

"If we've got to deal with a son like this, I can only imagine what kind of person his mother was," he heard Melinda say.

"Probably some drifter colony bum or drunk," Kade said.

Ryuu clenched his fingers and started to shake with rage.

"More likely she was a lowly slave girl," Dulglad said.

The glass in Ryuu's hand shattered under his grip.

Before his friends could stop him, he raced out the door and, launching himself from the porch, nailed Dulglad with a flying side kick. Dulglad lurched forward as Ryuu landed nimbly on his feet. For a second, Dulglad's friends looked at Ryuu, dumbfounded. Then Bamber and Melinda took out small rods that extended to bo staffs, and came at him.

Kade started with a punch, which Ryuu countered with a kick to his chest, sending him back before he side kicked Babieca to his right. He turned in time to grab Melinda's arm and threw her over his shoulder as she attacked with her staff. As he slipped her staff from her grasp, he ducked under a swing from Bamber.

As Ryuu turned to face Bamber, he kicked Kade back to the ground and blocked another attack from Bamber's staff. When Bamber withdrew his staff, Ryuu dropped down and swept his legs out from under him. After blocking a blow from Melinda with the staff, he then jumped to his feet, locked her arm up, and threw her to the ground.

Releasing the staff, he then did a couple handsprings, landing back on his feet. Babieca and Kade grabbed his arms as Bamber came at him, fist raised. He leapt up and wrapped his ankles around Bamber's neck, and using his body weight, he went to the ground and sent Bamber over him onto his back behind him. Leaping to his feet, he side kicked Kade back to the ground, ducked under a crescent kick from Babieca, and, standing, backhanded him across the face.

When none of them got up, Ryuu walked over to Dulglad, and the two faced off. Dulglad threw a crescent kick, which Ryuu ducked under, and tried to follow up with a spin kick, which Ryuu blocked. Then Ryuu counter-punched him in the face, sending him spinning. Stunned by the blow, Dulglad froze as Ryuu leapt up, nailing him across the face with a spin kick that sent him to the ground.

His anger still boiling, Ryuu reached down and dragged Dulglad to his feet, holding him by his collar. Then he turned Dulglad to face him.

"Call my mother a lowly slave, will you?" he demanded. He threw his opponent ten feet, where he landed hard on the roof of a hover car.

With one leap, Ryuu was on the hood, crouching over him. This time he grabbed Dulglad by the neck, fist pulled back to strike.

"RYUU!"

He froze and looked back. His friends were staring at him from the bottom of the steps.

"Ryuu, he may have it coming, but he's not worth it!" Bryan said.

Ryuu glanced down at Dulglad, who cowered beneath him.

Allison yelled, "Ryuu, we heard what he said—a lot of people did—and believe me, I'd do worse and you know it. But you have to ask yourself, would hitting him make you any different?"

"My sister's right, Ryuu," Eric insisted. "The taste won't be sweet, but bitter."

"Do the right thing and make both of your mothers proud," Aiolos said. "Be the bigger man and let him go."

Ryuu remained still, breathing hard, trying to get his inflamed temper in check. Then, with a brief yell, he shot his fist forward and struck the force field next to Dulglad's head. Slowly he let Dulglad go, stood, and hopped back down from the car.

"You're right," he muttered. He started to walk toward his friends.

"Coward!" Dulglad yelled from behind him.

"Hey!" Allison shouted. "He kicked all your asses! More important, by walking away he just proved he's more of a man than you'll ever be! So why don't you shut up?"

"Besides," Ryuu growled, "I still owe you one." As everyone looked at him, he spun around and threw a hard punch into Dulglad's face, launching the teen off his feet.

"That's for the flash bang and for nearly getting me killed!" he snapped, jabbing a finger.

Dulglad clutched his broken nose while people gawked.

There was a soft cough from the porch, and when they all turned toward the sound, Ryuu saw his parents. They were standing on the porch with their arms crossed. Jun held Ryuu's gaze for several long moments before they slowly turned and went inside.

"Oh, man," Ryuu muttered.

Aiolos patted his back. "If you survive, we'll see you later."

Ryuu managed a weak smile and nodded.

"I'll see you tomorrow, guys," he muttered. Then he took a final look at Dulglad and his friends. Bamba and Kade were still moaning on the ground, while Babieca was clearly nursing an injury. Turning his back, he went inside.

The living room was dimly lit, but most of the plates and glasses had already been cleared away. Sitting on their knees in the middle of the room were his parents, eyes closed.

Sighing, Ryuu started toward his room. Then his mother's voice called out, "Ryuu, come back in and sit by us."

Sighing again, he rubbed the back of his neck and stopped. Then he gave a quick moan and said, "It's still my birthday. Can't this wait?"

"Birthday or no birthday, you'll listen now," his father said firmly.

Ryuu remained still for a moment. Then slowly, face downcast, he walked forward and slipped down to his knees before them. When he was seated, they opened their eyes and looked at him. For a few seconds, he held each of their gazes in turn. Then he lowered his eyes to the floor.

"Tell us the most important thing we taught you," his father said.

Ryuu shifted his weight from side to side. "To possess the right frame of mind in order to gain strength, knowledge, and peace."

For a second, the room was filled with silence. Then his mother placed her hands lovingly on his cheeks and said, "Alac-Ryuu, we've tried so hard to channel your anger about the fact that your birth mother had to leave you. But so much is left. You've chosen to face it alone, but you must not forget your friends. And you must not forget us."

Then she cupped his chin and lifted his head so his gaze met her eyes. He looked at her, breathing in gasps, and a tear formed in the corner of his eye. Before it could fall, his mother pulled him into an embrace, and he cried into her. Soon his father's strong arms held them both tightly as Ryuu cried in wheezing gasps.

"Shhh," his mother soothed him. "We'll always be here, Ryuu. We always will." She rubbed his back.

"Why . . . why . . . why did she leave me?" he said, between gasps.

His parents looked at him and then at each other. After a few moments, his father said, "Because she loved you so much she would rather have died than to see you come to harm."

His mother took his hand in her own. "Either of us would do the same for you now."

Ryuu knew she spoke the truth.

The Next Generation

THAT NIGHT RYUU lay on his mat, his thoughts on his birth mother. He still stung with the shame of the fight with Dulglad, but more than that, he couldn't stop going over what his parents said.

Did they know her? he asked himself repeatedly. Why did she bring me here?

Finally, a clock in the hall chimed midnight, and he rolled over and went to sleep.

About an hour later, he awoke with a jerk as his ears filled with a loud ringing sound. Twisting around, he used his feet to turn his clock to check the time. He growled when he saw it was only one in the morning.

Still moaning, he slammed himself back down and stuffed his head under his pillow. For half an hour, he tossed and turned, trying to get rid of the sound.

Finally, he gave up. As he got to his feet, he growled, "Whoever is making that noise had better find themselves a tombstone!"

He continued to block his ears as he searched the house for the cause of the noise. Ten minutes later, he silently crept to his parent's room. He froze when he looked in; they were sleeping as if nothing was happening. To him, however, the sound was so painful he began to grit his teeth.

Leaving his parents undisturbed, he turned and quietly walked into the bathroom. As he crossed the threshold, the lights turned on. He stepped in front of the mirror, and a little holographic woman appeared on the counter.

"Good evening, Ryuu. Please state your requirement."

"Medical," he muttered. From the ceiling, a ring descended and ran down him.

"Bio temperature: normal. Digestive tract: normal. Skeletal: normal. Brain activity: normal. Abrasions: negative—"

"Primary focus, ear canal, left and right, intense ringing sound," he said through clenched teeth, and the ring raised itself to hover around his head level.

The computer was silent for a moment. Then, "Ear canals: normal; cause of ringing sound: unknown. Do you still require assistance?"

"No," Ryuu moaned. He moved out of the bathroom before the computer called him crazy.

Back out in the hall, his hands clamped around his ears, he slowly made his way to the front door and slipped outside to the porch. Taking a couple steps forward, he moaned again. It seemed like the noise was even louder outside the house. After taking a couple steps forward, he stumbled down the stairs and landed hard on his back.

He quickly rolled onto his elbows, hands flying to his ears. When he looked up, he was surprised to see his friends walking down the street toward him, hands over their ears.

"You all right?" Allison yelled when they reached him. He got to his feet.

"Yeah, mostly!" he shouted back. "You hear it too?" he shouted at Bryan when he got close.

"What?" he barked back. For a second, Bryan uncovered his ear. Then he snapped his hand back in place.

Almost doubled over, Aiolos stumbled a bit as he stepped forward, ears covered. "Whoever is making this noise had better have a death wish, because I'm going to kill him," he shouted.

"What?" the others yelled.

72

Ryuu waved his head left and right. "It's coming from that way!" He tilted his head and nodded toward the forest.

"What?" his friends demanded.

He sighed, removed his hand from his right ear, and pointed. As soon as he did, the group moved in that direction. Moments later, they were walking out of the village and into the forest. Deaf to the world around them, they stumbled through the forest. Eric emerged first, but as he did so, he nearly fell into the ravine they raced through and jumped over during the exam.

Ryuu and Allison darted forward and grabbed him as he flailed his arms for balance. For what seemed like an hour, the three teetered along the edge before they were able to pull him back to solid ground. Breathing hard, Ryuu clamped his hands over his sore ears as Eric grasped his sister in a tight bear hug. Ryuu looked around as the others came out of the forest, and Allison gently pushed Eric away before he smothered her.

Ryuu looked over the edge and cursed silently. The sound was coming from down the ravine, but he could see no way down. As he turned to shout this information to his friends, he eyed a cliff that ran to one side. Narrowing his eyes, he examined it more closely, and after a moment, gritting his teeth in pain, he picked up a stone from the ground and tossed it.

He watched the stone disappear over a dip and then reappear on another ledge. Excited, he stepped closer, looked down, and saw that a series of rocks jutted from the side of the cliff and ran down it. Smiling, he turned and saw the others hip deep in a silent debate.

He tried to signal them. When that failed, he flicked his foot and sent a pebble flying in their direction. He cringed when it struck Aiolos on the side of his head.

Aiolos gave a yelp and faced Ryuu, who, after a moment, bobbed his head in the direction of what he found. They came over, Aiolos nursing the spot where he had been hit, and looked down. They turned and some gave him the thumbs up and waved for him to go first.

He nodded, stepped in front of them, and, taking a deep breath, took the first step on to what appeared to be thin air, but was actually the first rock in the series of steps leading to the bottom of the ravine. For ten minutes, they walked down the cliff, and as they did, Ryuu was able to lower his hands. The volume of the ringing sound descended as they did. When they finally came to the end, they all stood on a lone cliff edge in the middle of the ravine.

"Well, at least it's quieter down here," Bryan said.

Ryuu looked around. There, shadowing them all, was a cave set into the wall of the ravine.

After a moment, Aiolos waved his hand and mouthed, "After you."

Sighing, Ryuu walked into the gloom. Inside, he blinked a couple of times to get his eyes used to the darkness. Then the others joined him.

"So, did anyone here bring a flashlight?" Aiolos asked.

"You'd think after all these centuries, they'd come up with a better name," Eric said.

"Eric, I didn't ask for a linguistics discussion; I just want to know if anyone brought one."

"Nope."

"Didn't think I'd need one."

"Negative."

"I was concentrating on saving my hearing."

"Never seem to need one."

Aiolos scowled and turned to Ryuu. "Well, Mr. Owl Eyes, lead the way!"

They laughed as they walked through the cave. Ryuu guided them as best he could, but every now and then, they still stumbled or bumped their heads. After several more minutes, Aiolos let out a large groan and rubbed his scalp.

"Okay, that's it. If I get hit in the head one more time—"

"What are you going to do, Aiolos, scream like a girl?" Allison asked.

"No, that would be your department, considering you're a girl."

"I'll show you what kind of girl I am!"

Ryuu turned in time to see Allison pounce in Aiolos's direction, but he dodged out of the way, so instead she attacked Bryan. Ryuu rolled his eyes as Bryan tried to fend her off.

"Allison, let Bryan go. Aiolos is at your nine o'clock," he said.

Allison, who just put Bryan into a chokehold, froze.

"Oh, thanks a lot, man," Aiolos muttered, and Allison whipped her head around in his direction.

Smiling, Ryuu turned to continue to examine the area. The noise was just an annoying low buzz to him now. He'd barely turned his head when he froze.

"Allison, let him go," he said, narrowing his eyes to look more closely at what he was seeing.

"Not a chance. I'm not done yet," she said. She still held Aiolos in her grasp, even though he kept moaning "uncle" over and over.

In one motion, Ryuu pulled them apart and held them up so their feet were dangling.

"I said, ENOUGH! I think we're here!" he snapped. The others turned toward him, and Allison stopped fighting to free herself.

"What makes you say that?" Eric asked.

Ryuu put his friends down and walked over to two stalagmites on a flat-topped rock. On the rock, which was about waist high, was a gold-embroidered, wooden box.

What the hell is this doing in here? he thought as he opened the lid.

An instant later, he jumped back, his hands flying up to shield his eyes from the sudden burst of multicolored light that radiated out of the box. The others also shielded their eyes, but they recovered more quickly as Ryuu stumbled about, blinded. Before he could hit the wall headfirst, Allison and Bryan grabbed him and held him back.

"Keep your eyes closed. Then slowly open them," Allison said, beside him.

He followed her directions, blinked a couple of times, and stood straight.

"I hate it when that happens," he muttered, turning to face the others. "Still want my Owl Eyes, Aiolos?"

Aiolos shrugged. Then they all turned their focus back to the box.

Now the cave was filled with the iridescent light from the box, and they could see clearly. The box contained seven bracelets, each imbedded with a crystal that glowed a different color.

"What the hell are those?" Eric asked.

"I have no idea," Ryuu said slowly. He raised a hand to reach in.

At once, the light from the crystals began to pulse, and the bracelets rose from the box. Stepping back, Ryuu and the others watched in awe as they rose into the air to hover near the ceiling of the cave. As the seconds crept by, the pulsing light increased until it seemed consistent. Then, without warning, all but three of the bracelets shot at them and wrapped themselves around the friends' wrists.

Ryuu and the others yelped in surprise and jumped back. Ryuu then closed his eyes as the light became blinding again. Twisting his arm to keep the light out of his eyes, he clutched his wrist and raised it above his head.

A booming voice declared in his mind, "AS FORETOLD BY ANCIENTS PAST! SO SHALL ARISE THE NEXT GENERATION OF DRAGON KNIGHTS!"

Mercifully, the light dimmed and went out. Ryuu opened his eyes to see the cave dark once more. Breathing hard, he blinked a couple times to get used to the dark. Then he looked at the bracelet on his wrist. When he glanced up again, he saw that the last three bands had disappeared.

Slowly, he turned toward his friends.

"Everyone okay?" he asked, and they each gave an affirmative. "Did anyone else hear that?" Bryan asked. "As foretold . . ."

". . . by ancients past . . ." Aiolos continued.

". . . so shall arise . . ." Eric said.

". . . the next generation..." Allison added.

". . . of Dragon Knights."

As Ryuu finished, the cave rang with silence.

✳✳✳

On a distant planet.

Eirian's eyes shot open and she raised her head, and slipping from the covers of her bed, went to the window and looked up at one of the stars. "It has begun," she muttered, shifting some hair from her face.

✳✳✳

On another planet.

Another eye opened that was fiery red surrounded by darkness. "So," a voice said in a growling tone. "A new generation has taken up the mantle."

The Anubis and the Dark Elf

RYUU WAS SO tired, he hardly stumbling back home, although he did recall the friends had speculated in great length about the potential recipients of the other three bracelets. Did they live in neighboring villages on other planets? When would they all meet? And did the Black Dragon know about this? How much danger were they now in?

He slipped into his room as the sun came up. Giving a big yawn, he made for his bed with all the intention of a nice long sleep.

He was just pulling back the blankets when he heard his mother's voice.

"Alac-Ryuu, is that you?"

Ryuu gave a small moan. "Just making the bed," he mumbled as his door opened.

"Well, breakfast will be ready in a few minutes," she said. She gave him a brief smile and then left.

He looked longingly at his bed and then turned, went to his dresser, and pulled out some clothes. When he was dressed, he walked down to the kitchen and sat at the table beside his father, who was already drinking his tea and reading the holo-paper.

Behind him, Chikako was just taking breakfast off the stove.

Hearing Ryuu come in, his father looked up and smiled.

"Some party yesterday," he said. The holographic paper vanished, and he placed the emitter pad aside.

"You're not kidding," Ryuu said. He stifled a huge yawn as his mother put his breakfast in front of him as both eyed him. "Didn't get much sleep last night," he explained, and his parents nodded.

"Must have been the cake; too much sugar or something," his mother said.

"Yeah, maybe," Ryuu said. He took a bite of French toast. As usual, it spoke to Chikako's skill in the kitchen. It was delicious.

The rest of the meal began as normal, with the three joking and talking. As it progressed, Ryuu noticed that his parents kept shooting glances at him, yet every time he felt their eyes on him, they quickly looked away, and conversation went on.

When his plate was empty, Ryuu stood and began to carry it to the counter.

"We'll take care of it, Alac-Ryuu. You go and meet your friends," his mother said. She reached for the plate.

"Okay, see you guys later," he said. He grabbed his sky surfer and bolted toward the door.

On his way out, he saw his father place his elbows on the table, interlace his fingers, and rest his chin on them.

"Too much sugar . . . hmmm." These were the last words he heard his father say as he closed the door behind him.

***

Not long after, Ryuu lay on his hovering sky surfer near the stone archway and crystal. He'd nodded off a little while ago and was still half asleep. For almost an hour, he remained in that position, catching up on his rest and listening to the sounds around him.

"I had a feeling you guys would be coming here," he said suddenly. He opened his eyes and looked at his friends.

"How do you do that?" Allison demanded. The others' expressions posed similar questions as they collapsed their sky surfers and faced him.

Soon they were all sitting in silence, simply staring at each other.

"So, are we going to talk about what happened last night?" Aiolos finally asked. He pulled back his sleeve and revealed his bracelet, which had a clear white crystal.

"I still don't know what happened to begin with," Ryuu said. He looked at his own bracelet, which bore a ruby-red crystal.

"What did the voice mean by 'Next Generation of Dragon Knights'?" Eric asked. He rubbed his own bracelet, which had a blue crystal.

"Not quite sure." Bryan looked down at his deep-green crystal. "And what do these have to do with the knights?"

After giving his bracelet a close look, Ryuu paused, taking it in. There seemed to be weapons engraved on the sides.

"You know . . . maybe, just maybe . . ."

A second later, Allison smirked and said, "You gotta be kidding me! You think these are the legendary armors of the Dragon Knights?" Her violet crystal seemed to flash in the sunlight.

Ryuu shrugged and said, "Well, what else could they be?"

She rolled her eyes. "If these bracelets were the only armor of the original Dragon Knights, they must have won their battles by sending their enemies into fatal peals of laughter," she said.

"But remember what Mr. Orleaus said," Ryuu persisted. "The original Dragon Knights were a blend of advanced technology and magic."

"Ryuu, it's not possible," Eric said gently. "It takes six bands to make our hockey armor—"

But before he could finish his sentence, the crystals on their bracelets began to pulse.

***

Inside the cave by the cliff, Ryuu's father, with a grim expression on his face, followed the beam of his flashlight. Eventually, the beam fell on the open lid of the box, and he paused. For a moment, he stood in shocked silence. Then, slowly, he drew closer and stared down at the empty box.

"And so it begins . . ." Jun muttered. "I just pray you're ready,

Ryuu." He turned to leave. "Spirits above and below, please be ready."

Jun headed home in a daze, ignoring the folks who called out to him in greeting and missing their startled expressions when he didn't respond. Inside, he found Chikako where he'd\\ left her at the kitchen table, a cup of untouched tea before her.

"It happened, didn't it?" she asked.

All he could do was nod.

Her eyes closed. "Do you think he's ready?" she asked finally, looking at him.

With a sigh, he sat beside her. "We taught him well . . ." He took her hand in both of his. "But it's out of our hands now."

For a few seconds, there was nothing but silence between them. Then he said, "I think it's time to tell him."

✱✱✱

As Ryuu looked down at the pulsing crystal on this bracelet, the alarms at the village began blaring.

"The planetary sensors must have been triggered!" he barked, and they leapt to their feet.

Another sound caused him to look up. Spinning around, he watched, open mouthed, as four bright, flame-red specks streaked across the sky.

He followed their progress closely as they flew over the village. Then he caught his breath. The streaks had altered course and were coming around.

"Scouts or slavers; they're heading toward the village," Ryuu shouted.

He grabbed his sky surfer, and his friends followed quickly behind as he headed into the forest to keep out of sight and observe what was unfolding. As he raced along, he watched the sky. When he stopped at the edge of the woods, a transport ship and several fighter ships descended from the balls of fire and moved directly toward the village.

The transport was a little bigger than a large house. Its wide forward section was almost oval in shape, with sharp, angular edges. At the rear, a tail jutted out, thinning with a pair of short wings at the end. The cockpit had laser cannons on rotating torrents and missile tubes on either side of it, as well as a larger torrent on top and bottom.

Each fighter was the size of a hover car, with the main body almost circular in shape and two wings attached to the sides that jutted forward and slightly back. There were also lasers between the wings and missile tubes embedded within them.

Ryuu felt a chill creep down his spine. The front of each vessel included the design of a dragon skull.

"The Black Dragon," he muttered.

They watched as the ships lowered their landing skids and touched down just outside the village.

"We've got to do something!" Bryan yelled.

"I say we kick butt," Allison said. She snapped her fist into her hand.

"And how do you plan to do that? Throw rocks at them?" Eric moved to hold her back as the ramp of the transport lowered.

When the door opened, twenty robotic Sentinels disembarked. They looked like muscular men, but they were a little taller than average-sized men, and they stood on raised heels of clawed feet. Their metal armor was smooth, with various slots around their arms and thighs. There were gears on the side of the arms as well as a line of blades.

Ryuu's attention was immediately drawn to their heads, for they weren't shaped like humans, elves, or any dark creature. Instead, each head was formed like the head of a two-horned dragon with red eyes.

Ryuu and his friends watched as the Sentinels moved into formation beside the ship and began to march into the village. Then a chill moved through him again as another figure came down the ramp and started moving toward the forest. It was as tall as a man, with skin as black as night over toned, hard muscles, clawed hands, and clawed feet. A gold cape whipped in the wind behind the figure, and gold bands and manacles decorated its arms. Black hair so thick it seemed a solid mass ran along the back of its head, which was in the shape of a wolf or a jackal.

Next to it walked a woman wearing black and blood-red clothes. She had long white hair that reached down to her hips. Poking out of her hair were the pointed ears of an elf. As her head turned and Ryuu saw a glimpse of her face from afar, he realized her skin was deep purple, and her white eyes had a ridge in the shape of a crescent moon between them.

"An Anubis and a Dark Elf," Ryuu said under his breath.

He took cover behind a cluster of trees, and his friends joined him.

"If they have an Anubis and a Dark Elf with them, then they must not plan to take any prisoners," Eric muttered.

"Or very few. But how'd they find us with the new dampening system? The last group we had to fend off was years ago, and we made sure they didn't transmit anything," Bryan muttered.

Ryuu's eyes slowly shifted to the bracelet on his wrist. Then his eyes shot back as the Anubis turned toward the village and began to speak in a deep, growling voice.

"I'm Maltanore," he declared. "We know you're here. We detected you from orbit two days ago. Come out now and surrender. If you cooperate, we will spare your lives and sell you as slaves."

Ryuu felt his face harden. He looked at his friends. Now they had their answer.

Before he could move, citizens came out of hiding places in the village below. Shooting blasters and defenses and started firing at the Sentinels. As one, the Sentinels each raised an arm. A slot on each arm raised up revealing a blaster cannon, and the Sentinels returned fire as they charged into the village.

The friends watched from afar as people fell under a barrage of laser fire.

"WELL, WE'VE GOT TO DO SOMETHING!" Ryuu yelled. Then, as he and his friends moved toward the village, the crystal on his wristband began to pulse again.

***

Ryuu's father dragged a wounded man behind an overturned hover car. Blood leaked from a wound in the man's shoulder, and Jun ripped some of his own clothes to make a bandage.

"You're going to be just fine," he told the man.

He turned at the sound of heavy feet and saw a Sentinel move to face them. As it slowly raised its cannon, there was a flash of movement across its neck, from shoulder to hip and across the waist. The Sentinel was still for a moment. Then those sections fell to the ground, revealing Chikako, a laser-edged Kanata in both her hands.

"Now don't go all to pieces on me," she said, rushing over to take the bandage and apply it to the man's wound.

Jun fired a few rounds over the top of the car.

"They're winning, aren't they?" the man demanded.

"What do you think?" an eerie voice answered from behind them.

Jun looked up to see the Dark Elf hovering over them. When she slowly raised her hand, a ball of swirling black energy appeared in her palm.

Jun tackled Chikako out of the way. As he covered her, he felt the heat wave of an explosion. Something hard hit the ground in front of them.

Uncovering his head, Jun looked around. The man's disemboweled torso lay on the ground before him, his blank, empty eyes staring at the sky.

As Jun reached for Chikako's hand, a pair of clawed feet stepped into view. He looked up into the face of Maltanore, flanked by a pair of Sentinels.

"Mortals," the Anubis muttered, and Jun felt gripped by a wave of fear.

To his surprise, Maltanore's attention suddenly turned toward the sky. Following his gaze, Jun saw five objects streak down from the sky in an arrow formation. Pulling up, they flew into the village, and as they drew near it, Jun saw that there appeared to be several young people on sky surfers.

As the leader neared a passing Sentinel, he drew back a fist, and as he passed, he punched a big chunk from the Sentinel, causing it to twist from the blow. Sparks flew everywhere as it fell to the ground.

Jun and Chikako joined a small crowd of people who had gathered to watch the flyers. Overhead, two of the flyers rolled, which caused them to drop to the ground. After flipping in midair, they each landed on bended knees. Then they stood up as the remaining flyers hovered above.

In appearance, they looked like well-muscled humans. They each had separated armored plates along the major muscle groups; these plates were surrounded by a black material that moved smoothly as the figures moved. Low on the hips were a pair of metallic rods with the same black material making up the grip, with emitters on both sides of the rods.

However, there were differences between them. One in particular had the slim but powerful build of a young woman. The main feature Jun noticed was their helmets and masks.

All of them were the shape of a dragon's head. The male on the ground had a round, blunt snout with a small ridge between the eyes. On both corners of his head he had a slightly swept-back horn, with a third in the middle of the head.

The female, who was one of the two figures on the ground, had a more pointed snout. She had a single sweptback horn in the middle of the top of her head. On the side of her head, she had long, large, pointed sweptback ears.

One of the flyers who was still in the air had a head with an elongated wolfish snout dragon face. With catfish-like whiskers that weaved through the air as if they were being billowed in a strong wind. Two swept back horns were set in the corners of his head.

The fourth—and most muscled—of the group had a slightly wider and squat face than the rest, with a thick, shallow dome in the center of the forehead and a line of spikes running along the side of the head.

The last one had two front and back sweeping frills on either side of its head; and two horns swept back over his head.

"It can't be . . ." Maltanore gaped.

"Oh, it is," the male figure on the ground said.

"Dragon Knights," Jun said in wonder.

Maltanore roared, "SENTINELS ATTACK! KILL EVERYONE! FIGHTERS INTO THE AIR! BOMBARD THE VILLAGE!"

At once, several Sentinels turned and raised their arms to fire at the Dragon Knights. In a flash of movement, the two knights on the ground charged forward. In a shower of sparks, the male forced the arm of the nearest Sentinel back as the cannon fired, blowing its own head off.

Beside him, the female Dragon Knight ripped off the arm of a Sentinel and then used the arm to knock off its head.

The other fighters started to lift off, and the male Dragon Knight pointed as he yelled, "Get them!" in an altered voice.

At once, two of the Knights in the air rocketed up after the fighters, while the one with the largest muscles dropped down to join the fight on the group. The leaner male nailed a Sentinel with a spin kick, knocking its head off the jaw spinning away, but when he turned, Maltanore nailed him with a hard uppercut to the chest, launching him off his feet.

"Ryuu..." Jun muttered in fear and worry as he watched him soar over the village by the blow with Maltanore leaping after him. As he glanced at the Knights both on the ground and in the sky he had a pretty good idea who was in the armors.

***

In the air, Aiolos weaved on his board, dodging laser fire from the fighter who was hot on his tail.

"This would be so much easier if I could shoot back!" he snapped, rolling to dodge more lasers. For a brief second, he shifted his attention to the fighter holo sensor and armor readouts in front of his face.

Suddenly a message flashed across the screen.

"Interface commencing?" he muttered, and at a sound, he looked down.

Below him, thin wires extended from the armor of his thigh and connected to his sky surfer. At once, his surfer began to change. Short, trapezoid wings with lasers embedded inside emerged from the base. Behind him, the engine grew slightly larger, and a set of missile tubes appeared underneath on either side of an intake ramp. "Now this I like," he said with a grin.

After glancing over his shoulder, he pulled his board into a sharp turn, firing the lasers at the fighter as it passed, blowing off a section over the missiles. Righting the board behind the fighter, he rocketed after it, and a targeting scanner appeared.

"See how you like it! FIRE MISSILES!" he yelled, and his missiles launched forward and slammed into the exposed missiles, detonating them and blowing the wing off.

"OH, YEAH! WHO'S THE MAN?" Aiolos shouted. He thrust his hands into the air in triumph as the fighter dropped from the sky, spinning like a top.

***

Ryuu tumbled over the village and came down in the forest, snapping branches as he went until he hit the ground. As he came to a skidding and rolling stop, he moaned and pushed himself onto one knee. Around him was a great clatter of wildlife as the forest animals rushed to flee the scene.

"Ow," he muttered. He clutched his armored chest while the torso section of his holo armor read out flashed .

He looked up just as Maltanore landed in front of him on crouched legs.

"So you're the next generation of Dragon Knights," he said as Ryuu climbed to his feet. "What makes you think you'll have any success where others have failed?"

Before Ryuu could reply, the sounds of an explosion filled the air above them. Looking up, Ryuu saw one of the fighters lose a wing and fall, spinning to the ground out of sight as the blast of the crash reverberated through the air.

"Looks to me like we're doing just fine," Ryuu said.

Maltanore chuckled and whipped off his cape. Now he was dressed only in a cloth, which was wrapped around his waist, and his jewelry.

"A few Sentinels and fighters are easily replaced," the Anubis said. "Personally, I'd like to see for myself if the legend of the Knights is true."

"Well, then I guess I better prove it to you," Ryuu said and charged him.

In a flash of movement, Maltanore met him halfway and double kicked Ryuu hard in the chest. Ryuu was launched off his feet back to the ground, where he slid across the forest floor. Clutching his chest, he looked up in time to see Maltanore flipping back to land onto his feet and slip into a low stance.

What the hell did I get myself into? Ryuu asked himself as he curled up and leapt to his feet.

Charging each other, the two met as Ryuu tried to kick his opponent in the knee. Maltanore blocked this move with a kick, leapt up, and nailed Ryuu in the head with a kick of his own. Then he kicked Ryuu in the gut. Moaning softly, Ryuu ducked under a spin kick and, standing straight, threw a kick to Maltanore's head. Ducking under it, Maltanore swept his leg out from under Ryuu, sending him spinning face-first into the dirt.

As he started to get up, Maltanore seized him and threw him back through the air. Landing low in a stance on a boulder, Ryuu blocked a couple kicks as Maltanore leapt after him.

After ducking under a crescent kick, Maltanore blocked a second with the same leg. Then he seized Ryuu by the throat.

Thrusting his palm into Maltanore's elbow, Ryuu forced him to one knee. Then, rolling his shoulder, Maltanore stepped back and forced Ryuu down, locking Ryuu's elbow back over his shoulder.

Ryuu tried to strike out but his fist was blocked and then doubled up as Maltanore drove his forearm into his side and flipped Ryuu off his feet. Going with it, Ryuu landed on his feet and, dropping down, tried to sweep Maltanore's feet out from under him.

Standing straight, he kicked out at Maltanore, who forced the kick down, sending Ryuu flipping forward. Halfway through, he grabbed Maltanore by the ears and threw him from the boulder. Landing on his feet, he was in time to see Maltanore roll onto his back. Then, curling up,

Maltanore thrust forward, landing on one knee, his leg stretched before him.

Turning to face Ryuu, he charged as Ryuu leapt over him. After blocking several more kicks, Maltanore grabbed Ryuu's arm and kicked him in his side, forcing Ryuu back before leaping at him with a hard kick. The blow launched Ryuu off his feet, and as he landed, he slammed into a thick tree trunk.

As he pushed himself to one knee, Maltanore charged him on all fours. Leaping up, Ryuu spun like a top and landed on a thick branch twenty feet up.

"Where the hell did that come from?" he asked, dazed at what he had just done. Then he spun around as he heard Maltanore land on the branch behind him.

"Before I bring this pointless but amusing exercise to an end with your death," the Anubis called, "I have a question that needs answering."

He threw a kick to Ryuu's leg, but Ryuu stepped back and it missed him.

"Oh, yeah? What's that?" Ryuu said. He stepped forward again and threw a punch.

Maltanore blocked and deflected it with both hands then backhanded Ryuu across the face. As he moved to strike again with his elbow, Ryuu blocked it, and Maltanore flicked his wrist, forcing Ryuu's strike down before backhanding him again in the head. Twisting more toward Ryuu, he nailed him with a punch to his side, sending him spinning from the branch.

As he fell, he reached out and grabbed the branch at Maltanore's feet, and as he started to pull himself up, Maltanore again seized him by the throat.

"Well?" Maltanore said. "Ready for my question?"

Before Ryuu could reply, he said, "Here it is: Why, oh why, do pests like you fight the inevitable? Why don't you just be good little insects and DIE?"

He followed up the last part with a palm strike to Ryuu's chest.

The blow sent Ryuu tumbling through the air. Hitting the ground with a roll, he stopped hard as his back scraped against a tree. Groaning, Ryuu climbed to his hands and knees.

Maltanore dropped from the branch and landed on one knee.

"Well, ANSWER ME!" he shouted as he stalked forward.

"Because . . . this . . . is . . . our . . . HOME!" Ryuu shouted. The very mention of home strengthened his resolve, and he climbed back to his feet.

Again, Maltanore charged him, and flipping like an acrobat, Ryuu sailed over him to land behind him. After blocking a kick with his knee, he kicked out at Maltanore's other knee, then bringing the same leg high, he brought his heel down on his head. In rapid succession, his leg still in the air, he kicked Maltanore several times in the chest and head before Maltanore caught a side kick.

Flipping forward as his leg was brought up he broke free before jumping up, spinning back to face him, throwing a kick which Maltanore ducked under. Landing back on his feet, Ryuu was swept off his feet by one of Maltanore's clawed hands. Landing hard on his back, he was barely able to grab Maltanore's clawed foot as he brought it down on his armored chest.

Growing with the effort, Ryuu twisted it, sending Maltanore spinning to the ground beside him. As he started to get up, he was kicked in the face, launching him back. After spinning to his feet, he was grabbed from behind and hurled against a tree.

As he started to climb to his feet, again Maltanore grabbed his shoulder and drove his fist into his gut repeatedly before punching him twice on both sides of his head. After being hit hard again in the chest, Ryuu soared back against a tree before leaping to his feet in a stance. With a roar, Maltanore leapt at him, and Ryuu brought his leg up and kicked him in his side, sending him to the ground away from him.

Ryuu leapt forward, and after pushing off from a tree, he nailed Maltanore across the face with a kick. Then he fell back onto his hands to avoid a blow before springing back to his feet. From there, he kicked the

Anubis in the knee, then in the head. He followed up by spinning on his own head, nailing Maltanore across the face with a kick.

Disoriented by the blows, Maltanore fell back. With a cry, Ryuu spun himself sideways through the air and brought his leg down hard across his opponent's back.

As Maltanore climbed to his feet, he rushed forward, seized Ryuu by the throat, and threw him hard against a tree.

"WARNING! WARNING!" an alarm called out in Ryuu's ear. "Further physical impacts will lead to armor retraction!"

"Good to know," he moaned. When he looked up, his eyes went wide as Maltanore ripped a tree from the ground.

"I'VE HAD ENOUGH OF THIS!" Maltanore shouted. He held the uprooted tree in both arms and swung it at Ryuu.

To dodge the swing, Ryuu leapt up into the air. But one of the roots still caught him in his midsection and sent him careening into the underbrush where he met a hard landing.

"Armor Retraction Commencing! ETA Until Operational Use: Fifteen Minutes."

"A lot can happen in fifteen minutes!" Ryuu growled as a sound of metal on metal met his ears.

Some of the armor retracted off his opposite hand, moving up his arm and across his shoulder. Next, more of the armor began to retract up his legs and across his chest. As this happened, the horns on his helmet retracted into the head. Then, from the base of his throat, the helmet withdrew up and over his head. Once it reached the base of his skull, the parts over his ears slid in before it merged with the rest of the armor, which retracted across and up his chest and down his arm.

As the last of the armor melded into his bracelet, Ryuu climbed to his feet, clutching his chest. Moaning, he moved as quietly as he could through the underbrush.

At that sound of a heavy crash, he looked in the direction of Maltanore. Then he dropped flat on his chest, so that he was covered by a bush. As he inched forward, he heard a small thud nearby. It was followed by loud sniffs.

"I know you're here," he heard Maltanore say. "I may not see you ... but I can smell you. And my sense of smell is almost as good as a Dragon's."

Ryuu's eyes darted left and right and then focused on a flower. Holding his breath slowly, he reached for it.

Just as his fingers closed around the head, Maltanore whipped aside the bushes he'd been hiding under. Ryuu held the crushed head of the flower in his open hand and blew it hard into his enemy's face.

As Maltanore started coughing and sneezing, Ryuu took the opportunity to drop down into a dry river bed.

"That should buy me some time," he muttered. "Last time I was anywhere near that flower, I couldn't stop sneezing all day."

Minutes later, just as he arrived at the testing ground he was in the night before, Maltanore dropped right in front of him, and Ryuu managed to block his punch. He did not, however, manage to avoid the powerful kick to his side. Spinning through the air, he came to a skidding, rolling stop.

Moaning as he clutched his side, Ryuu pushed himself up to watch Maltanore advance on him. His enemy was laughing.

"Well, this is certainly the icing on the cake, as humans say. Out of all the people in the known galaxies, the Legendary Armors chose a child."

"Hey, I'm still trying to figure it out myself," Ryuu countered. "Maybe it's the fact that my name means Dragon."

Hissing in pain, he pulled himself back and said, "So what happens now? You going to just kill me or make me beg, because I doubt you're going to get a better chance for bragging rights than killing a Dragon Knight!"

Maltanore started to take a step forward, but froze.

Slowly his eye traveled down to the wire at his ankle level. Ryuu's eyes widened in horror as his eyes followed the wire to the spiked log ready to swing down to impale its victim.

Chuckling, Maltanore turned back to a wide eyed Ryuu. Crossing his legs, he stepped to the side and walked around Ryuu, giving the trip wire a wide berth.

Until he stopped at Ryuu's side and grinned wickedly down at him. "Did you really think I would fall for the oldest trick in the book?" he leered, and with a small ringing sound \he drew a rod from the small of his back, which expanded outward with a pair of wicked looking axe blades on either end.

For a second, Ryuu just stared at him wide eyed in fear. "No," he finally said, a grin forming.

Before Maltanore could do more than blink at him. Twisting Ryuu slammed his hand down on the wire just behind him. And the blaster in a tree across from Maltanore fired the shot knocking him to the ground.

As he turned back, Ryuu's armor started to expand up his arm.

"Oh, so now you work?" Ryuu muttered as the armor extended across his chest and his other arm.

At a roar, Ryuu whipped around. To see Maltanore soar through the air, arms outstretched to grab him. Reacting, he leapt into a tree and out of sight.

Leaping after him, Maltanore crashed onto the same branch, finding Ryuu no longer there. "NO MORE TRICKS! THIS ENDS NOW!" he roared, spinning on the spot as he searched for Ryuu. "WHERE ARE YOU?"

In response, Ryuu, now fully armored, ran down the trunk of the tree. A rod at his hip shot into his hands.

"HERE, DOGGY, DOGGY!" Ryuu shouted. He leapt from the tree at Maltanore, who turned to face him, both slashing out at each other.

Ryuu landed with a roll on the ground below Maltanore, and stopped on one knee. Behind him, he heard a soft thump, followed by a heavier thump. When Ryuu turned around, he saw Maltanore's body lying on the ground, the head of the Anubis on the mossy ground beside him.

Slowly, his eyes moved down to look at the rod in his hand. The katana blade that extended from the rod was made of an almost transparent light. He watched as the blade slowly retracted back into the rod. When the blade disappeared entirely, he let it go, and the rod reattached itself to his hip.

"Boy, am I glad that's over. He was really kicking my butt," Ryuu muttered. Breathing hard, he sagged down, hands on his thighs.

***

Back in the village, Allison was fighting with the Dark Elf. As she landed on the ground, she heard the Dark Elf say, "You know, I find myself disappointed. If this is the best the Knights of old could do, they must have won their battles by intimidation alone."

"Well, at least I'm not a betrayer of my own people!" Allison snapped. She climbed to her feet and charged at her opponent.

With an amused look on her face, the Dark Elf stepped to the side, avoiding Allison's kick. Then she snatched Allison out of midair and threw her against a hover car that was turned on its side. The car crumpled under the impact, and the Dark Elf drew her hand through the air, producing a dark, elegant sword in a flash of light.

"Bold words for a little girl about to die," she said. She advanced toward Allison, sword in hand.

***

Suddenly, Ryuu appeared out of nowhere sailing through the air and nailed the Dark Elf with a hard flying side kick. It launched the Elf off her feet, and she rolled across the ground

"You forgot one thing about Knights," he snapped. "We always come in packs!"

"You okay?" he asked as Allison stumbled toward him.

"I had her right where I wanted her," she muttered, clutching her shoulder.

"I don't doubt it," Ryuu replied.

94

The Elf climbed to her feet. "You! Where's Maltanore?"

"Oh, you mean this guy?" Ryuu lifted the object in his hand, and the Elf recoiled when she saw it was Maltanore's disembodied head.

"Guess he didn't have the head for this job," he said. Then he tossed the head at her feet.

The Elf looked from the head of the Anubis to Ryuu. Then her gaze wandered as a crowd of people, including Eric, gathered behind them.

"Might I have the pleasure of your name? So I know a walking dead man," she said, placing one hand behind her.

Ryuu was silent for a moment, not sure of what to say. Then, standing straight, he declared, "Just call me Robin Hood."

As the Elf started to laugh, Allison leaned closer to Ryuu.

She whispered, "Robin Hood? Are you kidding me?"

Glancing at his friend, he muttered, "What? That's been my nickname from you guys for years."

"Yeah, a nickname, not an alias!"

The Elf snickered. Then she said, "So, young man, you wish to remake a legend. If that's the case, I personally prefer heroes with a sense of tragedy in their past."

Seconds later, she thrust her hand out from behind her back. Resting in the middle of her palm was a fiery ball of energy, which she launched from her hand. Eyes growing wide, Ryuu watched in slow motion as the ball soared through the air and collided into Eric, who raised his arms as if to shield himself. When it exploded, the shock sent both Ryuu and Allison flying. Ryuu landed hard. As he rolled across the ground, he looked back to the smoke-filled crater. There was no way to tell if Eric had survived.

Glancing down at Allison, he saw her freeze in horror. Baring his teeth, Ryuu turned to pursue the Dark Elf, who was now running toward the transport.

"This thing have any long-range weapons?" he yelled into his helmet mask. As he glanced at his holo armor readout, he saw that the icons of his lower arms, hips, and the small of his back started to flash.

95

"Well, this will have to do," he said, reaching behind him.

From the small of his back, he pulled a rod with a slight angled indentation on either side of the grip. As he brought it forward, limbs of a bow shot out from each end, with a laser string shooting from the top to the bottom. Skidding to a stop, he reached over his shoulder for an arrow, but felt nothing.

"Great, now what am I to do with this? Hit her with it?" he shouted as he flicked the string.

At once, what looked like an arrow made of light appeared and shot from the bow. It launched through the air and caused an overturned hover car to jump into the sky and fall back to the ground, making a fiery wreck.

"Okay, that'll work!" he said. Then he drew back the string, turned, and aimed at the back of the retreating Elf.

As he did, a movement in the sky caught his eye. He watched frozen as Aiolos and Bryan weaved through the air, dodging laser fire from the last fighter. Glancing back down, he saw the Elf was almost back at the transport.

After a couple seconds of shifting his aim, he gave a cry and fired. He watched as the arrow streaked through the air and slammed onto one of the wings of the fighter, which tumbled, spinning from the air, and crashed into the ground between the transport and the Elf.

"OH, YEAH! NOW THAT WAS A HELL OF A SHOT!" Ryuu yelled. He jumped into the air, whooping and brandishing the bow.

"YES!"

Turning around, he let loose a giant sigh of relief, Allison raced toward Eric, who was now visible through the smoke that continued to rise in front of some of the villagers. The ground before them looked like it had been scooped away. Eric's arms were still crossed in front of his face, and the crystal on his bracelet was pulsing to the same rhythm as a flashing shield, which had formed in front of him. Slowly he lowered his arms, and the shield vanished just as Allison reached him, knocking him to the ground in a ferocious hug.

A shout from Bryan caught Ryuu's attention, and when he turned he saw Bryan and Aiolos on the ground, standing over the Dark Elf.

"Don't even think about it!" Bryan snapped as the Dark Elf started to get up.

Ryuu moved toward them, and Allison and Eric quickly followed.

As Ryuu reached them, his bow retracted, and he replaced it at the small of his back. He faced the Dark Elf and said, "Now what was that you were saying about us being pests? Got to be careful, because they have a habit of multiplying."

Then a new voice came from behind him. "And I thought I taught you better than to gloat over a wounded enemy." It was Jun.

Ryuu whipped around to face his father. "Hey, after what they did, we deserve a little glo—" He caught himself halfway and stopped. "I have no idea what you're talking about," he quickly said, trying to cover up.

"Son, you were never a good liar to me or your mother. We know your tells too good, no matter how slight."

Ryuu was silent for a moment before his shoulders slumped.

"Sorry, Dad."

"Too much sugar, eh?" his father said, crossing his arms.

Ryuu made sure enough blasters were on the Dark Elf. Then he gave his father his full attention. Behind his helmet mask, Ryuu gave a weak smile.

"Eh, I can explain . . . but for right now . . . eh, how do you get this armor off? I doubt it's like we can say deactivate."

Before he could continue, a voice in his ear interrupted his train of thought. "Armor Retraction Commencing."

At once, with the sound of metal on metal, the armor retracted into itself.

Raising his hand, Ryuu watched as the last of the armor melded into the bracelet. Staring in amazement and shock, he shifted his eyes up to his friends, who were staring back at him. One by one, they deactivated their armor. Then they gathered around Ryuu's family, who were standing at the front of a group of villagers.

Looking at his father, Ryuu opened his mouth to speak, but his father raised his hand.

Jun said, "I was going to be angry, but that was before the next generation of Dragon Knights stood before us." Then he slowly knelt before them.

Stepping back in surprise, Ryuu looked at his mother. She beamed at him before she, too, knelt before them. The friends exchanged puzzled glances as row by row the villagers knelt before them. At the very back was Dulglad and his father, and after a few seconds, they, too, knelt.

Live for Freedom...Die for Freedom

AIOLOS MUTTERED. "OKAY, THIS is a little awkward,"

Before Ryuu could reply, he was knocked off his feet as the ground beneath him shook.

"WHAT THE—" he started to shout. He stopped when he saw the trails of hundreds of missiles and the clouds of their explosions. "Armageddon Missiles," he muttered in fear, as great cracks in the earth opened up around him.

"EVERYONE IN THE TRANSPORT, NOW!" his father screamed, pointing at the remaining ship on the ground.

Almost immediately, the villagers started running for the ship. Ryuu and the others regained their feet and followed.

"There must be other ships in orbit!" Allison yelled. "They must have some idea what happened down here, or else they wouldn't be doing this!"

"Well, this is typical of the Black Dragon's forces!" Ryuu replied, running full out for the boarding ramp. "Blow up a whole planet just because they believe an enemy to be on it!"

Less than ten feet from the ship, Ryuu came to a skidding stop as he heard a scream come from behind him. He turned and saw the ground beneath the Elf crumble and vanish under her feet, and she fell with another piercing scream.

Before he had time to think about it, he leapt forward toward the edge of the chasm. Landing flat on the ground, he thrust a hand down and caught her by the wrist.

"I've got you!" he shouted as she stared at him in amazement.

Before she could say anything, a crumbling sound met their ears. Looking under him, he saw the ledge he was on begin to fall away.

"You can let go, human . . . I'd understand," she said in a hollow voice.

Looking back at her, he desperately shouted, "Somebody! Help me!"

When no one came, she gave him a small smile and closed her eyes. At once, her features underwent a transformation. The ridge on her head vanished, and her skin turned white and fair. When she opened her eyes, Ryuu saw that they were now a deep violet.

"Prove them wrong, young knight," she muttered. Then she released her grip on him and slipped from his grasp.

"NO!" he bellowed, wide-eyed with horror as she fell into the abyss.

For a few seconds, he remained there, too stunned to move. The sound of the ledge beginning to fall snapped him back to reality as he tipped forward. Suddenly, a pair of strong hands grabbed him by his shirt and, with a mighty tug, dragged him to safety.

He landed on his side and turned to look into his rescuer's eyes.

"Alac-Ryuu, don't you ever freeze up like that again!" his father shouted, giving him a rough shake by the upper arms. "You're too important to lose!"

Then Jun nodded toward the transport ship. "I can't explain now, but you, your friends, your mother, and the rest of the village must take that ship."

"But Dad, what about you?" Ryuu said.

Jun grasped Ryuu's arm. "I'll out-run any other ship they have in orbit in one of the escape transports," he finished. "Then I will rendezvous with you all when I can."

"You'll never make it!" Ryuu cried. He looked up just as the mountain above them seemed to split in half and magma began flowing.

"We don't have time for an argument," Jun shouted at him. "Now move!" He pushed Ryuu toward the transport before turning.

"No, Dad! I won't let you go! It's suicide!" Ryuu grabbed Jun by the shoulder.

At that, Jun lowered his head. "I'm sorry," he muttered, and before Ryuu could do or say anything, his father whirled around, raised a fist, and Ryuu's world went black.

***

After knocking out Ryuu with a single strike, Jun gently reached out and took the young man in his arms before he could fall to the ground.

"Jun, what the hell is the matter with you?" Chikako demanded, running up with another villager.

He looked at her with tears in his eyes. Then he said, "Our boy and his friends have been chosen to fulfill a great destiny! They're Dragon Knights now, and they must be protected at all costs. It could mean our survival! And the survival of all free people. This was the only way I could get Ryuu to go."

For a few seconds, they looked at each other. Then tears began to stream down Chikako's cheeks.

"You're right," she said quietly. Then she reached out, took Ryuu from her husband, and handed him to the villager.

"Please carry my son to the transport," she said.

Jun took her hand. "Now I'm going to be the decoy. Once they're after me, you get the hell out!" he said.

Slowly Chikako nodded. She started to walk toward the transport. Then she ran back and flung herself into his arms.

Jun kissed his wife gently and said, "Until we meet again, my love."

This time, when they parted, she ran all the way to the transport. Jun watched as she disappeared inside as the ramp was raised.

As the world came apart around him, Jun stood still for a few seconds. Then he darted around the chasms and made his way to the forest. At the edge, he stopped before a tree and pressed hard onto a knot. The tree split open, revealing an elevator. He jumped in, and it immediately lowered below ground, stopping at the entrance to a large hangar.

Inside the hangar, a line of ships awaited on landing skids. Most were as large as a bus, with a point pod section in the front and a smooth shaft that extended in the back, where a set of stubby wings with engines at the tips reached out from all four sides. With his heart racing, Jun ran up the ramp of the nearest ship.

Once inside, he hit a holo button on the side. Immediately the ramp retracted and the hatch closed, sealing itself. Not stopping, Jun raced to the front and into the cockpit, which was a plain, two seated area with the controls in front and above the seats. Jumping into the pilot's seat Jun flipped switches and pressed holo buttons, and the ship came to life. The viewing screens in front and to the sides of the seats flicked on, as well as a holographic globe, which floated between the two seats and displayed various sensor readouts.

At a crashing sound, he looked out the screen to his right and saw the far wall break open. Lava poured into the hangar, melting the ships as it went. Grabbing the throttle, he threw it all the way back, and the ship rocketed forward. The movement threw him back against his seat, and the auto straps shot out and secured him to the chair. Yoke in his hands, he flew at a breakneck speed through the caverns, which were falling apart around him.

Coming around a sharp turn to the opening, he saw lava and rocks pouring back into the cave and fire spurting out around the edges. He gritted his teeth and opened the throttle all the way. He gave a sharp cry as the ship shot forward through the flames, rocketing into the sky.

When he glanced out at the nearest view screen, his eyes widened at the horrendous sight before him. The forest that had covered the area surrounding the village and mountains where the school had been was now gone. It looked like a giant had come through and ripped and burned the trees from the land that they had been a part of.

Climbing higher and higher into the sky, he could see just how deep and far the cracks extended, and even from inside the ship, he could hear the roar of the earth as the existing cracks grew and new ones appeared. The sound of the small eruptions as it spurted up out of the ground and the roar of the lava, which bubbled like many geysers, pulled at his heart. To him, in every sense of the phrase, it was indeed hell.

Unable to look at the sight anymore, he faced forward again as he soared through the clouds and into the stars. Closing his eyes, he wiped a tear away and sagged against the safety straps that held him to the chair.

Moments later, the shrill sound of the alarms blaring caused him to sit bolt upright and look at the sensor globe.

Seeing the ships coming after him, he banked his vessel hard to the right, activating the shields.

"Dad! Dad, do you read me?" Ryuu's voice came over the com link.

"Alac?" he said.

"Six ships in pursuit!"

Looking back at the globe, he could see the blips closing the distance between them. "I know," he muttered.

"But you can't out-run them in that bucket of bolts! Adjust heading one, one, three, five, and we'll cover you," Ryuu shouted at him.

Jun was silent for a moment as he watched the ships draw ever closer. Then he turned and looked out the forward view screen again.

"Ryuu, I'm sorry. Now you and your friends must listen to me carefully. There's not much time." As he spoke, the ships started firing on him, and he maneuvered his vessel carefully.

"Fate has entrusted you and your friends with a sacred mission, Alac. The spirits of the Dragons of old have chosen you and your friends to be the next generation of Dragon Knights, the greatest of responsibilities, Ryuu. You all must surrender to your shared destiny wherever it may lead you."

He took a deep breath and continued, "As for me, I have one last fatherly duty to perform for you, my son." He was jolted in his seat as the ship rocked from a direct hit and the alarms sounded.

"DAD!"

Pressing buttons to seal off the breaches, he turned back to check his shield gauges and saw they were failing.

"Now I give my final instructions to you as your father and your sensei. You must find the Sherwood, the other parts of you, your birth mother, and the next Gold Dragon. Find them and this war will end."

A new blip appeared on the sensor readout as one of the ships fired a missile.

"Live for freedom . . . die for freedom," he muttered. Then he closed his eyes and the vessel exploded.

Robin Hood

ON THE TRANSPORT, Ryuu, his friends, and his mother stared frozen in horror at the com as nothing but static came through. Ryuu lowered his head and sobbed. On his wrist, the crystal on his bracelet pulsed as his tears struck it.

When he finally raised his head and looked outside the ship, he saw that the cracks on their planet were growing larger and deeper, spreading across the surface with a deep-red glow. Moments later, the planet exploded, sending a shockwave of debris straight at the transport. Getting closer and closer, it raced at the little ship like a giant wave that's set to smash a small shell into pieces.

The second before the shockwave reached the ship, Ryuu heard the engines give a small clap like thunder and a throbbing pulse. Then it jumped into hyperspace, to safety.

**

Hours later, they were still in hyperspace. Ryuu stood alone in a corridor of the ship, leaning against the force field portal, his hands on either side of his head as grief continued to flood through him. With his tears still falling, he was overwhelmed with images and memories of his father: his recent birthday, his training, their homework sessions, the family game nights, and love. Always love.

Behind him, he heard his friends and mother come into the corridor. For a moment, they stood in silence. Then his mother walked forward until they were side by side.

His mother rubbed a comforting hand along his shoulder and he closed his eyes for a moment. When he opened them again, he looked out at the blurred stars that were flashing by. On his wrist, the crystal on his bracelet pulsed a few times.

Finally, his mother spoke. "As long as a shred of evil exists in the universe, there will always be a fight for freedom. That's what your father believed." She sniffed loudly. "And the fact is he and your birth mother fought together in the Resistance against The Black Dragon." She lowered her gaze, and he looked at her in surprise.

"He never said anything," Ryuu muttered.

"Before we settled down, the fighters used to say if the armors hadn't been seized by the Black Dragon, Jun would have been a Dragon Knight. He never would have admitted it, but it was his dream," his mother continued. Ryuu glanced at his bracelet, which pulsed again.

She looked out at the sky and said, "Goodbye, my love. May clear stars guide you home." Then she wiped some tears from her face.

"What did he mean?" Ryuu asked. "When he said, 'find . . . the other parts of you,' what did he mean?"

She was still for a moment. Then she turned to face him, and he could see that she was crying again.

"When your birth mother came to us, you weren't the only one she gave birth to. You have a brother and sister," she said. "You were all born on the same day."

Ryuu and his friends all stared at her. His jaw dropped, his eyes widened, and his tears stopped. "Wha . . . I have a brother . . . and a sister . . ." He paused and tried to absorb what he had heard. "Why didn't you tell me?"

"Your birth mother made us promise not to tell you until you were ready. We were going to tell you today when we realized . . . then all this." She waved her hands about.

"I'll give you some time alone," she said quietly. Then she turned and left.

Ryuu's friends gathered around him.

"Well, this has been a hell of a day," Allison said.

For a couple moments, the group stood there in silence before Bryan broke it.

"You know, I think I understand how you must feel, Ryuu—"

"That's not my name anymore," Ryuu said flatly.

He looked at his friends, who flinched.

"Alac-Ryuu Jun Yamamoto died back on Amal. From here on out, my name is Robin Hood," Ryuu, now Robin Hood, said. His voice and face were hard.

One by one, his friends looked from him to each other.

"Well, it was already a nickname, so Little John suits me just fine," Bryan, now Little John, said. He crossed his arms.

"I guess it would be appropriate for me to bear the name Tuck," Eric, now Tuck, said.

"I could settle for Willa Scarlet," Allison, now Willa, said, after glancing at her brother.

Looking around at his friends, Aiolos smiled. "I guess it's up to me to be the cool Much."

Robin smiled briefly at his friends and then turned to look out again at the stars.

For a couple seconds, Robin was still. Then he looked down at his bracelet. Raising it, he ran his fingertips over the pulsing crystal.

"We'll find them," he promised. "We'll find the Sherwood, the other knights, my brother and sister, and my birth mother. And most of all, we'll make the Black Dragon pay for what he did on this wretched day."

BLOOD CALLS

DRAGON KNIGHT CHRONICLES

BOOK 2

The Ancient Way

NEARING THE END of his shift, Robin sat alone in the pilot seat of the transport as they sped through hyperspace. With his eyes locked on the band on his wrist, he willed the bracelet to expand into his Dragon Knight armor. If he couldn't figure out how to get their armor to work as it did back on Amal, they will have little chance of succeeding against the Black Dragon and its forces.

Sighing, he sank back into the pilot seat. Not that our chances are good in the first place, he thought. Maltanore was probably the weakest of the Black Dragon's forces, and he toyed with me until practically the end. Let's not forget we have to find the remaining Knights and the new Gold Dragon.

"Come on, work! Damn it, work!" he barked in frustration. It remained as it was. The pulsing crystal almost seemed to mock him. "Come on! Activate! Turn on! Armor up!" he snapped, to no effect. "Look, I'm going to get shot!" Still nothing.

Growling, he threw himself back into the seat. Well, it was worth a shot, he thought as he let loose a puff of air, his lips vibrating.

He had no idea why the bracelet stopped working when it retracted back on Amal. Now he had no way to access his armor.

He glanced at the controls and then gazed into the almost-solid whiteness beyond the view screen.

Beep... Beep...

He eyed the flashing commlink. With a sigh, he reached over and pressed it.

"Yeah?" he said. A holographic version of Little John's head appeared. "Robin, you'd better get down here—we may have a problem," LJ said.

"Great, that's all we need," Robin moaned. He rubbed his hand over his face. "Get Much up here to take my place. I'll be right down."

He pressed a button on the armrest. The seat slid back, and he climbed to his feet.

He exited the cockpit through the door, which released a soft hiss at the rear, and started down the smooth-walled corridor. At each corner stood rigid frames to support the halls if the ship got attacked. Every now and then he passed a maintenance access port. A solid column of lights ran along the corners, more lights shining above at regular intervals.

As he walked, the metal floor tinning under his booted feet, his thoughts drifted to what might be going on. As he passed his friend Much in the corridor, Much muttered, "Good luck."

Oh, that's reassuring, Robin thought sarcastically. He arrived at the cargo hold door and pressed the release, where he was bombarded by various angry voices shouting all at once.

Spotting his mother, Little John, and Willa amid the angry crowd, which was headed by his former rival, Dulglad, and Dulglad's father, Shuji, he pushed his way forward and quickly stood at Willa's side.

"Willa, LJ, what's going on here?" he demanded.

"Well, we can tell you what's not happening," Dulglad's father interrupted. "No one here—including myself—will take orders from you or your friends."

Robin's mother, Chikako, stepped forward. "Then who would you suggest, Shuji?" she asked.

"This is not the time for this petty dispute!" Robin shouted, annoyed that this had come up. "Right now, we need to decide our next course of action."

Dulglad said, "I say we head for the nearest pirate base or village we know about. There, we either join with the resistance or at least take shelter."

Some of the people around him nodded.

"Tell me," Robin challenged, "has anyone seen this ship's schematics?" Everyone turned to Robin.

"I have," Tuck said, standing close to his sister, Willa.

Willa nodded, as did LJ.

"What does that matter?" Dulglad demanded.

"It matters," Robin said, "because if you had seen the schematics, you would know this ship has a tracking beacon." He crossed his arms.

Releasing a puff of laughter, Dulglad looked from one to the other.

"And you think that's a problem? All we have to do is turn it off or destroy it," he said smugly.

With a thoughtful look, Robin nodded. "Yes, we could do that... But there's one problem with that plan."

Before Dulglad could respond, Little John explained. "The beacon isn't in the ship. It's outside, attached to the hull."

Dulglad shrugged. "Then somebody will have to go out there and take care of it."

Unable to keep the smile off his face, Robin chuckled, shaking his head. "Do you have any idea what could happen if somebody tried to exit a ship moving at hyperspeed?"

"He or she would be lucky if death came just as fast," Willa said.

"Then drop out of hyperspeed to deal with it," Dulglad answered defensively.

Robin explained, "The second we drop out of hyperspeed, they can track us. And we have no idea how fast they can spring up on us. For all we know, we could drop right into a system hosting half the Black Dragon's fleet. And we have no means of proving we're friends. Even if we head for one of the familiar outposts, do you honestly believe they would welcome us, knowing we're giving the Black Dragon a map to their location?"

Dulglad's face hardened as he realized the truth behind the words. "All right—fine!" he snapped. "But we can't stay in hyperspace forever!"

"You're right, we can't," Tuck responded. "And that's why every starship has a navigation computer on board. Human error runs about twenty-five percent. But if both we and the computer are off by just one percent, we could fly right into a supernova or into the maw of a black hole. We'd all be dead before we knew what happened."

"Yeah, you're right about that," Shuji said.

"This isn't about who's right or wrong...or who wins or loses," Chikako added.

"This is about staying alive," Robin said. "And right now, that is more important than picking who's in charge."

Dulglad retorted, pointing at Robin and his friends. "It's because of these 'knights' that our village and planet were destroyed!"

"There's no way to know that!" Willa shouted. "We all heard what Maltanore said when he and the Dark Elf arrived. They detected the village from orbit two days before they even showed up! That's long before we were chosen to be knights!"

"It doesn't matter!" Shuji snapped. "Just because you and your friends were chosen as the next Dragon Knights does not make you our leaders."

"Then let's settle this the ancient way!" Robin said. Everyone looked at him. "Democracy. We'll put it to a vote and settle this once and for all."

For a second, Shuji and Robin glared at each other. Then Robin turned on the spot to look at the crowd. "Does anyone have a nomination?" he asked.

"I nominate myself and my son," Shuji said, placing his hand on Dulglad's shoulder.

Not surprised, Robin turned to face them.

"I nominate Robin," Chikako asserted.

Robin turned to his mother, blinking.

"Robin?" Dulglad muttered, frowning. He and his father shared a look.

Chikako gave Robin a brief, encouraging smile and nodded. Then she turned and faced the crowd. "All in favor of Shuji and Dulglad?"

At once, both father and son raised their hands. For a second, there was nothing but silence as they looked around at the people around them.

Only a few of Dulglad's friends had also raised their hands.

"Opposed?" One by one, everyone else raised their hand.

Nodding slowly, Chikako looked at the people. "All in favor of Robin?" she asked.

Scanning the group, Robin waited, holding his breath. A man sitting on the catwalk above, legs dangling, slowly raised one hand. As if that was a signal everyone else was waiting for, other people raised their hands. Turning on the spot, Robin watched as more and more people raised their hands. He faced his friends, who gave him small smiles and then raised their hands.

"Well, I guess that's one for democracy," Chikako said, facing Dulglad and his father. "Now that's settled, shouldn't we start planning our next move?"

Charting A Course

BACK IN THE cockpit, Robin sat alone in the navigation station. His head rested lightly in his hand as he tapped his cheek in thought.

For the last hour or so, he had poured over the star charts, trying to find a safe point to exit hyperspace.

He had reviewed and eliminated space ports, space stations, planets, and systems. Sighing, he sat back in his chair. "Where to go, where to go, where to go?" he muttered.

At the sound of the door hissing open, he rotated his chair. His friends came into the cockpit.

"So how's the newly elected fearless leader?" Willa asked, sitting across from him.

"About to request a recount," Robin answered.

"Hey, better you than Dulglad and Shuji," Much said, leaning against Willa's chair.

"Well, I'm not so sure people will agree with that once they see the only destination available to us," Robin responded.

"What do you mean?" Tuck asked, frowning, from his place near the controls.

In answer, Robin pressed a couple of buttons. At once, a holographic image of a rotating planet appeared before him.

It was a planet about the size of the one they had left behind. One of the moons orbiting around it hosted a magnificent set of rings, in contrast to the vast desert that covered the surface.

"I think we all know this planet," Robin said. He zoomed in on the moon planet.

For a few seconds, silence rang through the cockpit.

"The Bazaar System?" Willa asked. She looked shocked. "You want us to go to one of the biggest trade planets in the galaxy? Second only to the ones around Centurium?"

As his friends looked at each other, Robin knew they were trying not to think about the reference to the markets on the moons orbiting the capital of the Black Dragon's Empire, previously known as Illuminances. This had once been a place of light and justice, but now it was full of darkness and tyranny.

Robin answered, "We may not have much of a choice."

"'Not much of a choice?'" Little John repeated. "You're suggesting we fly right into the lion's den."

He stepped forward to lean against the navigation console. "We're talking about one of the largest trading ports in the Black Dragon's Empire for almost ten sectors. At one point or another, half the goods and people are sold there."

"Exactly," Robin said. "With all the transports, merchants, and lowlife buyers who go there, who's going to notice one more transport carrying slaves? All we need to do is have some of the people on board act like slaves. We can mingle and get lost in the crowds there. We can also get or steal a ship—one that doesn't have a tracking beacon on it."

Robin looked from one face to another. He added, "We already have everything we need on board to pull it off—including five sentinel substitutes to act as guards. I don't like this plan any more than you do, but I've spent the last few hours going over these star charts, and I can't think of anything else. If you have a better idea, I'm more than willing to listen." He waved his hand at the hologram, which went dim.

At first, the group was silent. Then Willa asked, "Any idea where we'd go afterward? If we're still alive, that is."

Blowing out a puff of air, Robin sat back. "Probably the safest place we can go, and perhaps find our way to the resistance..."

He looked at her. "Tortuga."

Much chuckled. "How fitting that we, a band of outcasts on the run, would find refuge within the hidden capital of pirates and thieves. And lucky for us, the Black Dragon shouldn't have any idea where it is." Nodding, Little John turned to look out the portal.

"But we still have one problem," Willa said. When they turned to look at her, she raised her wrist to display her bracelet. "This whole plan centers around whether or not we can turn these things back on." Silence again fell in the cockpit. She was right.

Determined, Robin climbed to his feet. He raised his hand to stare at the palm side of his wrist and the back end of the bracelet. As each second passed, he stared at the unmoving band, and his frown deepened. Unwilling to let the bracelet beat him, he focused increasingly harder.

Just as he bared his teeth in frustration, it finally happened. With a sliding metallic sound, the metal extended from the band, covering his hand and moving up his arm.

The friends watched in amazement as the metal covered Robin's chest, moved down his waist to cover his legs, and crossed to cover his other arm. Finally, sliding over his ears, the plates passed up and over his head. Then they expanded to form a dragon head and face.

After the horns and face had finished expanding, Robin looked from one friend to another.

"Well, I guess that solves one problem," he said in an altered voice. "The final question that remains is: who gets to tell the people on board about this plan?"

The helmet retracted from his face.

"I guess we'll have to decide like civilized, responsible people," Little John said.

For a couple of seconds, silence rang in the room.

"Odds or evens?" Much asked.

The Calling

LATER, AFTER SEVERAL rounds of the game, Tuck raised his arms in defeat. "I should have gone with evens," he moaned. Then he took a deep breath, like someone about to dive into a tiger pit, and left to break the news to the others on board.

For a couple seconds, Robin heard only silence. Then he heard cries of outrage from the other side of the thick metal doors. When the door finally hissed and started to open, Tuck quickly slid through, trying to shield his head from the objects the people in the angry crowd were throwing at him.

Robin grabbed Tuck and dove for cover as more things were thrown after him. Then he pressed the release, and the half-open door closed with a hiss. Breathing hard, he looked at Tuck, who finally lowered his arms.

After a few moments, Robin opened the door again and went out to the crowd. He raised his hands and gestured for silence. When the people finally calmed down enough to listen, Robin began to explain the plan in more detail.

Initially, both Shuji and Dulglad wore smug looks on their faces. However, their expressions turned sour when people started nodding at Robin, agreeing this was the best plan of action. Then Robin returned to his friends.

For a few hours, the five knights practiced expanding and retracting their armor. When they were confident they had a reasonable level of control again, they set the course.

While the main group waited in the cargo hold for the vessel to exit hyperspace, Robin and the other knights sat in the cockpit, covered by their armor. With each passing second, Robin's nerves became more on edge, and whenever he glanced at his friends, he could see they felt the same way.

"We're approaching the exit point," Little John said, his armored dragon head turning to face Robin.

Breathing deeply, Robin gathered his courage before he pressed the commlink to speak to those waiting in the hold.

"Everyone, get ready. We're about to exit hyperspace," he said. "And remember, you're supposed to be slaves. When you leave the ship, look subdued and beaten."

"We're ready," came his mother's voice.

Killing the link, he set his gaze straight ahead.

"Reaching exit point in three... two... one," Much said from his post.

"Kill hyperdrive engine!" Robin ordered.

At once, the ship responded with a great shudder and jerk as they exited hyperspace. Before them was the desert planet Bazaar.

Robin's eyes swiveled to the ships going to and from the planet, as well as the various orbiting stations and defense platforms. Trying to keep calm, he took the controls and throttled forward.

As they drew closer to the planet, the commlink on the controls started to flash.

With a light gulp, Robin looked at it. "Here we go," he muttered, and he pressed the flashing light.

At once, a hologram of a sentinel's head appeared above the console. "Shuttle approaching planet, identify."

"Shuttle 5587 requesting permission to land," Robin said, trying to make his voice sound robotic.

"Status of Maltanore and Velissa?"

"Deceased."

The sentinel was silent for a long moment. "Purpose for landing?" it finally asked.

"Relaying cargo for Centurium," Robin replied.

If a sentinel could blink, Robin was sure it would have done so. "Type of cargo?"

Robin closed his eyes, his half-hope dying. He felt the longer the exchange went on, the smaller their chance of success. If only the sentinel would believe the image of the crowd in the cargo hold, his former family and neighbors who were now pretending to be slaves.

He pressed more buttons, and at once another hologram appeared between them. "Captured non-magical beings," Robin said.

The sentinel eyed the image of the villagers in the cargo hold, each head demurely bowed, each bound by a laser shackle on one wrist.

As each second ticked by, Robin's anxiety grew. Would the sentinel buy it? Would it see through it? Had he led these people to their deaths?

"You're clear to land in section 184," the sentinel finally said, and the hologram vanished.

Sitting back in his chair, Robin released the pent-up breath he hadn't known he'd been holding.

"So far, so good," he muttered. He increased speed and looked over at the other knights. They stared at him. "What?" he asked.

Their helmets revealed nothing of the expressions on their faces as they turned to look at each other.

"You do realize you sounded like a twentieth-century antique robot, right?" Willa finally asked.

"At least it worked!" Robin replied.

When they landed, Robin and the other knights gathered with the villagers in the hold. As the 'slaves' lined up, Robin barked, "Okay, people, remember. Keep your eyes down, don't say a word, and, above all, keep together!"

The villagers were connected in pairs by laser manacles. Pretending to be sentinels, the knights took guard positions on the sides, front, and back.

Robin turned to face the cargo hatch, and as he pressed the release, the ramp dropped.

"Move it!" the knights commanded as they escorted the chained villagers off the ship onto the landing platform.

Quietly, the group moved through the crowds of people. Robin eyed everyone around him as they moved forward. Among the crowd, he saw elves in their dark beauty, with some of the same markings that Velissa had had. He noticed Anubis's, centaurs, trolls, goblins, ogres, and minotaur's.

Alongside them were other races from the stars, like the four-armed green-and-black-skinned Valeaking race. He saw the wide and strong-jawed dog-like and eyeless canberus, who observed the world in sound through the embedded ears at the base of their neck. There were droves of the ant-like, four-legged, two-armed, winged Dromeanias.

But most of the crowd were humans, some in wizard or witch robes, with staves or without; others wore plain clothes, with precious jewels decorating their fingers or necks.

There were also hundreds upon hundreds of sentinels. All led bound slaves from the auctions to the owners or to the ship that would take them to their new destinations.

As he eyed them, Robin noticed something odd: though many of the same races were now being escorted in bondage, a great many of the magical races and others were doubly bound by collars, small squares glowing yellow through integrations of the metal band.

As Robin thought about the possible purpose for the collars, a thin lined square isolated one of the collars on the display in front of him. The image of it was drawn to the side, where it rotated. Then words appeared right above it.

Clerical Collar

Used to disable a wielder's magic.

"Well, that answers..." Robin started to say aloud. Then he paused.

He noticed the free centaurs had ram-like horns curling from their heads. Spiky horns emerged from the minotaurs' chins. Golden lines ran along the chained Anubises' bodies and connected at the base of their jaws, which were solid gold.

So not all magical beings stand with the Black Dragon, he thought. He enslaves even his own people.

The crowds parted to let them through.

"Keep moving!" Robin snapped, taking advantage of the circumstances to give Dulglad a quick shove. Then he froze.

Robin felt as if an electric current was flowing through his body. Under his armor, his toothed necklace started to grow warm.

Immediately, he looked left and right. His eyes fell on a group of slaves on the other side of the platform. Frowning, he paused to watch them.

Suddenly, a lighted box on the display in his helmet focused on the group of slaves and zoomed in. The box encircled the head of a girl with long black hair amid the crowd, and her head occupied Robin's vision.

She looked about the same age as his friends. From what he could see, hers was a sharp beauty, her eyebrows, cheekbones, and jawline sharply angled.

Slowly, as if sensing his gaze, she turned and seemed to look right at him. Robin gasped. She had the same hazel eyes as his, and, like his, their color seemed to shift in the light.

Suddenly, she jolted in pain as one of the sentinels near her cracked her with a laser whip. As her hair shifted, he noticed she had the same three-pointed ears he did. Zooming out, he watched. She directed her gaze right at him.

"Robin?"

He heard a voice over the private commlink, and he turned as Willa approached.

"What's wrong?" she asked.

He turned to look back at the girl. "I have to stay," he said, turning to Willa.

"What? Why?" she demanded.

Hardly daring to breathe, he turned and nodded toward the slaves.

"See that girl who looks about your age? Long black hair?"

She looked. "Yeah. Why?"

"I think... I think she's my sister."

Captured

WILLA STARED AT him. "Robin are you nuts?" she demanded. "Of all of us, you know the odds that of all the planets in the known galaxies we'd land—"

"I know!" he hissed, glaring at her. "And yet we have, and she's over there, being dragged away from me." Robin nodded in that direction. "I can't let her go...not when I'm this close."

For a second, Willa was silent, looking toward the other group, where the girl was being led away.

"What if it was Eric?" Robin asked, resorting to Tuck's real name. When she eyed him, he said, "What would you do?"

Willa paused for a moment. "And just how are we supposed to know where you are?" she finally asked.

Robin was still; the question stumped him. On the screen visor before him, the armor readout flashed at the corner of his hip. Reaching one hand toward his hip, he pulled free a little crescent moon-shaped object.

"What is that?" Willa asked. Robin held it up and examined it.

"A little something that will help you keep track of my movements." He handed it to her. "Attach it to your armor bracelet. You can track my location to within a few millimeters."

After a second's hesitation, she took it.

"Tell my mother what's happening. I'll be back soon," he said.

"You'd better be, or she'll kill me."

With this reminder of his mother, Robin took a moment to find her face in the crowd. As he locked eyes with her questioning gaze, he raised one hand in front of his chest, fingers erect. Then he curled his middle and ring fingers down. An ancient symbol that meant: I love you.

Her eyes went wide with fear.

As he watched, Willa approached his mother. She put her hand on Chikako's shoulder and urged her forward before she could move toward Robin.

Trying not to think about the worried look in his mother's eye, he murmured, "Okay, I need a weapon, or weapons, that will stick with me after the armor deactivates."

As before, his armor readout began to flash in the hip area. "What the heck?" he murmured. He glanced down, trying not to move his head as he looked at the rods settled there.

"Ah, how are those going to help me?" he said. "They create energy melee weapons. They're not blasters."

As suddenly as before, an image of the rod was drawn from the readout. This time it became a mirror image in every detail. Lines linked to several sections, giving detailed functions. A name flashed above.

Force Plasma Saber

"Okay, I was wrong." He studied the readout. "Not only can these things create plasma energy melee weapons, but they're also a plasma blaster on each side, and they extend into fighting sticks with useful features. Plus, they can combine to form a staff." A smile expanded across his face. "Aside from that bow, I think I just found my new favorite toys."

As he ran a finger over the sabers, his focus returned to his sister. He eyed the group of slaves and their escort. "Now it's time to mingle," he said.

Robin moved closer to take a position beside the girl. He tensed up when a sentinel turned its head to look at him, but then it turned away, thinking he was one of their own. So far, so good.

A large cargo freighter came into view, and Robin assumed they were reaching their destination. He paused and glanced over at the girl. She watched him too.

Out of the corner of his eye, Robin saw the movement of a laser whip. Immediately, he shifted and took the hit himself.

He caught the girl looking at him again, and he winked. He hoped she saw it. When he saw her frown deepen, he knew she had.

Staying next to her, he walked up the ramp with the group. Pausing at the top, he turned to look for the others. Unsuccessful, he decided to view this as a blessing.

Inside the ship, he watched as the girl was led into the hold. The doors sealed behind them, and he started to back down a side hall on his own. Then he saw something that made him pause.

"Oh, great, that's all I need," he muttered as he spotted a canberus wearing a sash that dangled around its eyeless head. A bull-horned centaur stood next to it.

But then again, what I'm planning is crazy enough. He sank into the shadows. I just hope I can take one of those slavers down before it's done. Then he moved into the shadows.

Acting quickly, he felt the plasma sabers drop into his hands, and he felt and heard the armor retract.

"Okay," Robin whispered to himself. He held the weapons on either side of his head and moved his back against the corner.

"Let's do this!" He whipped around and fired.

At once, two sentinels, covered in holes, fell under the surprise barrage. The centaur grabbed a sentinel as a shield, and the canberus dove for cover.

"Non-magical scum!" the centaur barked before tossing the sparking robot aside. Then he spotted Robin. "How did he get loose?"

Darting down the hall, Robin heard the thunder of hooves as the centaur tore after him.

"Obviously, you never played that old human card game, poker!" the centaur snarled before Robin rounded another corner. "Four legs always beats a pair!"

Peeking around the corner, Robin saw the centaur race his way as he formed the staff mode. Taking his staff in both hands and carefully timing it he swung out.

The blow collided against his forelegs with a crunch that knocked him off his hooves by Robin's staff. The blow sent the centaur tumbling to the deck. Behind him, Robin spun the staff, formed from two plasma sabers, knocking the centaur over the head.

"True," Robin gloated as the centaur fell, knocked out cold. "But you can get up a lot faster with just a pair of legs!"

Detaching the two parts of the staff, he tore off in another direction. He stopped halfway down a hallway at the sound of approaching metal feet. He ducked through a hatch to his right into another corridor. He closed and locked the hatch just as a line of sentinels stomped by.

"I guess they don't make them too smart," he said aloud. Then the lights in the corridor went out.

After a couple of seconds, his eyes adjusted to the near blackness eliminating it, and he quietly moved forward to a spot where the halls intersected. At a sound, he froze. Looking right, he held his breath as the canberus advanced toward him on all fours. Stopping mere feet from Robin, it turned its head left and right, trying to hear him, giving a small growl of frustration.

"You're a bold one," it finally barked. "I will admit that. I mean, what was your plan?"

It took another step forward.

"Sneak aboard, kill us all, and fly away with the ship?" It chuckled. "You non-magical beings are all the same. Always overestimating your abilities, thinking you can win. But these ships require access codes to take off. And even if you can break the code, the ship can be tracked. There's no escape."

As the canberus drew closer and closer, Robin held his breath, not making a sound. Silently he stepped back to avoid the canberus bumping into him.

"The question is," the canberus continued, "can you see in the dark?"

It turned its head in Robin's direction. Robin held one of the plasma sabers close to his head, the end facing the canberus

For a couple seconds, the canberus seemed to look at Robin. Then slowly it turned away and continued down the hall. Robin released the smallest of breaths. The canberus whipped around to face him with a roar. Robin fired. The canberus stumbled back, orange blood seeping from the wound in its shoulder.

"Actually, I can see in the dark," Robin said, taking proper aim at the canberus's head. "Quite clearly."

Suddenly the lights came on. Robin stumbled, blinded, his arms covering his eyes.

"Drop your weapons!"

Lowering his shielding arms, Robin saw the centaur and the remaining sentinels surrounding him.

"Do what we say, and you might be spared," the centaur said.

After eyeing the forces around him, Robin tossed the plasma sabers down. They clattered on the deck. Then he raised his hands slightly above his head. The centaur gaped as the weapons dissolved among mirrored lights.

"So," the centaur said, stepping forward to begin circling him, "just what was your plan? Was it as my companion said: kill us all and steal the ship?" He rested the blade of his spear on Robin's shoulder, the edge against his neck.

"Something like that," Robin said, eyeing the edge of the spear head.

The centaur chuckled. "Not a good plan."

"Well, maybe you were separated from your herd too young to understand," Robin said.

Seconds later, Robin barely saw the canberus lash out, catching him in the temple.

He knew no more.

Processing

AN UNCOUNTABLE AMOUNT of time later, Robin woke with a splitting headache. He felt dried blood on the side of his head. It hurt too much to open his eyes just yet.

Spirits above and below, that canberus has got a heck of a right hook.

He lay still a moment longer before he tried to move his arms and legs. Something seemed to be restraining them. His eyes snapped open. He found he was strapped, naked but for tight shorts and his necklace, to a table. His head was framed by curved metal plates.

"Finally awake." The centaur's voice carried through a loudspeaker.

Before Robin could reply, he heard a whining sound. Below him, the table shifted, and he found himself looking up at a blinding light.

"723237181890, tell us your age."

Blinking under the light, Robin humphed at being dehumanized and objectified.

"Couldn't you come up with something more original than a number? How about a name?"

For a second, there was silence. Then Robin gritted his teeth in pain as an electric current shot through him. When it stopped, his body went slack, and he breathed deep.

"What is your age?"

"Figure it out yourself," Robin growled. He was shocked again.

When the current stopped, Robin sagged again. The voice remarked, "This will be a less painful process if you just cooperate."

Robin chuckled. "Excuse me if I prefer to keep my individuality and humanity." The current flooded him again. "Age: 16-20."

Close enough, Robin thought.

With another whirring sound, a probe dropped into his line of vision. With a barely audible hum, a wide beam of light scanned him from the top of his head to the bottom of his feet. A second later, a holographic image of him appeared in the air.

"Physical attributes:

"Muscle tonnage: 10:10.

"Muscular structure: 20:10.

"Skeletal structure: 18:10.

"Sensory attributes: Sight: 20/1."

"Is that your best guess?" Robin demanded. His holographic skin and muscles were stripped away to reveal his bare muscles and skeleton. He was shocked again.

"Sensory inputs and outputs." His face was zoomed in on.

"Light sensitivity: beyond excellent.

"Audio sensitivity: beyond excellent.

"Scent sensitivity: beyond excellent.

"Tectorial response: beyond excellent.

"Taste response: beyond excellent.

"Neural attributes..." His neural system was exposed.

"Brain activity: 400 percent.

"Neural reflex action: 500 percent."

"Does it also say my IQ is like 260?" Robin muttered. He received another shock. "I'm getting a little tired of that!" he barked. Then he was shocked again.

"Organ functions," the voice said, and his organs were revealed. Robin heard murmurs when the image showed his eight-chambered heart and extra pair of lungs.

"Heart rate: 15 RBPM.

"Lung capacity: 20 liters.

"Blood pressure: 20/80.

"Immune system: 400 percent.

"Digestive track: beyond excellent.

"Metabolism: beyond excellent."

After the report was finished, silence rang. Then there came the clacking of the centaur's hooves. Both he and the canberus came into Robin's view.

At first, the pair just stared at Robin. Then the canberus began a growling laugh.

"Well, this is certainly our lucky day," he said eagerly. "We now possess two slaves of great quality."

Robin eyed him, trying hard to hide his disgust as the canberus drooled a little in excitement.

Then it said, "Both he and the other are at least ten times stronger and faster, and they can see, hear, taste, touch, and smell far greater than our standard merchandise."

"I think caution is warranted, Valarka," the centaur said. "We don't even know what they are. And you forget those sensory strengths are also weaknesses, considering sudden bursts could hinder and disable them."

Valarka looked up at the centaur. "Isn't it obvious, Karon, that they're biologically engineered? Probably before they were born."

Karon shot Valarka a look and then stepped closer to Robin.

"What is this?" the centaur demanded, tapping Robin's bracelet with the tip of his spear. "The other has one quite similar to it."

"It monitors my organ functions," Robin said, by thinking fast. "Without constant monitoring, they fail."

Robin locked eyes with the centaur. "In other words, take it off or damage it, and I could have a heart attack just walking."

For a couple seconds, there was silence. Karon stepped closer. "And why should we believe that?"

Robin smiled. "We all know how temperamental and unpredictable bioengineering is. Can you really take the risk?"

The pair looked at each other. Finally, Karon commanded, "Computer, scan the bracelet around his wrist and decipher its functions!"

The scanner dropped down to be level with the bracelet. After scanning it, a holographic image appeared and rotated in the air. "Analyses:

"Metallurgy: unknown.

"Power source: unknown.

"Function: Neuro connections, heart monitor, organ monitor..."

"Enough!" Valarka barked, coming forward. "It seems he was telling the truth." He turned his eyeless sockets. "Now we know we can sell them for the highest price, let's get this over with. Computer, finish processing."

Looking at the scanner, Robin watched as a spray injector was brought forward.

"What the heck is that for?" He started to struggle.

"A little this, a little that," Karon said as it came closer and closer to Robin's upper arm. "But you'll always remember this as your last moment of freedom."

As the tip came into contact with Robin's deltoid, it made a slight hissing sound. Robin bared his teeth in slight pain and discomfort.

"Knock him out and put him with the rest!" Karon snapped. The pair turned and left.

As soon as the door closed, Robin saw nozzles slide out from the wall.

As some type of gas hissed from the nozzles, he was knocked out cold.

Freya

ROBIN WOKE UP ON a hard surface and rolled onto his back.

"Easy there, son," a gentle voice said.

"What the heck was that?" Robin moaned, his hand covering his eyes.

"Knockout gas," the voice said. "Though, frankly, I've never seen them use so much to knock out a single person."

"I'm not sure I should take that as a compliment," Robin said. He sat up and pinched the bridge of his nose. "Especially the way my head feels."

He opened his eyes and immediately noticed the ragged clothes he was now wearing. Then he jerked back. An Anubis was sitting before him, bent over him in concern. "You're a... you're a..."

"An Anubis," he said, nodding and resting his back against the wall. "And judging from your reaction, the last time you met one of my people, it wasn't a pleasant experience." He raised one arm, resting his hand on a bent knee.

Letting his eyes roam over the Anubis, Robin nodded. "You could say that." He shifted to move fast if he had to.

"I'm sorry to hear that," the Anubis said, and Robin thought he heard genuine sorrow in his voice. "Please, there is no need to fear me. After all..." He lifted his arm to show the laser shackle. "We're both prisoners." Robin took note of the drone collar around his neck, his gold veins, and his lower jaw.

"I guess you're right about that," Robin said, feeling himself relax a little.

The Anubis cocked a smile. "Not to worry. You're not the first to react like that. And you won't be the last."

For a moment, the pair looked at each other. Then Robin smiled, shaking his head.

"I guess that's true," he said and offered his hand. "I'm... I'm Robin." The Anubis paused and then took Robin's hand in a firm handshake.

"You may know me as Tekmet," he said. "But I suggest from here on out you call me 1967191799."

Robin chuckled. "Like hell am I going to refer to anyone by a number or answer to one."

"We thought that way at one point," Tekmet said, "but eventually we all had to submit. It is the injection."

"What was it?"

"Nanites."

Robin stared at the Anubis. "Well, that explains a few things," he finally said. "With those little bastards in our blood, they can track us, give us a nasty shock, or..." He looked away.

"Blow us up," Tekmet finished. "If we try to escape."

"Does anyone have any idea what their range is?" Robin asked.

Tekmet looked at him. "No one has lived long enough to find out," he said solemnly. "And I suggest you don't join the ranks of those who try."

"You're certainly more cautious than the last Anubis I met. At least he didn't encourage us to just give up."

"Really..." Tekmet said slowly. "Tell me, who was that Anubis?"

"Maltanore," Robin said, and Tekmet jerked forward, his mouth parted. "Only he didn't fare as well as I did."

"How so?" Tekmet demanded.

Smiling, Robin said, "Well, to explain, I think I'll fill you in on the oldest and best possible way to pass on a secret. Lean forward."

When Tekmet leaned forward, Robin said, "I'll whisper in your ear."

Then he whispered, "I separated his head from his shoulders." When he drew back, Tekmet was staring at him.

"Is there a girl here?" Robin asked.

Tekmet waved his hands. "Quite a few."

"How about one with long black hair, my height, eyes that change color, and three-pointed ears?"

Tekmet frowned, rubbing his chin in thought. "That sounds like 918—" he started, stopping halfway. He and Robin looked at each other.

"That sounds like Freya," he finally said.

"Freya?" Robin asked. He could feel his heart fill with hope.

"Yeah, I've known her since she was a child. Which isn't saying much, considering how old she is. We went through several masters and mistresses together."

He jabbed his thumb to the side. "She's over there, seeing to an injured woman."

Robin's head whipped around. He spotted Freya. She was tying a strip of cloth from her clothes around a cut on a woman's leg.

"Thanks," Robin said. He climbed to his feet and started toward her.

A thousand thoughts flashed through his mind. What kind of person is she? Have they broken her? How long has she been living this life? Will she believe what I am about to tell her? Does she have one of the missing armors?

As he drew close, Freya paused and slowly looked up at him. Her ragged clothes were so worn, Robin was surprised they were still in one piece. As she shifted her arm, he caught sight of the unmistakable bracelet around her wrist. It bore a light, sky-blue crystal that, like his, pulsed regularly with colored light.

"I haven't seen you before," she said, her eyes going up and down his frame. "You must be new."

"You could say that," Robin said. He sat next to her. "It seems you have a healer's touch."

She said, "Considering treatments are far and few between, we all have to look out for each other."

She finished tying off the makeshift bandage. The woman nodded her thanks, carefully climbed to her feet, and limped away to join another group.

"Tekmet tells me your name is Freya," he said, and she froze.

Slowly she turned to look at Robin and then at Tekmet.

"It's rare for him to open up to people," she finally said. "Especially new arrivals. He would tell you my name when my designation is—"

She shifted slightly back, as if she felt a little uncomfortable under the intensity of Robin's gaze.

"I will not call you by a number," Robin interrupted firmly. "And I don't want you to do so ever again."

Instead of replying, she finally stared boldly back at him. Eventually she said, "Even though you know what would happen if I do that? Anyway, why do you care?"

Biting his lip, he tried to steady his nerves. "Because... I think we both know I'm your brother."

Never Take My Soul

FREYA STARED AT Robin with a deep frown. "And what makes you think you're my brother?" she asked skeptically.

Despite the disbelieving tone in her voice, Robin couldn't keep the smile from his face. He shook his head and asked, "How many people do you know with eyes that change color like ours?" Her eyes narrowed as she looked into his.

"Or three-pointed ears like these," Robin said, shifting his hair to reveal his ears. "Or a necklace like this," he said, lifting his chain to bring the dragon tooth into her line of sight.

She clasped her necklace in her hand.

Then Robin added, "And we both know you've known since the first time we saw each other." She blinked in confusion. "When was that?"

"When you were being transferred," Robin answered.

Again she blinked. He continued, "But then I was covered in high tech armor. You looked at me quite frequently."

For a second, she remained silent. Then she turned to fully face him.

"No, that can't be right..." she said, eyeing him. "That was a sentinel."

Robin explained. "Like I said, I wore high-tech armor. Have you ever seen a sentinel that looked how I looked then?"

She lowered her gaze. Finally, she said, "Can't say I have." Then her eyes narrowed suspiciously. "So where is this supposed armor you wore?"

Robin glanced around and nodded toward Tekmet. He gestured for Freya to follow him to the Anubis.

"Let's discuss it back there, not here."

To his relief, she followed him, and they both sat down beside Tekmet.

"Okay," Freya said. "It's just us for now. Where is this armor?"

For a moment, Tekmet looked at them both with confusion. Then, before Robin could reply, the Anubis held up Robin's hand.

"Freya," Tekmet said, "this boy's bracelet is just like yours. It's here." He showed her the bracelet.

Freya quickly lowered her gaze to the bracelet on her wrist. Then she snorted.

"Ha, ha, this is our armor? What happened to the rest of it?" She continued to laugh. "Did your armor vanish into thin air?" Robin was only half-paying attention to her. His eyes were on Tekmet. "You know what this is, don't you?" he asked in a low tone.

The Anubis frowned. "Actually, I do. But I was beginning to believe they were only a myth."

His serious tone and expression seemed to silence Freya. She said, "Tekmet, what are—"

He quickly placed his hand over her mouth.

"Quiet, Child!" he hissed, his eyes searching everywhere. "No one else must hear us. And cover those bracelets up, both of you!"

He tore two strips of cloth from his clothes and handed one to each of them.

"Tekmet, what is going on?" Freya asked. She covered her bracelet just as Robin finished wrapping his.

"If he's telling the truth," Tekmet said, "then these bracelets contain the legendary armors of the knights."

Freya stared. "The knights? As in the Dragon Knights in the fairy tales you used to tell me and the other children?"

"As I have told you many times, Freya, fairy tales and legends often have the ring of truth to them. And they can in the darkest times bring us into the light."

Tekmet looked at Robin. "Why are you here? How were you captured if you are a Dragon Knight?"

"I came for my sister," Robin answered simply, tilting his head toward Freya.

"Sister..." Tekmet muttered, eyes wide. "Are you Jun and Chikako's boy?"

Robin blinked in shock when he heard his parents' names. "How do you... how do you know them?"

"I only met Jun once," Tekmet said. "On the other hand, I have known Chikako for years. She even saved my life a couple times." Robin stared.

"Now tell me the truth," Tekmet said. He leaned his snouted face so close that Robin could smell his dog breath. The Anubis whispered, "Are these truly the legendary armors?" He glanced at Freya. "Does this mean both of you are knights?"

Knowing his answer would bear the weight of a starship and would forever change lives, Robin nodded.

"Yes," he said simply. "We are both Dragon Knights."

Tekmet inhaled a puff of air and sat back. His voice grew lighter as he said, "Then I hope you have a plan for getting out of here."

"Well, step one is complete," Robin replied. He turned to Freya. "Get to Freya."

"And step two?" Freya asked.

Smiling, Robin uncovered his bracelet. "Give them hell," he answered. The crystal pulsed steadily. He focused to expand his armor. However, like before, nothing happened.

"Not again," Robin growled. He rapped the bracelet with his knuckles. "I thought I had this solved back on the ship!"

Freya looked at him for a moment. Then her gaze shifted to Tekmet and back to Robin.

"Well," she said. They both looked at her. "I don't know about the two of you, but I've had all the excitement I can take for one day." She climbed to her feet.

"Freya..." Tekmet said, reaching for her.

"They're fairy tales!" she hissed quietly, whipping around to face them. "They're nothing!"

Then she turned to Robin. "As for you...you may be my brother, you may not be. But remember this... I am a slave! I have been a slave since I was a small child, when our village was taken because I wandered among a couple scouts that landed on our world. For that I deserve this life!"

She waved her finger at him angrily. "Whoever you are, you are trying to give me the worst gift for a slave! You are trying to give me hope! To give a person hope and then let it get ripped away...that would break even the strongest person."

Then she whipped around and stalked away, leaving silence in her wake as the two watched her go.

After a moment, Robin slowly turned to Tekmet. "Is it true?"

Tekmet looked at the floor. "No matter how many times I've told her it wasn't her fault, and despite what everyone else says, she still blames herself for what happened," he said. "She may have looked like a teenager, but she was still just a child. To shoulder that kind of blame and ridicule... Over the years, I've done my best to keep her hope and spirits alive...and I have always loved her as a father."

As Robin stared at Tekmet, the Anubis climbed to his feet and walked away, leaving Robin alone. He lowered his gaze to glare at his still-pulsing bracelet.

For an uncounted amount of time, Robin remained where he was, leaving only for food and water from their dispensers, getting to know a few people while he did. But when he approached Freya again, she turned and walked away from him without a word.

With no way to keep time after what seemed like days, Robin still sat alone, staring at the bracelet. It continued to refuse to deploy, and he glared at it.

"Still at it?" Tekmet asked as he approached.

Robin looked at him and nodded. "I don't know why it's not working... but I know it's our best chance to get out of this mess." He looked over at Freya, who was teaching a clapping game to a few small children. "She still won't talk to me?"

Tekmet shook his head.

Before Robin could speak again, a large grinding sound from above filled his ears.

"What's happening?" Robin heard someone ask.

"Unless I'm very much mistaken," Tekmet said, "a ship is docking."

Soon silence fell. All eyes went to the hatch on the far wall. Robin waited quietly with the group. At last, the door slid open with a mighty hiss, and Valarka appeared with a man bearing a staff.

The canberus spoke only to the man by his side. "As you can see, we have many great specimens." He waved one pawed hand. "Please, all are available for your temporary will."

Smiling, the man stepped closer to the group. "Yes...very nice," he said. He cupped the chin of a young girl so she would have to look at him.

Robin froze in horror as the man moved through the crowd and stopped before Freya. He watched as he examined her, turning her head left and right.

"Well, aren't you a beauty?" he said. "You'll do." Then he turned back toward the door, grasping Freya by her upper arm.

"Hey!" At once the man froze. All eyes turned to Robin as he strode forward. "Get your hands—"

He was cut off when a surge of pain shot through him. It was like his blood was being electrocuted and on fire all at once. He dropped to all fours, teeth bared and clenched hard in pain.

At the door, Valarka pressed a button on his remote. "I apologize," the canberus said to the man as he released the button.

The pain slowly ebbed, and Robin breathed deeply. Valarka continued, "He's newly captured and has yet to learn his place."

Robin raised his murderous gaze to the pair.

"Well, then it's time he learned," the man said as Robin regained his feet.

The man lifted one hand. Robin was raised off his feet, and with a flick of the man's wrist, Robin was slammed against the far wall. First, he slumped to the floor. Then, just as he began to push himself up, he saw the man pull Freya out through the hatch. "Freya—"

Then everything went black.

A while later, he woke with a jerk as Tekmet was tending to him.

"Easy, Robin," Tekmet said as Robin started to sit up.

"How long was I out?" Robin asked, holding his head in his hands.

"Almost an hour," Tekmet said. "That was quite a hit you took." He glanced behind him.

Following his gaze. Robin noticed many people were shooting him odd glances every now and then.

"You certainly gained their respect," Tekmet said.

Robin lowered his gaze in shame. "I wasn't able to save my sister from whatever they're going to do to her," he said, climbing slowly to his feet.

Before Tekmet could reply, the hiss of the door interrupted him. Turning, they watched as Karon shoved Freya through the door. She stumbled to the floor. With another hiss, the door snapped closed behind her.

Robin rushed to her side. Gently, he reached down and touched her shoulder. When she looked up, he saw shame, tears, and anger in her eyes. He waited quietly for a moment, and then he helped her to her feet and slowly guided her to a secluded spot.

He helped her sit down and watched as she struggled to hold back her tears.

"I am sorry," he said. When she looked at him, he continued, "I am so sorry I wasn't able to protect you."

For a couple of seconds, she just eyed him. Then she said, "You know...ever since I accepted this life as mine, I made myself a promise. They can do whatever they want to my body, but they will never have my soul. Never."

Robin met her gaze, and then he nodded. He pulled her into a hug, and she finally let the tears fall as she clung to him.

Arrival

TIME HAD NO meaning for Robin as he leaned against the hull of the cargo hold. He tried to ignore the rumbles from his stomach and the irritation of his desert-dry throat.

Freya had finally fallen to sleep after shedding what seemed like a day and a night's worth of tears. He glanced down at her, her head resting on the pillow of his lap. He gently patted her head, trying not to hit her with the laser manacle on his arm.

The people around them moaned with hunger and thirst. The water and food units were bone dry.

"You'd think they'd take better care of such precious cargo..." His voice was a rough croak.

His thoughts were interrupted by the sounds of a scuffle. In a corner, he saw a woman named Hannah struggling with a rough-looking man over a few morsels of food the man managed to hoard. When the struggle started to become violent, Robin used what little strength he had left to shift Freya's head from his lap. He climbed to his feet, shuffled over to the pair, and pulled them apart.

"That's enough!" he barked. Several people turned and stared.

"All I wanted was a little bit of food for my child," Hannah explained. Robin kept one hand on her shoulder and the other on the man's broad chest.

"And I warned her if she touched my stash again, meat would be back on the menu for her child!" the man snapped. He continued to shield the meager amount of food with his hands.

Robin turned on him. "They've already taken our freedom. Should we let them take our humanity too? Because if we don't stick together, it will take them no time at all to break us or wipe us out."

For a few seconds, the man held his gaze. Then the man slowly lowered his eyes and opened his hands, revealing a chunk of stale bread no bigger than a fist.

Slowly, Robin extended his own hand and said, "What if it were your child?"

The man scowled. "If it were my child, I'd make sure it learned the best way to survive is to look out for yourself." But he handed Robin the bread and sat down.

Robin sighed and shook his head. Then he turned his focus to Hannah, who sobbed and fell to her knees. Dropping down next to her, he laid a comforting hand on her shoulder. When she finally looked at him, he said, "Come on, we have some food."

He helped her up, and the two went to her daughter.

A short while later, Robin and Freya watched as the mother eagerly fed the young toddler.

"If we weren't slaves, I'd suggest you go into politics," Freya said. "Damn near had me convinced, and I wasn't the only one."

He cocked a half grin. "It'd drive me crazy. Probably end up shooting myself my first term," he said, and she laughed.

Suddenly, the laser cord on Robin's manacle lit up, and the next thing he knew, an invisible force was dragging him across the floor by his arm. He came to a sudden stop next to Tekmet, and the band of lasers shackled the pair closely.

"This again," he moaned. When he sat up and looked around, he realized the others had been paired up as well. "I guess we've arrived."

He no sooner said the words than the cargo doors opened. Behind them stood three sentinels.

"On your feet, all of you!" they barked in mechanical voices. They slid laser whips from under their forearms into their hands and started cracking them.

Robin stole a glance at Freya, who was chained to the toddler's mother. Hannah was trying to keep close to her daughter, who was chained to a middle-aged man.

"We said, on your feet!"

The sharp sting of the whip brought Robin back. He bit back the pain, cringed slightly, and climbed to his feet.

"Now move!" the sentinel barked, and they were all marched out of the ship toward a roaring crowd.

The Auction

WHEN IS EYES adjusted to the sunlight outside, Robin gaped. He was on Centurium, the biggest trade planet on the galaxy, which was also the capital of the Black Dragon's Empire.

Looking around, he took in the city's levels, which seemed to stretch up to the sky. Crisscrossing above him, he saw lane upon lane of hover car traffic zipping to and fro, like lines of ants rushing to their destination.

The buildings around them came in all shapes and sizes and seemed to continue forever into the sky. Hanging from each of them, almost dancing in the wind, were deep gray banners featuring a black dragon flying upward, a white dragon skull overlaying it.

The symbol of the Black Dragon, Robin thought.

As they were marched along the stage, Robin couldn't help but feel dread move through him. Both he and Freya had to get off this planet—and fast. If the Black Dragon discovered them here, they'd be torn apart.

Robin, still connected to Tekmet, did his best to keep his eye on Freya, who stood forlornly with her partner in the corner.

Turning, Robin took in the crowd in front of the stage. As in the Bazaar system, he saw a mixture of species and people, each murmuring in their own language. All of these individuals turned in their direction, and Robin stiffened at the evil looks in some of the buyers' eyes.

"Come one, come all, ladies and gentlemen!" Valarka called, floating out of the ship on a hovering podium. "Come and see the best batch of non-magical slaves this side of the galaxy! We have men, we have women, we have children! We have them all, and we guarantee a lifetime of satisfaction!"

Suddenly, sirens blared. Robin's gaze shifted to the back of the crowd as a large, extravagant state transport arrived. He saw a Black Dragon crest on its door.

With a nervous gulp, Robin glanced down at his bracelet. *If you're listening, I really need you to work right about now!*

With a hiss, the doors of the state transport opened and stairs lowered to the ground. A tall man in a robe and billowing cape with a wand attached to his belt stepped out.

"Make way!" someone called as he moved forward, and the crowd parted. "Make way for Lord Balwin!" Robin's eyes widened.

Lord Balwin! The same Lord Balwin who runs the crystal mines! One of the Black Dragon's most loyal followers!

As the man walked toward the group, Valarka bowed to him. "My lord, it is indeed a—"

"You can dispense with the formalities," Lord Balwin said in a deep, oily voice. "I am here to claim my right of first pick of your merchandise."

"Of course," Valarka said, bowing low a second time with a wave of his hand.

Ignoring him, Balwin moved forward. "And of course, a look at our best specimens."

Valarka pressed a button on his remote. At once, the laser connecting Robin and Tekmet vanished with a hiss. A pair of sentinels pushed them forward. Robin quickly looked toward Freya; she was being pushed forward as well.

Balwin ran an eye over Robin as if he were a pet or a prize steed.

Valarka chimed in again. "As you know, my Lord Balwin, Anubises are quite strong. Great to carry whatever you choose or to do hard labor."

Then he waved a paw-like hand at Robin and Freya. "As for these two, both are genetically engineered beings. They are stronger, faster, and have

151

senses well beyond any other slaves we have here. It's as if they were created to be perfect slaves."

Balwin remained silent. He examined Tekmet. After a moment, he slapped Tekmet's chest as if to test its density. Then he took one of Tekmet's arms and bent it back, feeling the taut bicep.

"Open your mouth," he commanded.

Robin's eyes widened in disgust as he watched Lord Balwin examine Tekmet's teeth as he would an animal. "One thousand starrubbies," he finally said.

"Sold," Valarka answered.

Then Balwin moved in front of Robin. Not bothering to keep the disgust from his gaze, Robin glared at Balwin. He didn't move, and he did his best to keep his muscles slack while the man slapped his chest and squeezed his biceps.

When the man dropped Robin's arm, Robin glared at him.

"Open your mouth," Balwin commanded. Feeling more eyes on him, Robin did nothing. "Open your mouth!" Balwin commanded louder.

Robin kept his mouth closed, turning his lips into a hard line. He was promptly slapped, which barely jarred him. All he felt was hope that he could stand as an example for his sister to keep fighting.

Eyes blazing, Robin remained as he was.

Balwin returned his gaze with a look of rage. Hands on his hips, he ran his eyes up and down Robin. Robin mimicked him, which earned him another slap. Behind him, he heard a couple of people chuckling as quietly as possible.

With a growl of irritation, Balwin moved to Freya. His anger growing, Robin watched as Freya endured the same humiliation. However, she withstood the examination meekly.

"Same price," Balwin said.

"Sold," Valarka answered.

Feeling like he had fallen into a bottomless abyss, Robin realized his mistake. Instead of inspiring Freya, he'd lost her with his antics. He found his sister, but now she was being torn away from him. He watched in despair as she was led off the stage.

Cursing his pride, he stepped forward. "Freya!" he called. He was promptly shocked. Biting back the pain, he dropped to one knee.

Balwin paused, looking back at Robin.

"Apologies, my lord," Valarka said. "He was newly captured in the Bazaar System and has yet to be broken in."

"Then I suggest you do it immediately," the lord said, and with a wicked smile he led Freya and Tekmet into a transport, returning alone a few minutes later to continue the auction.

Before Robin could climb to his feet, a sentinel dragged him back. For the rest of the auction he watched as, one by one, the people around him were brought forward and sold to various buyers. Balwin bought even the toddler, ripped from Hannah's arms as they both screamed.

As Hannah was brought forward, tears streamed down her face. Robin watched with bated breath as buyers raised their hands and called out bids. After the mother was led away to her new owner, he was the only one left on the stage. A sentinel pushed him forward.

"Now, as you know, this is a prime specimen," Valarka said, again waving his paw-like hand. "Let's start the bidding at one thousand starrubbies."

For a couple of seconds, there was silence. "Come on, people, though unbroken, this is a bargain for such slave flesh. You will never find a better one."

"One thousand," a minotaur at the back called out.

"I heard one thousand, do I hear one thousand five hundred?"

Back and forth, the bidding continued. Robin shot a glare at Balwin's smug face when he refused to bid.

"I have five thousand. Going once... Going twice..."

"Ten thousand," a voice called. Heads whipped around, and Balwin stared, dumbstruck.

On the steps of Balwin's transport stood a young woman who seemed to be about Robin's age. She wore an elegant, flowing blue robe that was secured around the waist by a gilded girdle belt. Some of her long black hair was tied into an elegant bun, while the rest flowed down her back.

Even at a distance, Robin could see the elegant curves of her face, her full lips, and her slanted eyebrows.

He barely heard Valarka ask for an advance on her bid. When none came, he called out, "Sold to Princess Marian!"

Marian

ROBIN STARED IN stunned silence at the woman standing on the steps to the transport.

Princess? Princess! He blinked over and over, eyes locked on her. His mind was racing, and he barely noticed the laser shackle had extended and wrapped around his other wrist.

How can there be a princess? The Black Dragon would never allow... Unless... he thought, as he was practically dragged forward to her. Unless the rumors are true and this is one of the last heirs to the non-magical thrones. He was jerked to a stop.

"Here you are, Milady, plus his restraint control and frequency," Karon said, handing her a small remote device and bowing with a wave of his hand. "Though I suggest you take caution with this one. As you've seen, he's quite willful."

"That will be up to me to decide," she said, palming the remote, barely hiding the disgust in her voice. "Now away with you!" she snapped with a jerk of her hand.

Bowing, Karon backed away with a clip-clop of hooves.

Sighing, she looked down at Robin. He eyed her with a hard expression. "Would you step in?" she said, waving her hand toward the interior of the transport.

"Princess Marian!" a voice barked. Robin turned to see Balwin heading toward them. "I must protest—!"

"Sorry, Lord Balwin," she interrupted before she ushered the baffled Robin inside the luxury transport. "As you see to yours, I must also see to mine."

She closed the door. With a command to the driver, the transport took off.

As they pulled away, Robin looked out the back window. He could just make out Freya and Tekmet as they were led on to another transport.

Robin turned and met Marian's gaze as she watched him from her seat.

"You must be hungry," she said. "From what I hear, slave ships aren't known for their cuisine."

She opened a compartment and issued another command; fruit appeared. "Here, eat."

Robin's eyes looked from her to the food and back.

"Please," she said, and waved her hand. "I swear it's just food."

She lifted the remote and pressed a button. At once, the laser connecting Robin's wrists withdrew into itself. And with a clack, metal slid against metal, and the latch of the laser manacle opened. The cuffs fell to the floor.

Still eyeing her, Robin reached for the food and brought some to his nose. He sniffed deeply. For an instant, he saw indignation in her gaze, then understanding. Slowly he took the smallest bite.

Smelling and tasting nothing malicious, he swallowed and bit more deeply.

"You're either extremely brave or extremely foolish," she said, and he paused in the process of taking more food to look at her. "You're lucky I was here to intervene on your behalf."

He let loose a puff of quiet laughter. "I hardly consider it luck to be bought or sold by anyone," he said. "Especially those in league with the Black Dragon."

At once, Marian stiffened. "Was that before or after you were separated from your girlfriend?"

"She's not my girlfriend," Robin snapped.

Marian blinked, taken aback.

"She's my sister," he continued, and Marian's mouth parted slightly.

"And the time we spent on that ship was the longest we'd spent together since we were born."

For a second, silence rang in the transport.

"I'm sorry," Marian finally said, lowering her gaze.

"May I ask a question?" Robin asked, eyeing her sideways.

"Of course." She nodded and waved her hand.

"Why?" he asked.

She looked at him in confusion.

"Why me?" he clarified.

Sighing, she lowered her gaze before looking through the transport's forcefield window. "Because I admire your spirit," she answered. "And I couldn't bear to see it broken if I could prevent it."

"By anyone but you, I imagine," he added.

She glared at him.

"What about Tekmet and my sister, Freya?" Robin asked as he took more food. "What will happen to them?"

She turned away from him. "Balwin will have them sent to the crystal mines of Morhoth," she said, sorrowfully.

Robin's eyes widened in horror. The mines of Morhoth. On Amal, he heard stories about them. They were said to be hell among the stars. People seemed to disappear into their depths, never to return. There was no escape, other than death. Unless he could find a way to save her, Robin would never see Freya again.

"Where are we going?" he asked.

Marian's eyes shifted back to him and he held still, not willing to be seen as weak. If they were planning to break him, they'd have to kill him; he'd go out swinging.

He nodded at the remote in her hand and added, "Or will that question just get me another shock?"

Silently, she looked away again. Eventually she said, "To my personal yacht."

157

"We're leaving Centurium?" he asked. He hoped that until he was ready, they would put at least a hundred systems between him and the Black Dragon.

She sent him a hard look. "I'd rather not have to be here if I can help it," she said.

Before long, they arrived at another landing platform. On it was a luxury yacht, its mirror-like armor plating gleaming in the sunlight like a star in the night sky.

Following Marian out of the transport, Robin turned and saw Balwin's transport flew past to land on an adjacent platform. Absorbed in watching it land, he barely noticed when people came out of the yacht to greet Marian.

"Welcome back, Princess Marian," he heard one man say as he strode forward with a bow.

Continuing his focus on Balwin's transport, Robin watched Freya and Tekmet stagger out behind guards, along with a few others, including Hannah and her daughter. All were led toward a slave freighter.

Robin heard the man speak to Marian again. "Who's this?"

Keeping his attention on Balwin's group, Robin watched as Freya paused before turning to look right at him. Longing to go to his sister, Robin took a step forward. Could she see the love and hope for her return to his eyes?

Freya was shoved out of sight into the freighter. Shortly, with a roar of the engines, the freighter lifted off. Robin watched it rise higher and higher into the sky. He only lowered his gaze when it disappeared from sight. Then he closed his eyes, trying to bite back the sudden sensations of emptiness and loss.

When Robin was finally able to compose himself, he opened his eyes and looked at Marian. She was standing beside a man, and they were both watching him intently.

"I never did get your name," Marian said.

Returning their gazes with a hard face, Robin replied, "Do you want my name or the number they assigned me?"

"If I wanted the number, I would have asked for it," Marian said. "So why don't you give me what I asked for? Your name."

Robin's frown deepened. After a moment, he answered, "Ryuu. My name is Ryuu."

She looked at him for a moment. Then, nodding, she waved toward the ramp of the yacht.

"Would you accompany me aboard my ship, Ryuu?" she asked.

Hesitating a few beats, he looked at her. Then, without a word, he followed her aboard.

Friend or Foe

ALAN INDICATED TO Robin, "please this way," Frowning in confusion, Robin turned to Alan, who said, "Like the princess explained, you're welcome to either eat here or join her in her quarters for dinner. They are right down the hall." He indicated the way with a wave of his hand.

Then Alan turned and left, closing the door behind him.

For a few seconds, Robin remained where he was, his eyes on the door. Then he scanned the room. He walked to the wall near the holo screen projector and pressed a lit button on the wall. A panel slid open, revealing a food materializer.

"Water, room temperature," he commanded, and a glass of water appeared.

He sloshed the water around the glass and eyed it carefully. Seeing nothing, he swirled the tip of his finger in. He felt nothing. He lifted his finger to his mouth and sucked the liquid from it.

He tasted nothing out of the ordinary.

Shrugging, he brought the glass to his lips and drank down the contents. He put the empty glass down on the summoner, turned, and walked to the bed. He scanned the emitter with a sharp eye and flicked his finger against it. Then he removed a small black device he flicked from the base, which he immediately recognized as a covert listening bug. He reached under the bed, squatted, and eyed the frame under the hypo adaptive mattress. He removed a second bug, scooted over, and pressed the release on the drawers. They slid out.

He eyed the clothes inside. He ran his fingers around the sides, the front, and under the lip of the slide, discovering another device. He picked up a shirt and eyed it as it unfolded in his hands. In his other hand, he crushed the bugs he found.

A short while later, escorted by Alan, he walked into the princess's quarters, dressed in a black overlapping shirt tucked into form-fitting pants and calf-high buckled boots. Still tied around his wrist was the strap of cloth covering his bracelet.

When he entered, Marian looked up from the table where she was sitting. Smiling, she rose to her feet.

"Welcome," she said warmly. "I was hoping you would take me up on my dinner offer. Please, come sit down."

"It's not as if you need to ask," he said, stepping forward. "After all, many would say I am your property." He reached for the chair opposite her and sat down.

She lowered her gaze.

"Yes," she said in a low voice. Slowly she looked into his eyes. "I am sorry for that."

Silence fell between them. Then she raised her hands and clapped. At once, the doors opened, and servants came in carrying trays of rare roast beef, roasted chicken, fresh fruit, and steamed vegetables, which they placed on the table. Then they exited the way they'd come, leaving Robin alone with Marian once more.

Robin watched as Marian served herself. She paused when she saw Robin hadn't moved.

"I certainly hope the clothes in your quarters fit you well," she said, taking a bite. She chewed and swallowed.

Robin said, "Considering they're made from adaptive memory cloth, it's not surprising."

He served himself, and Marian eyed him.

"I see we have the same taste in food," she said, and his gaze rose to hers. "Or maybe it has something to do with that healthy appetite of mistrust and suspicion you've been feeding."

She selected a piece of food from every platter. "Now, may we enjoy this meal without further suspicion over one of us drugging or poisoning the other?" She cut a piece of meat on her plate.

For the next few minutes, they ate in silence, save for the clink of silverware on fine china.

Then Robin asked, "Is the purpose of this dinner for me to learn my duties before we return to your home?"

Raising her eyes for a second, she shook her head. "No. This is a simple meal I hope might bear the fruit of friendship."

She reached for her glass but misjudged the distance, accidentally knocking it off the table. In a split second, Robin leaned forward and snatched it in midair, without spilling the contents.

"Great reflexes," Marian complimented. She dabbed at her lips with her napkin.

"Thanks," Robin muttered, setting the glass back on the table.

A bell chimed at her door. "Enter," Marian said.

With a hiss, the door opened, and Alan walked in. "Sorry for the interruption, your majesty," he said with a bow, hand over his chest. "But there is an important matter I must discuss with you."

She waved him off. "Not to worry, Alan," she said. She turned to Robin. "You may return to your quarters. There's a long day ahead of us tomorrow."

Nodding, Robin climbed to his feet, turned, and left without a word.

Later that night, as Robin laid in bed, half asleep, he heard his door open quietly. He sensed someone watching him briefly; then the door closed again. As it closed, Robin allowed his eyes to snap open.

Throwing back his covers, he quietly crept from the room. He watched as a shadowed figure stopped outside the princess's quarters and went inside.

He moved silently to the door and closed his eyes, shifting some of his hair from his ear to better hear beyond the door.

"Is he asleep, Alan?" Marian asked.

"Yes, sound asleep," Alan replied.

"So what do you think of him?"

"I find him aggressive and insolent, your highness," Alan replied. "Yes," Marian said slowly. "I like him too."

"I never said I liked him, your highness," Alan protested.

Marian laughed. "It's time for my bath. Would you please prepare the water?" she said.

"Of course, your majesty," Alan replied.

For a few minutes, Robin heard them moving across the room. Then the sound of running water met his ears.

Certain he wasn't going to get more information, he quietly returned to his quarters to catch up on his sleep.

Gilded Cage

THE NEXT DAY, Robin woke when the door hissed open. Keeping his eyes closed, he listened to footsteps as someone walked in, and then he heard the swish of clothes. He listened as the person paused for a moment, and then he heard the soft ruffle of something soft being set down.

Eventually, the footsteps retreated and the door closed. He allowed his eyes to snap open.

He sat up and looked around. He saw the clothes he had worn yesterday, neatly folded and waiting for him on his chair.

He slipped out of bed, walked over, and picked them up to examine them. Seeing nothing out of the ordinary, he dropped the shirt on the chair and turned, rubbing his chin, pondering what he was supposed to do next. Only one thing was certain: he had to get Freya back.

Cursing his pride once more, he leaned against the back of the chair, gripping it hard enough his knuckles turned white. He had Freya within his grasp. He could have saved her from the life that had been forced on her. Now she was trapped in the mines of Morhoth, where she would be worked till the day she died.

How am I supposed to get her out of there?

He rubbed his chin in thought. *Simple fact is, I need allies. And perhaps Marian might be my best chance of fixing this.*

After washing and dressing, he once more examined the room. Finding no more listening bugs, he left.

Robin walked down the ship's corridor and passed several servants before he stopped outside Marian's quarters.

Taking a breath, he pressed the chime button next to the door.

"Enter," came Marian's voice.

He pressed the release, and the door hissed open. Marian was sitting in a chair, a holobook in her hands.

"Is there something you need?" she asked.

"Isn't that what I'm supposed to ask?" he said, standing straight, hands behind his back.

Frowning, she blinked at him. "What do you mean?" She turned her book off and placed it on the table beside her.

"I'm your property," he said simply, his expression hard. "Awaiting instruction."

Still frowning, she eyed him more closely. "Apart from preparing for our arrival, there's nothing for you to do." He nodded and moved toward what he assumed was a closet.

"What are you doing?" She sounded confused.

"What you instructed," he said. "I'm preparing your things."

"I meant your own things," she said, rising to her feet.

Taking a breath, he faced her. "Well, then maybe you should be a little more specific," he said.

"Or perhaps you could have asked," she countered. She walked over and put her book on a shelf, her back to him.

"Well, you need to consider I'm only worth ten thousand starrubbies. Maybe if you had bid more, I might show more insight."

Slowly, she turned to look at him. "Or maybe you could take some of that unneeded aggression and try turning it into common courtesy," she replied.

A voice came over the intercom. "Princess."

"Yes, Captain," she replied.

"We are about to drop out of hyperspace and will be arriving at Andurian in ten minutes."

"Thank you, Captain," she said. She faced Robin. "I suggest you return to your quarters and prepare for landing. And this time, let me be specific. Go back to your quarters. Place what clothes you need in a bag, sit down, and prepare to disembark when we touch down." She waved toward the door.

For a couple seconds, he remained where he was, just looking at her. Then, with a jerk, he turned and left the room.

In the hall, he walked toward his quarters. He stopped halfway and leaned against the wall, fingering the toothed necklace under his shirt. He cursed himself for a fool and lightly whacked his head against the wall behind him.

When the ship landed on a platform, Robin disembarked behind Marian. Without a word, he followed her, bag slung over his shoulder, discreetly eyeing his new surroundings.

In many ways, it reminded him of Amal: towering, white-topped mountains in the distance, a vast ocean of grass between the platform and their peaks. He watched a flock of birds riding the winds across the plains before his gaze dropped to the scattered clumps of trees. He looked at a herd of animals roaming across the prairie. Then he turned, feeling eyes on him, to meet Marian's soft gaze.

A short while later, he was again sitting across from her in a luxury transport.

"So, where are we going?" he asked, looking out the window at the many levels of transporter traffic going in various directions above and below.

"The place where I grew up," she said simply. She rested her chin on two fingers as she looked out the window. "It's not my ancestral home. That's on Earth... But it's close enough. My family's been thankful for a long time that it's a replica."

Frowning, Robin remained silent.

The rest of the ride passed silently until Robin caught sight of where they were going: a palace with the sun reflecting off its gilded walls.

It stood on the edge of a cliff face, and a large circular section with tall windows faced the cliff. Just behind it was a tall, curved tower reaching for the sky. Another section, connected to the back of the tower, faced the other direction. At various heights, the frame overlapped over view windows.

On either side, waterfalls flowed down rock formations, which the building had been built around. These reflected the lights from various other windows.

Awed at the splendor of the building, Robin looked at Marian. His eyes narrowed at the disdain and emptiness he saw in hers.

They landed before giant front doors with built-in gilded designs.

Before Marian could move, the door opened and two people appeared.

"Welcome home, your majesty," one said with a slight bow.

"John, Ellen." Marian nodded to each as she passed them, closely followed by Robin and Alan.

"Alan!" Ellen said, and she leaped into Alan's arms.

Robin glanced at Marian and saw she was also watching, a small smile on her face.

When the pair finally broke apart, Marian said, "Alan, after you show Ryuu his rooms, you can spend as much time as you want with your wife and your children."

The couple nodded their thanks, and Alan faced Robin. "This way, if you please," he said.

Robin watched Marian as she spoke with a few people. Then he turned and followed Alan inside.

Walking down the hall, Robin turned his gaze in every direction in an attempt to take in all the splendor around him. Elegant tapestries hung on the wall, and marble statues lined the hall. He saw elegant works of art and furniture.

They went up several grand staircases and down several halls before Alan stopped in front of a pair of double doors.

"These are your rooms," he said, pushing the doors open.

Robin slowly stepped into a very spacious, extravagantly furnished and decorated room. He walked over to a wooden settee with intricate images and patterns sewn into the cushioning. He ran his hand over the smooth wood and eyed the rest of the furniture.

"If there's nothing else you need..." Alan said. He turned to leave.

"Well, maybe you could answer me one question," Robin said, his back to Alan. "When will this charade end?" He turned to face the man. "I mean, what is the point of all this? To butter me up and get me to lower my guard to—"

Alan whipped around, a look of rage on his face. He stalked over and drove his fist into Robin's face. As he threw a second punch, Robin easily caught it in midair.

"Only the first one's free," Robin warned, bending Alan's wrist back, forcing the man to fold.

"Well, maybe the first will have knocked some sense into you!" Alan snapped. He freed his hand and stepped back to clutch his wrist.

"Princess Marian has done nothing but show you kindness and respect! And this is how you repay her? With accusations of deceit?"

Robin arched an eyebrow. "How else am I supposed to think about all of this?" he asked, waving his hands. "After all, I'm a slave, bought and paid for, and yet you people keep putting me in places like this? What am I supposed to think?"

"Maybe you should think you're not the only prisoner here!" Alan hissed. He stepped into the hall but turned back for some final words. "Maybe this place seems like a palace, but it's nothing more than a gilded prison!"

Then Alan slammed the doors shut, leaving Robin alone to ponder his words. They echoed in his head and, it seemed to him, the room around him.

Prisoners

LATER THAT NIGHT, Robin woke with a jerk. Breathing hard, like he had just finished a long run, he looked around his room. He fell back against the pillow and inhaled deeply, trying to slow his racing heart.

For a time, he simply lay there, holding his bracelet over his heart. The dream flashed through his mind, as it had the night before, and the night before that.

He was in his armor, surrounded by attacking enemies. In the distance, he saw his father looking out at him.

No matter how many enemies Robin fought and dispatched, four new ones took their place.

Slowly but surely, he drew closer and closer to his father despite their growing numbers. Yet piece by piece, his armor was stripped from him until all he had left was a single plasma saber.

As Robin dispatched another enemy, he leapt over a large crevasse. Around him, others fell into the darkness below. With arms and legs pumping, he soared through the air before coming down on the other side with a roll.

Regaining his feet, he raced forward. Whenever an obstacle appeared, he leapt, slid under, rolled, or powered through it. Finally it seemed like nothing was in his way to reach and save his father.

Then he realized that despite how fast he was running, things around him were slowing down. An invisible force was pulling him back.

"Dad!" he yelled, reaching for his father. "Dad, take my hand!"

His father slowly looked from Robin's hand to his face but made no move to take it.

"DAD!" he screamed again.

Then he was yanked back off his feet, and only darkness surrounded him.

The light of the crystal pulsed a fraction faster beneath the cloth that covered it. Alan's words reverberated through his mind. He reviewed the events of the past few days over and over. Still cursing himself over losing Freya, he briefly allowed his thoughts to drift back to his father. Then, as he struggled unsuccessfully to sleep on the softest, most comfortable bed ever, he tried to stop his memories from going deeper.

The next morning, Robin walked down the hall after his nearly sleepless night. He rounded the corner, but paused when a familiar scent filled his nose. Sniffing, he looked left and then right. His eyes rested on a set of gilded doors. For a second, he wondered what to do.

Steeling himself, he walked over and knocked on the door.

"Enter," Marian's voice replied.

He took a breath and did just that. As he closed the door behind him, he saw her enter the living room area from a side room, her dress swishing as she moved, a book in hand. "Is there something I can help you with?" she asked, fingering her necklace.

After eyeing the simple cheap knotted metal bobble, he dismissed it.

Thinking a child made it for her.

"No," he said, shaking his head. "But I believe I owe you something."

Clearly startled, she jutted her chin back and frowned at him. "What do you owe me?" she asked, still fingering her necklace.

"An apology," he admitted, and her frown deepened. "Since the auction when you... bought me..." he began, and he saw her lips twitch as he stepped further into the room, "I guess you could say I haven't been the most gracious of guests...to my fellow prisoners." He ran his hand along a sofa as he walked.

At first, Marian didn't respond. Then she murmured, "Come with me." She nodded toward her balcony doors.

Following her outside, Robin watched her lean against the marble railing.

"Tell me, Ryuu," she said, "what do you see?" She nodded at the land before them.

It was his turn to frown as he moved forward. "I see mountains, prairie, forests, herds of animals, small villages in the distance," he said, walking forward to stand beside her.

She kept her eyes on the scene before her. "I see all that you see," she said softly. "But I also see the two billion people on this planet. And the fact that all their lives rest in my hands."

For a second, he looked at her in confusion. Then he nodded in understanding. "Meaning if you—"

"If I or any member of my family resist the Black Dragon in any way," she said, interrupting him, "they will pay the price. And make no mistake, they will be slaughtered without mercy."

Breathing deeply, she shook her head. "This planet is nothing more than a gilded cage..."

She looked up at the palace in disgust. "This palace is nothing more than its lock...and my family is the key."

She sighed and looked out over the land again. "It's been like this since the last knight fell defending my family, after the other heirs were hidden. My father, Richard, always said the people are suffering because of us. So we must do what we must do to make their lives as pleasant as possible. Like the tradition my great-grandfather started..."

She looked at him with a smile. "Of course, that particular tradition is one I enjoy quite well."

"What is it?" he asked.

"Rotating the people in and out of the palace when my...guardians are away," she answered with a grin.

"Which explains the many families I kept running into," Robin said.

"Well…" she said with a shrug. "My great-grandfather thought it was a waste to have so many empty rooms."

Chuckling, Robin shook his head. "And it goes to show how big an apology I owe you."

Marian leaned her elbow against the railing and shook her head.

"Forget about it," she said reassuringly. "I actually would have been surprised and suspicious if you hadn't acted the way you did."

He chuckled again, but her face turned somber.

"Ryuu," she said, slowly placing her hand on his shoulder, "if I had known about your sister, I would have done everything I could to keep the two of you together. After all…" She gazed out over the prairie. "I also want my family safe."

Nodding in thanks, Robin lowered his eyes.

"Freya wouldn't have come," he said after a moment. "Not without Tekmet."

"Tekmet?" Marian asked, frowning. Then she nodded. "The Anubis," she said.

"As far as I know, he's the only father she's known in a long time," he explained. "My father—"

But then his voice broke and he found he couldn't continue.

"Ryuu?" Marian asked. He could hear the concern in her voice. "Is everything alright?"

Robin stepped back from the railing. "It's nothing."

"Ryuu," she said. She shook her head. "Please, we both know it's not nothing. Tell me."

He repeated firmly, "It's nothing!"

This time she slowly nodded. "Whenever you're ready," she said, stepping back. "Remember. I'm here if you need me…for anything, even if it's just a friendly ear to listen. Go or stay, it's your choice."

For a second, Robin remained where he was. Then he shifted his feet and walked across the balcony. He paused halfway and turned back toward her.

"I have two questions. One, when do you plan to rotate me out of the palace and the room I'm in now?"

Smiling, she faced him, lightly clapping her hands. "When I can think of a place where you can learn and apply a trade," she answered. "And the second?"

"You're not going to get in trouble because I found those listening bugs, are you?" he asked.

She frowned in confusion. "Listening bugs?" she said in a slow voice. "What bugs?"

"The ones in my rooms, both here and on the ship," he said, jabbing his thumb over his shoulder.

She stared at him, wide-eyed. "You...you found bugs?"

He looked at her through narrowed eyes. "You didn't know?"

Slowly she looked away. "I know the Black Dragon keeps an eye on me when it's away..."

For a second, she was silent. Then she looked at him again, fingering her necklace.

"Maybe you could show me how to find them. It would be nice to have some privacy."

Robin placed his arm across his chest and bowed. Then he headed back toward his room, his mind racing.

Prophecies

FOR ALMOST TWO weeks, Robin remained at Marian's palace. Each night when he finally found sleep, his nightmare returned. He frequently woke out of breath in the darkness, his heart pounding in his chest. As these unsettled nights added up, he became more and more depressed.

Each morning, the servants left his food on a small table, he was too despondent to eat. He spent his days wandering aimlessly around the palace, haunted by his recent shortcomings. Despite all his talents, he'd been unable to prevent the death of his father; he'd been unable to save his sister.

During his wanderings, he saw wide-eyed children watching him from corners. They scampered off each time he got near. He didn't speak with anyone, and he didn't see Marian again.

Near the end of the second week, after another restless night, he stood outside on his balcony, leaning against the railing. He heard his doors open behind him. Assuming it was a servant delivering his breakfast, he muttered, "Just leave it and go."

Robin expected to hear the door shut again, but he did not. He turned back into the room and said, "Is there something else you—"

Then he froze. It was Marian. She was sitting in a chair, dressed in a pair of pants and a long coat that brushed the floor on either side of her. Her elbows rested on the armrests, and the tips of some of her fingers touched while others were crossed. One leg rested on her knee. Her booted foot bobbed up and down.

"Actually, yes," she said, looking over her fingertips. "There is something I need. I've been told for almost a week you've been sending food back untouched."

She lowered her foot and leaned forward, eyeing him. "Why aren't you eating?"

"It's nothing you have to worry about," he said, coming into the room. "I can go for three weeks without food and sleep."

"Yes, you don't have to tell me about your biology," Marian said. "To say it's impressive is an understatement."

However, she looked concerned as Robin paced back and forth in front of her.

She said, "Despite what was said at the auction, you and your sister were not made to be slaves. You were born to be survivors."

Frowning, he turned to face her and snapped, "Yet with everything I can do, I couldn't stop it! I couldn't stop any of it!"

For a moment, silence rang in the room. Then Marian rose to her feet.

"I don't know everything that happened to you, Ryuu, but I'm sorry for what happened at the auction. I want you to know I will do all I can to get Freya and Tekmet back for you. But you won't do her any good if you lose your strength."

Marian turned and whipped the cloth cover off a platter of food on the table.

"You can either keep moping about or take a stand," she said. "It's up to you. Just let me know when you're through sulking; I have something for you to do."

As she left the room, Robin watched her go. For a long moment, he simply stared at the closed double doors. Then he plucked some food from the platter and popped it in his mouth.

Later in the day, Robin met briefly with Marian again. She gave him a list of items to retrieve from the city. For the rest of the week, he went to and fro, collecting things she said she needed.

Often, he would come back with sweets or small toys for the children he thought would brighten their days. Soon it was commonplace for children to surround him, rifling through his pockets for hidden treats.

However, each time Robin went into the city, he noticed a group of well-muscled men watching him. One had a shiny bald head; the other had a short crop of dark hair. Without his training, he might have missed their observations. He had to admit they were good. He wondered who they worked for and what their intentions could be.

One day, after returning from the city, Robin stood surrounded by a laughing horde in the courtyard set into the roof behind the tower. He held his arms raised high, laughing with the children as they searched him for loot. They gave a collective moan of disappointment when they found none.

Lowering his arms, Robin regarded the children around him.

"Hey, why all the long faces?" he asked, squatting down to their eye level.

"You didn't bring us anything," one little girl said with a pout.

"Ahh," he said sadly. Dramatically, he caressed her cheek. "But then..." he added, with a quick flick of his wrist across her ear, "you never know what might appear!"

The girl's eyes nearly popped out of her head in wonder when she saw the candy he held.

The next thing he knew, he was knocked to the ground when the kids tackled him, renewing their search, and he laughed. When they finally allowed him to sit up and thanked him for the treasures, he smiled.

Robin felt eyes on him and noticed Marian watching from a balcony. He gave her a small wave. She shrank back a little, but then returned the gesture with fluttering fingers. Seconds later, she disappeared from sight.

Leaving the children after promising to play more sky hockey with some later, he walked to her room. She was sitting on one of her sofas, reading.

"You're spoiling those children rotten," she commented, not looking up.

"And I thought you wanted me to bring them a little joy." He leaned his back against her bookcase.

"I'm not complaining," she said. She shut off her book and looked at him. "Yet I can see even bringing those children happiness or being useful doesn't mend the wounds you hide."

She sighed heavily and placed her book on the table. "I need you to go out again tomorrow," she said.

"Yes, Milady," he said, with a light bow.

"Please don't," she said. She slowly faced him and fingered her necklace. "Balwin is coming the day after tomorrow."

"What!" Robin said.

He thought, What can this mean? If the Black Dragon has any knowledge of me and my friends, Balwin will know by now. Has Balwin discovered that I am a knight?

Marian interrupted his thoughts.

"I want you to stay out of sight until he's gone," she said. "For the time being, you will have to sleep in the servants' quarters. Almost everyone here will be doing the same. When he is gone, you can return to your rooms."

Robin's brain raced at hyper speed. If Balwin has found out I am a knight, Freya's life might be in jeopardy as well.

"Ryuu."

Blinking, Robin looked at her again. "Sorry."

For a second, she eyed him. "It's all right, you have a lot on your mind. But remember—you have to stay out of sight during dinner. I'm hoping to use that time to bargain for Freya and Tekmet."

"And you're afraid I might hinder your style?"

She shook her head. "No, it's because you humiliated Balwin back at the auction. He might want to even the score."

The next day Robin was back in the market, picking up additional items that Marian had requested. He was gathering some things for the children when he glanced over and saw the same men discreetly watching him.

Despite the covert looks from these men, he continued to run his errands. A few moments later, a glittering crystal caught his eye. It belonged to an elderly woman, who was wearing loose clothes, a frilly headscarf, and fingerless gloves. In a mystical voice, she called out to the crowd from her booth.

"Come ask the question of Madam Verinous!" She waved her hands.

"For Madam Verinous knows all. You there..." Robin paused, looking at her. "Your aura: it is strong and powerful."

She fluttered the fingers of one hand at him; the other hand covered her eyes.

"Great troubles rage around you."

Chuckling, Robin shook his head. "I bet you say that to all the guys."

He bowed with a sweep of his arm. "And though I might wish to spend this day flirting with you, I must be off." He turned to leave.

"Great troubles," she repeated. "Especially for a sister." Robin froze. Slowly he turned back to her, frowning.

In the same mystic voice, she chanted, "One who was lost, then found...only to be lost again."

Robin felt like his head would explode in anger. He slowly approached and leaned against the booth.

"Lady," he growled, "I know everyone needs to make a living. But you're—as they say—treading on thin ice. That is information you could get from anyone in the palace."

Unfazed, she waved her hands over the crystal and gazed into its depths.

She said, "A brother you have yet to find...a father who is no more...a mother who loved you so, who for your protection had to leave the three of you..."

She slowly looked up, and he stared into her piercing, sightless eyes.

Then she said, "You are among the first of a new generation of ancient guardians."

Taken aback, Robin blanched.

"Who are you? How do you know these things?" he demanded in a whisper.

Smiling, she spread her arms wide. "I am Madam Verinous! I know all," she said dramatically. She waved her hands again over the crystal.

"The path before you is a dark and dangerous one. It is unclear whether you have the strength to survive... Dark forces that have engulfed the known worlds will rise to overwhelm you. But if you stand united, you may find part of what you seek—in the ancient temple of the gods." She sank back into her chair.

"Now go..." she ordered. Then her voice dropped to a whisper. "Remember my words, son."

Rooted to the spot, Robin stared at her, her words echoing in his mind. But before he could ask any more questions or even confirm what he had just heard, she dismissed him with a wave of her hands. Shaking his head slowly, he straightened and walked away.

The Ambush

ROBIN HEADED TO the bookstore, which was the next destination on Marian's list. Along the way, his mind raced around what Madam Verinous had told him. What is the ancient temple of the gods? What would I find there? My brother or something else? Someone else?

After picking up Marian's books on an upper level of the market, he lifted his eyes skyward and inhaled deeply. Then he turned down the street, weaving through crowds of people going about their business.

A little while later, he waited for an elevator after he picked up some holo books at the top for Marian. When it arrived, he saw that there were four people already in it. He nodded at a couple who were holding hands and chatting, and two men. One of the men with a scar down his cheek was carrying a metal crate; the other who was missing a finger on his callused hand carried rolls of fabric.

With a small smile, Robin stepped in and turned to face the doors. When they closed, all conversation in the elevator ceased.

He hummed with the music that played in the still air. His eyes drifted casually to the people beside him: a man carrying a metal crate by his side, a couple smiling at each other each, their hands on the small of each other's back. The man to his right carried rolls of fabric.

The elevator dinged, with a whoosh the doors opened, and two more bulging muscled men stepped in. They quickly turned their backs to

Robin, but he immediately recognized them. It was the men who had been watching him earlier in the city.

Again, Robin eyed the people around him. He noticed how well they moved in their clothing.

"I'm on the next floor," he told the computer.

The people around him shot him brief glances. As he faced forward, he said aloud, "Are you all sure about this?"

He heard people shift around him. Into the silence, he said, "We have five floors to go… There's still time for you to walk away." They arrived at the next floor. The doors opened. Nobody got out.

Robin sighed, eyes on the ceiling.

"Well…none of you can say I didn't try," he muttered as the doors closed. "Just try not to damage the books. They're not mine."

As soon as the doors closed, the people around him reacted. The man with nine fingers to his right dropped the rolls of fabric. He kept one small square length in one hand. Robin smelled a faint odor from it as he twisted toward Robin.

On Robin's other side, the crate fell to the floor with a crash. After the handles detaching from the crate remained in Scarface's hands as he turned to Robin.

Robin twisted and threw a punch at the man who was holding the cloth. At the same time, he kicked the man behind him. As they dropped, Robin spun to face the couple. They drew taser sticks from each other's back pockets.

Blocking the man with one arm, Robin pushed his arm away. The taser connected to the woman's chest and sent her jerking to the floor.

After Robin knocked the taser stick to the ground, he was grabbed from behind by big beefy arms and jerked off his feet.

"Calm down, kid, and this will be over," the man growled into his ear.

Then the man who was part of the couple came at him again along with the bald headed man.

"Like that's going to happen!" Robin barked. He kicked the beefy man, sending him tripping over the woman against the opposite wall. Robin kicked the face of the man who was part of the couple, and the momentum sent the three of them to the floor.

Now on one knee, Robin spun around, kicking Scarface in front of him hard across the face, then spinning back to face the man behind him. He was in time to catch the nine-fingered man by the wrists when he came at him again.

Robin threw the man across him, where he landed hard. Then he delivered a powerful elbow to his face, which sent him back hard against the wall of the elevator. As the man dropped both handles, Robin caught them in midair.

When he brought one around the man's wrist; the handle extended to enclose the man's arm. Robin locked the other handle around the ankle of the man who was part of the couple and, with a jerk, both handles were brought together with a loud clack.

"Magcuffs," he muttered, blinking in surprise.

Rising onto his feet, he blocked a blow from the bald-headed beefy man. Robin grabbed the back of his head and drove his knee into the man's gut. Then he heaved him up to the ceiling.

Robin hopped forward and side kicked the dark-haired man in the chest when he started to get up again. The other man crashed to the floor behind him on top of the other two men, who were struggling to move in their awkward positions.

Holding his foot against the man to keep him in place, Robin eyed the people around him. They were all in various states of unconsciousness, the woman still twitching slightly.

As Robin retraced his foot, the man started to slump forward. Robin caught him by his hair.

"Hey, pay attention!" he snapped, tapping the man's face and forcing him to look at Robin. The man's eyes were half glazed over.

"Tell Balwin for me that if he touches a hair on my sister's head, I'll tear his heart out!"

"Wait..." the man moaned in a low voice. Robin stopped the voice by driving the man's head against the elevator wall with both hands.

Sighing, Robin straightened and brushed himself off. He rolled the bald man off and picked up the books he'd dropped. As he examined them for damage, the doors dinged open.

Robin froze as he locked eyes with the people waiting in the corridor. They were as still as statues, staring open-mouthed at the scene before them.

"Ah...wrong elevator," Robin said with a shrug. Then, with a smile, he got off the elevator and stepped around them.

Dinner Guests

THE REST OF the return to the Palace was uneventful. Robin was relieved when each book turned on and worked without a problem.

After his encounter with the children claiming their sweets and toys, he made his way to Marian's room and knocked on her door.

"Enter," she called.

He opened the door and stepped in. For the briefest second, he saw surprise in her eye.

"I brought you your books," he said, holding them out to her.

"Yes, thank you," she said, taking them. "Now remember, you need to keep out of sight while Balwin is here."

Before Robin turned to leave, he paused. "What is that?" he asked.

She followed his pointing finger to the sofa in her bedroom. The dress laid out across it was black, with two long slits that went to the bottom of the skirt. The short-sleeved top was only connected to the skirt by two strips of cloth on the sides that would cling to her like a second skin. Everything below her chest and back would be revealed to all.

"That..." she said as she walked over and picked it up, "is the dress I am required to wear to dinner. If it weren't for the company I would probably enjoy wearing it...and not burn it afterwards." She held it up in front of her. "What do you think?"

Facing her, he eyed it. "I have to agree with you. And it's a shame it will be wasted on the company you'll be having. Anyone else you might have worn it for would have been lucky."

A small smile graced her lips, and he continued. "But why would they require you to wear that?"

Sighing, she turned and tossed the dress on the bed. "To show both me and my dancing off to the others who are coming," she explained.

"'Dance'?" Robin asked, frowning. "I've never seen you dance."

Smiling she waved her hands. "All things considered, can you blame me? They ruin it for me entirely."

He nodded in understanding and went to move his clothes to the servants' quarters, which would be his home for the immediate future.

The servants' quarters contained row after row of bunk beds. As he lay on one of the top bunks, he sandwiched his hand between his head and the pillow.

Various scenarios played over in his mind at a million miles a minute. Balwin could be coming here because he had figured out Robin was a knight. He could be coming just to torment Robin by rubbing in the fact that Balwin had his sister. Or he might intend to have his men deliver Robin to Balwin. Or Balwin could be bringing Freya here just to kill her in front of Robin.

"I need more information," he growled in frustration. "And there's only one way to do that," he finished. He turned and slipped from the bed.

A short while later, dressed in a server's uniform and fidgeting with the cuffs and collar, Robin walked toward the area where people were gathered to greet Balwin. As he exited the double front doors of the palace, Robin froze.

Below him, at the bottom of the steps, Marian stood, wearing the black dress. The skirt slits shifted, allowing free movement of her legs. He caught sight of booted heels stretching over most of her calves, straps crisscrossing the front. The top clung to her body but allowed free movement.

Her hair was done up in a complex braid falling down her back. It hid the clasp of the diamond necklace, which matched a diamond-speckled cloth around one wrist. Atop her head was a silver and gold headpiece, with strands dropping down above her ears. The strands looped and connected at the back.

Turning in his direction, Marian froze. For a brief second, she stared, wide-eyed. Then her eyes narrowed, and she stalked up the stairs to him.

"Just what in the name of the Gold Dragon are you doing?" she demanded.

"Well, for starters I'm admiring the view," he answered, his eyes roaming over her. He whistled and shook his head. "It's a shame such walking art is wasted on this pending company."

Again, her eyes narrowed. "Flattery won't help you here," she hissed. "I told you to stay out of sight!"

"And I need to know more about the status of my sister!" he hissed back. "The faster I know things, the faster I can help decide on a course of action! You need me here! The more eyes watching Balwin, the more likely we can figure out his next move!"

Before she could respond, she was interrupted by a sound like a clap of thunder. Marian and Robin both looked up, and he saw a ship enter the atmosphere.

Growling through her teeth, Marian faced him again. "Fine, you got your wish," she said dangerously. "But don't draw attention to yourself! And don't agitate him!" She whirled around and descended the stairs again.

Making sure his ears were covered by his hair, Robin slipped among the ranks of the waiting servants, trying to disappear in plain sight.

Though he faced forward, Robin's eyes tracked the progress of the ship across the sky. As it drew closer, Robin's focus shifted to the woman beside him.

She bit her lip, wringing her hands.

In an undertone, he said, "It's Jenna, right?" When she looked at him, he added, "Everything all right?"

Biting her bottom lip, she turned to look back up at the approaching craft. "I'm worried about my children," she said.

Frowning, he said, "I thought they were hidden away?"

"They were," she replied, and she looked back at him. "But the last time Balwin was here, some of them were discovered. He treated them very roughly, claiming it was play. He levitated them for long periods of time, he spun them like tops in the air—all to remind the parents of his power."

"That's monstrous," Robin said. "Torture."

"I know," she said, turning back to watch the ship draw closer. "I don't want it to happen again. We're all grateful none of the children sustained lasting injuries."

"We should all be grateful for that," Robin muttered. Then returned his gaze skyward.

The ship was twice the size of the transport the village had used to escape. It was similar in design but sleeker, with wider, swept-back wings. Though Robin could see no weapons, he didn't doubt it was armed to the teeth.

He watched its progress across the sky until it hovered over the landing pad. Then it slowly lowered, dropping its landing skids before it touched down.

As the ramp came down, Robin shifted back so Jenna hid him from sight. He watched as Balwin descended the ramp, his boots clacking on the hard surface. His cape was attached by a pair of silver pins between two rings shaped in the image of the Gold Dragon. It matched his black clothes with gilded seams. There were two other men beside him, similarly dressed.

When Balwin reached the bottom of the ramp, Marian dropped to the ground on her hands and knees.

"We are all honored by your visit, my lords Balwin, Prim, and Valdo," she said in a humble voice. Under it, however, Robin could hear her malice.

Balwin smiled broadly down at her and chuckled.

"Come now, Princess, there's no need for false pleasantries," he said, towering over her. "We all know we're the last people you want here."

Slowly Marian looked up at him, and Robin caught the look of steel in her eye. "I can think of one other person to top the list," he heard her murmur.

Balwin laughed. "And speaking of our beloved leader," he said, turning to face the other lords behind him. "My mines are to be visited for an inspection..."

Everything else faded away as Robin's blood turned to ice. If he was going to get to Freya, he had to do something fast

.

You Do What You Have To

ROBIN SNAPPED BACK to awareness when Balwin and the others started to ascend the palace stairs. He lowered his eyes so Balwin wouldn't recognize him. Focusing on the carpet, he discreetly shuffled back.

When he saw the booted feet pass him, he slowly raised his gaze, tracking them. Then he followed the other servants inside.

His mind tried to quickly form a plan as he walked in line into the dining room. Quickly he joined the group along the windows, opposite a raised platform on the other side of the table. He noted the sunlight was right behind him, blocking Balwin from getting a good look. Stopping by one of the dangling curtains, he faced the room with the others.

He watched as Balwin's party took their places behind their chairs. When Balwin moved to the head, Marian moved behind him to an ornate gilded chair.

Robin watched as, with a flick of his cape, Balwin turned to face the rest of his party. Then, without pause, the lord sat, quickly followed by the rest of his party. Robin fought hard to control his anger as he watched Marian push the lord's chair in.

"I welcome all honored guests," Balwin said, waving his hand to the people before him. He ignored Marian, who was standing next to him.

"As your host, I would like to offer some entertainment before we enjoy our feast." He turned to Marian. "If you would be so kind, Princess," he prompted with a snap of his fingers.

Her face neutral, Marian bowed. Then she walked over and stepped onto the platform, her back to the room.

Soft music filled Robin's ears. With a quick glance, he spotted a small string and flute orchestra.

Looking back to the platform, he saw Marian draw her hands up her sides and sway her hips. Then, with a jerk, she widened her arms above her head. She brought them back to her side and thrust them forward, palms up, and took a deep step back before spinning low to the ground to face everyone, one leg bent and the other out to her side, one arm crossed her chest. Bending along her outstretched leg, she gracefully reached out with one hand, bringing the other leg up high behind her. As if her feet were walking on air, she gracefully moved toward her audience. Her arms and torso matched her movements as she dipped and swayed. Eyes closed, she moved to the music.

At the edge, she stopped and, bringing one leg high above her head, spun around. Stepping forward, she pushed off with her hands, then held one hand out. After tapping the back of her hand against the upheld palm, she brought it around in a circle to lightly tap her hand at her elbow.

At one point, she thrust out a leg and then spun in place a few times. For a second, Robin could have sworn he felt her eyes on him. Then she dropped into a split.

Arching her back, she brought her hands behind her to touch the floor. Then, with total ease, she flipped onto her feet. Again, she went low to the ground, one leg stretched out as she lightly touched the platform.

Finally, rising to her full height, with her hands above her head, she brought one leg up high. Robin heard a slight whirring sound and the flap of cloth as she side-flipped through the air, again landing in a split. Shifting to her feet, she brought her leg in a circle around her. Then she stood still, hands lightly spread at her side, eyes closed, and pointed her chin toward one shoulder.

Mesmerized by what he had just seen, Robin stood rooted to the spot. He was finally drawn back by the sound of clapping. Blinking, he looked at the table as Balwin and his party applauded.

"And now we feast!" Balwin called out, clapping his hands as Marian stepped off the platform. A light layer of sweat glistened on her brow as she took her place near Balwin. The doors behind Robin opened, and servants walked out carrying trays of food.

Once everyone had been served and drinks had been poured, silence fell. After the last servant disappeared behind the doors to the kitchen. All eyes turned to Balwin. He lifted his golden goblet.

"To the Black Dragon!" he declared. "And the destruction of this pitiful rebellion."

"To the Black Dragon," his party called, and they all drank.

Robin continued to observe as the dinner progressed. With more and more drinks served, the group took every opportunity to humiliate Marian.

One man purposely knocked a roll to the floor with a snap of his fingers, and Marian had to crawl over to pick it up. Livid, Robin's hand fisted at his side as she did as ordered; they all jeered at seeing her crawl.

A servant carried a jug of wine past Robin to refill Balwin's goblet, and—as if it had always been there—a plan snapped into place in his mind.

Placing a hand on the serving woman's shoulder, he whispered in her ear, "Please allow me." He slipped the jug from her hands and approached Balwin.

Marian glanced up and froze as she locked eyes with him. He could see the plea in her eyes before he turned to pour.

"Well, well, if it isn't my little friend from the Centurium auction," Balwin said as he smiled at Robin. Robin ignored the comment, but gripped the jug more tightly.

The rest of Balwin's party turned to look at Robin. "So this is the boy you spoke of, Lord Balwin," one of the men said.

"Yes indeed," Balwin said, sitting back in his chair. "I am curious if he has finally learned his place."

With a jerk, he picked up his goblet and threw the contents in Robin's face. While the table roared with laughter, Robin blinked away the wine.

"Well, don't just stand there, dog," Balwin said, cocking a grin. "Clean this mess."

Robin gave Balwin a hard stare for a moment. Then he placed the jug on the table, dropped down, and began to wipe the spill.

"Now do you see?" Balwin said smugly above him. "This is where you belong...a dog at my feet."

Slowly, Robin raised his hot eyes to meet Balwin's. He could feel Marian behind him, as if she was sending him a silent plea. Robin dropped his eyes, and he could almost hear a tiny sigh of relief from Marian. Then Robin gave a humph.

At once, Balwin seized him by his hair. Pulling hard, he arched Robin's head back. Taking advantage of Robin's gasp of pain, he forced Robin's mouth wide.

"What was that?" he growled down at him. "I must have misheard you, dog. You must be smart enough not to commit the same mistake twice. As if you have enough brains to think...or even have a soul."

For a couple seconds, Robin remained where he was, Balwin's fingers holding his mouth open. Then he let loose a series of gurgled words.

"What was that?" Balwin asked, leaning close.

Again, Robin gurgled. Then, with a jerk, he snapped his mouth closed. Balwin barked in pain as Robin bit down hard on his fingers. The copper taste of blood leaked into Robin's mouth.

"Do you still want to see my teeth?" Robin said after Balwin dislodged his fingers and stared at the deep cuts Robin had made.

In less than a second, Balwin and his party sprang to their feet, knocking chairs to the floor. Spitting blood from his mouth, Robin stepped back, eyeing them.

"Why, you!" Balwin growled in a deadly voice as his fingers healed themselves.

192

Jumping forward, Marian got between Robin and Balwin. "Please, my lord..."

With a wave of his hand, Balwin sent her hurtling across the floor.

Immediately, Robin pulled his fist back and rammed it full into Balwin's face. The force of the blow lifted Balwin off his feet back a few steps. When he tripped over his cape and the chair he knocked over, Balwin flipped backward and sprawled face-first on the floor in a tangled heap with his cape.

Before Robin could move again, Balwin's guards pounced on him. In seconds, he was pinned to the floor, his arms bound behind his back.

Grunting, Robin looked up. Balwin regained his footing and untangled his cape. His eyes were ablaze with rage and humiliation.

"I'll kill you for that!" he barked, raising his hand.

"You can't!"

All eyes turned to Marian. "He is still my slave! Only I can decide his fate. Only I have the codes to detonate him! By the laws of the Black Dragon, you cannot harm him! He is my property!"

She paused for a breath and continued. "And you know what will happen, even to you, if you break the Black Dragon's decrees!"

For a second, Balwin stared at her. Then he slowly faced Robin again.

"Very well," he roared. "I may not be able to kill you, but you are going to wish I had. To the mines of Morhoth with you!"

The guards jerked Robin to his feet and led him out of the room.

Robin soon found himself sitting on the floor in Balwin's ship. He was chained by a collar and his wrists to a wall. Around him, more chains with collars and manacles hung at intervals on the walls. He contemplated what he was going to do next.

A small sound jerked him from his thoughts, and he glanced at the door. With a small hiss, it opened, and Marian stood in the frame, Balwin right behind her.

"Say good-bye to your little pet, Princess," Balwin said, shoving her in so she fell to the floor. "It's the last time you'll ever see him." He sealed the door behind her.

For a second, Marian simply stared at Robin.

"Why'd you do it, Ryuu?" she asked in a quiet voice. "I told you I was going to do my best to get them back. So why?"

"You do what you have to do to protect the ones you love," he answered solemnly.

When she seemed to recognize he wasn't going to say more, she climbed to her feet and turned.

"I'm sorry," he said.

She paused, her back to him.

"I'm sorry it had to be this way," he finished.

Marian was still before she turned to face him again.

"So am I," she said.

She walked to the door and pounded her fist against it. When it opened, she left him alone to face his fate.

The Mines of Morhoth

AS THE SHIP took off, the chains started rocking, which showed the ship had been amped up to hyper speed.

Okay, time to start planning, Robin thought. He didn't speak aloud, in case someone was listening. Obviously, my first task is to find Freya and Tekmet. After that... He was stumped. And he was afraid he'd have to do what he usually did.

Wing it.

He reviewed the umpteenth scenario as the ship jerked again. I guess we're here.

He took several deep breaths. The ship jerked several times as it entered the atmosphere. Then it landed.

No one came for Robin for half an hour. But just when he was starting to think they'd forgotten about him, the collar around his neck sent such a large current through him, he was jolted to the floor. The pain from the shock collar was the last thing he felt before he lost consciousness.

Eventually he moaned, his head rolling and pounding with a racket that sounded like thousands of hammers driving into his skull. Opening his eyes, he saw that he was lying on solid rock.

Moaning again, he pushed himself up and looked around. He saw lines of raggedly dressed people using laser picks, shovels, and drills on tunnel walls of solid rock. In the other direction, he saw a large, open space, as though the tunnel were lit by an unknown source of light cast the whole place in low gloom.

On the far side, he saw people hard at work with laser drills emitting flickering lights at odd intervals. Above them, more people worked on a section of rock that branched out into open air. A conveyor belt carried loads from top to bottom.

Spread out here and there were patrolling sentinels.

As Robin started to push himself up, he felt the ground vibrate under his palms.

Looking up, he saw a line of hover carts moving right at him. He rolled forward. They missed him by barely millimeters. Now on all fours, he turned to face the carts as they rocked by, loaded with glowing crystals.

He released a pent-up breath and stood straight. None of the people had stopped working or moved from what they were doing. Yet he was certain they were checking him out.

Suddenly, he felt a sharp, stinging pain across his back, which dropped him to one knee. Teeth bared, he fought back the pain and looked behind him.

"Stop dawdling! Get to work!" a sentinel barked in its robotic voice as the laser whip retracted into its arm.

Robin glanced around and picked up a laser drill and bucket beside him. He noticed his servant's clothes from the palace had been replaced with patched pants, worn boots, and a torn, spotted sleeveless shirt.

"Great, the bastard undressed me. That's an image I needed in my head," he muttered. Slowly, his eyes drifted to his wrist and the exposed bracelet and crystal. "Or maybe not," he finished, knowing what would have happened if Balwin had seen the bracelet.

As quickly and as discreetly as possible, Robin expanded a hole in his shirt and tore away a patch of cloth from the shoulder. That part of his shirt dangled a little, exposing toned muscle as he quickly tied the cloth over his bracelet.

He rose, slung the drill over his shoulder, and walked closer to the workers. He set the drill stock against his chest and, locking in his position, prepared to drill into the rock. He placed the bucket on the ground below him to collect the crystals he would extract with the drill. Pretending to adjust a setting, he leaned close to the man beside him and murmured, "I need your help."

The man barely shot Robin a look before turning back to what he was doing.

"Look," Robin continued, "she's about my height, with long, dark hair, and eyes and ears like mine." He shifted his hair so the man could see his ears.

Again, the man remained silent.

Robin tried again. "Look, buddy she's—"

"Quiet!" the man hissed, turning his head to look at Robin. "I know you're new here, but—"

"No talking!" a voice barked. Robin glanced behind him at the sentinel. "The gods forbid it!"

The sentinel cracked its whip at them.

Frowning, Robin mouthed, "Gods?"

He turned back and activated the drill, which bit into the rock face, joining the other flickering lights around him.

For over an hour he worked hard, filling the bucket with crystals.

When it was half full, he paused to arch his cramped back.

Hearing a voice, he turned.

"Grandfather, you have to slow down," a teenage girl muttered worriedly to an elderly man, who was using a shovel. "You're too old to work as hard as you are."

"I've been digging for almost seventy years," the old man said, wiping his brow. "Take my advice. Slowing down will only...make things worse." He went back to work.

Robin stared at them for a second before glancing down at his bucket. He looked around, picked it up, and crossed over to them. Then he discreetly emptied his bucket into the old man's. As he straightened, he saw the girl look up at him, a grateful gleam in her eye.

Smiling, he pressed his finger to his mouth. Before he had time to move away, she beckoned him to work next to her.

"Thank you for what you did for my grandfather," she said.

"Don't worry about it," he answered, shrugging it off. "Who are you?" he asked, placing the bucket on the ground.

"7181940," she answered.

"I meant your name," he clarified.

She held his gaze before glancing around and back. "Gina," she finally said.

"Nice to meet you," Robin said, nodding. "I'm Robin."

"I heard what you were asking that man earlier," she said in an undertone as she set up her own bucket and drill. "Before I say anything, what is this girl to you?"

"She's my sister," he said, turning on the drill. He felt her eyes on her and stopped the drill again.

"There were a few new arrivals before you," she said. Robin shifted crystals out of the wall and into the bucket. "I see them every now and then. There's a girl who seems to stick to one of the Anubises here."

"Is she about my height, dark hair, ears like mine?" he asked, shifting his hair to show her.

After looking at his ears, Gina shifted her gaze back to her work. "I don't know about the ears...but the rest sounds like her."

Robin sighed in relief. "At least I know she's here," he muttered.

Then he heard a familiar voice.

"Water! Water!"

He turned and saw Hannah, the mother of the toddler, walking along the tunnel. She had her daughter beside her, and she was carrying a bucket of water.

"Hannah," he muttered. He raised his hand to get her attention.

She approached Robin, set down the bucket of water, and then scooped some into a ladle. She turned to offer some to him. When she got a good look at him, she froze, staring.

"Shhh," he urged, finger pressed to his lips. Quickly taking the ladle, he drank some water and poured the rest down his back. "Where's Freya?" he asked quietly.

Gesturing with her eyes, she answered, "She's working in that section with Tekmet."

Glancing over, he recognized the area across the open space he'd spied earlier. As he started thinking of a way to get over there, a great gonging sound resonated through the chambers, and he covered his ears against the bass vibration. His head felt like it would split open.

"What the heck?" he barked, looking around for the source. He paused when he saw everyone drop their tools and move along. "What's going on?" he asked when he could finally uncover his ears.

"It's calling us to gather," Hannah said.

"For what?" he asked. He dropped his drill and followed her.

"To worship the gods or god of Morhoth."

The Gods of Morhoth

ROBIN FOLLOWED HANNAH and her child through the maze of tunnels until they reached a vast cliff, which loomed before them. An eerie, shimmering black-and-red glow outlined the edge of the cliff.

On the far wall, the head of a dragon with forward-swept horns was carved into the rock. The shimmering light below it cast the upper half in shadow. But Robin could still see the detail of the carving, right down to the smallest scales. The eyes glowed red from an internal source. Smoke rose from its wide nostrils.

Tearing his eyes from the sight before him, Robin scanned the mob of people for Freya and Tekmet. However, the crowd behind him would not let him stop to get a proper look. He stepped near the edge of the cliff. Glancing down, he gaped at the river of lava that flowed below. Standing on his toes, he tried to see over the crowd of people.

A grinding noise of stone on stone filled his ear. He turned back to the statue and froze. The mouth was slowly opening, and he saw a wall of flames inside burst forth, stopping halfway between the statue and the cliff before the flame was drawn back into the gaping maul. It seemed to explode over the edges, and a figure appeared. A cape billowed in the heat.

Narrowing his eyes, Robin focused on the figure, but the flames behind it lit the figure in silhouette. He could not see it clearly beyond the fact it was a man.

He sensed shifting movement around him and realized people were dropping to their knees. All chanted, "Apep! Apep!" over and over.

As Robin looked over the sea of chanting people, some with arms raised as if in worship, he paused. There, at least a hundred feet away to his right, stood Freya, Tekmet at her side, looking right back at him.

"On your knees!" a voice barked behind him. Robin didn't resist the metallic hand forcing him down.

He briefly glared at the sentinel behind him before facing forward again. He watched as the figure in the cape stepped up to the edge of the mouth. Following the man's gaze, Robin saw the last of the hovering mine carts dump its contents into a large container carved out of the rock.

A booming voice sent a chill down Robin's spine. "The ancient gods of the Underworld are angry!"

"Balwin!" he growled.

"The great fires given by the great god Apep have burned since the beginning of time, keeping you all alive with life-giving energy!" Balwin continued. "As Apep's high priest, I warn you the gods ask very little of you! You must feed them! Dig deeper! Work harder! Feed the crystals that fuel the flames of life!"

As if he were a god himself, Balwin pointed a finger at them. "Or die!" With a flick of his cape, he swiveled and walked back through the fire.

Again, Robin heard the grinding of stone on stone. He watched as the large indent in the rock, which the crystals had been kept in, separated from the cliff and floated toward the gaping maw. He tracked its movement through the air until it disappeared into the flames.

For a second, the flames seemed to flare and grow stronger and brighter. As they died down, the indentation reappeared and floated back to where it had once been. Instead of crystals, it was full of wrapped bundles.

At the sight of the bundles, the people around Robin leaped to their feet with cries of joy.

The sentinel behind Robin cracked its whip. "Pick up your gifts and get back to work!"

Curiosity getting the better of him, Robin followed the others into the sinkhole. At the bottom, he watched as a few fought over a bundle. Snagging one, he climbed back up, turning in time to see Freya and Tekmet climb up across from him.

Moving forward, he maneuvered through the crowd and pushed people aside, making his way to them. It seemed to take forever until he was at his sister's side.

"Freya!" he said, holding her upper arm.

She stared and gripped her bundle.

"I was afraid it was you, Robin," she finally said. "What the heck are you doing here?"

As soon as they could, the trio found a secluded spot to talk. They set their drills nearby, and Robin unwrapped his bundle, revealing a loaf of bread. As he broke off a piece, he eyed the pair, who hadn't touched theirs.

"How'd you find your way back to us?" Tekmet asked.

"Long story," Robin answered. "I don't think our break will be long, but let me say it involved biting Balwin's fingers and knocking him off his feet."

When he lifted the piece of bread to his mouth, the pair beside him snorted.

Then he froze, the bread halfway to his mouth. A faint oily odor filled his nose. He eyed the bread carefully before bringing it close to his nose and sniffing deeply.

"This bread has been—"

"Drugged," Freya finished for him.

"Probably to make the people here more open to suggestion," Tekmet said, looking around. "So we've been eating and drinking as little as possible to avoid the effects."

"It's in the water, too?" Robin asked, cursing himself for not smelling it earlier.

"It might be," Freya answered. "So far we haven't detected it. But I warned Hannah and her daughter, Kylie. They're following our lead." "It's lucky those two were able to stick together," Robin muttered.

Looking around, he noticed some people worked while others ate.

He said, "So, have you guys been working on a way to get out of here?"

Freya scowled. "Don't tell me you're still on that fairy tale?"

"Freya," Tekmet said, placing a hand on her shoulder. Then he turned to Robin. "Like us, you'll find getting out of here to be rather... difficult," he said, hesitantly.

"What do you mean?" Robin asked, sensing there was more to what he was saying.

"You see the guy over there?" Freya asked, pointing.

Following the direction of her finger, he eyed a man hard at work not far from them.

"Yeah," he answered, nodding.

"When we first arrived, he was trying to rally the people to revolt," Freya explained. "Claiming Apep was a false god and there was more to the universe than these caverns."

Robin's admiration for the man grew.

"Then one day he vanished," she said, cutting into Robin's thoughts. "For two work cycles he was gone. Then he reappeared as he is now." She shook her head. "One of Apep's biggest followers."

Robin stared at her in disbelief before he looked over at the man. "Brainwashing?" he asked.

"What else could it be?" Tekmet answered. "Instead of killing him and giving his argument credence, they did something to him that made him like this. After all, what better way to prevent uprisings than to have your slaves believe you're a god?"

Robin had to agree with him. "But still, there has to be a way," he muttered, looking around him. "Because we have got to get out."

"Even if it were possible, why are you so eager?" Freya asked.

"Because the Black Dragon is coming here," he answered.

Tekmet jerked suddenly. Grasping Robin by his upper arm, he demanded, "Are you sure?"

"Balwin said the Black Dragon was doing an inspection of the mines," Robin explained.

Gulping, Tekmet looked around, as if expecting to see the Black Dragon somewhere around them. "Then you're right, we have to get out of here," he muttered. "Especially you two. Neither one of you is ready to be anywhere within five systems of that monster."

"I can't believe that you two—" Freya began, but she stopped when Tekmet turned to her.

"Freya, you may believe it or not," he said. He twisted her arm upright so her covered bracelet was at her eye level. "But this is real. This is—and has always been—your destiny. And it's about time you embraced it!" She glanced at the strip of clothing covering her bracelet. Then she looked from one face to the other and slowly shook her head. With a jerk, she freed herself and bolted. Robin and Tekmet watched her go. Tears streamed down her face as she ran.

At the end of their work cycle, Robin lay in the vast sleeping cavern in an alcove cut from a slab of rock. All around him at various levels were similar alcoves full of resting and sleeping people.

He brushed pebbles out from under the small of his back. Then, using his hand as a pillow, he tried to get comfortable. After a moment, he rolled onto his back and brought his cloth-covered bracelet into his line of sight.

He looked around before he slowly unwrapped it. Then he eyed the pulsing crystal. The beat moved faster than ever, to the point it was almost a steady stream of light.

He asked aloud, "What does this mean?"

Measure of a God

OVER THE NEXT couple of days, Robin and Tekmet worked together closely in one of the new tunnels, trying to get Freya to speak to them. But she had yet to say a single word to either.

"How long do you think she'll keep this silence up?" Robin asked during his fourth work cycle.

"She's your sister," Tekmet said, shrugging. He took a tiny sip of water before handing his flask to Robin.

Shaking his head, Robin looked over at Freya, who was working with her back to them. "She's basically your daughter, so you've known her longer," he pointed out.

"Yeah, but I'm still learning," Tekmet said with a chuckle. "Especially now that she's a teenager. And now I suspect she's as stubborn and bold at times as you can be."

"But she has a tender side as well," Robin pointed out. They watched Freya turn as Hannah and Kylie approached her and took some water.

Then Tekmet lowered his voice and said, "Have you had any luck getting that armor to work?"

Sighing, Robin shook his head. "Nothing so far," he admitted. "The crystal is pulsing faster, though."

"Pulsing faster?" Tekmet looked thoughtful.

"Something on your mind?" Robin asked.

Blinking, Tekmet looked back at him. "Sorry. Can you tell me about the last time you were able to use the armor?"

Robin thought about the unexpected question. "Right before I was captured in Bazzar by Karon and Valarka, and..."

He allowed his voice to trail off as he tried to make some connections. Then he held up his wrist and said, "You think this thing has been deactivating the nanites from their injection?"

The Anubis shrugged. "What else could it be doing?"

"But Tekmet," Robin continued, "if that's true, why hasn't it done it faster?"

"It would be a delicate process," Tekmet said. "Like deactivating any bomb. One wrong move and you blow yourself up. Remember, the nanites have explosive powers. And until two days ago, Freya's crystal was behaving the same as yours. I think it was deactivating her nanites, too."

"Two days," Robin muttered, looking away in thought. "How fast was her crystal pulsing before it stopped?"

Tekmet pointed to Robin's cloth-covered band and said, "Let me see."

Glancing around again to make sure they weren't being watched, Robin shuffled closer and drew back the cloth. The pulsing light was practically iridescent.

Tekmet said, "Could be any day now."

Robin quickly covered his bracelet again. Then he said, "If the nanites aren't active anymore, then we may have a chance to escape. But the main problem is—"

He was interrupted by heavy footsteps and a flash of pain.

Cringing, he looked at the sentinel as it cracked its whip again.

"Get back to work, you two!" it barked before striking out at them with the whip.

"Those guys patrol everywhere," Robin finished. "I can't armor up out here. They could turn on some random person." Tekmet nodded.

Before Robin could pick up his tools, a deep rumbling filled his ears. The ground beneath his feet vibrated along with it. He looked up and saw fine lines of dust and dirt falling from above.

"Cave in!" Robin shouted. The pair dropped their tools and bolted.

As they approached Freya, Robin skidded to a stop. His eyes locked on a teenage boy who was running from the new tunnel, hands over his head as rocks started falling around him.

Robin sprinted toward the boy and tackled him, knocking him back as part of the ceiling came down.

For several long moments, Robin lost consciousness. When he awakened slowly, he could barely see the darkness was so complete if not for the shards of light that managed to get through the wall of rocks trapping them. Bit by bit, he pushed the rocks off of them. With one of the boy's arms wrapped around his shoulder, Robin carried him over the pile of rocks that were now blocking the tunnel. Pushing aside the ones in the way.

When he reached the ground, Robin handed the boy off to a distraught woman who was clearly his mother.

"He's unconscious, and he may have a busted leg, but he's alive," Robin reassured her as the woman gratefully took her son from him and held him tightly.

"Gods be praised! Thank you! Thank you!" the woman sobbed. She and two others carried the boy away.

Breathing deeply, Robin hunched over, hands on his thighs. "Well, that was—"

Suddenly, Freya flung herself on him, arms wound around his neck.

"Don't you ever scare me like that again!" she cried, sobbing into his shoulder. Then she stepped back and punched his shoulder. "I just got you back again! I don't want to lose you!"

"Hey, tough girl," he said.

When she finally smiled he said, "I'm all right. Just a few scratches and maybe a bruise or two."

Their moment was interrupted by the crack and sting of a sentinel's whip. "Back to work!"

Later, in the sleeping cavern, Robin watched as Freya gently looked the boy over.

"How is he?" Robin asked when she came over.

"He's lucky," she answered. "His leg isn't broken. He just has a bad bone bruise, perhaps a crack. He needs to take it easy so it can heal right." At Freya's words, his mother began sobbing again. "How is he supposed to take it easy? If the Underworld Guardians—"

"Sentinels?" Robin interrupted.

She looked at him like he was speaking a foreign language.

"You mean the Sentinels?" he said again, facing her. "What are they going to do, kill him?"

Her silence spoke volumes.

"Are you saying the sentinels and 'Apep' would demand his death because he has an injured leg?" He could feel his temper rising.

"What use is he to anyone if he can't work?" a voice said from behind him.

Turning, Robin found himself face to face with the man who previously tried to stage an uprising. An idea suddenly popped into Robin's head.

"What good is he?" Robin asked. "He's a living being, and he has a right to live!"

"It is against the commandments to interfere with the Guardians' decisions!" the man snapped. "It is against the law of Apep!"

"Then why do you follow him?" Robin demanded, pushing the man back. "Why would any of you follow a god who would call for the death of a person you know, a boy whom you grew up with, because he's injured?"

"Apep is a caring and loving god!" the man defended. "If it weren't for Apep—"

"What?" Robin snarled. "We'd be dead?"

Robin noticed a small crowd forming around him. "What kind of life is this? We are worked till the day we die or our backs give out, with no hope for a brighter future."

"What better future could there be?" the man argued.

"I know there is more to life beyond these dark caverns!" Robin asserted.

Several people murmured to one another, but he couldn't tell if they were on his side or not.

He continued, "I have seen the stars shine like diamonds in the night sky! I know what it's like to laugh and play in the sunshine! And I have known free air!" He paused and looked at each face in turn. "Isn't that the life a god would want for their children? Not to—"

He was silenced as a laser whip wrapped around his neck. Instantly, Robin jerked and gagged. His hands flew up to grasp the whip, but he was yanked off his feet with a jerk.

He landed hard on his back, the wind knocked out of him.

"You are guilty of speaking out against the gods!" the sentinel above him snarled.

"Fluently," Robin said as the whip retracted.

Before he could react further, two sentinels grabbed him by his upper arms. As they dragged him away, a flash of movement caught his eye.

"Let him go!" Freya demanded, drawing back the pick in her hands.

A sentinel blocked the blow with its arm. Before she could draw the tool back for another attack, the guard seized her by the throat.

"And you will join him!"

The sentinels tugged Robin and Freya through several tunnels before they stopped at a rock face. With the sound of rock grinding against rock, the wall slid open, revealing a long hallway lined with steel doors that were inset with small, barred windows. The sentinels dragged them down the hallway, where they were separated, and pushed into two rooms across from one another.

Robin sprang to his feet just as the door slammed shut behind the sentinel. He brushed himself off and walked to the window. Two sentinels remained, standing guard at the entrance.

"I told you," Freya called out from the cell next to him. "I told you this would happen."

Robin saw her standing behind her door's window.

"Then what are you doing here?" he asked.

"Maybe what you have is contagious," she finally said.

Chuckling, Robin moved over to lie on the cot attached to the wall near the door. Unwrapping the cloth, he watched as the crystal on his bracelet continued to pulse iridescently. Eventually, the incessant pattern lulled him to sleep

.

Escape

ROBIN WOKE WITH a jerk. He glanced around the darkened room as he tried to remember what happened. Then he closed his eyes with a growl of frustration.

Giving himself a shake and cursing himself for slipping into sleep, he sat up and rubbed the bridge of his nose. Lowering his hand, he scanned the darkened room again. The only light came from the barred window.

He froze and stared at his bracelet. A giant grin spread across his face when he realized the crystal was no longer pulsing.

"Time to put the theory to the test," he muttered, raising his hand.

He focused on what he wanted to happen. His grin grew wider as armor expanded from the bracelet, covering his hand and forearm and stopping just under his elbow.

"I'm back!" he cheered in celebration.

"What?" Freya called from her cell. "I didn't know you had gone."

Ignoring her, Robin climbed to his feet and went to the window.

Peering out, he eyed the two sentinels at the end of the hall.

"Oh, buckethead! I have something for you!" he called.

For a second, they didn't move. Then the one closest to his cell stepped forward.

Drawing back, Robin concentrated. At once a beam of light shot forward from a slot on the forearm, forming a sword blade. When the sentinel arrived in front of the door, Robin thrust the blade forward, through the door and through the sentinel. The robot stood there, looking at him. Then Robin withdrew the blade, and it crumpled to the floor in a shower of sparks.

"What's going on out there? What was that?" Freya demanded.

Without answering, Robin used the illuminated blade to cut a large hole in his door. He kicked the section free and stepped through to face the second sentinel. It charged him, with its blaster aimed at Robin.

Acting on reflex, Robin rolled forward as his blade retracted. The tips of his fingers were covered by sharp, armored claws.

He lashed at the sentinel's ankle, severing the support hydraulic. As it fell to its knees, Robin stepped behind it. He drove his covered fist through its back and out its chest. Pulling back, he ripped out the power unit. The sentinel crumpled to the floor.

Robin breathed hard and looked up at Freya's cell. She gaped at him from the window.

Quickly making his way there, he ordered, "Get away from the door!"

The blade extended again, and he cut a hole big enough for her to pass through. As he helped her climb out, she stared at the sentinel's crumpled remains, then at Robin.

"How?"

Smiling, he raised his armored forearm and hand.

"Told ya so."

The armor expanded up the rest of his arm. She looked amazed when it covered his chest, the other arm, his legs, and his head.

"Some fairy tale, eh?" he teased as the holo readout flicked on.

Mutely, she nodded.

"Good. Now that we're on the same page, let's get the heck out of here!" He turned toward the exit.

"Wait," Freya called.

Robin turned back.

"I'm not going anywhere without Tekmet, Hannah, and Kylie," she said firmly.

Robin faced her, hand on one hip.

"Tekmet is the only father I've ever known," she continued, and Robin felt a pang in his heart for Jun. "Hannah is my old friend, and I helped bring Kylie into this world. I always wanted her to know freedom." Robin looked at her. "Is that all?" he asked.

For a second, Freya returned his stare. Then she nodded.

"Fine. Then let's go," he said. He pointed toward the door and stepped toward it.

For a second, Freya frowned and blinked in confusion.

"What?" she asked. She seemed stunned he hadn't offered an argument.

"You didn't honestly believe I'd leave them behind, did you?" Robin said. Then he punched a hole through the door and forced it open.

Freya walked submissively behind Robin as they wandered the tunnels and caverns, searching for Freya's friends and family. Each time they encountered work groups, Robin glared as they averted their eyes.

That's starting to get annoying, Robin thought after the fifth group. At the same time, he was relieved they didn't see any sentinels.

They finally found Tekmet among a group of Anubises.

"Wait here," Robin said to Freya in his altered voice. "I'm the one in disguise."

As Robin drew close, Tekmet straightened, his eyes blazing with hate.

"You must come with me!" Robin said.

Tekmet arched an eyebrow.

"I don't see why," he said, slinging his drill over his shoulder. "I'm not a sound engineer."

Behind his mask, Robin rolled his eyes. Again with the twentieth-century robot jokes.

Suddenly three sentinels approached. One grasped Freya by her arm.

He turned to Robin and said, "What are you doing with these two?"

"Taking them to the high priest," Robin replied without thinking.

For a second, the sentinel was silent. Then he barked, "No such orders have been issued. What is your designation?"

"Ah..." Robin said. He waved his hand in front of the sentinel's face. "I am not the droid you're looking for."

Robin saw Freya blink, and he felt Tekmet's eyes on him. The sentinel just stared.

Sighing, Robin slumped. "I really hoped to avoid this," he muttered. Then he drove his foot into the sentinel's chest, knocking it off its feet.

Before the other sentinels could react, he opened his hands to deploy his plasma saber. A message flashed across his face.

Abundant explosive substance detected at unknown vicinities. Explosive weapons inoperable, he read.

"Great, now you tell me!" he said aloud. "So what's left?" Before he could get another message, two of the sentinels charged him.

Spinning, Robin drove his elbow into the back of a sentinel's head, leaving a sparking mess behind.

Then he eyed the flashing parts of his own armor. "Well, let's try that one!"

He blocked a blow from the other sentinel and quickly threw a kick that knocked the sentinel's head off its shoulders.

Following the blow, he spun around to face the third sentinel, which still restrained Freya, thrusting his left arm forward. From under his arm, a thin, tightly wound metal cord tipped with a metal spike flew out. It passed through the sentinel's midriff, and Robin heard a metal clang as claws expanded from the spike. Yanking hard on the cord, Robin yanked the sentinel off its feet. Robin's other fisted hand connected hard with its face and detached its head.

"Well, that was fun!" Robin said. The cord withdrew under his arm.

Frowning, Freya walked up to him.

"'I am not the droid you're looking for'?" she mimicked. "What the heck was that all about?"

He shrugged. "I saw it in what was known as a movie in my ancient Earth studies," he answered.

"Robin?" Tekmet asked, his jaw open. He walked around Robin to look him in the eye.

"Hi, Tekmet," Robin said, nodding. "I got it to work." He raised his arm, displaying his bracelet.

Suddenly a warning flashed across Robin's holo screen.

"Oh, great!" he said.

"What?" Freya asked.

"I think an alarm has been tripped." He watched as what appeared to be a map of the surrounding area displayed on his screen.

"Looks like we're going to have company real fast!"

On the display, he saw a mass of fast-moving red dots coming at them. "But what about Hannah and Kylie?" Freya demanded.

"If we don't leave now, we're not going to leave at all!" Robin barked.

Before she could do or say anything else, he scooped her up and slung her over his shoulder.

Freya banged her fists against Robin's back as he ran through the tunnels, Tekmet matching his strides.

Now and then a sentinel appeared in front of them, and Robin disabled each one with a kick or a punch as they passed.

Eventually, they burst into the main cavern.

"Robin, behind us!" Freya cried.

He whipped around, one hand instinctively open. This time, his plasma saber emerged into his palm as he faced the horde of sentinels rushing at them. He fired shot after shot, knocking as many as he could out of action, trying not to hit the workers who were milling around behind them.

"Tekmet, take Freya!" Robin barked, handing his sister off to the Anubis so he could receive the other plasma saber and open fire.

"Okay, what now?" Tekmet asked, holding Freya protectively.

"I don't know! I'm kinda making this up as I go!" Robin answered. The blade of one of the plasma sabers ignited, and he cut a sentinel in half, still shooting with the other plasma saber.

A moment later, Robin turned at the sound of stone grinding on stone. He saw the offering indentation move forward and the statue dragon's mouth open to receive it.

His gaze shifted to Tekmet, and silent communication passed between them. At once Tekmet clasped Freya and leaped into the bed of crystals.

"Robin!" Freya screamed, popping her head above the rim. "What about you?"

"Don't worry, I'll cover you!" he called. He blasted more sentinels. Quickly, the guards began collecting people to use as shields.

When Robin couldn't see a clear shot anymore, he retracted the plasma sabers' blades, and the metal parts extended into fighting sticks.

Soon, he was a blur of motion as he deflected and struck out with the sticks. After kicking a sentinel aside and caving in its head with a whack from one the sticks, he turned to face the rest, only to find the sentinels, shielded by workers' bodies, moving toward him.

"Okay, that's not fair," Robin muttered. He took a step back from the advancing horde.

Glancing behind him, he realized that the offering indention was halfway through its journey. Reacting quickly, he brought the ends of his plasma sabers together, forming a staff.

"I'd love to stay and fight, but I've got a rock to catch!" he shouted.

Robin darted to the edge of the platform. Digging the tip of his staff into the ground near the edge, he vaulted into the air.

Time seemed to slow as he soared through the air, arms and legs flailing. Freya and Tekmet's eyes locked on him as he soared over the ravine, the river of lava beneath him. He reached the apex of the arc and gravity started pulling him back down.

He fell closer and closer in the direction of the offering area. Reaching out, he grasped the edge before his armored body slammed against it. The sudden impact against the surface jolted his hands loose, and he slid partway down the rock face. He gripped a slight overhang before his left hand lost its grip altogether.

Instantly, Freya reached over the edge and gripped his wrist to stop him from falling further. For a second, he looked at her eyes. Then his weight began pulling her over the lip.

"Get out," he muttered loud enough for her hear.

Her eyes widened.

"Robin!" she screamed.

His hand slipped from her grasp, and he began to drop.

Wind rushed past him as he tumbled to the river of lava below. His body twisted in midair to face it, and he watched as the river seemed to rush up to meet him. Seconds away from impact, he crossed his arms over his face. He shut his eyes, ready for the impact and the melting white heat.

It didn't come.

Slowly, he cracked one eye open. He seemed to have stopped in midair.

Blinking in confusion, Robin looked around to see if someone or something had caught him.

He saw that a pair of giant, bat-like metallic wings had sprouted from his back. He saw the words scrawled across his holo screen:

Flight mode activated.

Robin released the biggest sigh of his entire life. If there is a manual for this armor, I have got to find it.

With experimental flaps of the wings, he shot up through the air. Bursting over the cliff rim, he turned to face the gaping crowd. With a mighty snap of the opening wings.

At once, various red circles and lines highlighted and pointed out people on the screen in front of him. Soon the faces of Hannah and Kylie zoomed in.

Quickly making up his mind, he shot toward them, weaving through the air as the sentinels raised their arms and fired on him.

He approached the pair and snatched them from the ground.

"Hang on to me!" he yelled over the rush of air. Then he circled around and dashed back toward the mouth of the statue dragon.

As soon as they arrived above Freya and Tekmet, Robin straightened and deactivated flight mode. As they dropped into the bed of crystals, he released the pair, who Freya quickly embraced as the wings retracted into his armor.

Just as his wings vanished, Freya turned and smacked Robin's shoulder.

"Ow!" she squealed, clutching her hand. "Why didn't you tell me you could fly! You scared me half to death!"

"Hey, it was news to me too!" he snapped back. "But I think we have bigger issues!" He turned at the wall of flame. "Get behind me!"

Before anyone could say anything, he pushed Freya behind him. Focusing hard, he crossed his arms above his head. A second later, just as they were about to be engulfed by the flames, a red bubble shield projected from the crystal on his bracelet, surrounding them all and keeping them safe.

After they passed through the wall of flames, he lowered his arms, which dissolved the shield. They were now in an open possessing area, with giant alcove after alcove piled high with crystals.

Large containers, either empty or loaded with crystals, rolled at intervals along a giant conveyor belt before they were dumped into alcoves.

"Over the edge!" Tekmet barked as they neared the belt.

Scrambling to the edge, Robin lifted Kylie in his arms, and they all vaulted over the side.

"Now what?" Tekmet asked, looking around.

Robin realized they had passed through a series of valved pipes that shot jets of flame. A mix of magic and showmanship, he thought. "I guess we find a way out of here and steal a ship."

Knight Versus Knight

ROBIN HAD BARELY taken a step forward when a shot landed at his feet. He looked straight up. On a catwalk above them stood an armored figure.

"What the heck is that?" Freya demanded.

The figure flipped over the edge of the catwalk, twisted through the air, and landed right in front of them, crouched down.

Slowly it stood to face them. The muscular female body was as tall as Robin, with a pair of force plasma sabers slung low on its hips.

Its head, like Robin's, was dragon-shaped, triangular from the side, with four horns on the corners connected with webbing. At the bottom corners of the webbing were pairs of smaller horns. The webbing overlapped behind the main connections, with the smallest horn at the base of the jaw. Beneath the chin was a small barbed horn.

"The last Dragon Knight..." Robin muttered. He relaxed and set Kylie down. "I wasn't expecting it, but it's nice to have—"

Then her plasma sabers shot into her hands. She activated them, and a pair of short swords appeared. Moving quickly, she slashed at Robin.

Moving just as quickly, he deflected the blows. She dropped down, using the momentum to try to cut his legs out from under him. After blocking her attack with a kick, Robin leaped up and flipped over her as she regrouped for a double attack.

He kicked her in the back as he passed over her, and she stumbled forward and dropped. Rolling across the ground, she slashed again, only to find him above her.

Robin landed, and she rose to her feet. They faced off.

"Lady, what the heck is your deal?" Robin demanded. She charged, and he pushed her back with a pair of kicks to her chest.

"In case you haven't noticed..." he shouted. He rolled across the ground as she formed a staff with a large slashing spearhead. "We're on the same side!"

He sprang back to his feet, deflecting a slash. His plasma sabers dropped into his hands, and he drew them together to form a staff. Spinning it around, he blocked several attacks. The staves became blurs as they attacked and defended.

Robin ducked a slash and turned to face his opponent. Their staves met midair. Ducking again, he rose and pointed a finger at her.

"Look, lady, I think we have a serious problem. It's called miscommunication!" he snapped.

His words had no effect. She slashed at him again. Robin blocked it before she nailed him hard with a side kick, slamming him with enormous force against a wall. Shaking his head to clear it, he watched as she adjusted her grip on her staff.

Then she hurled the staff at him.

Dropping down and rolling away, Robin barely managed to miss being impaled by the spearhead. Her spear flew back to her hand. He detached one plasma saber, forming a sword, and blocked the longer, thinner staff spearhead.

He ducked to the side to avoid a thrust and blocked a couple more attacks, spinning around her. He rolled away when she jumped up, twisting, to slam the staff down where he had been.

"This is really not getting through your thick head!" Robin said to her as he rolled to the side, dodging another attack. "I don't want to fight you!" He rolled and then pinned the staff down with his sword.

"Look, lady! I'll say it again! I don't want to fight you! But if you try to hit me again, I'm going to kick your butt!"

She paused and stared at him. Thinking it was over, Robin climbed to his feet. She immediately leaped into a spinning kick, nailing him hard in the chest and knocking him back down.

"Okay, that's it!" he growled. He curled up and jumped to his feet. Charging at her, he threw a low roundhouse kick. She dodged it, but he nailed her across the head with a spinning kick. She climbed to her feet and threw a punch, which he blocked. He nailed her with a punch and followed that with a spinning backhand to her head.

She blocked the punch and slammed him with an elbow to the face. Grabbing his head, she drove her knee into his skull.

He dropped to one knee, expended the other leg, and spun around, sweeping her legs out from under her. Then he jumped forward to tackle her, but she grabbed him in mid-flight and tossed him aside.

He rolled onto one knee and held out his hands. His plasma sabers became swords, and he turned to face her. She morphed her staff to include spear blades on both ends and spun it over her head.

They charged at each other once more. He deflected a couple jabs with his swords.

Then she retreated, deflecting or blocking his attacks. Deactivating one blade, she used it to throw a kick, nailing him in the chest. She raised her staff high to block a downward slash. But she didn't see the attack from his other sword. Slicing the staff in two.

Stepping back, she stared at the sparking ends of her plasma sabers. But she didn't have time to ponder long. Robin brought both his blades down. She brought both broken ends up and blocked the attack.

Drawing close, he glared at her through his helmet; she glared right back.

Then, at a sound behind them, he turned his head and watched a lift descending to their level

.

The Black Dragon

AS ROBIN CONTINUED to watch the lift, he saw that it held two passengers: Balwin, who was wearing what Robin guessed were his finest clothes, and a well-dressed woman, whom Robin didn't recognize. She was wearing onyx clothing, including an overlapping jacket with a silver sash around her waist, a shirt, and black pants. A flowing black cape was attached to her shoulders with silver brooches. Around her forearms were intricate silver armguards, and she had highly polished black boots on her feet.

As the lift drew closer, Robin noticed her face was narrow and angular, her eyebrows defined and pointed, her lips full and hard, her jaw strong. On her head was a silver diadem that connected at the back and restrained her long dark hair from her face.

"Oh no..." the other knight whispered in terror. She quickly disengaged and leaped away.

"What the..." Robin said, as she disappeared from sight.

Before he could go after her, the lift reached the bottom. Robin turned to face the occupants as they disembarked.

Robin moved to stand in front of the others, and Tekmet joined him. For a brief moment, the pair from the lift eyed Robin.

"Well, well, well," the woman said, stepping forward. "I never would have thought I would meet the new generation of knights so soon." Her tone was eager, like a child on Christmas Day.

Balwin moved forward. She raised an arm to block him.

"This is my pleasure!" she warned the lord with a growl.

With a low bow and sweep of his arm, Balwin moved back. Robin frowned.

Reversing his grip on a sword, Robin grunted. "Lady, I don't know who you are. But you're going to wish you'd stayed out of my way."

Her smile widened. "You have no idea how wrong and how out of your league you are," she said. She stepped forward, lifting a hand to the shoulder brooches. With a flutter, the fabric fell to the floor.

For a second, both stood stock-still, facing off. Then they charged at each other. Robin slashed at her with his swords, but she easily dodged them, as if he weren't even moving. She knocked them from his hands, sending them rolling across the floor. The blades sucked back in.

Next Robin threw a hard tornado kick, which she caught in midair. She sent him hurtling over her shoulder across the floor.

Stopping on one knee, Robin looked at her in surprise. Then he leaped up high to the catwalk above, only to find her waiting there for him.

How can she be so fast? he thought. His heart was pounding in his ears.

He threw a kick she easily blocked. After blocking one punch, she sent one toward his face but missed. Growing more confident, Robin threw another kick.

She easily stepped out of the way and close-lined him as he passed, knocking him hard to the floor. But before she could drive a fist into him, he kicked out. She blocked and stepped back. Robin jumped to his feet.

He went on attack, throwing punches and a roundhouse kick she easily blocked. He jumped and flipped over her. Catching her backhand to him, she dragged him back in front of her and soundly kicked him, first in the gut and then in the face with the same leg.

Stumbling back, Robin landed hard against the railing. Clutching the bar, he looked up and quickly rolled down the walkway just before she propelled her leg down on the railing where he had been.

Robin was startled to see the railing snap in two under the force of the blow. She's toying with me, he realized, eyes widening. When he jerked his left arm forward, the cord again shot forward. She stepped to the side to dodge it and caught the cord in both hands. Then she wrapped the cord around his forearm with a flick of her wrist. Before he could stop her, with the cord still in her grasp swung him off his feet and across the room.

With a clang that reverberated throughout the processing room, Robin collided with a large processor and left a sizable dent in the side.

He dropped twenty feet onto the intake tubes and laid there, motionless. "Ow!" he moaned in agony. Slowly he pushed himself up onto all fours.

Hearing a howl, he looked up and saw the woman kicking toward him, her foot outstretched for the strike. He ducked, and she sailed over him, leaving another large dent in the processor frame. He spun around to face her again and dodged another kick to his head. Then he ducked as her raised leg hooked toward his head. She nailed him with a roundhouse from the same leg.

She grabbed him, spun around, and threw him against the processor, putting a third large dent in it. He started to take a step forward but was met by a powerful side kick to his gut. Crossing his arms, he blocked two follow-up punches, but she nailed him in the gut again.

He slipped behind her and tried to lock her arms. Instead, she grabbed him, in one fluid motion she ran up the processor, and threw him over her shoulder.

Robin twisted in midair as his wings released, and he flew up to the catwalk to find her waiting for him.

Before he could move out of the way, she leaped onto his back. Grabbing both wings, she twisted him around and sent him hurtling hard to the floor. Still on his back, she drove her knee against the joint of his wing. With a quick jerk of her hands, his wing broke with a snap.

She rolled off to face him as he climbed to his feet. His wings retracted.

"I have to say..." she started, walking forward and throwing a punch Robin barely managed to block. The next one connected with his cheek. Then she boxed his ears hard enough that he heard it inside his helmet.

Before he could collapse, she gripped him by the throat with one hand. "The last Dragon Knight I killed put up more of a fight," she finished, sounding disappointed.

Robin's eyes opened wide with terror. "Yo-you c-can't be," he stuttered through the force of her grip.

She laughed.

"The Black Dragon..." he said, the color draining from his face.

"And if you're the best the new knights have," she continued, adding her other hand to his thigh and lifting him high over her head, "I have nothing to worry about.

"

Not Meant To Survive

BEFORE ROBIN COULD reply, the Black Dragon slammed him down, back first, over her bent knee. He cried out in agony as he heard and felt something give a loud crunch.

He rolled to the floor with a moan. Pushing his chest off the ground, he looked up at her. Like the predator she was, she was circling her prey.

Suddenly there was a cry from behind her. Whipping around, she blocked the pipe Hannah was thrusting at her. With her other hand, she seized Hannah by the throat.

"No!" Freya cried, as the Black Dragon lifted Hannah off her feet. "Let her go, please!" she begged.

After glancing at Freya, the Black Dragon grinned up at Hannah, as she gripped her wrist as she struggled for breath. "I can't allow dissent among my slaves," she said. She twisted her wrist. A loud snap followed, and Hannah went still, hands dropping to her side.

"No!" Freya screamed.

Letting Hannah's body crumple at her feet, the Black Dragon turned back to Robin. He was on his back, pointing his bow at her, string drawn back, arrow in place. And he fired.

Twisting, she dodged the shot. But Robin hit what he was aiming at. The alcove of crystals behind her exploded.

The force of the explosion knocked everyone to the floor. The Black

Dragon was flung through the air and came down on the other side of the room. Portions of the ceiling crumbled down around her. When the smoke cleared, there was a gaping hole in the earth where the alcove used to be.

"Let's get out of here!" Tekmet yelled, picking Kylie up and rushing for the hole.

"Robin, come on!" Freya urged.

"I can't move my legs!" he called back. He struggled to pull himself along the floor with his arms. His useless legs dragged behind him.

Returning, Freya and Tekmet each grabbed him by the wrists and dragged him across the floor into the gaping maw in the wall. Before the Black Dragon could follow them, a rumbling swirled above them. Part of the ceiling collapsed, sealing them off from their enemies.

When the dust settled and the rumbling stopped, with effort Robin turned over on his back, eyeing the wall of rock separating them from Balwin and the Black Dragon. In one corner, Tekmet held Kylie, who was crying for her mother.

"No wonder the other knight booked it," Robin muttered. His armor retracted.

"What's happening?" Freya asked, watching it withdraw into his bracelet.

"Took too much damage. It's repairing itself. Won't be able to use it for a while."

Robin moaned in pain.

"Let me have a look," Freya said. She gently turned him over to assess how badly he had been hurt.

First, Freya gently ran her fingers along his spine. She pulled back when she touched an indentation at the base of his spine and he barked in pain.

She shifted to speak in his ear. "Robin, your back is broken. If it doesn't heal right, if we don't get you proper medical treatment, you may never walk again."

Dread sank deeply into Robin's center.

"Freya," Tekmet said, his voice cutting into Robin's despair. "You have to."

"Have to what?" Robin asked, trying to look at them.

"Tekmet..." Freya objected.

"Have to what?" Robin asked again.

"Freya, do you really think you're in danger of being discovered now?" Tekmet demanded. "They probably think we're dead."

"Have to what?" Robin loudly demanded.

Freya finally said, "Robin, whatever you do, don't move. I've never done this before."

"Never done what?" he asked, trying to look over his shoulder at her, but Tekmet, who was still holding Kylie, kept him in place with pressure on his shoulders.

For a few seconds, Robin heard nothing but silence. "Would one of you just... Arghh!" He screamed in pain as he heard and felt a large scrape and pop in his back.

Pushing he whipped around glaring at Freya. "What the heck...?"

He froze when he noticed that his legs moved. One knee bent close to him.

"How?' he asked in wonder. He moved his legs around experimentally before rolling onto his feet.

His hand went to the small of his back. The lump was gone. His spine felt strong and intact.

Slowly he looked at Freya. "That boy's leg was broken?" he asked.

After a second, she nodded. "You healed it like you just did with me?" She nodded again.

"You can use magic?" he asked, eyes opening wide.

Again she nodded.

"Dang... You really do have a healer's touch. How... how were you able to keep that hidden?" he demanded.

"Very carefully," Tekmet answered, climbing to his feet. "Otherwise, she also would have been fitted for a clerical collar. The collar would have disabled her magic."

"It's the reason it hurts the injured or sick person so much when I heal," Freya said, standing. "They become too suspicious when I set a bone without screams of pain."

"I can understand that," Robin said, looking around.

"So now what do we do?" Freya asked.

"Well, we can either stay here in our grave," Robin said, looking at her, "or dig our way out."

Working in shifts, they dug higher and higher up. As they made progress, they created small ledges to stand on as they continued to dig. While one or two people worked, the others slept, ate, and drank what food and water they had left. Kylie often sat in a corner of the ledge, stacking the smaller rocks into towers, knocking them over, and starting the process again.

"How long do you think we've been working?" Robin in his repaired armor eventually asked, looking at Freya as the plasma sabers he had been using to dig reattached to his hips.

Slinging Tekmet's drill across her back, Freya shrugged. "Maybe a day, maybe two," she said, wiping sweat from her brow.

"And how much food and water is left?"

"For them, maybe a day and half," Freya answered, looking at Kylie and Tekmet.

"And how far do you think we've dug?" Robin asked, gripping the rock he had been leaning against to look down at the hole beneath them. It seemed like they had climbed pretty far up.

"Somewhere between two hundred and a thousand feet," she answered, also looking down. "I haven't really been keeping track. Found it depressing." She shrugged.

Nodding, Robin looked at the others on the ledge. "Come on. We can handle it. Let's try to get an extra shift in." A plasma saber dropped into his hand.

The pair worked until the others woke. Then, at Tekmet's insistence, Robin and Freya rested on the small ledge while the Anubis took their shift.

A couple hours later Robin woke with a jerk as he heard Tekmet calling their names. "Robin! Freya!"

Rubbing his eyes, with a sound of scraping metal on metal, reminding him he was in his armor, he saw Tekmet was pointing up. "I think we're near the surface!" he called with excitement. "These look like plant roots!"

They quickly climbed up to the next ledge to look for themselves. Robin's spirits lifted when he noticed the thick, corded roots embedded in the dirt. He ran his armored fingers over them.

As Robin examined the roots, one twitched in his fingers. A series of strange readouts passed over his holoscreen.

"Uh, I don't think these are roots!" Robin yelled. He scrambled back as the root-like creature moved through the dirt in front of them.

Plasma saber in hand, Robin eyed the dirt and rock walls around them. "What is it?" Kylie gasped.

Before Robin could answer, the creature burst through the wall next to her with a high-pitched screech. Its pointed head opened wide, revealing a gaping maw with rows of deadly teeth and three toothed tongues waving through the air.

Robin twisted around, aimed, and fired. The creature's head exploded like a balloon, splattering them all with body fluids and gore.

Before he could celebrate or think of what to do next, a series of screeches reverberated through the air.

"Sounds like it has friends," Robin muttered, and his other plasma saber shot into his free hand.

"You're the only one with weapons," Freya said, covering Kylie. Robin and Tekmet stood back to back.

Without warning, another creature burst from the wall and soared through the air, jaws wide open. As it sailed for Tekmet's head, Kylie screamed.

Turning, Tekmet blasted it with the drill. Another creature burst through the wall at his side, and its jaws latched onto the drill. The force of the impact knocked the tool from Tekmet's hand.

Leaping forward, arms outstretched, Freya tried to catch it, but it slipped out of sight into the darkness.

When another monster launched from the wall, Robin raised his arm to block the attack to his face. Its jaws locked around his forearm instead.

"Hey, get your meal somewhere else!" Robin barked. Pointing his other plasma saber, he blasted the bottom half of the creature.

As it stopped flapping, two more burst from the dirt, aimed directly at Freya and Kylie. Freya pushed Kylie down, covering her as the creatures slammed into the rock where they had been standing.

Stunned, the creatures dropped to the ground. Before they could recover, Freya grabbed a big rock and lifted it over her head. She brought it down hard on their heads, flattening them.

"How many more do you think there are?" Freya asked, looking around.

Another monster burst out of the wall in front of Robin. He caught it in mid-flight. For a second it squirmed in his grasp. Then Robin squeezed it hard, and it burst.

Breathing hard, Robin shaking the gore off his hand looked between Tekmet, who was against one wall, also breathing hard, and Freya, who was trying to comfort a terrified Kylie.

Robin knelt at the side of the ledge, looking down into the abyss.

"What now?" Freya asked. He looked over his shoulder at her as she continued. "I mean, those creatures must mean we're near the surface?"

"Or we could still have hundreds of feet left to go," he murmured.

"Robin—" Tekmet started.

"My bullheadedness nearly got us all killed," Robin said. He stood and turned to face them. "First by the Black Dragon and now by those things!"

"Hey, you fought the Black Dragon and survived!" Tekmet said, stepping forward.

"Only because she wanted to toy with me!" Robin snapped. Tekmet stepped back at the force of Robin's voice. "She could have killed me at any time during that fight! Just like when I fought Maltanore, probably the least powerful of her followers, which I also barely survived after he toyed with me!"

Robin looked at them and hung his head. "Freya was right," he said after a moment, and she blinked. "It's time to face facts."

He turned back to look into the abyss again. "We ran out of food yesterday. And without that drill, we won't be able to dig our way out before we run out of air. We aren't meant to survive." Silence echoed his words.

Then Freya spoke up. "Oh, yes, we are!"

Robin turned back and stared at his sister, who glared at him.

She said, "We're here, aren't we? How dare you! Out of all of us, you have more of a will to go on!"

Her cheeks were flushed. "And you know the worst of it? Despite the fact I resigned myself to my fate at these mines, during the past few days I found myself daring to believe...to hope...that I was needed in the universe! That my fate was to be more than a slave!" She continued shouting. "And you know what? You were right!"

She stepped right up to his face and yelled, "And I'm going to keep believing it! So I, for one, am neither ready nor willing to die here!"

Then she raised her hands above her head and jerked them, elbows bent at her side.

As her words echoed around them, her armor expanded from her bracelet. Robin watched in awe as first it covered her body, then her head. The helmet formed into a wolf-like snout with two horns curling back from either side.

Freya looked at her armor-covered hands for a second before she raised her eyes to Robin. Then she spun around and stalked to the wall. She drove

232

her hands and feet into the rock and climbed to the top. Where she drew back a fist and started punching the area with enough force to shake the walls.

Quickly following her lead, Robin climbed to a position across from her. "Let's bust our way out of here!" he said.

"Now you're talking, brother!" Together they repeatedly punched the ceiling.

On the ledge below them, Tekmet shielded Kylie from the falling debris that was shaken loose by their blows.

For nearly ten minutes, Robin and Freya delivered punch after punch to the same spot, which slowly expanded. Then, with matching grunts, they delivered two mighty blows. The section gave way, and their arms shot through it.

Drawing back, Robin froze beside his sister and stared in wonder at the starry sky above.

Reunion

IN SHORT ORDER, they expanded the hole so it was wide enough for them all to pass through. In no time, they all stood above ground, staring at the sight before them.

They had emerged from the underground in the middle of a prairie, bathed in moon shadows and starlight. Not far off was a thick forest, with trees that seemed to reach for the sky.

Smiling, Robin looked over at Freya as she boosted Kylie up on her shoulder. "What is it?" the little girl asked.

"Freedom," Freya answered, and the girl stared with tears in her eyes. "It's freedom."

Still smiling, Robin nodded. "Let's find a ship so we can get the heck out of here," he said, and the group trudged through the open space toward the forest.

Within the shelter of the forest, their progress was slower as they climbed over or around large tree roots and rocks and untangled themselves when they became snagged on a branch or bush.

"Perhaps some of us shouldn't go too far," Tekmet said, when they took a break at a spot where a large tree's branches overhung the rushing river. Vines dipped into the water below.

The Anubis continued, "Unlike you and Freya, me and Kylie still have nanites in our blood. We can be tracked. If we're lucky, the Black Dragon thinks we all died down there, but we should keep a low profile just in case she does not."

"I guess you have a point there," Robin said. "We'll need to find a good place for you guys to hide until Freya and I find a ship." "Why?" Kylie asked innocently.

Robin retracted his helmet to reveal his face. He smiled again as he knelt in front of the little girl.

"Because, Kylie, we don't know what's out there. So we have to tuck you away to keep you safe." He brushed the tip of her nose with his finger, and she giggled.

Suddenly Robin was jerked forward. He fell flat on his face, and Kylie screamed as he was dragged a short distance and lifted off the ground to hang upside down. A thick, vine-like tentacle was wrapped around his ankle.

"Case in point!" Robin quipped. His helmet closed over his face. Freya and Tekmet pulled Kylie to a safe distance as she continued to scream.

Robin realized in shock that part of the tree had separated from the main trunk, revealing some kind of creature. Many of the vines that dipped into the water were actually tentacles, like the one that had snagged him. Other tentacles secured the creature to the tree. If Robin had been standing, he guessed it would have been twice as tall as he was.

Shimmering like water, the skin of the giant creature transformed from resembling tree bark to appearing amphibious. The creature opened a pair of large, watery yellow eyes, and it revealed a huge gaping mouth with long serrated teeth.

Slowly the tentacle around Robin's ankle tugged him so close to one of the creature's great eyes that Robin could see his reflection in it.

"What are you looking at?" he growled as he pulled his bow from the small of his back. He leveled the arrow and shot it through the creature's eye.

Howling in pain and fury, the creature flailed, sending Robin wildly swinging. Eventually, he was able to get a hold on his plasma saber and cut himself free.

Robin flipped around and landed on his feet. Standing tall, he faced the creature, which now had a murderous rage in its remaining eye.

Before Robin could make another move, the creature exploded. Robin's armor expanded to shield him from the flood of body fluids and parts. Then he heard a familiar voice.

"You're a hard person to track."

Willa stood in the river in her armor, her arm raised. What looked like a small launcher smoked on her arm.

"I mean, you disappear for almost four months and can't stay out of trouble." She lowered her arm and put a hand on her hip. "It always has to be me who pulls your butt out the fire."

Laughing, Robin shook his head. "And you're still one for overkill," he said, walking toward her into the water.

She met him halfway, and they embraced.

"It's good to have you back, man," she said, stepping back and grasping him by his upper arms. "Your mom was driving us nuts with her worrying."

Robin laughed.

"Robin?"

Turning, he saw Freya standing at the edge of the river with Tekmet and Kylie.

"Who is this?" Freya asked.

Robin pushed Willa forward.

"This is one of my best friends, Willa Scarlet. Willa, this is my sister, Freya."

Robin waved a hand between the two and then rested his arm across Freya's shoulders.

Willa retracted her helmet and looked Freya's armor up and down. "I don't see any family resemblance. Though being a Dragon Knight must run in the family."

Then Willa nodded toward the pair on the river bank. "And them?" But before he could reply, he heard someone call his name.

"Robin!"

As Robin turned his head toward the voice, he saw his mother rushing toward him, followed by the rest of his friends. Before he could react, she waded into the river and jumped toward him. She would have knocked him into the water if it wasn't for his armor.

"Don't you ever scare me like that again! Do you understand me, young man?" she shouted as she shook him roughly.

Robin looked at her fondly for a second. Then he pointed to Freya in her armor on the riverbank.

"Mom, I believe you know Freya."

"Freya?" his mother said. She slowly turned to look at his sister.

Freya looked from Robin to his mother.

"Oh, deactivate," Robin said, and his armor began to withdraw. Water started to fill his boots.

"What's a little water?" he joked. "I was going to change out of these boots anyway."

Following his lead, Freya retracted her armor. Everyone stared.

"Okay, now I see a resemblance," Willa said, nodding.

Stepping forward, his mother gently took Freya's face in her hands. "The last time I saw you, you were just a few days old," she said, tears in her eyes.

"I still look back on that day fondly," Tekmet said, as he approached and she turned to him.

"Tekmet?" she murmured. "You raised her beautifully, my friend," his mother said, embracing the Anubis. "Though I am so sorry about what happened."

"All that matters is she and I were able to stick together," Tekmet said. "And this fine man you raised got us out."

Before Robin could break in to share the credit, Much stepped forward. "Ah, excuse me!" he said.

Everyone looked at Much.

"Not to ruin the moment, but shouldn't we get back to the ship and get the heck off this planet before we're discovered? We're supposed to meet the others in Tortuga."

"Right!" Robin said. "Let's move! Tekmet and Kylie can join us now we have a ship."

They moved through the forest with the best speed they could muster.

After a while, Robin turned to Tuck and said, "We're going to need a way to get rid of some nanites. Kylie and Tekmet still have them in their bloodstreams."

Tuck dodged some roots and came to walk directly beside Robin. He said, "I think I have an idea! But I'm going to need a camera. I have one back on the ship."

A short time later, they arrived at the ship. It was hidden by overarching foliage, which made it invisible from the sky.

The ship was a medium-sized transport that looked oval from the front, with the cockpit in the middle and two sections jutting forward on either side. A ramp dropped from the midsection.

As they darted toward the ramp, Robin realized the rear section and engines were attached by a square structure that jutted out at a sharp angle when it met the engineering section, which, like the forward section, curved back to form two large engine propulsion nozzles. A pair of large spoilers was attached on top of and below the engine section, with missile tubes along the middle.

"Where'd you get this rust bucket?" Robin demanded as they darted up the gangway.

"Hey, she may be old, but she's hearty!" Tuck answered, giving the skin of the ship a fond pat.

Inside Robin paused when he noticed the name of the ship on a plaque. "The Will of Odysseus?" he questioned.

"I thought it fit," LJ said.

Tuck stepped away for a few moments and then returned with a holocamera. Moments later, he started taking it apart.

"Uh, should we be asking what you're doing?" Freya wondered aloud.

"I am using the parts to create an improvised...EMP device," he said, speaking around a wire in his mouth.

"An EMP device?" Tekmet asked. Robin noticed the Anubis sounded nervous.

"Yes," Tuck nodded as he worked. "It works like the Gremlin missile, which is used to temporarily knock out a fighter or small ships systems," he explained as he worked. "except on a more permanent basis. It renders the nanites inoperable. That is, if this works."

"And if it doesn't?" Freya asked nervously.

"We blow up," Tuck answered simply.

Tekmet leaned closer to Robin. "Are you sure he knows what he's doing?" the Anubis asked in an undertone.

"Mostly," Robin admitted, half grimacing.

Tuck sent them a sharp look.

"Well, why don't you have some faith in me?" His voice was indignant. "Start shutting down systems so they won't be affected."

Half an hour later, virtually every one of the ship's systems had been shut down. The crew gathered around Tuck and his contraption: a dismantled holocamera with wires attached to a switch.

"Moment of truth," Tuck said, rubbing his hands. He picked up a flashlight and turned it on.

"You step closer," he commanded, indicating Tekmet and Kylie.

"Ready?" he asked, hand on the switch.

"No, but go ahead," Tekmet said. He reached for Kylie's hand, turned his head away, and closed his eyes.

Tuck threw the switch. The light he held abruptly went dark. Staying dark even when he flicked it on and off several times.

For a few seconds, Tekmet remained as still as a statue. "Are we dead?" he asked.

"Far from it," Tuck answered with a triumphant smile. "Now for that collar," he said as he began to bring the ship's systems back online.

Alarms blared immediately.

"What's going on?" Kylie asked, covering her ears.

LJ darted to a console. "We got incoming!" he shouted. "At least eight ships coming our way—fast! They'll be all over us in five minutes!"

"Willa! LJ! Man the guns!" Robin barked, darting toward the cockpit.

"Make sure to keep the ship as steady as possible!" Tuck said, as he strapped himself in next to Tekmet, tools in hand. "I still need to release this collar. The process is delicate!"

Taking the pilot's seat, which slid forward, Robin took the controls. Soon he heard the engine hum to life.

"Top guns locked and loaded!" Willa said. A holo readout showed the laser turrets atop and below the ship move into position.

"Bottom guns manned and ready!" LJ reported.

"Weapons online! Engines at fifty percent!" Robin declared. "Now let's get the heck out of here!"

With a roar, the ship lifted off, and the landing skids retracted.

Once they were above the treeline, Robin threw the throttle forward. The ship shot ahead.

"Whoa!" he cried, surprised and exhilarated by the acceleration.

"Dang, this thing has a heck of a kick!"

"Told you so!" Tuck gloated.

"We see them, Robin! Eight fighters!" Willa reported.

As they rocketed over the trees, more alarms sounded.

"And it looks like they see us!" Robin snapped.

Keeping close to the trees to offer less of a target, Robin weaved left to dodge the pulsing laser salvos. Willa and LJ returned fire. Suddenly, the ship rotated on its side in a hard bank. With a small clap of thunderous noise, the thrusters went full power, and they shot forward.

As the fighters banked to follow from his rotating orb like station eyes locked on the holo targeting system. LJ pulled the trigger on the yoke in one hand, firing his cannons.

Lasers rocketed forward at high velocity, clipping a fighter wing.

Sending it tumbling from the sky.

"Whoa!" Little John hooted. "And the score is one-zip!"

Then Willa's cannon fired and hit its target. The fighter tumbled and crashed into another as it fell.

"Buy one, get one free!" Willa crowed as the fiery wrecks crashed to the ground.

From the pilot's seat, Robin kept his eyes on the view portal. The ground below was a green blur that quickly became a dusty, rocky blur. As they approached a looming canyon at an alarming rate, he called, "Everyone hang on!"

With a whoosh and a roar of the engine, the ship rolled and dropped down into the canyon.

Tuck, who was holding his tool in his mouth so he could use both hands to work on Tekmet's collar, groaned in frustration at the rocking and rolling ship.

"Robin what did I tell you about keeping the ship steady!" he shouted around the tool.

The ship weaved left and right through the canyon, avoiding rock formations as laser explosions erupted against the canyon walls.

As they quickly approached another pillar formation, Robin yelled, "Willa! Low bridge!"

Willa swiveled her seat completely around until she faced the way they were going, and she fired, exploding the base of the formation.

The pillar tilted forward and began to collapse. The ship dropped and dodged the falling rock. Looking at the screen that showed what was behind them, Robin saw it a second later, as the fighters came around the bend, one collided with the pillar as it fell on it. "We've still got three on our six!" LJ said as the ship weaved again. Robin's eyes widened when he saw the narrow bend coming up fast.

"I think I have something for that!" Tuck said, As with a small clack, the collar around Tekmet's neck released and issued a beep as the lights turned red and flashed. Tekmet carefully slipped free.

"Then you better do it fast!" Robin said, turning the ship onto its side to slip through the narrow gap.

Still holding the collar, which was now beeping and flashing red lights louder and faster, Tuck moved toward the airlock hatch, gripped the frame firmly, and opened the airlock. The roar of the wind was deafening. Tuck's knuckles gripping the frame turned white as he dropped the collar through and into the open space.

The ship roared through the narrow gap with the fighters in close pursuit. Then, as the falling collar exploded, shock waves suddenly rocked the ship, and the narrow canyon walls crumbled as the Odysseus burst past.

Looking behind them once more, Robin saw that two of the remaining fighters were slammed and buried under falling rock.

The engine blasted again, and the Odysseus rocketed out of the canyon, one fighter in pursuit.

"Who's got a bead on that fighter?" Robin called as he drove the ship up toward the atmosphere.

"I got him!" LJ responded.

As Robin and Much set the hyperspace settings for Tortuga, shots from the fighter passed by them.

"Any time now, LJ!" Robin warned as the missile-lock warning sounded.

"I said I've got him!" LJ barked, firing his cannon.

The fighter fired a few more shots, and Robin pulled hard on the yoke and throttle. The ship flipped backward over the fighter behind it. The holo targeting system activated as the fighter entered Robin's sights.

Robin cued the forward weapons, which emerged from either side of the cockpit. Then he acquired a lock and fired. The fighter blew to pieces.

"I told you I had him," LJ said.

"I know," Robin answered. "You were just taking too long." LJ chuckled and shook his head just as the ship made the hyperjump.

Once they were safely away, the planet receding through the rearview screen, Robin and the other knights joined his mother, Freya, Tekmet, and Kylie in the main room. Freya was tucking Kylie into a small sleeping alcove.

"So, how does it feel to be de-collared?" Robin asked the Anubis.

"It feels great!" Tekmet answered, rubbing his neck.

Chuckling, Robin looked at Freya. He said, "Well, this is not quite how I originally planned your rescue, but—"

Freya flung her arms around him. "Thank you," she whispered into his ear. "Thank you for coming to get me." Robin returned her embrace. "What are brothers for?"

Smiling, she shook her head and patted his arm.

A moment later, Robin froze as the crystals on his bracelet began to pulse. Looking at the other knights, he saw that their bracelets were pulsing too.

"What's happening?" Willa asked, looking at her wrist.

"There's one way to find out," Robin said.

The six knights stood in a circle, grasping each other's forearms. Faster and faster, the crystals pulsed. Behind him, Robin saw Chikako and Tekmet were watching the bracelets from over the knights' shoulders.

Beams of light shot up from the crystals and tilted until they connected. Light seemed to explode and reform around them into what seemed like a series of multi-sided dots. Some appeared to flash around others. A red line zigzagged between them.

"What is it?" Freya asked.

Eyeing the moving dots of light, Robin said, "It's a star map."

"To where?" Tekmet asked.

Robin's focus drifted to the far end of the light grid.

"I don't know," he answered, eyeing the large gaps at the far ends of the map. "Let's find out."

THE HUNTED

DRAGON KNIGHT CHRONICLES

BOOK 3

Tortuga

LJ LOOKED OVER HIS shoulder "We're nearing the exit point," he said, looking at Robin, who walked into the cockpit dressed in clothes similar to those he wore when on Alberan. He had discarded the rags he'd been forced into in the mines of Morehoth, grateful he, his sister, Tekmet, and Kylie escaped from that hell hole.

He sat in the pilot seat of *The Will of Odysseus*. "Killing hyperdrive engines!" Robin called out when he was strapped in his seat.

With a great shudder and a clap of what sounded like thunder from the engines, they dropped into normal space into an asteroid belt

"WHOA!" Robin barked as he turned the ship sharply, barely avoiding an impact. "A little warning would have been nice!" he snapped, glancing at his friends.

"Well, we wanted to see if your reflexes were still good," Much said with a grin.

"Yeah, right," Robin growled, maneuvering around a pair of asteroids with a spin of the ship. "I can see why Tortuga was hidden here," he added, reaching overhead to throw and kill switches and make a few adjustments.

"Any ship larger than the *Odysseus* gets pummeled in this big a field." The others nodded around them.

"As you can see," Willa said, and everyone in the cockpit gazed out the corner viewscreen as they flew by a severed section of a battle cruiser, "some learn the hard way."

"We're almost there," LJ said as they flew around more asteroids, one of which was the size of a small moon. "Better go alert the others."

"I'll do it," Robin said, pressing a button on his chair and making it slide back. Before the others could say anything, he was on his feet and through the hatch.

When he entered the main room, he looked around at his mother, who sat on a bench behind a small table and talked with Tekmet.

He also spied Freya, who watched over Kylie as she slept. She gently stroked her when she grew restless in her dreams, twitching and murmuring in her sleep. It calmed her at once, and she returned to a peaceful slumber.

Turning, Freya looked at Robin. "Are we there?" she asked, climbing to her feet.

"Almost," he answered. Everyone but the sleeping Kylie looked at him. "Better get ready." They nodded as he turned back toward the cockpit.

A short while later, back in his seat, the group maneuvered the ship through the belt. Finally, they came to an open area that was large enough for the ruined space station that dwarfed their ship with asteroids circling it. The hull of the station was greatly marred by battle damage. At the bottom of the floating fortress, one of the three sensor fins was broken in half from a long-ago fight.

Robin's eyebrows arched in surprise. "That," he started slowly as they moved closer to it. "Is that Tortuga?"

LJ glanced at him and frowned. "Not what you were expecting?"

"Kind of, yeah," Robin answered as he made a few more adjustments, "but I expected it to be more heavily armed and guarded." He eyed the area again. "Did you tell them who we are?"

After sharing a glance with him, LJ answered, "We thought it would be best for us all to decide that."

Before Robin could say anything, alarms blared. Checking the readouts, he saw they were being targeted. Looking upward, they found what appeared to be a double-barreled cannon drop out of a slot at the bottom of the ship. It swiveled to point right at them.

As hundreds of smaller cannons appeared from hidden slots, fighters flew out from behind large asteroids and bays opened on the side of the station.

"Maybe for now, we should stay behind masks," Robin said as he eyed the fast-approaching fighters. "That is, unless Dulglad and Suji shot their mouths off while we were away."

"If they did, they'd have to deal with the whole village," Willa growled, "and then whatever's left of them would have to deal with me."

The main body of the fighters was a shaft with a smooth top coming to a cone-like point. At the back, right before the engines, was the cockpit, and on either side of it were two halves of a ring with a pair of trapezoid wings attached.

Another fighter that caught Robin's eye was shorter in length. It had a broad, rounded front with a second level on top of it and a massive Gatling blaster attached. There were similar guns on its four stout wings with a set of afterburner engines on the main wings, with fins attached above and below each tip. Right above the main engine was a rotating double-barrel gun turret.

"This is Buccaneer lead!" a voice called out over the coms. "Identify or be blown out of the stars!"

Eyeing the fighters, Robin opened the channel. "This is *The Will of Odysseus*," he answered the lead fighter. "Requesting permission to land."

"Passcode," the lead fighter commanded.

Blinking, Robin looked at the others. His eyebrow shot up, and an exasperated look cloaked his face.

Leaning over, LJ said, "Passcode: James De Wolf."

For a second, there was silence. "Passcode accepted," the squadron leader said as the guns on the station were retracted. While lights started coming on all over the station, the fighters took flanking positions on either side. "You will follow us in," the squadron leader told them. "For all first timers, I welcome you to Tortuga."

"Roger, Buccaneer leader," Robin said as he followed them toward the main hangar. "Matching speed and will follow your lead."

When they neared the hangar, the armored doors split and slid open. They passed through the force field barrier with a small flash of light, and Robin lowered the landing skids and set the ship down with a small shudder.

After lowering the ramp, the group exited into the hangar. Robin eyed the fighters that had landed around them, noting the pilots in their flight suits as they climbed out and removed their helmets after detaching the face masks.

He felt at ease when he saw not only humans but also elves, Valeakings, a couple Dromeanias, and even a few broad-muscled dwarves. One of them exited the more heavily armed fighter and moved quickly in their direction, his helmet under his arm.

"Good to see you all back. Bryan," the dwarf said, "I certainly have missed your crazy streak." He looked at Willa, who propped a hand on her hip. "And you must be the famous leader, Ryuu." The dwarf looked up at Robin. "Though, what kind of leader abandons his people?" He eyed him while the rest of the squadron gathered around.

Giving the dwarf a side look, Robin rested his hand on Freya's shoulder; her hand rested on Kylie's.

"The kind who would do what he has to do to rescue family," he answered, and the man eyed Freya. "That's something I would have thought a dwarf would understand, considering your people put their clans first." For a few seconds, Robin locked eyes with the dwarf, and then the man issued a great burst of laughter.

"That's certainly the kind of leader I could get behind," the dwarf said, slapping Robin on the arm. "One who would put himself in danger to save those he cares about." He stuck out a hand. "Roaran, son of Orin."

Smiling, Robin took the dwarf's firm grip in an equally firm one. "I look forward to that"—he looked at the rest of the squadron—"but only if you can tell me how a dwarf took command of a squadron with elves in it."

Over the sound of a door hissing open, a gruff voice said, "I believe you can imagine through the same stubbornness that got you here."

Robin turned to see a large black minotaur walk toward him.

"Pure stubbornness and guts."

The King of Pirates

THE MINOTAUR LOOKED him up and down before offering his hand. "You must be the famous Ryuu."

"I seem to be getting that a lot," Robin said before taking it.

"I am curious; what made you decide to leave the people who entrusted you to lead them?" the minotaur asked. "After coming up with a plan for them to come here, you would just run off and abandon them?"

In answer, Robin stepped aside to show them Freya. "She did," he said, as both the dwarf and minotaur looked at her. "This is my sister Freya," he explained, and they looked back at him. "Now, I think anyone would do what they could to save their family from the Black Dragon."

Slowly, the pair nodded. "Personally, I'd say that earned you a drink from me." Roaran nodded his approval before he turned to walk away.

"I suggest you take him up on that," the minotaur said. "The sooner you do, the sooner you'll be tired of it. He may be one of my best pilots, but he uses any excuse to have a drink."

"Do not!" Roaran called back before he slipped through the sliding hatch doors.

"Sir," said Robin, "it seems a little unfair that you would know my name but I don't know yours."

Nodding, the minotaur faced him. "You may call me Hector," he said, offering his hand. "Tortuga base commander."

Nodding in return, Robin took his hand in a firm grip. "Then I guess that would make you the Pirate King."

"That's one way of putting it," Hector said as he led the way through the hangar doors. "Only we have to keep putting my kingdom back together or it will fall apart."

At his words, Robin eyed the people around him. Many of them were repair teams going about their jobs, sparks flying from their work. Around them, people moved about, some in and out of makeshift shelters.

"Ever thought of expanding?" Robin asked, stepping aside as a young child on a rusted hover tricycle went by.

"Certainly, we've thought about it," Hector answered. "The problem is finding and moving a second base into position to weld them together." After a pause, he added, "After all, more people arrive each day. We've started hollowing out the surrounding stable asteroids, just not fast enough."

Robin nodded in understanding. "So that's where those fighters came from..."

"Guarding the workforce," LJ said.

"At least we caught them at the change of watch," Much said, and they all looked at him.

"Excuse me," Freya interrupted. "Is there somewhere I can get Kylie settled in?" She boosted the little girl into her arms.

"On that note," Robin began, "how are my people settling in?"

"They seemed to be settling fine before we left," Chikako started.

"Well, things are a little different now." They all looked at Hector, who continued, "Since a few days after you left, one of your members has been working hard to turn people against you all."

Moaning, Robin raised his gaze to the ceiling. "Let me guess... this person is about this high"—he held up one hand—"with dark hair and eyes, one heck of an attitude, and a thing for himself?"

"Sounds like the right person," Hector said as they came to a closed hatch.

After pressing the release, the door opened with a *hiss* and they were met by Dulglad's voice.

"...abandons us," he was saying to a small group of the village with his back to the new arrivals.

At once, the people sitting or standing before the campaigning teen reacted to the sight of them when Robin and the others motioned them to sit and be quiet.

"What kind of a leader is that?" he asked the lot of them as Robin and the others moved closer. "He just left us there—when you all put your faith in him!"

"Then I say, when he gets back, we take him out back and beat the heck out of him!" Much said, and Dulglad jumped nearly a foot in the air before whipping around to face them.

Giving him a hard look, Robin asked, "So, have you been planning a funeral as well?"

Dulglad returned his gaze. "This coming from a guy who first got our planet destroyed and then left us?" he demanded. "So, what's the excuse this time?"

Rolling his eyes again, Robin stepped aside to reveal Freya behind him. "Dulglad, meet my sister, Freya," he said simply. "Now," he said, stepping back into his rival's face, "how many people do you know who would abandon family when the chance to rescue them arises?"

When he looked back, he saw people exchanging glances, none of them with malice. A few nodded in approval.

"Great, now there are two of you to cause trouble for us," Dulglad growled as Robin returned his gaze. "You brought an Anubis with you," he continued as he eyed Tekmet, who crossed his arms. "After all, Ro," he started, but was silenced by a hand falling on his shoulder.

Robin's gaze fell on one of the bigger men of the village. "It's good to have you back, Ryuu," he said, a small smile on his face. "Isn't that right?" He squeezed Dulglad's shoulder, causing the teen to flinch slightly.

After the teen gave a small nod, the man released the pressure. After a few seconds' silence, Dulglad pushed past him and stormed out of the room.

Shaking his head, Robin locked eyes with Hector, who said, "I don't envy you for having to deal with him." He turned to leave and then added, "But after you speak with your people, you and I are going to have to talk." With a clatter of hooves on the deck, he left.

After watching him go, Robin turned back to the big man. "Thanks for that, Dolph," he said, and the man nodded in return. "Can you gather the rest of the village? I have some things that need to be said."

Dolph nodded and left through the hatch.

Blinking, they all looked back at Robin. "What are you thinking?" Willa demanded as he leaned against a table, arms crossed.

"That the village put their trust in me and I left when we were on Bazaar, like Dulglad said," he answered her. "I have to face them for that."

"Robin," began Freya as she let Kylie down, "what's going to happen now?"

"Honestly," he answered, "I don't know."

The Judgement

IN WHAT FELT like no time, Robin was brought to one of the storage hangars by Willa and LJ. Meanwhile, around him, people of the village filed inside. Catching eyes, he saw looks of surprise, wonder, amazement, and in a few, derision.

Scanning the growing crowd, Robin spotted Dulglad, Suji, Babieca, Bamber, Kade, and Melinda. After eyeing the smug looks on their faces, he sighed, thinking about what was to come.

When everyone had gathered and the doors had closed behind the last arrival, Robin stepped forward, wondering if there was going to be anything left of him after this dive.

"Thank you all for coming," he said, and all the voices of the people around him quieted as they turned to look at him. "For everyone who didn't know before they walked through those doors"—he nodded in their direction—"I'm back!" He raised his arms before letting them drop to his sides.

Aside from a couple of grins, none of them reacted.

Sighing, he looked at them all. "I know some of you are sour because I left without an explanation, despite making sure you were left in good hands." After a pause, he added, "Some have been campaigning that what happened makes me unfit,"—he looked at Dulglad and the boy's father and friends—"and in some ways, they're right." The smug looks on their faces just got worse. "You all deserve to know why I left. This is why." Turning, he motioned for Freya, Tekmet, and Kylie to come forward.

As they did, people gasped, eyebrows raised, as they stared in wonder at Freya, with fondness for Kylie, and let out deep frowns of uncertainty, suspicion, or derision over Tekmet—some even inched away.

"Everyone, meet Freya," he said, placing his hand protectively on her shoulder, "my sister." People shifted in surprise, eyes going wide as they looked at her more closely. "This is Tekmet, the only father she's ever known, and that makes him a member of my family." After grinning at him, Robin placed a hand on Kylie's shoulder. "And this is Kylie. Right now, I don't know whether to introduce her as my niece or younger sister, going by the way my mother has been looking at her." He looked at Chikako and then at Freya, who shrugged. "I guess that's going to have to be settled between these two." He waved a finger between the women.

"The simple fact is that, while we were on Bazaar, I saw Freya amongst a group of slaves being put on a ship for transport," he explained, walking out from behind the three. "Realizing she was my sister, I knew I only had one chance to save her," he continued, "and I knew I had to take that chance."

Again, murmurings rose from the people, some leaning close to whisper in another's ear.

"Now I know you all entrusted me to look after your safety," Robin said, and the murmurs died down, "and in some ways, I violated that trust." His gaze shifted to Dulglad and the others with him. "If you want me removed as leader, I understand."

"I, for one, think it would be a bad idea!" Freya called out, and Robin looked at her in surprise.

"I agree," Tekmet piped in. "I praise the day this young man came into our lives." He nodded. "You want a leader who would do anything for his people? You've got one in Robin. He let himself be captured and enslaved for people and family he didn't know," Tekmet continued. "He even willingly got himself thrown into the Mines of Morhoth, so he could get back to us when we were separated."

"He fought Lord Balwin to return to us!" Freya picked up where Tekmet had left off. "He even broke his back fighting the Black Dragon herself..." She stopped when Robin shot her a look.

"*You* fought the Black Dragon?" a disbelieving Dulglad piped in while his friends and father laughed lightly. "You expect us to believe that? For starters, you're walking!" Other people started nodding. "If you fought the Black Dragon *herself*," Dulglad continued, making air quotes with the last word, "and *she* broke your back, then how are you still walking?"

Before Robin could answer, something shot out of Dulglad's pocket. He watched as it soared through the air, coming to a stop and hovering above Freya's palm.

"Got a bit of a sweet tooth there?" she asked, and a couple people chuckled. The half-eaten candy bar spun in the air above her hand. "I was able to hide the fact I can use magic," Freya said. "I was able to heal him." She looked at them all before the candy bar floated back to Dulglad. "You can believe us or not," Freya said as the teen jammed the candy bar back into his pocket, "but I know what my brother did for me, and that's enough. I will forever be grateful to him. Anyone who says he is anything less..." There was a warning in her tone.

"For once, I agree with you." Dulglad climbed to his feet. "You see someone across a series of landing platforms and you risk all of us to save her!" he exclaimed, pointing at Robin. "What kind of leader are you to risk our lives like that?"

"One I can get behind." Dolph stood amid a group of men. For a second, he just stood there, looking at everyone. Finally, he spoke again. "Robin may have left, but he made sure we were in good hands before he did." He nodded in the directions of Willa, Little John, Much, and Tuck. "And I like to think that, if anyone here were to see family anywhere being led away for enslavement, they would do anything to save them."

Robin saw husbands, wives, brothers, and sisters squeeze hands or hold each other close.

"I know I would have done the same thing if I had been in his shoes!" He jabbed a finger at Robin. "If he did that much for people he didn't know, imagine what he would go through to save one of us!" At his words, people started murmuring again while others shared looks. "So, I don't know about the rest of you, but I *will* stand behind my leader!" He pumped his fist into the air. "ROBIN!" he declared, and began to chant.

With a clatter of movement, people leapt to their feet, fists raised in the air, all following the chant. It reverberated through the air, vibrating all the walls around them.

Surprised, Robin looked at his friends, who held his gaze before they each raised a fist in the air, the crystals of their bracelets flashing in the light.

Tekmet slammed his fist against his chest and bowed his head in respect while Freya raised her fist and joined in the chant.

Taken aback and humbled, Robin looked back at the crowd. When he saw the hard looks from Dulglad, Suji, Babieca, Bamber, Kade, and Melinda, though, he clenched his jaw and he stood straighter.

Settling In

HOURS LATER, ROBIN stood in one of the hallways, looking out of a force field viewing portal. People moved about around him, some going to makeshift shelters and others going down different corridors. Some were just kids, laughing and playing as they were chased by their friends.

Robin still stood there, watching the tumbling asteroids beyond as they floated through space. With one hand, he fingered his toothed necklace and medallion. He chuckled and a grin appeared on his face, amazed that, after everything, he managed to keep both. His smile slowly faded as his thoughts turned to his father.

"Ryuu." Head turning, he eyed Freya as she drew close. She followed his gaze, a smile on her lips, and looked out the portal. "It's weird having to call you that," she finally said, "especially since I know you by another name."

Robin nodded. "The person who bore it is long dead," he said, and she looked at him. "It's only a mask now."

Her eyes returned to space. "I guess we all have to wear masks at one point."

After a few seconds, his hand slowly moved to rest on her shoulder, and she lay her head on his shoulder

"How are you, Tekmet, and Kylie settling in?" he asked.

"As soon as people heard I was a healer, the medical teams wouldn't leave me alone," she answered. "Then they learned I could use magic."

"Did it get worse after that?" he asked.

"Depends on the person." Again, silence fell on the pair. "What's on your mind?" she asked.

"That we still have a brother out there," he replied, and he felt her surprised eyes on him. "That it's a big universe out there—a lot of places my father could have hidden him."

"Are you saying we're triplets?" she demanded, her mouth open. He slowly nodded, looking her in the eye. She let out a puff of air and shook her head. "Better late than never that you told me," she said, her voice hardening.

"Another way to tell you two are related," a voice said behind them, and they turned to face Much, LJ, Willa, and Tuck. "You both have a short fuse," Much continued, and Willa smacked the back of his head.

"No, he's right," Robin admitted. "We do."

After giving him a smile, Freya looked away. "I would say mine is a bit longer," she added smugly.

"Maybe by a millimeter, if that," he retorted.

She slapped his chest as everyone around them laughed. Robin chuckled, looking down at her.

"Nice to see you all settling in," came Hector's voice.

"Time to have that discussion you mentioned earlier?" Robin asked, facing him.

"Yes." The minotaur nodded.

Robin lowered his gaze. "I'll see you all later," he said, and moved down the corridor at Hector's side.

The man caught two boys running as they rounded a corner. "Walk," he said sharply after turning them both to face him. "Don't run! Walk!" With that, he let them go on their way.

Robin smiled as the kids left. "You do realize they're going to be running again as soon as you're out of sight, right?"

"Yes," the minotaur answered, "but hopefully the next people they bump into won't be a work crew and blow up half the station." Robin chuckled at that.

After rounding a couple more corners, Hector led him to a pair of doors. He pressed the release on the side, and the doors opened.

Stepping in, Robin looked around the room, eyeing the bed built into the wall. Some of the wiring and tubing dipped down from the ceiling. He shifted things out of his way as he looked around.

There was an old emitter for the computer with a foldout stool, as well as what looked like an ancient simulator pod consisting of a foldout stool, a yoke, and an old eye viewer.

"After everything you've been through, this must seem like a palace," Hector said, stepping forward, his hooves clanging on the metal floor.

"You'd be surprised," Robin muttered, thinking about the palace on Andurian. Memories of Marian surfaced, and he frowned.

"I'm assigning you quarters similar to this," Hector said, snapping him back.

He whipped around, looking at him. "You don't need to do that."

"As leader of your band, it is customary," Hector said, overriding his objections. "There will be things you will have to discuss with your people in private, and this is better than having to kick people out of places." He sat on the bed. "That's another thing I wanted to speak to you about," the minotaur continued, eyeing him. "What are your plans for you and your people, now that you're all here?"

After looking at him, Robin moved to the old projector. "We were hoping, after arriving here safely, to find our way to the Resistance," Robin said, turning on the projector and pulling up a star map.

"Well, then you all have a pretty big problem," Hector said, and Robin frowned. "Most of the people in this base would willingly join the Resistance."

"Why don't they?" Robin asked, facing him.

"There's your answer," Hector said, pointing at the floating star map and climbing to his hooves. "There's a lot of space out there to get lost in." He eyed the floating stars. "In short, you don't find the Resistance..."

"They find you," Robin finished for him with a sigh of frustration, running his fingers through his long hair.

"It's virtually the only reason they've survived this long," Hector said. "So, what will your plans be until they find you?"

"I guess we'll be sticking around for a while."

"Then there's something I need to make clear." The minotaur nodded somberly. "You may be the leader of your village, but *I* am in charge here. If you are going to stay, you're going to have to contribute—everyone has to pitch in to keep this place from falling apart."

"I figured as much," Robin said, hands going to his hips.

"Is there anything you can do?" Hector asked.

"Well, I have this." He showed him his medallion.

Taking it in his big hand, the man eyed it closely. "Jun taught you?" he finally asked, looking back up at Robin.

"He was my father," Robin said, tucking the medallion back under his shirt.

"He was a good man. I was sorry to hear he died."

Nodding in thanks, Robin's gaze dropped to the floor as thoughts of what happened flooded his mind.

"Unfortunately, that won't help you much here," Hector continued, and Robin stared at him. "Many come here already trained."

"But I still have to have time to train my sister."

"Then what can you do to give yourself that time?" Hector asked, arms folded across his massive chest.

Robin thought for a few seconds. "I'm a good pilot," he finally said.

Hector arched an eyebrow. "Really? You're offering yourself up as a freight pilot?"

Tilting his head to one side, Robin grinned.

Buccaneer Squadron

A SHORT WHILE later, strapped to the seat of a fighter in flight gear, Robin was flying through space at high speed with one hand on the throttle and the other on the yoke. All the while, he dodged the various-sized asteroids that tumbled around him, stopping them from either crushing or colliding with him.

"Oh, yeah—this was a great way to test my fighter pilot skills," he growled to himself as he dodged another floating rock. When an alarm sounded, he glanced down at the rear view screen. Roaran's fighter was moving in behind him. As the missile lock warning sounded, he jerked hard on the yoke. The fighter shot around an asteroid with Roaran in close pursuit.

"Is that really your strategy?" the dwarf demanded as Robin dodged around another flying boulder. "Using the asteroids against me?"

After glancing at the rear view screen again, his eyes shot up and a grin spread across his face. "No," he replied as he banked his fighter hard. A trio of asteroids was coming on course in front of him, about to collide with each other.

Robin sensed his plan of action, and his fighter was bombarded by blaster cannon fire. Weaving left and right through space, he dodged the fire from Roaran's fighter. Once more, the missile lock warning sounded.

He remembered the rules of this dogfight: the first one hit by blaster cannon fire or locked on for a missile launch would be the loser.

After glancing at Roaran's pursuing fighter, he locked eyes on the rapidly shrinking gap between the three asteroids. He then pressed a button on the throttle.

Right away, the afterburners fired with a roar of the engines, and he shot forward. He knew he had a miniscule time window to survive what he was going to do, and the time he could safely stop and save himself was no less thin than a sheet of paper...

Larger and larger the asteroids loomed around him while Roaran maneuvered to follow. Looking back up, Robin's eyes widened when he saw he was out of position. With a cry, he spun his fighter and barely made it in time to scrape through the shrinking gap of the asteroids and shoot through to the other side.

Sighing in relief, Robin sagged in his seat. "But they sure do help in shaking a tail—or missile lock," he finished, killing the afterburner engines and pulling up on the yoke.

As he was clearing the top of the asteroid, Roaran's fighter shot into his view. In a flash, he was behind him, turning the hunter into the hunted.

As the fighters weaved through space, Robin opened fire. "So, how does it feel to be on the receiving end?" he asked as he maneuvered to gain a missile lock.

"I'll let you know!" Roaran replied, and his fighter suddenly shot backward.

"WHOA!" Robin barked in surprise as he jerked his fighter to the side, dodging Roaran's.

With the dwarf back in pursuit, Robin jerked hard on the yoke and throttle. He put the fighter into a dive-and-roll while he was closely followed. "You did not just pull an old man's maneuver on me!" Robin exclaimed, throwing a couple of switches.

"Don't you be calling me old!" Roaran barked back.

After rolling his fighter to avoid more blaster fire, he again put the fighter into a dive. Knowing he didn't have much time, Robin quickly took cover behind a couple of large asteroids. He pulled the fighter to a full stop and started throwing switches, virtually shutting down all systems.

As he drifted, he looked up between a crack in the shifting asteroids, spying Roaran coming into his line of sight. With bated breath, he eyed the fighter as it slowed and started searching for him. For what seemed like hours, Robin watched until he saw him start to pull away.

Slowly, Robin put the maneuvering thrusters back online and moved into position. Then, as Roaran disappeared over the lip of the asteroid, he reacted to the main systems. He slammed his foot down on one of the strafing pedals and shot up with his fighter on its side. He was right behind Roaran now and rolled to right himself. Before the dwarf could react, Robin had him in a missile lock.

"Bang! You're dead!" Robin cheered, jerking one fist up in triumph.

Over the commlink, Roaran growled in frustration. "Well, I guess I should welcome the newest member of Buccaneer squadron," he admitted as Robin pulled up alongside him and they turned toward Tortuga.

Apprentices

AFTER THE PAIR landed in the main hangar and climbed out of their fighters, they started chatting about the dogfight.

"That last maneuver you did—you've got to tell me what that was!"

"Let's just say I got inspired," Robin replied as they walked toward the hatch.

"By what?" Roaran demanded, exasperated.

"An old toy for young children on Earth," Robin answered. "I believe they called it a jack-in-the-box."

Walking through the main hatch, the pair were met by Hector in the hall. The two stood, their helmets tucked under their arms.

"Ryuu," said Hector, "that was quite impressive, young man. You weren't exaggerating when you said you were a good pilot..."

"Bragging about it, I bet," came a stage whisper, as the three eyed Dulglad as he walked in.

"Actually, all he said was that he was a good pilot," Hector said, "and then he pointed out we could use all the fighter pilots we could get."

"Besides," Roaran said to Dulglad, running his finger through his thick, braided beard and chuckling, "I seem to remember blowing you out of the stars merely five minutes into the dogfight."

At the dwarf's words, Dulglad's face hardened in rage, and he whipped around and stormed off. Willa, Little John, Much, Tuck, and his mother walked toward Robin. Surprisingly, he didn't see Freya or Tekmet anywhere.

After changing out of his flight gear, he wandered down the hall, looking for them. He turned down one corridor and paused when he saw a crowd of children at the end of the hall. Tekmet stood alone, gazing out at one of the forcefield portals, hands clasped behind his back.

After glancing at the crowd again, Robin called, "Tekmet!"

At once, the man turned and smiled as Robin approached. "It's good to see you, Ryuu," he said in greeting. "Shall we find a place more private?"

Robin looked back at the children and nodded in agreement. "Now I know what a goldfish must feel like," he commented as they walked away.

"It's strange calling you that," the other man said as they rounded the corner. "Who is this *Ryuu*?"

At the question, Robin lowered his gaze. "A boy who died not long ago," he answered. "Now his memory has become nothing more than a mask I have to wear."

At his words, Tekmet looked at him. "I saw part of your test to get in the squadron," he said, changing the subject, for which Robin was grateful. "It was quite impressive."

"Thanks," he said. "In some ways, I always felt at home flying."

"It shows. Was there something you wanted to talk to me about?"

Sighing, Robin nodded as they stopped beside another portal. "Yes." He turned and looked out. "Since Freya can use magic, does that mean my brother and I can, as well?"

After looking at him for a second, Tekmet moved to Robin's side, rubbing his chin. "Perhaps," he finally said. "Usually, family members do share the gift, and it's possible, now that you're..." He glanced down both ends of the hall, "you know," he finished, nodding toward Robin's covered bracelet.

At his words, he lowered his gaze. "I don't know if I ever had that gift."

"Did you ever try?"

***

The next day, after showering and changing into some loose clothing in his room, Robin was meditating on his knees as he heard a knock at his door.

"Come in," he said, opening his eyes.

The door opened, and Freya came in. "Hey," she said with a smile he returned. "I heard you wanted to see me."

"I did," he said, shifting to his feet and sitting on his bed. After pressing a button on the wall, the foldout chair slid out of the wall and folded into position, she sat.

After a couple seconds of silence, she patted her thighs, looking around. Meanwhile, he tried to think of the right words to say.

"I heard you got into Buccaneer squadron," she said, and he waved it off.

"I didn't ask you here to talk about that."

"Then why did you?"

Sighing, he ran his fingers through his hair. "I heard you got in with the healers," he commented, and she nodded. "As a Dragon Knight, though, you also have to learn how to fight."

Biting her lip, she lowered her gaze in thought. "I guess you're right," she said before looking at him again. "And I guess you're going to have to teach me?"

"Can you think of anyone better—or anyone else you trust more?"

Lowering her gaze again, she sighed and ran her fingers through her hair. "I guess not," she finally said. Freya looked him in the eye then. "When do we start?"

"As soon as you change into something you can train in."

Shortly thereafter, they found themselves in one of the cargo holds that served as the armory and training area. Freya, in loose clothing with her hair tied back in a ponytail, landed hard on the ground. The air rushed out of her while, above her, Willa, who was similarly dressed, circled her.

"At least you're getting plenty of practice falling," the other girl said, offering her a hand to help her up.

"Thanks," Freya moaned, taking the offered hand and getting to her feet. "And here I was thinking I was wasting my time."

She turned to Robin, who watched from the side, and tried to not think of when they had stretched and she struggled to do a split when all he'd had to do was shift his hips from one split to another to get the result.

"So, what's next?" she asked, hands going to the small of her back as she arched it with a series of small pops.

Rolling his eyes, Robin stepped forward. For a second, he just looked at her, and then, without warning and in a flash of movement, he tapped her first in the chest and then the temple with the back of his fist.

"Those are called strikes," he said as she recoiled, her hands going up in defense. "Now we work on blocks." He turned his back on her, walking away.

Eyes blazing, Freya charged at him. Robin was faster; he spun her, so she charged right past him. She whipped around and glared at him. "Anger doesn't give you an edge!" he snapped at her before turning.

Again, she charged at him. Spinning back to face her, he again deflected her outstretched hands. One hand slid up her arms as she went past, and the next thing she knew, the crook of his elbow was wrapped around her neck, cutting off her blood supply.

"It blunts it!" he hissed in her ear before flexing his arm to make the point. She pushed him off and coughed, unsteady on her feet as the blood rushed to her head. "Now, let's get started." He looked from Willa to Freya. "She will strike," he explained as Willa stepped in front of Freya, "and you will block."

For the next half hour, Robin watched Willa throw strikes at less than half her typical speed while Freya attempted to defend herself. He instructed her from the side every now and then, sometimes stepping in mid-action to adjust Freya's movements. Thankfully, she only had to be directed once before she got it.

"She learns fast," Willa commented, drinking water as the pair watched Freya practice in the air.

Robin nodded and then shrugged. "Must run in the family." His face fell then as he thought of his father and the brother he had yet to find.

The Haystack

BACK IN HIS quarters, Robin fingered his toothed necklace and eyed the holographic projection of the galaxy that floated around him.

"Talk about a needle in a haystack," he murmured, "and I don't even know which haystack to start with." As his mind churned with thoughts, his doorbell chimed. "Come in," he said.

With a hiss, the door opened and Freya stepped in. She closed her eyes as she massaged her aching muscles.

"If the rest of the sessions are going to be like that," she moaned, "then I'm not sure..." She opened her eyes and paused at the sight around her. "Redecorating?" she asked, eyeing the floating planets and stars.

"Not really," he answered as she stared at him. "We still have a brother out there. The problem is trying to figure out where he is in all that." He gestured toward the planets and stars. "There's a lot of space out there to get lost in."

"Is there anything else I should know about this family?" she demanded.

Glancing at her for a second, he smiled softly. "Aside from having no idea where our mother is? Not much."

For a second, she held his gaze in stunned silence. "But I thought..." She trailed off, pointing at the door. "Then who is Chikako?"

"She and her husband, Jun, adopted and raised me," he explained, "right after our mother gave birth to all three of us and disappeared. She told them the three of us would have to be separated."

Again, she stared at him, her mouth open, and plopped down on the bed next to him, sighing. "What's she like?" she asked.

Lowering his gaze, Robin shrugged. "I don't know, but I wish I did." He climbed to his feet, his hands patting his knees. "The question is," he started as he walked through a couple of the projections, "where could my father have hidden our brother?"

As if in answer, he felt the tooth of his necklace grow warm. With a start, he took it in his hand and faced Freya, who held her own. Before either could speculate about what was happening, both necklaces shot out of their hands into the air. They watched in amazement as they circled the room before stopping with a jerk. The two necklaces pointed at each other with a giant rotating planet between them.

Robin stepped closer, eyeing the rotating holographic mass in space.

"I think we've found it," Freya murmured. "He's in the Bedie System."

A Course to Danger

LEAVING FREYA TO gather the others, Robin left his quarters. Soon, he arrived outside Hector's door and pressed the chime button on the side.

"Enter," came the minotaur's voice.

Robin pressed the release, waited for the door to open, and stepped in. Hector sat on his bed, a great axe across his leg as he sharpened one of the blades with a grinder.

"Yes, Ryuu," he said, putting the tools aside. "Is there something I can help you with?"

"I need to leave," Robin said, and the other man blinked.

"You've barely been here a couple days." He put the axe back in its place of honor on the wall and the grinders away in a cupboard and stared at Robin, frowning.

"I'll probably only be gone a few days. It's just—I got word of my brother's location. I have to go after him."

After looking at him closely for a few seconds, Hector closed the cupboard. "Are you sure it's him?"

"Let's say I have a reliable source," Robin answered as Hector walked past him.

The black minotaur was silent as he leaned against the wall, away from Robin, whose nerves grew tighter and tighter with every passing second.

"I must say you are devoted," Hector finally said, facing him, "which means you would probably leave, even if I didn't give you permission."

Robin's shoulders loosened at his words. "Does that mean I can go after him?"

"I might as well not fight the tide when it comes to you—especially after everything I've heard about you," Hector said and held out his hand. "But you better come back alive," he added as the pair shook hands. "Like you said, we need all the fighter pilots we have, and I'd hate to lose you."

At his words, Robin nodded and turned to leave.

"By the way," Hector called to him, and the man paused. "What system did your source say he was in?"

"The Bedie System," Robin answered and then frowned at the deep frown of concern on the minotaur's face. "What is it?"

"I just got a report from a scouting party," he said, going to his computer and pulling it up. "It says half the Black Dragon's fleet is heading for the Bedie System."

Robin's eyes widened.

Difference of Opinion

BACK IN THE storage area, as before, the rest of Robin's friends, Tekmet, and his mother gathered around him. The villagers stood ahead, murmuring at everything he had just told them.

"So, now you're leaving us again!" Dulglad barked, stepping forward.

"I have to," Robin answered. "The location of my brother has been narrowed to the Bedie System."

People murmured at that.

"So, once more, you're chasing after your family rather than doing what you ought to!" Dulglad continued while his father and friends nodded with sly grins. "With this, I say we recast—"

"SHUT IT!" one of the villagers shouted at him, and Dulglad froze, stunned. "Instead of you blabbering about him abandoning us, why don't we hear why he has to go?"

After blinking in surprise at his defender, Robin continued, "Aside from the fact that this is my brother, it's more than likely he is the last Dragon Knight."

Murmurs arose again.

"There's no proof that..." Suji started but was silenced by a look from a villager.

"The fact his sister was also made a Knight is a strong indicator!" Willa shot to the crowd.

"There's more reason to suspect it," Robin continued, and they all looked at him. "Hector recently told me, for reasons unknown, the Black Dragon recently deployed half her fleet there." Again, hushed voices began talking. "We all know the Bedie System has virtually nothing to offer!" Robin called over the crowd, which fell silent to listen. "I don't know why or how, but if rumors have reached her that a Dragon Knight is in this system, then they're hunting for him.

"We need to reach him first; if he is the Knight; we need to find him and bring him back here. That way, we can be a stronger force against her tyranny!" He stared at his people and then continued, "With another Knight in our ranks, we will have a better chance against her forces until we can find the Sherwood and the Resistance!" People looked at each other, some nodding in agreement.

"Okay, fearless leader," Dulglad said slyly, "who will you leave in charge, pray tell?"

After shooting him an exasperated look, Robin turned to the others after raising his gaze to the heavens. "Willa, Little John, and Freya," he said, and the three stepped forward, "you're coming with me." Willa and LJ nodded, while Freya stared at him. "Tuck and Much, you two are in charge," he continued, and they nodded. Robin and Tekmet shared a look, and then Tekmet gave him a slight nod.

Later, Robin had begun packing a few clothes when his door chimed. "Come in," he called out, buckling a belt with holsters holding his buster sabers.

LJ came in as he buckled the holsters to his thighs. "I think we have a problem."

"What's that?" he asked, practicing drawing and holstering the plasma sabers.

"Freya is refusing to come."

Robin looked at him, blinking, and then followed Little John down the halls to where Freya stood, looking out into space. Her arms were crossed and her face was hard.

Sighing, Robin stepped closer. "What did LJ mean when he said you weren't coming?" he demanded.

"I'm not going anywhere without Tekmet," she growled.

He nodded in understanding, albeit with a sigh. "I understand why you don't want to leave them," he said, and she glanced at him, "but I need Tekmet here."

"Why?"

"We don't have time for this." Robin ran a hand down his face. "Right now, we have to get to the *Odysseus*. Our brother needs us, and we have a better chance of finding him together than alone." He jerked his thumb over his shoulder down the hall.

"Why?" she asked. "You found me just fine."

"That was pure luck," he countered with a jab of his finger. In response, Freya turned back to the portal. Robin's eyes turned upward, and a memory popped into his head. Before she could say anything, he drew one of his plasma sabers with a twirl. "Hold this for me," he said simply after pressing a small button and tossing it to her.

She barely had time to ask, "Why?" before she caught it in one hand and then went stiff as a stunning electrical current raced through her.

Eyeing her grimacing face, teeth bared in shock and pain, Robin slipped the plasma saber from her hand. Her stunned eyes rolled back, and she started to fall forward; he bent down and scooped her over his shoulder.

"Unless you know how to fight them, never argue with a guy with a blaster," he told her unconscious form as he walked down the hall. People stared after him in surprise.

"Lucky for her, you had that thing set to stun," LJ murmured as they entered the hangar.

When they boarded the *Odysseus*, Willa gasped and asked, "What happened to her?"

"A difference of opinion," Robin answered, depositing Freya in a seat and strapping her in.

Shortly after, the *Odysseus* left the hangar and, after clearing the asteroid belt, jumped to Hyperspace.

A Sister's Wrath

AS THEY SPED through Hyperspace, Robin made adjustments from his seat.

"What are you doing?" Little John asked, watching him.

"Making sure everything is running smoothly," he answered, making a couple more adjustments—either trying to put things off or anticipate her retaliation. "In case I'm not here to do it later."

At that, LJ chuckled, patting him on the back. "If Freya is anything like you," he said, chuckling, "I'd be more concerned about having my will in order."

Robin shot him a slight snide look. After glancing around at the controls and settings around him, he sighed. "Might as well get it over with," he murmured, pressing a button on his chair and sliding it back.

"Got any next of kin I should notify?" LJ asked over his shoulder. As he walked through the hatch, Robin rolled his eyes.

As in the transport before, rigid frames supported the halls if the ship got attacked. Every now and then, he eyed a maintenance access port with line-covered wires exposed. A solid column of lights ran along the corners.

At the end of the short hall, he opened the hatch to the main room. Frowning, he glanced around, and saw only Willa sitting at the bench, a hovering table before her.

"Where's Freya?" As if in answer, a fist suddenly connected with his cheek, and he stumbled to the side. Regaining his composure, he caught the kick Freya threw as a follow-up. "At least I know you've been paying attention," he mumbled, keeping his grip on her leg as he rubbed his stinging cheek.

"Let go of my leg, and I will give you more than that!" Freya hissed. "Especially since you kidnapped me!"

"You didn't leave me much choice," Robin countered, "and that is precisely why I am going to be holding onto it a little while longer."

He looked at Willa. "You could have warned me!"

She shrugged and smiled. "We girls have gotta stick together."

At that, Robin rolled his eyes. "And I thought you were my friend."

"I am," Willa said, leaning back in her seat with her hands behind her head, like she was enjoying herself, "but you had that coming."

"Let me go!" Freya snapped, and the other two looked back at her.

"You promise not to hurt me?" Robin asked, eyebrows arched. In answer, she growled at him. "Fine," he said, and she yelped as he lifted her foot higher and placed it on top of a console.

Robin and Willa watched her hop to keep her balance for a second before she freed her foot and jumped back.

"At least she's flexible," Willa said with a nod.

Glaring, Freya marched up to Robin. "This isn't over," she growled in his face.

"Fine," he shot back, drawing one of his plasma sabers with a twirl. He held it out to her. "Here's your chance to settle it."

She looked at it and then back at him. Reaching up with one hand, she tapped it a couple times. When it seemed safe, she jerked it from his hand and pointed it right between his eyes.

In a flash of movement, Robin seized her by the wrist, pushing it to the side. He spun her around and his elbow connected with her side, causing her to arch back. With an arm hooked under her shoulder, Robin threw his sister to the ground in front of him. His plasma saber returned to his hand at his side.

"Are we done now?" he asked.

Moaning, she looked up at him as she slowly climbed to her feet. "For now."

"I'll take what I can get," he muttered as he holstered the weapon.

The hatch opened and LJ came through. "Am I missing something?" he asked, looking at all of them.

"Just giving another lesson," Robin answered. "Now, shouldn't we decide an approach?" He jerked his head toward the table before Willa.

"It was a good show while it lasted," she said, calling up a star map that hovered over the table.

"What are you doing?" Freya asked, moving closer to the floating stars.

"With all the activity Hector said was going on in the Bedie System," Robin started, "we're going to figure out how to get there without their knowledge." He focused on the system in question, eyeing the giant gas planet with four moons, each bearing life.

"This means the regular routes are out," LJ said, lowering his gaze with a sigh and running his hand through his hair.

"And we didn't think to install a cloaking device before we left," Willa said, "not that there would have been one in Tortuga. If there had been, it's not like they could've spared it."

"Which means we only have one option," Robin said nervously.

"Charybdis' Maw."

Both Willa and LJ shifted nervously.

"What's that?" Freya asked, looking at them.

"To some, it's been the most dangerous section of space for over a thousand systems," Little John answered.

Freya frowned.

"It's a nebula," Robin clarified, "formed by ten young stars in its center. Many have tried to navigate through it...but only a few have been lucky enough to make it out alive." He paused and then continued after a moment. "Most were lost. Nobody knows what happened to them—probably crushed by interlocking gravity wells or compromised by all the radiation ionizing the gas there."

"And," Willa continued where he stopped, "it certainly doesn't help that one of the ships that made it through said a ring of ice formed near one. Also, navigation computers don't work there, and it's going to take us a week to cross it." She threw her arms up in frustration.

"Well, that doesn't seem so bad," Freya said, and they all looked at her like she was crazy. "What?" she asked with a shrug.

"I think you're missing one little thing," LJ said before pressing a few buttons. The map zoomed in on their present speeding location.

"That's us for the next few hours," Robin said, before pressing some buttons himself.

At once, the map expanded, and Freya's eyes widened in horror. She stared, open-mouthed, at what looked like a sheer circular wall of a shifting, multicolored cloud that made planets seem like nothing more than specks of dust.

"That's Charybdis' Maw," Robin said, "and it's our only way to reach our brother—if it doesn't kill us first, that is."

Charybdis' Maw

WITH A CRACK of thunder from the engines, they came out of hyperspace right on the border of the nebula.

Through the viewing screen, Robin eyed the shifting colors of the burning gases. To him, they seemed like an immense wall that stretched for lightyears, blocking all signs of the stars above and below them.

"It's beautiful," Freya murmured, and they all glanced at her.

"If anyone wants to turn back"—Robin looked back to the nebula—"now's the time."

For a second, there was silence.

"Not a chance," Willa said, sounding braver than she looked. "I eat nebulae for breakfast."

"I ain't afraid of no nebula," Little John said, nodding. "You're not getting rid of me that easy."

Nodding in return, Robin looked at his sister, who still gazed up at the nebula. Her eyes slowly lowered to meet his and then LJ's and Willa's.

"It's up to you," Robin said, and she looked at him again. "Either we all agree to go or we don't go at all."

She blinked, and again her gaze went up to the nebula before them. Freya slowly looked back at them again. "If there was any other way, I'd take it," she finally said. "Let's do it."

Robin brought his hands together. "All right, people, let's move it! We've got work to do!" They sprang into action. "Little John, Willa!" he snapped, and his friends looked at him as he took his post. "We're all going to have to keep an eye on the radiation levels, so one eye on the sensors at all times.

"Willa"—he turned to her—"also keep an eye on the shield gauges. If they go into a section of the nebula with high radiation, we're finished." She nodded. "LJ, you keep an eye on those engines. We can't stop moving, no matter what, or we could be in a hurt box." LJ nodded, his chair sliding into position. "And most important," he finished, "we've got to make sure the sensors keep running. If they go, we're all dead."

"I'm starting to wish we had brought Tuck along," LJ muttered as he was strapped in.

"We can handle basic engine problems," Robin reassured him. "We don't have to rebuild the engine."

"Let's hope it doesn't come to that," Willa murmured, "or he'd kill us."

"What about me?" asked Freya. "What do I do?"

"Your job is the most important," Robin said, taking the pilot's seat and sliding forward. "Keep an eye on us and make sure we don't have any problems medically—and make sure we don't overdo it." She nodded.

Robin shot LJ a look taking a deep breath. "Okay," he said, resting one hand on the throttle between them. "Taking her to one-third power." He accelerated the ship. "Let's take her in!"

A second later, they were enveloped by the nebula.

Coming to Terms

A COUPLE DAYS later, in the pilot's seat of the *Odysseus,* Robin eyed the rainbow colors of the nebula through the view port and made adjustments on the control panel. In the copilot's seat, Little John kept an eye on the sensor readouts.

"At least your father didn't hide your brother in a place that was easier to get to," LJ said as he focused in on one readout.

"I would have been more surprised if he hadn't," Robin agreed. He adjusted their course and added, "If it's hard for us to get to my brother, imagine how hard it will be for the Black Dragon." Then he asked, "How are the radiation levels?"

"All in the green," LJ answered. "From these readings, I'd say we're in the safest part of the nebula." Silence fell. After a few moments, Little John looked at his friend and then back at the closed double doors behind them. "So..." he said, slowly turning back to the view portal, "how are things with Freya?"

Adjusting the throttle, Robin glanced at him. "As well as can be, considering we've spent more time together in the past few days than we have since we were born."

Nodding, LJ looked back at the portal. "Is she still giving you the cold shoulder?"

He shrugged. "We barely know each other—and I'm not sure she's forgiven me quite yet."

"Well, there's one sure way of fixing that."

Robin looked at his friend, who grinned slightly. "I know, if she were my sister, I would make every excuse I could to be near her." Before he could reply, the door hissed open. It was Freya.

"Something wrong?" Robin asked her. She bit her lip and nervously wrung her hands. "Whatever it is, you can tell me," he assured her.

For a little while, she just looked from him to LJ. Finally, she shrugged and said, "I'm bored."

Robin stared and then laughed. "For the first time in years, you can do whatever you want and you're *bored*?"

Her face hardened. "Look, if you don't—"

"Wait," he said, glancing at LJ. "How about a lesson?"

She moaned. "Please, no. I'm still recovering from the last one."

"I was actually thinking of your first flying lesson." Robin waved her closer to the console.

She stood rooted to the spot. "Really?" she asked, as if to convince herself, before she moved to his side.

"Really," he said, relieved to see her smile. "These are the yokes." He patted the joystick handles in front of him. "They direct the ship up, down, left, and right." As he explained, he went through the motions; she paid close attention. "This is the throttle," he continued, and he laid a hand on the large lever between him and LJ. "Move it back to go forward and forward to go back. The farther you move it, the faster you go; middle puts you at a full stop." He gestured to the pedals at his feet. "Strafe peddle, left and right," he finished, and pressed the button on his seat, which slid back. "Take her for a spin."

"Really?" Freya looked stunned.

Waving at the seat, he nodded. She grinned from ear to ear and climbed into the pilot's seat. As it slid forward, LJ and Robin shared a smile. "What happens if I turn just one of the sticks?" she asked.

"You roll the ship," Robin answered. "Let's wait on that, okay?"

Before his sister could really get started, a deep, rumbling groan reverberated through the ship.

"What was that?" Freya asked, her mouth falling open.

As he turned to eye the door, a chill ran down Robin's spine. "I don't know," he said quietly.

The groaning sounded again. As the ship vibrated under his feet, he clenched one hand into a fist and felt his armor expand.

Guiding Angels

THE GROANING GREW louder and louder. Again, the hatch hissed, and Willa barreled in from where she had been taking a nap.

"What's going on?" she asked, her armor expanding up her arm.

Again, Robin shook his head.

They all frowned then as a ghostly humming sound met their ears; it reminded Robin of the songs of giant marine mammals on Earth. Before they could speculate about what it was, something shot across the view screen.

"What was that?" Freya asked.

Frowning, mouth slightly open, Robin stepped closer. With one hand resting on the top of the pilot seat, he sat in it, trying to see what she saw.

The humming sound met his ear again, and another figure seemed to meld out of the nebula and into their line of sight. Its body shimmered with the colors of the nebula, and with four wings flapping in sync, it glided alongside the ship. Robin's gaze met one of its forward-facing, stalked eyes. Opening its mouth, it issued more of the haunting melody.

Robin's shoulders slumped, and he sighed in relief as his armor retracted from his forearm.

"What are they?" Freya asked, looking worried.

"Star angels," he said, and she looked up at him as more star angels appeared and seemed to dance around them. "They follow ships into deep space, feeding off the exhaust from the engines."

"Do they live in nebulae?" Freya asked, now watching them in wonder.

"No, not really," Willa answered. "The gravity can be hazardous to them, and some of the radiation can be poisonous."

"But they blend into the nebula so well," Freya said, looking back at them and their ever-shifting colors.

"That's more their way of saying hi," Little John explained, "and that's probably how they all got trapped here."

They looked out at the pod again, which circled and danced around them.

After a few minutes, Robin turned to Freya. "I've heard many consider them good luck—and they've been known to guide lost ships to port."

At his words, she stared up at him. "Do you think they'll do the same for us?"

"Well, there's one way to find out," he replied and jerked his head at the screen with a grin. "Give them a run," he encouraged. "If they follow us, then we've got ourselves a guide." Freya looked up at him. "Are you sure?"

Nodding, he sat in a chair next to Willa. "We'll keep an eye on the sensor readouts," he reassured her, "but when we say don't go somewhere or stop, you do it. Got it?" Grinning, Freya nodded. "Willa," Robin looked at her, "keep an eye on the shields; Little John, the engines; and I'll take the sensors." They all nodded.

"Okay, here we go," Freya said, and threw the throttle back.

At once, the *Odysseus* shot forward, and she banked into a gas cloud. As they came out on the other side, they were surrounded by columns of gassy clouds with lightning-like energy shooting from one to the other. Above them, they could see more flashes of the same energy.

Keeping an eye on the viewscreen, Robin watched as Freya weaved left and right around the columns. The star angels were keeping up easily.

"Come on, open her up!" Robin yelled, a grin on his face, as he made some adjustments. "Don't lose them, but make these angels work for this meal!"

"You asked for it!" Freya barked and threw the throttle all the way back.

With a roar, they shot forward and the weaving grew tighter. The angels pulled ahead of them, their skin shifting rapidly with bright colors.

Suddenly, the *Odysseus* spun onto its side and dipped back into the cloud. For a couple seconds, they sped through the clouds, the colors swirling around them, and then they burst back up and out. At once, the star angels regrouped around them.

"Not bad for her first time," Willa said, adjusting the shields as Freya put the ship into a spin, the angels spinning with them.

"Flying must run in the family," Robin added when his sister stopped the spin on the ship's side and strafed until the side scraped the ceiling of the open area they were in.

Dipping back down, they left a rippling ring of energy in their wake, and again Freya weaved through the pillars. Every now and then, they scraped against one, causing it to collapse in both directions.

Robin then spied two pillars before them, closely grouped together, and they were racing right at them.

"Are you sure you don't want to take control?" Willa asked in an undertone.

Robin shook his head. "I think she's got it." He shared a look with LJ, who nodded in understanding.

At the last second, Freya rolled the ship onto its side and, still spinning, they soared right between the pillars, skimming both as they collapsed behind them.

With a cheer, Freya thrust one hand into the air. Suddenly, the star angels broke away before them.

Frowning, Robin checked the sensors again. "Okay, Freya, that's enough," he said when he saw the spiked radiation levels. "Follow them out."

She quickly turned the *Odysseus*, and they were clear of the radiation as they leveled out with ten angels still moving around them.

"At least we now have guides out of here," Robin said as he watched them. He met Willa's and Little John's eyes.

"You know what? I'm hungry," Little John said, sliding his chair back. "What about you, Willa?" he asked. Before she could answer, he had her by her upper arm and pulled her from the cockpit.

After watching the doors hiss closed behind them, Robin looked back at where Freya still sat. Sighing, he climbed to his feet and moved behind her. "Not bad for your first time."

She looked up at him. "Thanks."

Robin took a breath, like he was about to take a deep plunge. "So, are you going to listen to me without throwing punches?"

"Well, considering I'm at the controls and one wrong move means we could all suffer a horrible, fiery death..."

Rolling his eyes, Robin murmured, "A little morbid, but I'll take it." He glanced out the screen again. "Look, you have every right to be angry with me. You and Tekmet have never really been apart, and I know how you feel about Kylie, but I need you here with me."

"Why?" she asked. "Just so you can keep throwing me all over the place?"

"Partially," he admitted, and she shot him a look. "You are learning fast, though, which is a very good thing. That roundhouse kick alone proves that."

"Thanks," she said, "I think."

"I need you here with me," he continued, and she glanced at him again. "If it wasn't for the fleet, I would have left you behind, if that's what you wanted. But when I heard of the Black Dragon's plans... He's our brother, and I can't take chances with his life."

Lowering her gaze, she nodded in understanding. "I guess I should have listened to you." Freya looked back at the screen to the twisting and turning star angels. "It's...it's just hard..."

"Gathering feelings for someone you've never met," he finished for her. She nodded. "I guess we're going to have to take a chance," he said with a shrug. "The same one I took when I went after you."

Sighing, she sat back, running a hand through her hair. "I guess you have a point." When he cleared his throat, she looked at him again, and he jerked his head at the yokes. "Oh," she said, taking them again. "Hands on the controls at all times."

"No, you can take them off." He reached over and pressed a button. "Just make sure to engage the autopilot," he finished.

She chuckled, relaxing against the seat.

"There were other reasons," Robin continued their conversation. "You and Tekmet are the only magic users I know. I needed him to stay with the others, and I needed people I could trust..."

"And though you think you know the pirates of Tortuga, you don't *know* them," she finished for him, and he nodded. "I guess we magic users have been tarnished by a certain dark-scaled lizard breath."

"That brings me to the other reason I need you here." She looked at him again. "I need you...to teach me, LJ, and Willa," he finally said as she blinked, a frown on her face, "how to use magic."

"Have any of you shown signs of having the gift?" she asked.

"No," he admitted, "but we've also never tried."

For a second, she just stared at him before she slowly nodded. "Okay. I'll see what you have to work with." Robin nodded. "It'll be fun ordering you around for once. I take it that's the other reason you had Tekmet stay behind."

He nodded. "I asked him to teach Tuck and Much."

She nodded. "Well, before anything happens, we have things to settle." Robin noted the gleam in her eye and frowned. "Can I borrow your plasma saber?" she asked, holding out her hand.

A little worried about what she had planned, he started to draw one. Suddenly, he grimaced in pain as an electrical current shot through him; the next thing he knew, his legs buckled under him and he fell to the floor. The last thing he saw before he blacked out was Freya's smug face.

The Balance of Magic

WITH A MOAN, Robin regained consciousness, his hand going to his aching forehand.

"How's your head?" a self-satisfied voice asked. Opening his eyes a crack, he met Freya's gaze. Chuckling, he sat up in one of the bunks built into the wall of the ship. "It feels like I've got a colony of bees buzzing in there."

She nodded, a big smile on her face, and he saw LJ behind her, pinching the bridge of his nose as he held back a smile. Willa must have been in the cockpit at the controls.

"I guess I had that coming," Robin said finally.

"Nice to hear you say that." His sister climbed to her feet. "And now...we're even." With that, she smugly walked away with a sashay of her hips.

After watching her go, LJ moved close to him. "I like her style." Robin shot him a look, slapping his stomach. "What?" he asked defensively. "It's nice she's learning fast enough to pull one on you."

The next day, Robin and LJ—to keep an eye on him with his sister—sat at the table. They were quickly joined by Freya, three eggs in her hands. After sitting, she handed two eggs to the pair before her.

"So, what are we learning today?" LJ asked.

"You are learning nothing for now," she answered, leaning back in her seat at the bench. "Right now, I need to know if you have it to begin with."

"How?" Robin asked.

In response, she held up her egg between two fingers before shifting it back to her palm. For a second, they watched her and then the egg as it lifted into the air. It spun on its small end, hovering in place, and then shifted into a small, perfect crystal ball that shimmered in the light. Finally, it shifted back to an egg and floated into her hand.

"How...?" LJ started.

"You just have to believe," Freya said, interrupting him. "Magic is a perfect balance of fire, earth, water, and air. A true user of magic understands and respects that balance." The men looked at each other.

"Is that how dark magic users are created?" Robin asked. "They don't respect it?"

"That's part of it," Freya answered, "but they also believe themselves superior, because they've been granted a gift." She tilted her hand to allow the egg to drop and splatter on the floor. "It's true magic allows one to shape reality, at least partially, to our whims and fancies..." The bits of egg lifted into the air, becoming one again. "But the magic they practice has a heavy price, as they are ruled by lust for power." The egg floated back to her hand. "Some might call it the soul...others, their humanity; for me, it's their sanity." She looked at them. "You have to admit they are rather crazy."

The boys chuckled at that.

When they quieted down again, she shot them hard looks. "Now, you try," she instructed, "and remember: believe."

Face screwed up in concentration, Robin eyed the egg. Nothing happened. At once, he and LJ shared a look of disappointment before promptly switching eggs.

"Anything specific we should be believing?" Little John asked.

"That you can do anything," she answered simply.

The Beast of Bedie

AFTER WHAT FELT like a few days, Robin was back in the cockpit. As usual, the star angels danced outside the viewscreen.

Now Freya had gotten even, her attitude toward Robin was more pleasant. When he wasn't on shift in the cockpit and she wasn't teaching the two of them, they spent what time they had with each other, talking about their pasts or anything that came to mind.

On who knew on what day, Little John had been at the controls of the ship, still following their special guide pod. Meanwhile, Robin held a small, light object in the palm of his hand—the eggs had been safely left in the fridge.

"Still trying?" LJ had asked after shooting a glance in his friend's direction.

"Until I know for sure," Robin had answered, still determined.

"What did Tekmet tell you before we left?"

"That, since Freya and I are"—he'd shrugged—"well...triplets, or when it comes to siblings chances are that all three of us can do it."

"Then how is it," LJ said before raising a hand to make an adjustment, "that whatever you put in your palm stays in your palm?"

Laying down the object, Robin looked with a shrug. "Hey, I'm still learning—hopefully, as fast as I usually do," he defended as he adjusted their course following the star angels. They sat in silence for a couple of seconds and Robin glanced over at him. "Besides," he finally said, "it's not like you and Willa are doing any better."

LJ chuckled at that. "No, I can't deny that."

Falling silent, Robin's mind drifted. Believe, he thought. I already believe I can do anything I put my mind to, so what am I missing?

Just then, the star angels shot forward. "What the heck?" he said, speeding up to follow. "What's got them so excited?"

"Not a clue," LJ said, trying to get a read on what was in front of them. "Whatever it is, I can't detect it."

Suddenly, one of the sensors caught Robin's eye. "Full stop!"

"Robin!" his friend snapped as he pulled the throttle to the center position. "What are you doing? We can't stop!"

Before Robin could reply, though, the hatch hissed and opened behind them. "What's going on?" Willa demanded. "The engines stopped!"

"The navigation computer just came back online." Robin simply pointed to the readout. "We must be near the edge."

Mouth slightly ajar, LJ turned back to the viewscreen. "No wonder they were so eager to get the heck out of here," he commented.

"Okay," Robin said, his hand going to the throttle, "let's ease forward. LJ, passive sensors only. We don't want anyone to know we're here—but tell me the second you detect anything in front of us."

As Little John nodded, Robin eased the throttle. Slowly, the ship inched forward with each of them on edge.

"I got something!" LJ finally barked, and Robin killed the engines at once.

"What is it?" he asked, trying to get a look for himself.

In answer, Little John pressed a few buttons, and a floating hologram of a planetary system appeared with two suns. The fourth planet looked to be made of endless lakes and rivers, surrounded by countless islands, the largest of which he knew to have cities. In orbit around the planet floated several moons, one with a large population despite it being the exact opposite of the planet as it was a vast desert.

"The Bedie System," Robin said, a smile forming on his face. They were one step closer to finding his brother.

"Something else is coming up on the scope!" Little John barked. "What?"

"It's big, whatever it is," LJ said slowly. "Should we try to get a visual?"

"Carefully."

Again, they began to inch forward. As they did, the sensor readout slowly came into focus until the object became a large ship.

It was made of two large isosceles trapezoid sections, the downward angled sides looking like short wings. The smaller one was attached atop the rear of the first, which was more than twice its length, and there they saw a small command structure with a rotating sensor array beside it. On either side was a pair of block-like shield generators attached to the main superstructure. Attached to the underbelly of the larger section were larger sensor arrays. Along the body, they could see torpedo tubes and other openings from which numerous weapons might direct their fire.

At the sight of it, Robin grabbed the throttle, sending the *Odysseus* back into the nebula as quickly as possible.

"What? What is it?" Freya asked.

"That was a Black Wing class battlecruiser," Robin explained, "one of the most powerful ships in the Black Dragon's fleet."

"Looks like the reports are true," LJ said. "She really is massing the bulk of her fleet here."

"Now how do we slip past that monster?" Willa asked. "Because we sure can't fight it."

Thinking fast, Robin asked, "How close was that beast to Charybdis' Maw?"

Magic Hats

ROBIN MANEUVERED THE ship into position at the edge of the nebula "So, what are we going to do now?". Freya asked.

"It's a trick called magic hats," Robin explained, making adjustments to the engines. "Basically, we're going to fly right between the engine nozzles of that big boy out there." He looked at her. "That way, they won't be able to detect us when we're right under them."

"Why don't we come up from the bottom then?" Freya asked.

"Because we'd never fool them that way," Willa answered. "If we come up underneath them, they'll see us the whole time."

"But if we go between the thrusters," Robin continued, "they'll pick us up for a few seconds and then lose us in the exhaust of the nozzles. The sensors below the ship won't be able to tell the difference between the ship it's attached to and us."

Freya nodded, thinking his words over. "Why do I have the feeling there's a very big but?" she finally said.

The other three looked at each other, wishing she hadn't brought that up.

"One wrong move from us or any sudden turns from them and we're toast," Robin admitted, "literally."

Using the passive sensors at the edge of the nebula, he and the others watched the battlecruiser, waiting for the right moment to make its move.

"Come on, come on," Robin murmured as the giant ship passed them. "Now!" he snapped when it started to turn, and he inched the throttle back. As the back of the ship faced them, they burst from the nebula, heading right for the propulsion nozzles.

"Willa, keep an eye on those shields!" Robin barked as they drew closer and the ship began to vibrate from the exhaust.

"What about me?" Freya asked.

"Watch what LJ and Willa are doing!" he shouted, making adjustments. "If something happens to one of them, take over!"

"Got it!" she shouted back.

Closer and closer they flew at the cruiser. All the while, the vibrations grew stronger, making it harder for Robin to hold the course.

"Shields at eighty percent!" Willa reported when they were less than a thousand feet from the nozzles. "Micro fractures are starting to appear!"

"Here comes the fun part, everyone!" Robin called, and he started positioning the ship.

Suddenly, there was rumbling and the ship jerked. "What was that?" Robin barked.

"Port thruster malfunction!" LJ reported.

"Willa! Freya!" Robin barked, as they started drifting toward the right. At once, both girls leapt to their feet and then darted out of the room as he shouted, "Get that nozzle working or we die!"

Bursting into the engine room, Willa headed right for the console, flashing red against a section connected to the main engine.

"What's wrong?" Freya asked, looking over her shoulder.

"It's in auto shut down! It's overheating! Robin must have maneuvered a hair too close! The auto-cooling system could have also been compromised because of the nebula's radiation."

"What do we do?" Freya demanded as Willa darted to another console for a valve and opened it fully. "We've gotta find a way to keep the rest of the injecting fuel cool, or the only thing left of us will be microbes!"

Back in the cockpit, teeth still bared in frustration, Robin struggled to correct their still-shifting course. "LJ!" he barked, and his friend looked at him. "Get me to the engine room!"

"Go!" Little John barked, opening the channel.

"Willa, I need that engine going!"

"No kidding! I'm already having a Sunday feast of you pressuring me!" Willa shouted into the comm before she killed the connection. She then looked at Freya after she said, "I have an idea!"

Back in the cockpit, the alarms started blaring. "What's that for?" Robin demanded.

After his seat drew back, LJ reported, "Multiple things! Shields are failing, more microfractures...and they may be detecting us!"

"Okay, I admit this may have been a bad idea."

Suddenly, the *Odysseus* jerked to the left. "Nozzle back online!" Willa called over the comm.

"Roger that!" Robin replied. "Hang on!"

Rolling the ship onto its side, he righted their course; throwing the engine fully open, they slipped through. As they cleared the nozzles, the vibrations slowly faded.

Rolling the ship fully over, Robin brought the *Odysseus* close to the bottom of the ship. With a flick of a switch, he deployed magnetic mooring cables which attached to the underside of the ship, securing them in place.

Sighing in relief, Robin fell back against his chair. He was breathing hard, like he'd run a few miles, and his body grew limp as the adrenaline faded from his system.

When he could lift a hand, he opened a link to the engine room. "That was one heck of a job, Willa," he said.

"It wasn't just me," she replied, and Robin frowned. "Come see for yourself." He looked over his shoulder at LJ.

A short while later, with Little John at the controls, Robin walked into the engine room where he was greeted by Willa and Freya. Everything looked alright.

"So, what am I supposed to be seeing?" he asked.

Willa motioned with her finger for him to follow her. She then showed him the fuel injector for the nozzle and the light layer of frost covering it.

"Willa said you had to keep the fuel to the nozzle cool," Freya said as her brother turned to her.

After a second of just staring, he shook his head, chuckling. "Well, you certainly achieved that. Lucky you didn't use too much magic and freeze it solid."

"I'm just glad the ground is more stable under my feet," Willa said. "I should have the line checked soon."

Robin nodded. "Should be easy, now that we're under the hat." Both girls nodded. "Once you're done, I want you manning the top gun, just in case," he said, and Willa agreed. "Other than that, the only thing we have to worry about are Crazy Ivans." He then turned to leave.

As he walked through the hatch, he heard Freya ask, "What are *Crazy Ivans?*"

The Great Fall

FOR THE NEXT few hours, the group worked to repair the engines so they could make their move when the time came.

"It doesn't have to be pretty," Robin said as they examined the makeshift overlapping patch on the fuel coolant injector. "I mean, it's not exactly Tuck's standards..."

"Who will be spitting nails when he sees this," Willa murmured under her breath.

"Well, we have to make do with what we have," Robin said, and they left the engine room. "Right now, we have to figure out how we're going to get to the surface," he added, as they sat around the small table that rose out of the floor in the common room.

"Well, the obvious thing to do is let the big ship we're attached to get us close to the planet," Freya said.

"Obviously," Robin agreed.

"But the main problem is that we can only use passive sensors," Little John injected, "otherwise, they could detect us by picking up our sensor sweeps." Again, Robin nodded. "Which means, when we make our move, we only have a small window in which to do it," LJ continued.

"But that also means we're only going to be able to know we're near the planet for maybe a few seconds at most," Willa pointed out. "That is, unless we knock out the sensors." They all looked at her, and Robin sat back. "Looks we're virtually at point-blank range to knock it out,"

"Which will cause the secondary systems to come on instantly," Robin interrupted her. "You know that, Willa…" He paused as he realized what she had in mind. "Which would give us enough time to make a break for the surface of the planet."

With a smug smile on her face, Willa nodded.

"Then I guess I'd better get familiar with the gunner," Robin said, slapping his hands against the surface of the table to get up.

"No, that would be my job," she said. "Robin, we all know you out of all of us, you're the best shot, but you're also our best pilot, and we don't know what will be thrown at us once the sensors are taken out." She held his gaze. "I've got the elf eyes, which will help me be the second best shot among us."

For a second, Robin looked at her, eyes narrowed in thought. "This has nothing to do with you wanting to make something go *boom*?" he asked.

With a self-satisfied, triumphant smile, she shrugged and admitted, "That's just an added bonus."

In short order, the group was in place. Robin, Little John, and Freya were in the cockpit with commlink mikes' ear pieces slipped into place, eyes locked onto the passive sensors' readouts.

"Come on," Robin murmured under his breath. "Come on…" Suddenly, the holographic image of the planet appeared floating before them. "Now, Willa!" he barked, hand reflexively going to his mouthpiece.

At once, Willa opened fire, blowing the sensor array at point blank range.

Reacting as quickly, Robin released the magnetic clamps. Dropping down, he rolled the ship right-side up as he threw the throttle open, shooting them forward like a torpedo from its tube.

"Everyone, hang on!" he snapped as they burst from under the cruiser and headed directly for the planet.

They were almost to the outer atmosphere when Freya said, "Uh…what's that?"

"What?" Robin asked, reaching up to make a few adjustments just as an alarm blared. "John!" he snapped.

At once, LJ reacted, and a holographic radar readout appeared.

"We've got fighters incoming!"

"Hang on!" Robin called out, and he banked the *Odysseus* away from the fighters.

"Sorry," Freya said.

"It's not your fault." Robin tried to reassure her. "It must have been a patrol. Now hang on—this is going to get bumpy!" he warned as he pressed a button and was strapped into the chair. "Hopefully we can lose them entering the atmosphere," he said, adjusting the angle of entry.

"Robin," Little John warned, "if we stay too long in the atmosphere, we can burn up!"

"Which would make them crazy to follow us!" the pilot pointed out. "Now keep that finger on the reverse thrusters!"

"On your signal!" LJ barked as the ship started shaking from atmosphere entry turbulence.

The seconds slowly ticked by as the shaking grew stronger.

"Are they still on our six?" Robin barked over the turbulence, which was getting so bad that it felt like his teeth were going to shake right out of his skull.

"They're either crazy or they're drones! They're still right behind us!" John barked back.

Robin issued a curse as his eyes roved everywhere, searching for a solution, before they froze on one of the instruments. A light went off in his head.

"John!" he barked, eyes shooting to his friend, and LJ glanced over. "How much longer can they last?"

Blinking, Little John frowned. "Not as long as us, but—"

"How long?"

"I don't know, a few seconds!"

"Okay," Robin said, looking down at the rear-view readout again, eyes locked on the fighters still following them. "Everyone, brace yourselves!"

"Why? What are you going to do?" Freya demanded.

Before he could answer, the fighters began breaking apart. "Brace! Brace! Brace!" he called out. At once, he pulled the throttle into neutral and the engines died. At once, the ship shook harder as they began to drop like a stone.

"What the hell, man?" LJ reached for the throttle as they started going into a spin.

"No, don't!" Robin barked.

"Are you crazy?" Freya shouted as she hung from her safety straps like a Christmas ornament.

"Maybe," he muttered under his breath as he was thrown in and out of his chair, the safety straps the only thing keeping him in it as the ship tumbled through the atmosphere. The debris of the fighters fell around them.

"LJ, give me a count!" he barked, hand going to the throttle.

"I hope you know what you're doing!" his friend called out before counting down their altitude. The seconds seemed to last an eternity. "30,000...25,000...20,000..." LJ reported as the ground got closer.

"Robin, if we don't pull up soon, we'll die!"

"Tell me when we reach 10,000!"

After shooting him a look that clearly showed he thought he was crazy, LJ looked back at the rapidly-falling count on the altitude reader. "NOW!" he barked.

At once, Robin opened the throttle. "Come on..." he growled as he began making out each tree in an oasis and several large boulders surrounding a small patch of water.

Just when he thought they would crash, they came to a fast stop a couple hundred feet above the ground. After landing the ship next to the oasis and sighing, Robin sagged in his seat, face turned toward the ceiling and eyes closed.

"Do you mind telling us what the heck you were thinking?" LJ demanded, glaring.

Letting loose another sigh, Robin opened his eyes, looking over at his friend. "It just came to me," he admitted, "to let the fighters fall apart and then hide in the falling debris," he explained as he climbed out of his seat to lean against it.

Breathing deeply, LJ shook his head, looking away. "Good plan," he muttered with a scowl, "but a little warning would have been nice!"

"I sure hope insanity doesn't run in the family," Freya murmured, still in her seat, as the safety straps retracted.

Before Robin could say anything, the hatch opened, and they all looked at a slack-faced Willa, who looked a little green around the gills.

Her face formed a snarl and she pointed at Robin. "You're lucky I have a strong stomach," she growled, "or you'd be cleaning the bottom gunner station!"

Raiders

SHORTLY AFTER, THE group again sat at the table, discussing their next move. The last to join was LJ, who had been going over the sensors.

At the sound of the hatch opening, they all turned to watch him come through. "Well, from what I gathered," he started before taking a seat, "we're a couple hundred miles from the nearest large settlement." He sighed, exasperated.

"Anything between here and there?" Robin asked.

Sighing again, LJ shrugged. "A few camps, from what I can tell." Robin leaned back in his seat, looking up at the ceiling in thought. "Well, obviously, Freya and I have to get to that larger settlement," he finally said, looking at them. "That way, we have double the chances of finding him. Hopefully, somehow, we can get transportation of some kind from one of these camps."

Locking eyes with him, Freya nodded. He then looked between Willa and Little John.

"LJ, you're with us," he finally said, and LJ nodded. "Willa, you stay here." She moaned. "What?" he asked, exasperated.

"Does this have anything to do with the fact that I grew up with Tuck, and you hope I picked up some engineering skills from him?" she demanded with a frown, her head resting in her hand.

"More like survival," Robin answered, getting to his feet, "because we may be coming hot or need to be picked up in a warzone. Frankly, I'd rather have someone I know is crazy enough to do it."

For a second, Willa looked at him before she sat back with ease. "Okay, I can live with that."

In short order, the three prepared to leave, picking out loose clothing for the heat, as well as face masks and sun goggles.

"Why don't we wear our armors?" Freya asked as she slipped her plasma sabers into their holsters strapped to her thighs.

"The same reason we're not carrying those," Robin answered, opening a compartment. Reaching in, he pulled out a double-barreled stacked blaster pistol with a rounded back. Ejecting the power magazine, he checked the levels before strapping on the gun belt. "They're too unique," he explained, buckling the holsters to his thighs. "They'd make us stand out like sore thumbs and rather easy to identify later. It's better to wait until we don't have a choice." At the end of his explanation, she nodded.

Soon, dressed appropriately and with food and water slung over their shoulders, the trio walked away from the oasis and into the desert beyond. The robes and loose clothing they wore swished in the breeze.

For hours they walked, keeping a steady pace. As night began to fall, the three flattened themselves against a dune and peeked over the edge at the small cluster of tents that made up the camp less than half a mile away.

Robin eyed the thick-necked, stiff-maned, horse-like animals, as well as the few sky riders parked at the edge of the camp. Glancing over at LJ and Freya on either side of him, he signaled, and they all shuffled back.

"What do you think?" LJ asked when they were at the bottom of the dune.

"I'm thinking I like those sky riders," Robin answered.

"And I'm thinking they could be Raiders," his friend countered.

"Raiders?" Freya asked.

"Basically, they're like pirates, or scavengers," Robin explained with a sigh.

"You mean they're from Tortuga?"

He shook his head. "Tortuga may be where most pirates are based, but that doesn't mean they all are."

"So, what's the plan for getting those riders?" LJ asked.

"For starters, we wait for the cover of night," Robin answered.

"Do we really have to steal from them?" Freya asked.

Little John looked at her and jabbed a thumb over his shoulder. "How do you think they got them?"

Shortly after dark, which was hardly different from the noon day sun for Robin with his eyes night vision, he and John lay low as they crept near the edge of the dune again. Peering over, they saw two sentries near them as they patrolled.

Drawing back, the pair sent hand signals with rapid movements, and then Little John nodded before they crept to the top again.

The pair watched the sentries move closer to them before they paused not far from the edge, their eyes straining to pierce the surrounding darkness. When the sentries turned back to the camp, they made their move.

In a flash of movement, Robin's hand covered the man's mouth while Robin's other arm wrapped around the man's neck to choke him out. Twisting, he kicked the man's legs out from under him, so all of his weight put pressure on his neck.

When the man went still, Robin dropped him to the ground. When he glanced over, he saw Little John paralyzing the other sentry's voice with a strike to his throat before boxing his ears and delivering a knockout blow to the temple. Breathing hard, LJ turned to him.

"Still brawn over brains, eh?" Robin said as they dragged the sentries over the dune by their ankles and sent them rolling down the slope.

After collecting Freya, the three moved forward through the camp with Little John covering the rear.

When they reached the riders, Robin and LJ checked them over.

"These puppies will seriously burn air," he said with a grin.

"Yeah, if we can get them started." Robin stared down at the lock on the ignition.

"Great," LJ groaned.

Robin eyed the locks for a second before he rolled up his sleeve, exposing his bracelet.

"What are you doing?" John asked.

As if in answer, thin tendril cords extended from the bracelet before attaching themselves to the lock and the section of the sky rider around it. Less than a second later, the rider's instruments lit up.

Smiling behind the cloth that masked his face, Robin turned back to the others. "Nothing like a little hot wiring," he said, swinging his leg over and slipping on and activating a helmet. "Get on," he said, looking at Freya. "As for you, if you're going to use that thing, use it.".

For a second, LJ looked at him with a puzzled look, and then they froze when the sound of a charging weapon met their ears. Both Robin and Freya, now also on the rider, slowly turned to look at the young teen pointing a rifle at them.

"Kid, put that down—it's not a toy," Robin said, masking his voice by making it deep and rough. "Now, put it away before you hurt yourself. We're just borrowing them—we'll do our best to bring them back in one piece."

The teen glared at them. "If you think I'm—" He was interrupted as the knife Robin shifted from its place in his sleeve hurtled through the air, knocking the rifle to the ground.

"Do you really want to do that?" Robin hissed when the kid reached for his fallen weapon. For a second, he hesitated as he eyed them before slowly stepping back. "Just tell them the truth," Robin said as he and LJ started the engines. "Tell them we disarmed you," he continued as LJ shot off into the night, "and that Robin Hood needed to borrow this." After gunning, the sky rider shot off after LJ, his and Freya's robes flapping through the air behind them.

The Hunt

AS THE SUN began to rise over the horizon, LJ looked over at Robin and Freya as he drew close on his rider, the dawn light reflecting off his helmet.

"What was it you said to that boy?" he asked over the helmet comms.

For a couple seconds, they rode over the desert in silence before Robin answered, "What was bound to be said sooner or later."

"If we do what we set out to do, we will spread through the stars like a burning nebula." Looking back out at the desert, he sighed. "So, any idea how we'll find your brother?"

Robin thought of the best way to answer. "I guess the same way we found Freya: by following my instincts." He gunned his engines, speeding ahead into the sunrise.

When they stopped around mid-morning to let the engines cool a bit, they drank from their limited water supply.

"So, how are the instincts?" LJ asked as Robin scanned the endless sea of sand.

Sighing, he shook his head when he still felt nothing. "Not as strong as I'd hoped," Robin admitted. "It was so easy back on Tortuga."

"And now we're just minnows in a sea of sand," Freya murmured as she fingered her toothed necklace. Robin nodded and then saw a light flicker on in her eye. "Maybe we can recreate…"

"What we did there," he finished, seeing where she was going. Reaching under his robes, he pulled his tooth necklace out.

"Come on!" he muttered under his breath as he focused, willing it to show the way.

His tooth necklace jerked in his grip. Glancing down, he opened his hand, and what he saw made him blink in surprise. The tooth dangling from the necklace lifted from his palm, spinning in a circle as it rose in the air. Faster and faster it spun, like a dancing compass. It came to a sudden stop, then, pointing right into the desert.

"Well, that settles it for me," LJ said with a nod. Climbing back on the sky riders, they tore off in the direction the necklace had indicated.

Hours later, the group stood on the edge of a cliff looking down at a walled city built on a small rise. Around the center and the edge, tall, round buildings had been built with smaller buildings in their shadows. They were surrounded by large, interconnected pipes that made up their aqueduct system, most of which was built above the city. Some pipes even wrapped around the tall towers. From the large gate, a sea of tents stretched out.

"What do you think?" Little John asked, lowering his digital binoculars.

"Right now, I'm just glad it's not a space port," Robin answered, down on one knee as he eyed the city. His sight seemed to zoom in when he focused like he imagined happened to birds of prey. "It seems quite active down there." He stood straight.

"Must be a trade city," LJ commented.

"That would explain all the goods I saw down there," Freya muttered. "Did you see any slavers?"

Robin glanced at her. "No," he said. "Is that good or bad for you?"

She glanced at him, a glint of steel in her eye. Sighing, he nodded.

"That's what I thought."

"Are you two getting any vibes from that place?" Little John asked, looking at the pair.

Robin took his toothed necklace in his hand along with his medallion. "Well, either way, that's where we've been led," he said when the tooth pointed at the city.

"So, what's the plan on getting in there?"

Sighing, Robin rubbed his chin. "Well...there's always the direct approach."

At once, the others looked at him. "Are you crazy?" LJ demanded. "You want us to walk through the front door? We've been trained to sneak in..."

"And risk being caught or found out and have them hunting us, as well," Robin explained. "It's better for now they think we're simple desert people."

For a few seconds, the pair just looked at him. "On sky riders?" LJ asked, jabbing his thumb over his shoulder at their rides.

Robin shrugged. "Hey, not all desert people ride animals," he said. "Besides, we'll need them for a quick exit."

LJ held his gaze before glancing away in thought. "I guess you have a point. What if we need a *really* fast exit?"

Robin thought for a second before he uncovered his bracelet. "Willa, can you hear us?" he asked, tapping the crystal.

"WILL YOU STOP THAT? I'M GETTING A HEADACHE!" her voice shouted in his head, causing him to cringe.

"I'll take that as a yes," he said openly while LJ and Freya frowned in confusion, "though I'm not so sure you had to shout."

"Well, what do you expect when it feels like someone is ringing a gong in my head?" she snapped in return. "Do you think you can stop doing that?"

"I thought you'd be more surprised that this thing can act as a commlink," he murmured.

"Not really, since we used it when you left to get Freya but could never raise you," she said.

316

His eyebrows arched in surprise that he hadn't thought of it sooner. Robin murmured, "Probably because it was busy disarming the millions of little nanites that were injected into me."

"That explains it. So, what do you need?" Willa asked.

"We're outside a small city and may need a fast exit, so be ready to come get us."

"Gotcha," she replied. "How hot could it be? Are we talking boiling or volcanic?"

"Truthfully, it has the potential to be nova," he answered solemnly, turning back toward the city, remembering all the sentinels he had seen on the streets.

Old and New Friends

IN SHORT ORDER, the group had made it to the large gathering of tent dwellings. As they peeked out at the main gate, their faces hardened in frustration at the sight of eight guards on either side of it.

"Why the heck would they quadruple the guards in the time it took us to get down here?" Robin hissed as they drew back.

"Maybe we should take it as a compliment," LJ suggested. Robin looked at him, half-heartedly agreeing.

"Maybe it has something to do with that," Freya said and pointed.

They gaped at the large caravan moving toward the city made of both people riding mounts and vehicles.

The grandest was a large, hovering litter with four silver, elegant pillars intricately carved with gold holding up closed silk curtains. It was being driven by a team of four of the horse-like creatures they'd seen at the Raiders' encampment.

The people they saw were dressed like the three of them in flowing robes that shifted with their movements and the desert breeze, as well as headscarves which protected most of their faces from the sun. Most, from what Robin could see, at least, were armed with rifles slung over their shoulders.

"That just might be our way in," Robin said, a smile on his face. "That is, if we can mingle in and pass as one of them. Let's circle around and come up behind them." Again, they climbed back on their riders and pulled a tight one-eighty.

Once they were out of sight of the city, Robin and LJ turned in the direction of the caravan. When they found the tracks of the animals some members of the caravan rode, they followed them back toward the city. Soon enough, the caravan came into sight, and when they drew close, the pair slowed to match the speed of a couple riders on the sides of the caravan.

To be even less noticeable, the three deactivated their helmets.

Robin paused when the air hit his covered face.

"What's wrong?" Freya asked when she felt him tense.

Not answering, he lifted one hand from the handlebar to the lower part of the fabric covering his face to expose his nose. He then took in a deep sniff of air.

Slowly, he turned to the litter, eyes wide in surprise. "It can't be," he murmured. "What are the friggin' odds?" Before they could stop him, he moved his rider to the side.

"Robin, what the heck are you doing?" Freya hissed as he moved toward the litter.

When he drew close, he said, "How was your journey, Milady?"

There was a brief pause. "How do you think?" a soft voice finally answered.

A grin grew on his face. "It's nice to see you off Anduria."

Again there was a pause, and then a hand suddenly appeared and whipped the curtain open. "Who are you?" Marian demanded, eyeing him.

In answer, Robin lifted the tinted goggles from his eyes before he lowered the cloth wrapped around the lower half of his face.

To say the look on her face was of shock was like saying the desert sand was dry. Her eyes grew so big that Robin was worried they were going to pop out of their sockets.

"Princess Marian?" a familiar voice said.

She turned as Robin replaced the cloth over his face.

"Is this man bothering you?" the voice asked. Robin saw it belonged to Alan.

"No," she quickly answered. "It's hot out, and I want him and his patrol to join me on the litter for now."

"But Princess..." Alan started to protest.

"Now!" she snapped and withdrew behind the curtain.

Without looking at Alan, Robin moved back to LJ. "We're getting a ride," he murmured, and his friend glanced at him. "While we're on it, call me Ryuu."

In no time, the three were seated on the litter designed like a giant bed or sofa with various sized pillows and cushions to lounge on. Almost as soon as he was seated, Robin was enveloped in Marian's arms, and she held him tight.

"I was so worried about you, Ryuu," she said into his ear.

"Nice to know," he said, raising his goggles and lowering the cloth again.

"Why wouldn't I be?" Marian asked, sitting back on the cushions around them and fingering her necklace. "The last I saw of you, you were chained to the wall of a ship like a dog."

"Well, that's how he treated people like me."

"Uh, excuse me?"

They looked at LJ as he raised his goggles and lowered the cloth covering his face, as well. "Could one of you tell me what the heck is going on?" he asked, looking from one to the other. "Ryuu, how do you know her? Who is she?"

"Do you want it answered in that order?" Robin asked, a slight grin on his face. Little John shot him an exasperated look, eyebrows arched high.

"Okay," Robin said, his grin growing. "I know her because she bought me." Blinking, LJ looked at her. "As for who she is," Robin continued, "she is Marian, one of the last princesses of the non-magical thrones." Again, LJ blinked, looking at Robin before his gaze shifted back to Marian.

"Marian," he continued, and she looked at him, "this is Bryan, a very old friend." He waved his hand toward LJ.

"Nice to meet you," Marian said with a nod.

"Likewise," a still-stunned Little John said, pausing. "Do I call you Your Majesty? Your Highness? Should I bow?"

"Marian would be fine," she reassured him with a smile before she turned to Freya. "And you?"

She turned her covered face to the princess. "I'm—"

"A friend," Robin interrupted before she could finish, and Marian looked at him. "She's a friend we recently picked up."

"I see," the princess said, eyeing the fabric over Freya's face. "I am curious." She looked at Robin. "How in the name of the Gold Dragon did you escape?"

Thinking fast, Robin shrugged at her question. "Hey, let's say it took a lot of digging."

She blinked, surprised. "And the nanites?"

"It took some time, but an improvised EMP device later, they were no more," he explained, and again she blinked in surprise. "After that, I linked back up with Bryan and my other friends, and we made our way to Tortuga. The rest, as they say, is history."

Lowering her gaze, Marian nodded. "I can't say how happy I am to now know you escaped," she said, looking up at him, "and I'm sorry about your sister."

Frowning, Robin's mouth parted slightly in worry. "Freya?" he asked. "What about Freya?"

She took a breath to steady herself. "I tried my best to barter for her and Tekmet to join me on Anduria, but I was told they and two others had been executed in an escape attempt," she said with sorrow. Robin fell back against the cushioned seating, his face slack in shock.

"I am so sorry."

Slowly, he looked at her. "Thank you for telling me," he said softly, his voice full of grief.

She nodded. "Now, what are you doing here? Why aren't you on Tortuga?"

Running a hand down his face, he looked back at her. "Because I'm looking for my brother."

Her head jutted back in disbelief. "Well, this day has no end to surprises."

Robin shrugged. "That's what happens with triplets. Now, why are you here?"

She shrugged with a wave of her hand. "I try to make visits to these backwater worlds. If the people get hope from seeing me, then I'll do it—maybe even bring them to a better place, if I can."

"Like Anduria?" he asked.

"I guess so," she agreed, looking away. "The last Dragon Knight died to keep my family safe. I guess it's my way of proving myself worthy of that sacrifice from such a brave man, like many of my ancestors have done before me. No matter how small, it always helps to see the grateful look in their eyes." She looked at them again.

"No wonder you spoiled those kids rotten at that replica of your ancient family home," Robin said, and she glanced his way, "or insisted I spoil them when you couldn't."

"I never insisted," Marian protested.

"Uh, excuse me?" They all looked at Freya's hidden face. "Don't we have more immediate things to worry about?"

"Right," Marian said, nodding. "But why did you come to me—and how did you know it was me?"

"Well, we need your help," Robin answered, "getting into the city." She lowered her gaze in thought as he peeked out the curtain. "And as for knowing it was you," he continued, looking at her again, "no two people smell the same."

Promises

AFTER MARIAN AND Robin had enough time to sort out a plan of action, Robin and LJ once more masked their faces and got back on their riders, taking up a defensive position around the litter. Freya rode behind LJ.

When they reached the gate, Robin held his breath as the guards questioned the caravan leader, relaxing only when they were waved through. When they were all inside the giant doorway, the three moved once more toward the litter.

"You have to leave again?" Marian asked, drawing back the curtain to look at them. "Once more we have to part."

Robin smiled, lowering the fabric covering the lower part of his face. "At least now one of us doesn't have to be carried away in chains," he said, and she cocked a grin.

"Do you think we'll get lucky enough to run into each other again?" she asked. "Somewhere out there, among the stars?"

He grinned back. "Keep those French doors in your rooms unlocked and I might find a way to drop in," he said with a slight nod. Robin then looked at his companions and lifted one hand over his head with a circular motion. After gunning the engines, the three turned into the city down a side road, away from the convoy.

Stopping at a corner, Robin turned in his seat and glanced back toward the caravan. The litter's curtains remained closed as it continued on its way. When it disappeared from his sight, he revved the engine and shot down the street to catch up with the others.

When he reached them, they sat idly, LJ looking at him with his elbow propped on the handlebars. Though his face was covered, Robin was willing to bet he had a wise guy grin across his face. When he looked at Freya, he wasn't sure what would be behind her cover.

"What?" he finally asked.

Slowly, Freya turned her back to him. She then hugged herself, hands going up and down her sides.

"Oh, Ryuu," she started to moan. "Oh, Marian..." she moaned again, deepening her voice, while LJ roared with laughter. "Oh, keep those French doors unlocked...I might find a way to drop in..."

Trying not to laugh, but exasperated, he shook his head, looking away from them. "Okay, that's enough." he looked back at them, "and you are a bad influence on my sister." He jabbed a finger at LJ as Freya turned, laughing.

Little John shook his head. "Robin, she's beautiful, rich, has the right name, and she's a princess," he counted off. "Don't you think your standards are just a little high?"

Chuckling, Robin shook his head. "There is nothing going on between me and her," he protested.

"Right," LJ said over the comms, "and that glint in your eye when you were looking at her was a reflection of the sun."

Rolling his eyes, Robin gave his friend a shove, sending him off his rider and onto the ground. Still laughing, he sped away.

Ask for a Thief

WHEN FREYA AND Little John caught up, Robin's eyes were on a swivel behind his goggles as he scanned the crowd, many of whom were dressed like the three of them. More than that, though, there were sentinels on every street and corner.

"The phrase *needle in a haystack* comes to mind," LJ said over the comms. "And what's with all the sentinels?"

"Good question," Robin said, pulling his rider to a stop. "Looks like they're looking for someone," he said when he saw them asking people to uncover their faces.

"That means Freya had better stay out of sight," LJ said. "After all, she's supposed to be dead."

He nodded in agreement. "Freya," he said, looking at her, "you stick close to John and keep out of sight."

She quickly responded, "And what's your plan for finding our brother before then?"

"Hopefully, the same way I found you," he answered, looking around again. "Is it just me or are the sentinels more interested in the covered women?" as they watched the sentinels practically ignore the men they encountered.

"So, more than likely, they're looking for a woman," LJ muttered, "or a very small man."

"Yeah." Robin glanced over at the sound of a group of people moving. "I don't think he has to worry about that."

They all turned and nearly busted a gut at the sight of a fat man in regal robes and a headdress. He walked down the street followed by several people. A few carried bags for whatever he pointed at, whether food or objects; others carried a small tent to keep him out of the sun.

"You think he runs the show here?" LJ asked.

"I think he wishes he did."

Suddenly, Robin saw a small child dressed in rags nearly falling off his body. With a hungry look in his eye, he reached into one of the food bags.

"THIEF!" the fat man barked, seizing the boy's arm. "How dare you steal from me? I will see you in prison!" the robed man shouted, shaking the child as he cowered under the man's fury. Face hardening, Robin slowly turned to the man.

"What are you doing?" Little John demanded.

Before he could answer, a feeling came over Robin—the same feeling he felt when he first met Freya.

As he looked at her, he saw her grow still as she started glancing around. Her eyes finally came to a stop on a person who had started toward the large man in robes—and who had stopped in his tracks to look right at them. He was dressed like them with his face completely covered. Robin guessed that, if they were standing side by side, they would be the same height.

Slowly, he turned his back to them and walked to the man. "Tell me, do you have children?" he asked in a strong, deep voice.

The man in robes turned to the figure. "What?" he demanded.

"I say any man who would refuse food to a starving child deserves none of his own!" he snarled, slapping the hand of the man to make him let go of the boy.

"HOW DARE YOU?" the man bellowed, forgetting about the boy as he darted away.

"Ask for a thief," the figure said.

"And you shall receive one!" Robin barked on cue as he sped close on his rider. As he passed, he stretched out one hand and snatched a bag of food from one of the men.

In a flash, he was out of there, the man shouting an alarm as he went. After rounding the corner, he came to a skidding stop at the sight of all the sentinels turning their weapons on him.

"Other way, other way!" he told himself, leaning the rider in a loop as he pressed the activation of the helmet ring around his neck and his head.

As he shot in the other direction, he rolled right-side up, dodging fire from the sentinels' weapons as he went. He turned another corner and as he sped down the street he spied a group of children like the boy in ragged clothing. He tossed the bag of food at their feet as he passed them.

"A gift from Robin Hood!" he called.

In the rear-view camera on his helmet, he watched the children snatch the bag and duck out of sight. Smiling, he looked up as he took another turn. His smile suddenly dropped away, however, at the sight of four sentinels taking aim at him.

Turning the rider, he skidded toward them, drawing his blaster, and opened fire. At once, two sentinels fell with shots to the head as they fired on him, hitting the rider where he had been. Leaping from the machine, Robin rolled across the ground as the sky rider collided with the sentinels and exploded.

After coming to a rolling stop, Robin moaned, pulling off his helmet. "I'm going to need a new ride," he said, rolling onto his back and coming face to face with the sentinel's cannon. Glancing around, he saw his blaster three feet away.

"You have been deemed hazardous," the sentinel said as he reached for the blaster. "Surrender or be terminated."

At a whining charging sound, he rolled and the blaster cannon fired, leaving a small crater where his head had been.

When he came to a stop, his blaster was several feet out of reach. Focusing, he reached for the weapon, willing it to shoot into his hand, but it remained motionless on the ground. Again, the sentinel turned his cannon on him. Remembering what Freya told him, he reached for the blaster as he focused on it.

The weapon gave a small twitch and then shot forward, into his hand. In a flash, he leveled the weapon and fired, leaving a hole in the middle of the sentinel's head. For a second, the sentinel just stood there; then, with a groan of metal, it toppled back, coming to a crashing stop against the ground.

Exhaling deeply, Robin's eyes shot to his hand holding the blaster. "I guess being a knight isn't the only thing that runs in the family," he muttered before climbing to his feet and darting down a side alley.

Holstering the weapon, he rested against the wall of the alley.

"Not bad," he suddenly heard someone say.

Adam

AT THOSE WORDS, Robin whipped around, pulling out the blaster pistol at his side. Taking aim down the alley, he eyed a silhouetted figure dressed smartly in loose clothing that billowed lightly in the wind.

"That's not going to do you much good," the figure said.

"Why not? I'm a pretty good shot," Robin countered.

"I'm not talking about me," said the figure, lifting one hand to point.

Glancing over his shoulder, Robin froze at the line of sentinels coming toward them. "I see your point!" Robin barked, darting toward the figure as the sentinels raised their arms and cannons popped up. As the pair rounded the corner, the machines opened fire.

"This way!" the man said, leading him to a manhole cover. "Get in!" he barked after lifting it up.

Without a word, Robin jumped in, arms crossed over his chest, and landed on a cobblestone platform that came to a sharp drop into what looked like a small river below. Glancing around, he eyed the old stone walls that curved up and around him.

The figure jumped in after him, still holding the manhole over his head, and then putting it back in place. "Let's go!" he said, grabbing Robin by the arm and leading him down the sewer.

"What is this place?" Robin asked as they darted around a bend. "I would have thought you'd have figured that out."

"I did—I was just hoping I was wrong," Robin replied. "The smell is certainly enough to knock me out for the count." He was doing his best to breathe through his mouth and not his nose.

They came to a skidding stop. A dead end of sand piled high with protruding stones loomed before them.

"I am sure you know this place better than I do, but I hope this is part of your plan," Robin said, turning to look back the way they came.

"Always," the figure said, and Robin glanced back to see him press his hand against a stone in the wall.

At once, the sand parted as a double door concealed under it opened. "Not bad," Robin said, and when they darted inside, the doors sealed behind them.

Breathing deeply, Robin looked back at the doors in the darkness before looking at the figure, who eyed him in the dark.

Robin took in the lean, muscular frame he could see under his robed clothing. Like him, he seemed barely winded after the escape they made.

"Follow me," the figure said and moved past him down the tunnel.

"Don't need a light?" Robin asked, turning to follow him.

"No more than you do, I suspect."

"You're sharp," Robin murmured under his breath.

"And I have good hearing," the figure piped up.

"Good to know. Got a name?"

"Adam," he answered.

"Robin. Nice to meet you."

"I'll save my greetings until we're safe," Adam said, turning to look at him, "and I know I can trust you."

Paranoid? Robin thought as he eyed Adam's back.

For the next thirty minutes, the pair walked down the tunnel, which wound this way and that like a corkscrew. Finally, Robin could make out a pinprick of light at the end of the tunnel. It grew larger and larger as they continued until they emerged into the sandy-floored tunnel.

After going down it, they came to a large metal door with an embedded lever. Grabbing the lever, Adam's fingers flew across the keypad next to it in a flash—so fast Robin barely caught the combination.

With a hiss, the door unsealed itself. Adam pulled the lever, and there was another hiss as the second seal was broken.

He eyed the large space beyond the door with crates piled one on top of the other. Some stacks went all the way to the ceiling; some barely made it above his waist.

As he turned in a circle, he caught sight of strung-up hammocks, a couple of discarded toys, and old-looking computer emitters.

"Not bad at all," Robin continued, looking at Adam as he closed the door behind him.

He was not surprised when a few dozen people of various ages, some quite young, popped out of various hiding positions, all training weapons on him.

"Now, I have some questions, and you're going to answer them," Adam said, reaching to start unraveling his head scarf.

Robin watched, mouth parting slightly, as more of Adam's face was revealed. A flow of long, black hair fell down to Adam's shoulders. The last thing he removed was his tinted goggles, and as he turned his head with the quick movement, Robin caught sight of three pointed ears.

For a solid second, all Robin could do was stare at what was almost a mirror image of his face with minor details making the difference.

"Now, who are you?" Adam demanded.

Giving himself a slight shake, Robin said, "You might not believe me."

In answer, Adam snatched a rifle from a girl next to him. Putting it to his shoulder, he took aim at him. "Try me," he growled. Sighing, Robin reached for his goggles. "Slowly," Adam warned.

Robin slowly pulled his goggles off and saw Adam's eyes narrow. Just as slowly, he uncovered his face. The rifle in the other man's arms dropped a little in surprise as he looked into Robin's eyes, which were shifting colors the same as his.

"Would you believe me if I said I'm your brother?" Robin asked.

Wanted

THE RIFLE ADAM held dropped to his side as his eyes moved up and down Robin as if, he was unwilling to believe what they were telling him was right before him.

"You have my attention," he said, powering down the weapon and handing it back to the girl as he signaled for the rest to stand down.

"I hope she knows that's not a toy," Robin muttered, watching the kid move away while the rest lowered their weapons and moved off. "What is this place?" he asked, looking around at the lit-up cave walls.

"This used to be part of the main underground river," Adam answered.

Robin blinked in surprise as he glanced at Adam's back. "What happened to it?" he asked, wondering what would have caused the river to dry up. But he only met the sound of silence. "So, was it you they were looking for out there?"

Adam shrugged. "Maybe once upon a time. After all, I've had to steal for every meal."

Robin followed him as Adam slipped off his robe, exposing a sleeveless shirt. A strip of cloth covered one wrist, and a tattoo over his shoulder caught Robin's eye. It was a burning skull missing a jaw bone with the sharp ends of what he guessed was a trinity poking out the top corners and center bottom, all surrounded by a fire-red background with gold framing.

"You're a Raider," Robin said, and the other man looked at him. "That group out in the desert is with you?" Adam held his gaze for a second before he turned. "Why aren't you with them?" Robin asked, making him turn back to face him.

"Because I wouldn't leave them." He nodded to the people behind them. "Besides, they might be glad to get away from me for a while," he said as he continued on.

After blinking in surprise, Robin followed, catching up to him again near the disembodied head of a sentinel perched on a crate.

Again, Robin took him by the arm to turn him. "Why?" he demanded. "From what I know of Raiders, they don't leave their own behind!"

"We don't," Adam said. "We wouldn't even leave our dead behind."

"Then why did they leave you?"

Adam was silent before he explained, "They wanted a break from me." Robin frowned in confusion. "They call me their lucky charm."

"Wouldn't that mean they *would* want you around?"

Sighing, Adam looked away. "Let's just say, a lucky charm isn't always a good thing...at least, not in my case."

Before Robin could respond, he activated the computer and a woman's face appeared. Lost for words, he stared in awe. She had long, fiery red hair, high cheekbones, a strong jawline, and slanted eyebrows. Above her narrow lips was a dainty nose.

"Who is she?" Robin asked.

"We don't know," Adam answered, arms crossed. "All we know is the Black Dragon wants her. Since a report that she's been sighted here, the Black Dragon's forces have been coming in droves." Robin looked at him. "The Black Dragon wants her almost as much as the leader of the Resistance."

"Yeah, and nobody knows what he looks like," Robin muttered.

"Rumor has it he's a Dragon Knight," Adam said, and Robin's gaze shot to him, "but then again, rumors also say he's the Gold Dragon reborn. So, who can say what's true and what's not about him?"

Robin shrugged in agreement. "One of the main reasons he's still alive, probably," he commented, "is because no one really knows anything about him." Adam nodded, and Robin looked away. "But I know one thing about you."

Frowning, the other man looked at him. "What?"

Robin turned to face him. "You are a Dragon Knight."

Water Rustler

ADAM BLINKED. "WHAT?" he asked with a deepening frown. "What makes you say that?"

Before he could stop him, Robin seized his covered wrist. At once, Adam yanked it back, tearing a piece of the cloth. Robin's other hand shot out to grab it, but Adam caught him below the wrist.

They locked eyes for a second before Robin reached up and moved the cloth covering his own bracelet. Adam froze at the sight of it, and at once the spark of recognition appeared in his eye before he met Robin's gaze once more.

"Because we both have one of these," Robin answered, before glancing down and spying the other man's weapon engravings on his bracelet similar to his own.

After looking at each other for a second, they lowered their arms and relaxed. "What do you want?" Adam asked.

Robin eyed the kids, who shot him glances. Some practiced disassembling and reassembling their weapons while a few of the older teens stuck close to each other with looks of affection. All around them, kids ran around, laughing like kids should.

Taking Adam by the arm, they walked a short distance away.

"Right now, I need to hook up with some people I know. Is there anywhere nearby where you would feel safe meeting them?"

Adam frowned. "Why would I want to meet them?"

"Because we came a long way to find you," he answered. "We deserve to at least meet with you."

For a second, Adam was silent. "Val!" he called out, and a second later, a teenage boy arrived. "I have to go back out," he snapped with complete authority as he slipped on a hooded cape. "You're in charge until I get back." The teen nodded as Adam covered his face as before. "Follow me," he said, leading Robin into the caverns again.

Once they were above ground, Robin's face was covered with a different head scarf and shades instead of goggles. The pair walked through the streets as they eyed the sentinels still patrolling. He guessed they were looking for them.

"So, how many people live here for them to build those?" he asked, jabbing a thumb at one of the towers that caught his eye.

"Not as many as you'd think," Adam answered, not looking up as he walked. "People don't live there—they are water towers."

Blinking, Robin looked back at them. "Then you guys won't be running out of water any time soon," he said. "How did you find enough to fill them?"

"They are constantly being filled by what's left of the underground river," he said, looking at him before drawing close, "which carved out the tunnels we were just in." The two continued on. "Once that river spanned far and wide, and it used to be one of the many places in the city where people could collect water." He then nodded toward a grand, dried-up fountain. "Then Savic came and built his towers, and the river dried. Now, the only way to get water is by paying him."

Robin gasped at this. "Did he divert the river?" he asked, looking at his brother.

Adam nodded. "By the time these people found out what was going on, it was too late," he said, pausing at a corner to glance around it.

"And who is this *Savic*?" Robin asked.

337

"Remember that man you stole from earlier?"

Face hardening, Robin nodded as they walked around the corner. "Now I have a reason for us to meet again. Is that why the Raiders are here?"

"In some aspects," Adam said. "There's nothing like robbing a thief."

"And you were sent in to find where he keeps his money?" Again, Adam nodded. "Then what were you doing with all those kids?"

"Surviving," his brother said simply before entering a building.

Following him inside, Robin saw it was a saloon with a circular, lit bar in the center of the room surrounded by people seated on stools being served their drinks. Around the room, booths built into the walls with small tables were scattered here and there. On the far side, an empty dance floor was set up, with a band stand in front of it.

"You can tell your friends to meet us here," Adam said, walking down the small flight of stairs and passing the bar, where a slumped figure sat.

"We're already here," the figure said aloud, turning and grabbing Adam by the shoulder and pressing a pistol into his side.

Coming Together

ROBIN HISSED, shoving the blaster down, "LJ do you mind not pointing a gun at my brother?"

Sighing, Little John holstered his weapon. "How was I supposed to know this was him?" he said, embracing Robin. "Will you stop taking off like that?" he snapped, giving him a light shove.

"I always come back," Robin replied, glancing around. "Where's Freya?"

"In that booth," LJ led them over, "and it was she who got us here before you two." Freya sat waiting for them, her face still covered.

"Let me guess, by smelling me out," Robin said with a laugh and sat next to her.

"Something like that," she said as he lowered his face covering and removed his shades.

"Freya, Little John, this is Adam." Robin waved his hand as his brother removed his face covering. At the sight of his face, LJ gaped and Freya gasped at the likeness. "Adam, this is one of my best friends, Little John, or LJ." Freya started removing her goggles. With his eyes on Adam, Robin watched the surprise grow on his face. "I think it goes without saying," he continued, "that this is our sister." Freya nodded in greeting.

"You certainly look like each other," LJ said, nodding, before he looked at Robin again. "Is he," he started to ask, discreetly tapping his covered bracelet. Robin nodded. "Whoa," Little John said. "I guess it does run in the family with you guys. Looks we got them all now."

Lowering his gaze, Robin murmured, "Let's hope so," and they all looked at him. "Hey, some stories say the Knights were between eight and ten in number, so until we know for sure, we keep an open mind."

"So, what's the plan for getting off this planet?" LJ asked, leaning back in his booth seat.

"I'm not going anywhere," Adam snapped quickly. "Not without those kids."

For a second, they just looked at him before Robin moaned, his face going to his hand.

"Adam, you just made things really complicated," he said, rubbing his face.

"Wait," Freya said. "You're not saying he's a..." She raised her eyebrows.

He shook his head. "No, they're street kids he gathered under his protection," he clarified. After glancing around, he exposed his bracelet. "Willa, can you hear me?"

"Loud and clear, Robin," she replied. "What is it?"

"We found my brother."

"Great!" she said. "Great job! Now, when do we get the heck out of here? The heat is brutal."

"That depends on one thing," Robin answered.

"What?"

After sighing, he took a deep breath, bracing himself. "How many people can the *Odysseus* hold?"

In short order, the group was back down in Adam's hideout with the group of kids before them.

"So, where are we to go?" Val asked, arms crossed over his chest.

"We have a ship out in the desert," Robin answered. "Once we are all loaded, we will leave for Tortuga, where we will be safe."

340

"How can we be safer there than here?" a teenage girl with long, blonde hair asked.

"Because it's hidden," LJ answered, stepping forward, "and you will be defended better there."

The kids and teens murmured to each other.

"The choice is yours," Robin said, stepping forward, "but if you decide to stay, here is what will happen. Sooner or later, you will be found. They will throw themselves at the door, and it will hold, and you will fight them." Some of them nodded smugly. "But then the day will come when it will fail and, like a sandstorm, they will come. Most, if not all, of you will die trying to stop them, and those who are captured will wish they had." When he was done, virtually all the smug looks had faded away.

"If you decide to come with us, though, you will have a better chance of survival. It won't be just us looking after you—it will be a small army, and one day, we will find our way to the Resistance. With the Resistance will come the protection of the new generation of Dragon Knights!" he declared. Everyone stared at him before some laughed.

"The Dragon Knights?" one laughing teen asked. "What makes you so sure they've returned?"

Robin looked at Freya with a silent question. He turned to hold LJ's gaze and again received a nod. Breathing deeply, he faced the small crowd before him, clenching the hand donning his bracelet into a fist.

With the sound of metal on metal, his armor expanded. One by one, each kid stopped laughing and their eyes went wide in surprise and wonder. There was a ripping sound, and the loose desert clothing he wore dropped away in tatters; as his helmet began to encase his head and face, he slipped off his turban and face covering.

When the screen before his face activated, he looked at them all.

"Any questions?" he asked and was met with silence.

The Ice Raider

ROBIN STILL IN his armor said "We're probably going to need help," his helmet began to retract. Around him, people still glanced in wonder as they packed, readying themselves to leave.

"Why?" LJ asked, shrugging. "It's simple enough to get them out of the city: We take them out in groups with one of—" He was silenced by an alarm going off.

At once, the group rushed to where Adam had set up the sentinel's head. "What is it?" Freya asked as he turned it on and they read the data being fed to it.

"Remember that woman?" Adam asked, looking at Robin, who nodded. "Well, a strong possible sighting has been reported." He looked at them each in turn. "A small army is on the way."

Sighing, Robin looked at Freya and Little John. "Okay. We're going to need help," LJ admitted.

Adam lowered his gaze. "I might know who to ask."

With the lights dimmed and his helmet extended, Robin watched as Adam pulled up a holo comms channel, which he was trying to project between two rods. "So, who is this again?" he asked.

"They call him the Ice Raider," Adam answered. "He's one of the most revered and respected leaders the Raiders have ever had. Before he came, they were a disorganized, divided clan of thieves, stealing from anyone weaker than themselves. Then he came and united us—made us live by a code to be more than what we were," he continued.

"You sound like you admire him," he commented.

Adam looked at his brother. "I should," he answered. "When my parents were killed by the Black Dragon's forces, he took me in and raised me." He turned back to the comm unit.

"Who is he?" LJ asked, now in his armor.

"He is simply known," Adam said, glancing at him, "as the Ice Raider." Static came over the line then and the picture turned fuzzy. "Blue Ice calling Ice Raider. Come in, Ice Raider," he called in to the picture. There was no answer. "Blue Ice calling Ice Raider. Come in, Ice Raider," Adam repeated.

There was flicker, and then a face appeared on the holo screen. Its light blue eyes gazed out at them from skin that seemed to be made of blueish-clear ice that reflected the light of the room it was in. The creature's earless and hairless head swept back with the curve of its forehead, and it had a strong, angled jawline.

A Chillania on a desert section of a planet, Robin thought. Hope he doesn't melt.

"Blue Ice, this is the Ice Raider," the creature said in a surprisingly deep voice. "Good to see and hear from you, my boy." "It's good to see you, too, sir," Adam said.

"Did you find Savic's stash yet?" the Ice Raider asked.

"No, sir," Adam replied and, if it were possible, the Ice Raider's face hardened, "but I just learned the Black Dragon's forces are moving on the city—"

"Then I suggest you get out of there while you can," the Ice Raider interrupted him.

"I am, sir. It's just that there are people here who need help getting out, as well."

"We don't have time for that, my boy," the Ice Raider replied. "If the Black Dragon's forces are marching in, as you say, we have to get off this planet and fast."

"If you don't help, these kids are probably going to die," Robin said from behind Adam.

"Who said that?" the Ice Raider demanded. In answer, Adam stepped aside, and the creature looked right at Robin's silhouette. "Who are you?" he demanded.

"Someone who cares more than you, apparently," Robin answered, and the three looked at him in surprise. "If we don't help these kids, they won't stand a chance.

"Adam has told me you united the Raider clans—that they all revere and respect you," he continued. The Ice Raider's gaze shifted to his brother and back. "I would think someone who did that would leap at the opportunity to heighten his reputation and defy the Black Dragon. If you help these children in the process, they will always remember who saved them."

At his words, silence filled the room. Even the teens and children who were packing paused to look from the projected face to Robin and back.

"Who are you to say such things to me?" the Ice Raider asked.

Robin stepped forward into the light. At once, the creature stared in surprise at the armor covering his body. "I am Robin Hood."

The Ice Raider's eyes narrowed. "The same Robin Hood who stole a pair of sky riders from me?" Silence fell once more.

Robin remained still as Freya, LJ, and Adam eyed him, hoping what they did wouldn't rob him of this chance of a potential ally and destroy any hope for these people. For an eternity, the seconds seemed to tick by as Robin hoped for the best.

At long last, a smile grew on the Ice Raider's lips and he started to laugh. "You've got stones, boy. First, you steal from me and now you're asking for my help to take on the Black Dragon itself," he finally said. "What do you need?"

The Great Escape

ONCE AGAIN DRESSED in desert garb and face coverings, Robin sat on a crate with one leg propped up, facing the door Behind him, the others helped get the kids ready for travel.

"So, what's the plan?" Adam asked.

Robin, eyed the cave around him. "Was this where the river used to run?"

Adam nodded as he looked around. "Before, we probably couldn't even hold our heads above water in this room."

"Would Savic have an emergency flush system for the towers?"

Still looking at the cave around him, Adam said, "More than likely. Even he..." He paused, looking at Robin and then growled, exasperated, "What do you have in mind?"

Before he could answer the door, the alarm sounded. The response was immediate as the kids seized their weapons and took up hiding positions. Robin drew his blaster pistol, eyes on the door, and then it hissed open, revealing three figures dressed similarly.

In the middle stood a black leather clad figure with a poncho-like cape draped across his shoulders and a hood over his head. The parts of his body that showed were ice blue and sharp angled in some areas, like he was living crystal or ice. Reaching up, he lowered his hood and the cloth that covered the lower half of his face, revealing the Ice Raider.

His eyes roamed the room until they found Adam. "Tell the kids to stand down."

Adam was silent for a moment before he raised his fist and slowly opened it. At once, the kids and teens stepped or stood into sight, weapons lowered.

"You trained them well," the Ice Raider said, eyeing the group, as Little John and Freya, who were dressed and masked like Robin, moved next to him. "So, which one of you is this Robin Hood?"

"Can you blame us for hiding that?" Little John asked.

"After all," Robin said, standing, "pretty soon, we'll be the most wanted people in the Black Dragon's empire." He looked at the other two behind the Ice Raider, whose faces were still covered. "After all, she can't allow Dragon Knights to exist beyond her control."

Blinking with a quiet sound of ice clinking against ice, the creature looked at them before nodding in understanding. "Very well," he said. "Now, do you have a plan?"

"You could say that," Robin said, "but you'll have to decide for yourself whether to follow it."

A short while later, the group stood in a small circle with a diagram of Robin's plan etched into the ground at their feet.

He watched as the Ice Raider rubbed his chin in thought. "You certainly are a bold one," he finally said, "and a strategic mind..."

"We came up with this together," Robin said. "I've always thought a good leader acts on the opinions of his men.

"Can we count on your men to help with the distraction?" He pointed to a section of the diagram. "Adam will lead you to where the river has been diverted and blow it." He slammed his fist into the dirt. "That will provide time for us to get out of the city, and then we'll meet in the desert where our ship awaits to take us off planet," Robin finished.

"How do you plan to get these kids through the gate?" the Ice Raider asked, looking at him again.

"Did you bring what I asked for?"

"Yes," the Ice Raider said with a nod.

A short while later, Robin was back on a sky rider, once more acting as security for the caravan the Ice Raider had come to the city with. At the front, the creature rode one of the strange horses with Adam at his side. The others were spread out, either riding a sky rider like Robin or driving one of the caravan wagons; the teens and children were scattered and hidden throughout.

Slowly, they moved toward the southern gateway to the city. Robin's eyes were locked on the sentinels guarding it, hoping what was about to happen would work and draw them away.

Inch by inch, they moved toward the gate. Each passing second felt like an eternity until the ground shook. The people around him grabbed whatever they could to stay upright as things fell from market carts.

Just as he had hoped, the sentinels were called away from their places at the gate. Once they were gone, the caravan moved quickly through, though Robin did not relax until they were all safely outside the city.

Gunning the engine, he moved to the front next to Adam and the Ice Raider. "Just how many explosives did you use?" he demanded.

"Plenty," his brother replied simply.

They traveled through the desert until the sun started going down. Once the caravan came to a stop, Robin climbed off his rider, scanning the area.

"Unload!" he barked, and there was a flurry of motion.

"How long until your ship shows up?" the Ice Raider asked, drawing close as LJ, Freya, and Adam rounded up the kids.

As if in answer, a roar met their ears. Looking up, they saw the *Odysseus* come over the horizon, heading right for them.

"Does that answer your question?" Robin asked as the ship landed. "Let's get them aboard!" he called out as the hatch opened and Willa appeared, armored. At once, the kids filed up the ramp. Robin turned to the Ice Raider as he and his men kept watch. "I want to thank you for keeping my brother safe."

At his words, the creature looked at him, stunned. "You're Adam's brother?" he demanded. "Jun's boy?"

Before Robin could say anything, someone shouted, "SANDSTORM!" Following where he pointed, they saw the large dust plume headed in their direction.

After narrowing his eyes behind his shades to focus, they went wide at what he saw. Turning, he looked at Willa, who nodded, confirming she saw the same thing.

"That's no sandstorm," he murmured as his armor expanded up his arm and he slipped out of the loose desert robe. "They've found us."

The Chase

CLIMBING ON THE rider, Robin, back in his armor, barked to the others, "I'll draw them off!"

"Are you crazy?" LJ demanded. "On a sky rider? You'll

be torn to pieces—especially with only the weapons you have!"

Before Robin could answer him, thin cords emerged from his bracelet and connected to the rider. At once, with a sound of metal on metal, the machine began to shift. The section over the tire expanded with a second pair of engines growing out of it. Just in front of his legs, a two lines of missiles popped up; right above them, a pair of cannons emerged, the barrels extending, with another pair popping out right in front of the windshield. The weapons then slid back into place, as if they weren't even there.

Looking up, he gave them a grin behind his helmet. "I think I'll be fine," he said and revved the engines, the new ones spouting high-heat exhaust.

"I'm coming with you!" his brother said.

"Adam," he started.

"These kids are here because of me. I am not going to just sit on the sidelines!" he barked.

Before Robin could object further, a sound met his ears. Eyes traveling down, he watched Adam's hand become covered in armor.

Catching sight of it himself, Adam quickly stripped out of his desert robe, and then the armor covered his head. It expanded into a dragon head covered in spikes under the short snout, with a line of long horns protruding from the back of his head.

For a second, he looked at his armored self. "Any other objections about me not going?" he demanded as he looked at Robin and jabbed his thumb at his armored chest.

"You're not driving," Robin said after a moment of silence, and Adam climbed on behind him. "Now hang on!" The two took off.

"You could have at least given me time to get a grip!" his brother barked over the comms as the two sped through the desert, toward the approaching force. "So, what's the plan?"

"Make them want to chase us!" Robin replied as a targeting system popped up on the screen in front of him.

For a second, multiple bluish circles swiveled across the screen before they turned red and froze over various targets. After he called up the right weapon, the missile packs popped open again and unleashed their payload.

Robin watched the barrage of missiles streak through the air before impacting with explosions, either destroying or disabling what they hit, kicking up both sand and smoke in their wake.

"Hang on!" Robin yelled when they were almost on top of them and put the rider into a roll.

The guns popped out of the front and fired, and they came out of the roll on the other side of the advancing force and sped off toward the city.

"What's the rest of your plan?" Adam asked.

"Get the civilians out of harm's way!"

"How?"

"The old-fashioned way," Robin replied as he took aim with the rider blasters and fired.

As intended, the shots skimmed the top of the wall where no guards patrolled. "Now to knock on those doors."

He locked onto them with the last two missiles and fired. They shot from the slot, streaking through the air; smoke from the exhaust trailed behind them before they blew the doors right off the hinges. The smoking and bent metal remains landed hard in the sand. When the dust cleared, all that was left was a gaping hole.

"You sure have a funny definition of knocking," Adam said. "Now, what about those guys following us?"

"Nag, nag, nag," Robin muttered under his breath as a rear view appeared, blocked by Adam's dragon-faced helmet. "Lean to the side!" he snapped.

At once, Adam did so, and in less than a second, Robin locked onto a pair of armored riders coming after them and fired. Two compartments in the rear section opened, extending two missiles, which launched at their targets, leaving smoldering wrecks in the desert.

Robin burst through the door. "Whoa!" he barked, bringing the rider to a skidding stop, at the sight of the Knight he met on Morhoth on a weaponized rider of her own.

At once, both she and Robin had a plasma saber in hand aimed at each other. He wasn't sure what her motives were.

"Another Knight," his brother said in surprise. "What are you doing? Isn't that a good thing?"

"Not from what I gathered at our last meeting," Robin replied. He then said openly to her, "So, what now?" She remained silent. "Are you just going to attack me like you did last time, or are you going to talk to me this time?"

For a second, she was still; then her head tilted slightly upward, like she was looking at something behind him.

Taking a chance, Robin glanced over his shoulder using the rear camera and saw more gun platforms and riders coming their way.

"Or not listen to you while you stall for time for your allies," she finally said. Before he could deny her words, she opened fire.

"I don't have time for this!" he barked. Gunning the engine, he tore down a side street. "Any suggestions on where to go?"

"Up the pipes!" Adam barked. "The airships won't risk damaging the aqueducts—water is worth more than gold here!"

"Got it!" Robin said, gaining altitude and keeping close to the pipework, ducking under it whenever a gun platform drew overhead.

As they rounded one of the towers, they were surrounded by a barrage of blaster fire. The brothers dropped low to avoid them.

"Two on our tail!" Adam barked, looking behind them.

Going over his options in his head, Robin shouted, "Take the wheel!"

"What?" Adam started to protest.

"Just do it!" Robin snapped, taking his brother's hands and pushing them onto the handlebars.

Then, reaching for the small of his back, he drew out his bow. Turning in his seat, he pulled back the string, forming an arrow over Adam's shoulder. Taking a second to aim, he released the arrow.

He watched it sail through the air, colliding with the rider head on and blowing it to bits as the pilot fell to the ground.

"That's one down," Robin said, pulling back the string and forming another arrow. "And one...to...go!" he said as he fired again.

He hit the other rider, sending it, like the other, into a fiery wreck to the ground below.

He turned back in time to see more riders coming at them. "Hang on!" he barked, taking the controls again and rolling the sky rider onto its side, where he opened fire with the forward blasters just as they were fired upon.

"They're trying to bring us into the open," Robin said as he glanced behind and saw their pursuers make a quick U-turn after them, "so the gun ships will have a clean shot!"

"Any ideas?" Adam barked.

Robin glanced around, trying to think of something. Then he saw it. After coming to a skidding stop in midair, he shot off towards the towers.

"The towers belong to Savic, right?"

"Right!"

"And what would happen if they were knocked down?"

For a second, he was silent as the pair sped on. "You can do that?"

"Anyone can do anything when they put their mind to it!" Robin replied.

Before Adam could respond, his brother again put the rider into a roll. Once upside-down, the weapons platform he had seen coming up to meet them appeared; his plasma saber shot into his hand as the forward cannons opened fire. The people on the platform dove for cover under his barrage of blaster cannon fire.

It gave Robin time to drop low, igniting the blade of his sword and using it to make a deep cut down the middle of the platform. When he rolled over, clearing the other side, there was an explosion as the platform split in half, catching one of the riders pursuing them. Both wrecks fell to the ground below, and the platform pieces crashed into the base of one of the towers.

Robin and Adam circled up and around the second tower, the plasma saber now back on Robin's hip. Coming to a stop at the top one foot on the ground, he looked over at the other tower as a loud, metallic groaning met their ears.

At a clang to their side, the two turned and saw the other Knight. Again, she pointed her weapon at them.

"What's your game?" she demanded. "First, you try to ambush me with your allies and now you destroy these people's water supply!" She turned as more of the riders that had been chasing them appeared over the edge, leveling weapons. "And now you think to trap me!"

Face hardening behind his helmet, Robin growled in frustration at her persistence. His eyes then fell on what was coming up behind her. "I prefer to think of it as liberating!" he snapped as he drew his bow once again.

After it snapped open, he took aim and fired. Out of reflex, she ducked as the arrow shot past, impacting with the gun ship coming up behind her.

The resulting explosion shook the airship, sending it back a little before it tumbled forward into the tower. Robin raised his arm to activate a shield to block the shock of the exploding crash, which sent their pursuers tumbling over the edge.

They were surrounded by the flames and the twisted remnants of the gun ship that littered the ground around them.

"Maybe you overdid it," Adam muttered, looking around them, and Robin glanced his way.

At a sound of scraping metal, he looked over and saw the other Knight push wreckage aside as she emerged from underneath it. Clutching one arm, she glanced around before she looked in his direction.

A groan reverberated up their feet, and the tower began to tilt to the side. Losing balance, the three slid through the debris and toward the edge. After hitting the railing, Robin barely managed to hold onto the rider as he was sent over the side of the machine to slam against the side of the tower, the rider the only thing keeping him from falling.

The other Knight hung from the railing as she glanced over and met his gaze.

"You have ensured the destruction of this water source for these people, but I will save what's left!" Planting her feet against the tower, she kicked off it, sending her into the air. Robin watched her fall, but then her wings extended and she flew off toward the other tower.

Rolling his eyes, he started pulling himself up with Adam grasping him by his wrist—and then the railing snapped.

"AAAGGGGHHHH!" they screamed as they fell.

With the ground rushing up to meet them, Robin managed to pull himself back onto the rider. "Nice to see you behind the wheel again!" Adam barked. "Now, get us out of here!"

"Not yet!" his brother shouted back as he headed toward the control bunker. "Take over!"

"What?" Adam barely got out before Robin threw himself forward.

I'm Coming

AS HE HAD been trained, Robin kept his limbs tucked close to keep him streamlined, eyes locked on the screen, which told him how high he was. Above him, Adam pulled up and peeled away.

When he was a couple hundred feet above the ground, Robin flipped forward and deployed his wings. At once, they filled with air and his head snapped back hard. He came down on the roof, landing on one knee with one fist on the ground to keep his balance, and his wings retracted.

Rising to his full height, he opened his hands and his plasma sabers shot into his palms. Activating the blades, he spun on the spot, cutting away a circular section of the roof before falling to the floor below with a loud crash. Looking up, he saw the room was deserted.

Sighing in relief, he raced for the controls. "Come on," he said under his breath as he looked them over and rushed along the console. "Which one? Which one?" At more sounds of metal groaning on metal, he whipped around and looked up at the tower as it tilted closer to him.

He turned around and drew back a fist to drive it into the console before his eyes fell on his bracelet. Quickly lowering his hand, the thin strands extended and attached themselves to the console. At once, he was interfaced, and the flush sequence was brought up.

"STOP!" At the shout, Robin looked over his shoulder and saw Savic standing on the threshold, outlined by the dancing flames of the fires outside. "Just who do you think you are," he demanded, "coming here and taking what is mine? Thinking of killing me as so many have?" Robin was silent, and then, at his command, what lights remained switched on. At once, Savic blanched at the sight of him.

"I know who I am," he answered. "I am Robin Hood, and I am a Dragon Knight! I am returning what belongs to the people—not a tyrant like you!"

He activated the flush sequence, and as the sound of rushing water reverberated through the building, Robin spun around and launched himself at Savic, knocking him out the door. After extending his wings, they launched him into the air, where Robin held the man by his clothes.

Savic shook in fear as he looked into the masked face.

"I hope you live, so you can tell people what happened here. And you tell those like you I'm coming for them!" Diving low, Robin dropped him to the ground.

A Savior's Voice

STREAKING THROUGH THE sky, Robin quickly located the rider and dropped low over it. "Move back!" he snapped at Adam, who quickly did so, and his brother dropped in front of him.

"Now what?"

"We've done enough!" Robin said, turning the sky rider. "Let's get back to the others!"

He dived down to the streets toward the entrance, and when they leveled out near the ground, he was relieved to see all the people below running to safety out of the towers range. At more groaning sounds, Robin glanced over his shoulder and watched as the nearest tower slowly started toppling over.

Faster it fell until, with an impact that sent the ground shaking below them, it crashed, sending sand and parts of buildings into the air. Everything beneath it was crushed.

"Whoa!" Adam barked, watching as the second water tower fell, as well. "That'll show 'em!"

"Let's just hope we minimized the civilian casualties!" Robin replied, eyes on the giant fountain he had seen earlier as water shot from the spouts.

"Tell them that," Adam countered.

For a second, he wondered what his brother meant, but then he heard it: cheering.

357

Glancing down, he gasped. The people who had been running had now slowed or stopped and looked up at them, cheering. For a second, Robin was stunned at the sight; then, with a grin growing across his face, he brandished a fist in the air, and the crowd roared.

"If you can hear me, pay attention!" a voice Robin had never heard before sounded, and he paused. "A squad of the Black Dragon's forces have assembled at the gate to ambush you!" He froze, eyes on his bracelet, as it started flashing rapidly. "GET OUT OF THERE NOW!"

Quickly going over his options, he turned toward the crowd. "Get out of here! Go!" he shouted.

Then, grabbing the handlebars, he gained altitude as quickly as he could. He had barely cleared the top of the roofs when he was surrounded by laser fire.

"HOLD ON!" he shouted at Adam as he pushed the sky rider to go faster.

A few hundred feet off the rooftops, Robin was beginning to think they would get away when a few lucky shots hit the rider, taking pieces with them. Bit by bit, more shots hit home, blowing off more pieces of the sky rider; in no time, the only thing keeping them up was air.

Yelling, the two fell to the ground, limbs flailing, unable to deploy their wings with the blasters still firing on them.

Suddenly, something large streaked out of the sky, and Robin came to a jolting stop before gaining altitude again. After eyeing the large claw holding him, his head whipped around and he gaped at the purple-scaled dragon flapping its wings as it soared over the desert.

"What the..." Robin started as Adam gasped.

"You two sure know how to leave your mark!" the dragon said as the civilians on the ground gazed up in awe.

The Power of Three

THEY FLEW OVER the desert, which seemed endless from high up. Soon, the *Odysseus* came into sight, and the dragon glided down to it. Close to the ground with a few flaps of its wings, it touched down on its hind legs, dropping Robin and Adam into the sand. They whipped onto their backs in time to see the dragon come down on its forelegs and fold its wings. All they could do was gape. It looked down at the pair as it walked around them, as if it were studying them.

Robin studied it just as close, from its long snout with wide nostrils to the two large horns sprouting from the side of its head and sweeping back. A smaller line of horns ran from the top of its head to the tip of its tail, and it had three-clawed feet.

Slowly, Adam leaned close to Robin. "Is it going to eat us?" he asked quietly.

"If it was going to do that, we'd be dead already."

"Your brother is correct," the dragon said in a feminine voice. "What you did, the people will never forget," she continued.

For a second, all Robin could do was blink. "Thanks," he was finally able to say. "I take it that was you who warned me about the ambush?"

The dragon tilted her head. "It was the least I could do after all you did for these people," she said, and then her head whipped around toward the way they came.

A sound caught Robin and Adam's attention, and they saw a large force heading their way.

"If you don't leave now, you don't leave at all," the dragon snapped, looking at them again.

Nodding, the pair rushed up the ramp. Pausing halfway, Robin looked back.

"Will we see you again?" he asked over the roar of the engine as the *Odysseus* lifted off the ground.

"I hope so," she replied before she opened large, leathery wings and, with a few mighty flaps, took to the sky and soared into the desert.

As the *Odysseus* climbed higher, Robin stood on the ramp, watching her go, before he bolted up into the ship.

After closing the ramp, he raced for the cockpit through the sea of kids, which Freya and Adam tried to coral into some kind of order.

"Willa," he barked into his bracelet, "I can't get to the cockpit right now!"

"We're okay for now," she replied, "if you can get to the gunning station above or below!"

"Got it!" he said as he reached the ladder that would take him to either one and started to climb.

Reaching the top, he opened the hatch with a press of the button, and it slid into the frame. After pulling himself inside, he climbed into the gunner seat and started activating the weapon.

"Robin, so far, we're clear of fighters!" Adam said over the comms.

"It's not the fighters I'm worried about!" he said as the screen in front of him lit up as they cleared the last layer of the atmosphere and he gripped the yoke. "It's that!" He eyed the Black Wing cruiser still in orbit.

"Missiles loose! Missiles loose!" Willa barked over the comms, and Robin turned his guns to target them.

Opening fire, he blew them out of the sky, and then saw the ship was turning. "No! Stop!" he shouted. "Head right for them!"

"Are you crazy?" Willa demanded.

"That's what they'll think when they see what we're doing!"

"Yeah, they'll think we're playing chicken with them, and they are not going to blink!"

"They will, if we go right for the bridge!" Robin retorted as he shot more missiles. "Put everything you can into the shields and engines, and act like you're going to ram them!"

For a second, the *Odysseus* held its course, and then it turned on its side. "If we get out of this alive, remind me to kill you!" Willa barked as she turned back toward the cruiser.

Before he could answer, there was a clap of thunder, and Robin was thrown against his seat as the ship shot forward.

As they weaved left and right on each side, Robin shot virtually all the missiles fired on them; those that slipped through were repelled by the shields as they appeared to go under their enemies. With a roll, they flew up and over the edge of the lower section of the cruiser.

Robin opened fire, hoping to knock out a gun, and was rewarded by small explosions in each corner of the ship and a couple farther along the edge. Coming fully around, they headed for a square, raised section above the hangar doors ahead of them.

"Come on, come on," Robin muttered as Willa weaved to avoid as much fire as possible. Just as he was beginning to think he had gotten his friends killed, the ship started turning. "Now, Willa!" he shouted, and again they went into a roll, shooting above the bridge.

"Now where?" she demanded as Robin fired again on the surface and on the bridge.

"Head back for Charybdis!" he barked, hoping the explosions he saw were more guns being taken out. "We've been through it before, and they'd be crazy to follow us!"

"You're the boss," LJ replied over the comms.

"Yeah," Robin said, powering down the guns, "and I'm coming down!" He slipped down the ladder as they were enveloped by the nebula.

Once in the cockpit, Robin and Willa switched. "Are they following us?" he asked when she took her station.

"What do you think?" she answered. When a warning alarm sounded, Robin cursed.

Thinking quickly, his eyes landed on a sensor before he banked the handle to the side.

"Robin, what are you doing?" LJ demanded.

"Either saving us or killing us." He killed an alarm as it sounded and then pressed another button. "Freya, Adam, tell our passengers to strap in! It's going to get bumpy!" he said over the intercom.

He did his best to keep ahead of the cruiser pursuing them through the nebula while the reading he watched drew more and more toward the red.

"Willa, load a sensor beacon in a tube!" he barked as the ship began to shake from an invisible force.

"Why?"

"Just do it—and make sure it looks big!"

"Robin, what are you planning?" LJ demanded. "Micro fractures are starting to appear! We're being shaken apart!" he reported.

"LJ, on my call, put everything we have into the engines!" Robin barked.

Giving in, his friend moved his hands over the controls. "On your go!"

"Firing beacon!" Robin shouted, and he watched it disappear into the clouds.

"Robin, the cruiser picked up speed!" Willa reported. "They're in firing range!" Large laser cannon blasts shot past them.

"Not yet! Not yet!" Robin said, and they burst through a cloud of the nebula to see a trio of stars awaiting them. "NOW!" he shouted, pulling back hard on the yokes, and LJ threw the switch and the engines roared.

In a vertical position, they backed away from the stars, and through the view screen, they watched the cruiser shoot past them. Righting the ship, Robin headed the other way, and his eyes shot to the rearview screen.

"Why the hell didn't you tell us what you were planning?" LJ demanded as they watched the cruiser fight the gravity of the three stars to turn around.

"Thought you might have tried to stop me," Robin answered, and his friend rolled his eyes. "Remember what our old flight instructor told us about flying through space?"

Willa nodded. "The bigger you are, the faster you burn or get crushed."

"The Black Wing is too big," Robin said as the engines of the big ship gave all they had. "Charybdis has her!"

They watched as the ship seemed to come to a standstill. Then, the rear section of the ship was torn away and pulled into the star behind it; a whole section to one side was ripped away by another star. Piece by piece, the ship was torn apart by the three stars like it had been caught between three starving dogs.

Looking away, Robin eased back on the engines as they slipped into the cloud of the nebula again. "Let's get out of here."

A couple days later, after coming out of the other side of the nebula, the *Odysseus* exited Hyperspace on approach for landing on Tortuga.

After they landed and disembarked, people stared at the kids who'd accompanied them.

"I see you've been busy," Robin's mother said before embracing him, relieved to have him back alive. "Did you find him?" she asked, stepping back.

"What do you think?" he asked, turning as Adam came down the ramp with Freya. Chikako beamed.

When he saw the slack-jawed look on Tuck's face as he gazed up at the state of the *Odysseus*, he said, "Uhh, Mom, I'll catch up with you later. Right now, I need to run!" Turning, he bolted.

"RYUU!" Tuck's angry voice called after him as he fled through the doors of the hangar.

THE SEARCH

DRAGON KNIGHT CHRONICLES

BOOK 4

Buccaneer Squadron

IN HIS FIGHTER, Robin drifted through space behind an asteroid at the edge of the field. Most of his fighter's systems shut down so he wouldn't be detected as he eyed the approaching transport, which had to drop out of hyperspace to safely travel the asteroid field.

From the angle he was viewing, it looked long and cylindrical in shape. And he could see glimpses of the cargo containers attached to the large, indented sections of the ship. The front coming to a short point where the bridge was located. While on either side, a pair of fighters flew escort.

"HIT IT!" Roaran barked over the coms and his fighter's systems roared to life and he shot over the top of the asteroid.

Before the fighter could react, he had locked and fired on it. As it exploded as the missiles first penetrated its shield and the second impacted the hull. While simultaneously, the second fighter exploded under Willa's barrage of pulse blaster fire.

Weaving through space as the freighter's torrents opened fire on them. "Buccaneer three and four, the engines!" Roaran barked as he and Dugald's fighter shot down at the freighter and fired on the torrents, knocking them out. While Robin and Willa took out the shield generator atop the ship. Behind the freighter LJ and Much's fighter shot out from behind another couple of asteroids. And locking larger missiles fired them on the engines, which exploded on impact, crippling the ship.

"Boarding party, and mammoth, you're clear to move in!" Robin called out through the comms as he circled the freighter and took out one of the last torrents, while LJ and Much took out the other two.

A moment later, both a transport and a large cargo ship jumped in above them. Along with a group of smaller ships with a set of large interlocking claws.

The cargo ship was oval in shape with one large structure stretched forward in the front. While in the back held the command decks with a rotating sensor array at the bottom.

The transport maneuvered down to the side of the crippled freighter while the claw ships moved close to the cargo containers. Firing a series of grappling cables pulled the ships together at the air locks.

The transport...

Adam gripping his rifle in both hands wearing a combat suit charged through the airlock after the freighters were cut open. Bursting through the open fire cutting down a couple sentinels that turned toward them. As they fell, he and the rest of the boarding party rushed in shooting any other sentinels that came toward them.

"Bridge crew move out!" the boarding party CO called out and the selected team moved toward the bridge. "Cargo and fuel cell teams move it!" and the other teams moved out. "Keep it together people, we got a job to do!"

Robin...

Outside, Robin had taken up position with his fighter. While around him, others had as well. A couple circled the area to protect the cargo ship and the snatcher ships. His eyes on the cargo ship, his mind on Adam.

Suddenly the cargo containers detached from the ship and the gripper ships moved in. Robin watched as they maneuvered into position before beams of light shot from the center of the ships to connect with the containers. Hauling the containers into position before the claws closed around them and they moved up toward the mammoth to lock them into the empty structure of the ship.

Trip after trip the grippers went from the cargo ship to the mammoth.

Adam...

After clearing the bridge and setting their explosives, they returned to the airlock where they were still loading fuel cells. While a couple medics looked over a couple of the wounded.

"Bridge clear," he reported. "Explosives set, we have 10 mikes."

Suddenly one of the medics stiffened. Before pointing at some debris on the ground, then with a jerk pointed at him. The object shot at him through the air.

Reacting, Adam dropped down, weapon pointed at the person. While the object shot through the space he'd occupied. And tore off the head of the sentinel who appeared around the corner.

Looking from the still standing sentinel to the person. "Looks like you missed one," she said.

"Well, I guess I wanted to leave one for you, Freya," he replied as he climbed back on his feet.

Robin...

"This is Buccaneer six to transport," he said through his comms.

"This is transport," came the reply from the pilot.

"Any casualty reports?" he asked, biting his lips out of nervousness.

"Crew and boarding parties on board and accounted for," he reported, and Robin sighed in relief. "we're also heavy with a load of fuel cells."

"Okay Buccaneer squad," Roaran called out through the coms. "Take up flanking positions around the mammoth. And let's move out!"

"Rodger," Robin replied, and he and the rest of the fighters took their positions. And just as they jumped into hyperspace, the cargo ship exploded.

Extraordinary

AFTER LANDING BACK at Tortuga, Robin climbed out of his fighter like he had the last few times he paused. Smiling and running his finger across his name painted under the cockpit canopy. As well as his call sign.

Alec 'Dragon's Fire' Yamamoto

As his memory drifted back to when his father had given him the name, he climbed the rest of the way down the ladder.

"Not bad for a day's work," Roaran said, helmet under his arm as Robin slipped his off as they watched the transport land. The people aboard began to depart as soon as the ramp was lowered.

After watching both Adam and Freya walk down the ramp. Before his gaze lowered as his thoughts went over the raid. And it filled him with unease.

"Something wrong?" Roaran asked, catching the look on his face.

Glancing at him as they turned heading for the hatch. "Did it seem a little too easy to you?" he asked.

"Easy?" a voice behind them asked and they turned to look at Dulglad come over his flight jacket and suit partially unzipped and carrying his helmet in one hand. "Good guys came, good guys stole from bad guys; enough for me," he said.

Sighing, Robin nodded. "Yes, that basically sums it up," he said. "But I've been with the squadron for over a month," and he looked at Roaran.

"How often have you encountered a cargo ship with only a two-fighter escort or without a gunship?"

Roaran frowned in thought. "Come to think of it, it's a little odd," he admitted as the others came close.

After looking at them all, Dulglad sighed. "Little over paranoid," he started,

"Paranoia is a good thing." They turned to see Hector walk down the corridor with the clacking of his hooves. "Considering the alternative, which is why we are going over the haul piece by piece," and Robin nodded, feeling a little more at ease.

Then he turned back to Freya and Adam. "Then I guess we have things to do," he said, and they looked at each other.

Later after some time to themselves in one of the cargo holds Robin and his friends dressed in loose clothing continued training Freya and Adam. While Chikako and Tekmet watched from the far wall. "...then you scoop up his leg still on the ground," Robin instructed as he lifted LJ in his arms, demonstrating a counter against a kick. "...then let gravity do the rest," and he dropped him, and LJ took the fall like he was trained.

"Questions?" he asked looking at the two.

"Yeah, which move stops a blaster?" Adam asked.

Robin rolled his eyes. "Then how about we work on something that would disarm an attacker at close range," he offered.

Adam bent down and drew a blaster from an ankle holster. Frowning as he ejected the power magazine. Robin's eyes hardened and his friends stared in surprise as his brother walked close and put it under his chin.

"Now what?" he asked and glanced over as angry murmurs started.

Robin reacted first grabbing his wrist pushing the blaster away. With his hands still gripping his brother, he kicked his legs out from under him, causing him to fall to the ground hard. Next thing Adam knew he found the blaster still in his hand pointed right at his face.

"Bang! You're dead," Robin growled before yanking the blaster from his grasp and tossed it to his mother, who was marching over a murderous look on her face.

Caching it in one hand she reached down and pulled Adam to his feet by the scruff of his shirt. "Never do that again!" she growled out before shoving him back.

"I just don't see why we have to do this when all we need is a good blaster at our side," he complained.

"You saw the result of this training on Bedie," Willa snapped, stepping into his face, a deep scowl on hers. "So, stop complaining and start training!"

Later after doing a few more drills, techniques, and sparing where Adam was partnered with Willa. And after he tried to fight a little dirty, he found himself flat on his back with her knee on his throat.

"I hate to say it," Willa said as they wiped the sweat off from the training, the light shining on her ebony skin, her Elven-pointed ears uncovered by her braid. "But your brother's a creep. I mean who the heck brings a blaster to a training session!"

"Considering he was a Raider before he came here," he said. "he's been taught to win at any cost."

Blinking, she stepped forward. "He put a blaster under your chin and now... are you honestly defending what he did?" she snapped.

Returning her hard gaze, he faced her. "Not a chance," he growled. "And if he does something like that again. I'll give him a beating he won't forget."

For a couple seconds they remained there in silence as he watched with a keen eye and felt her eyes on him. "Is everything else okay?" she asked and he glanced at her.

"I'm fine," he reassured her before looking back.

She looked at him in silence. "You're wishing we could give some of those supplies we've been stealing from the Black Dragon back to the people she's been taking it from?" she finally asked.

Sighing, he looked away. "They need those supplies," he muttered looking back at her. "You know the stories and what it was like on Bedie and the Bazzar Systems." He looked away again, shaking his head. "We need to do more."

Sighing, she nodded looking around at the other pausing on her twin brother. "Robin.... we've been doing what we can..." she reassured. "But if we take the fighters out more than we have for 'patrols'..." she said, emphasizing it with air quotes. "...to steal more supplies that we've been getting to people. It could draw too much attention to what we've been doing. I mean the people here are talking more and more about the new Robin Hood as well as new arrivals...." And she sent him a half grin. "And the rumors of new Dragon Knights are soaring.... But then again, we haven't exactly been subtle at times."

"Not exactly like The Black Dragon would want people to know there are new Knights," he pointed out. "But the reward for the new Robin Hood is climbing..." A smirk grew on his face.

"Yes, it is..." she said slyly. "At first it was a commission as a junior officer in her forces..." and she sent him a side look "...but after he and his band hijacked that caravan meant for her palace but was distributed across several systems... the rank has gone up quite a bit..." and chuckling he shook his head. "I just wish the reward for the new Willa Scarlet was just as high..." and that brought a laugh out of him.

"Might be a little harder next time if she put more than sentinels on board those cargo ships. Might take more than one knight to take over one of them with a fighter for each circling outside," he said, and they started walking back to the group training. "But for right now, she knows Robin Hood is a knight... probably still best we keep the secret here... so if word gets back to her he is on Tortuga.... She won't send her entire Armada here if she finds it."

A short while later they were having a lesson in magic by Tekmet and Freya. This time they were charged to hold up cargo containers in the air.

374

"That's it… keep it steady," Tekmet said as he watched them. "Keep all distractions away from your mind. The more you can focus on your goal the faster and easier it will come."

As the pair walked between the two rows they made, seeing how they progressed. With LJ teeth bared as he struggled to keep the container struggled to keep it steady in the air. Willa and Tuck holding theirs steady but looks of deep concentration on their faces. While next to Robin, Adam could barely get it off the ground.

Tekmet put a hand on his shoulder. "Remember not to beat this into submission; silence your egos and surrender to the possibilities now within reach of your fingertips," he said before looking over at Robin. "And before you ask what use the training Robin was putting you through," and he nodded over where Robin stood with one hand up, the container in front of him and holding steady.

"And right now, I'm getting a little bored," Robin said, looking over at them before he sent it flipping over on itself.

"Show off," Much said as he struggled to keep the container up.

Nodding Freya stepped forward, a smile growing on her face. "I guess it is getting too easy for you," as his face slowly went slack, and he lightly gulped.

In no time, Robin was down on one knee, teeth bared in frustration. As he struggled to keep two containers up. One on each side with his arms spread wide toward each of them.

"I should have kept my mouth shut…" he groaned as one of the containers dropped a little.

"No please we're enjoying ourselves," Willa said smiling at him as she continued to hold up her container.

Meanwhile, Tekmet leaned against the wall next to Chikako. "He's learning fast," he murmured.

"He was always like that," she answered. "Did Freya learn that fast?" she asked, and she looked up at him.

"Actually, she did," he admitted. "Frankly, I never seen anyone learn this fast and Adam is not far behind," and he nodded over at him as his container started to tilt up before coming back to the deck. "That is if he can ever let go of his ego," and he sighed, shaking his head. "Did Jun ever tell you anything about their birth parents?"

She shook her head. "I only met their mother once the night she gave birth to them. I asked several times, but Jun wouldn't tell me anything," she answered. "Only that their mother was a friend."

Nodding he looked back at the teens. "Well, if those three are her children, I can't imagine how extraordinary their mother is," he murmured.

No Beginning or End in Sight

AFTER THE TRAINING session, Robin his siblings and friends were back in his quarters. Looking over the star map projected from their armors. Which now included Adam's part of the map.

"Well, your piece has helped a little," Much said as he looked at it. "It's nice we have the rest of its gut." He nodded toward the section of the middle that had been Adam's piece. "But we still don't have a beginning and an end," and he looked at the remaining missing sections.

Sighing, Robin eyed the map. "The beginning we can probably live without," he pointed out.

"It's the end we need most of all," Tuck said.

"And unfortunately, there's probably only one way to get it." Willa sighed in exasperation falling onto Robin's bed as the map vanished.

"We got to find the other Knight," Robin groaned, running his hads through his hair in frustration. "And we both know how open she is to working with us."

"Yeah," Freya said, arms crossed. "Each time we met up with her she would rather burn bridges than forge an alliance."

"And we have no clear way to find her," LJ put in.

"Maybe we do?" Robin murmured, his chin resting between his thumb and fisted fingers as he thought. "There is one common factor in both times we met her," and he slowly turned to them. "The people..." and they blinked at him before realization dawned. "On Morhoth, there's the slaves in the mines and on Bedie…"

"The people's water was stolen from them," Adam said before waving it away with a flick of his wrist. "In case you forget, this is the Black Dragon's Empire," he said, jabbing his finger at the deck. "There's no shortage of people suffering."

"Thanks for stating the obvious," LJ said. "Now let's try to be a little bit more productive."

"So, the question is how do we narrow down a couple galaxies full of haystacks," Much asked, running his hands through his hair in frustration. "I don't suppose those toothed necklaces could help out, again, can they?" he said, looking over at Robin and Freya.

Sighing, Robin shook his head rubbing the back of his neck trying to ease his nerves. "I don't think they were meant to work that way," Freya said, looking at him, hands on her hips.

"And besides." They all looked at Robin. "These people weren't just suffering, they were desperate. They virtually had no hope," he pointed out.

As they thought he pulled up a star map of the known galaxies. "So, we just have to find the most decimated planet which holds the most ragged population out there," Adam said, moving to lean against the wall of Robin's quarters. "Again, there's no shortage of those as well."

Robin looked at him. "at least it's a starting point," he replied.

As they started to leave Robin moved close to Willa and Tuck. "You guys still spending time with the elves on board?" he asked.

Willa nodded. "It's nice to learn something about our mothers' people," she replied. "there're even a few more half elves here. Some even heard of our parents and hold them in high regard. Even tell us stories of how they…" Willa started saying before she stopped by an elbow from Tuck.

Blinking, she looked at the look of longing and envy on Robin's face.

"Robin…" she said feeling uncomfortable. "I didn't mean," she started.

"It's okay," he reassured her, placing a hand on her shoulder. "It's a good thing and I'm happy you guys are learning about your mothers' people and heritage."

Before more could be said he turned at the sound of hooves on the deck and saw Hector come toward him. "We may have a serious problem," he said, and Robin faced him, fully growing nervous at the tone of his voice.

Problems

IN HECTOR'S QUARTERS, Robin stood with the other group leaders and command structure of Tortuga. Robin was easily the youngest person there as he studied all the battle hardened people, noting the hardness in their eyes and the many scares they bore for their people. Or in the Elven leaders case almost a deep far off look in his eyes as he just stared at Robin. While they studied him just as closely, the Dormeanias leader's mandibles went a mile a minute.

"...paranoia proved to be right," Hector said, looking at all of them while he paced back and forth. "We found a tracking device well hidden in the cargo we captured. It was so well hidden we missed it the first two times we checked."

A rapid series of pops and clicks came from one of the Dormeanian leaders. "Do they know our location?" came the automated translator voice.

"Not precisely," Hector answered. "The asteroid field lies in a dense gamma radiation field which obscures their sensors and any transmissions out of it."

"But they have the general area?" Robin asked.

Hector nodded. "Do we have a plan to make them think we're not here?" the Eleven leader asked in a soft, mystic voice.

"We have an idea," Hector said and turned to Roaran. "Buccaneer squadron will take the cargo containers, which will be full of explosives. If there are any Black Dragon forces following the tracking beacon..."

"Do a little return to sender," Roaran finished for him.

Hector nodded. "You'll also have a couple of torpedo bombers," he added. "The goal of the mission is to strike and run," and Roaran nodded.

As Hector nodded, he paused as he turned, catching the look on Robin's face. "Something wrong?" he asked.

All eyes turned to him. After trying to get rid of the feeling that his mouth just turned into a desert.

"How many fighters and bombers are you thinking of sending?" he finally asked.

"Enough to make them think that you're us on the move," Hector answered. "And have them take the bait."

"And that's what I don't like," Robin continued. "Without her fighters Tortuga is vulnerable. If they send ships to search the asteroid belt and discover the station the defenses will be compromised."

"He's right," the Elven leader agreed. "We should keep some fighters here in case that happens." He looked back at Hector.

Hector nodded. "Then it's agreed we'll keep a few here." Hector looked at Robin. "Like I had intended all along, you are young, but you have a sharp mind."

"Very," the Elven leader said, and Robin studied him out of the corner of his eye. "And I have a feeling he's younger than he appears." He finished the last part so quietly Robin barely heard him.

"You all know your orders," Hector said, snapping him back and people moved out. "Ryuu," he said, and Robin paused, looking back. "A word."

Nodding, Robin stayed behind while everyone else filed out. "As Jun's adopted son, you and what you have managed to do you have earned the respect of everyone that had been in this room," he said, and he stepped closer to him. "But remember what I said when you arrived. I am the commanding officer of Tortuga, or as you had called me... the King of the Pirates."

Sighing, Robin nodded in agreement. "It was not my intent if it came off that way I apologize," he said walking over to run his fingers against the top of a chair. "I was merely thinking like everyone else who had been in here. The safety of my people."

"And that's understandable," Hector remarked. "But so was I and everyone else on this station."

"As was I," Robin said. "Old habit of mine."

"Then don't lose the habit," Hector said. "It's served you well so far." He stepped forward. "But you have to remember you're not the only one with this habit. Or think like you do," he finished.

"I didn't doubt you Hector," Robin said looking at him. "I wasn't going to say anything to begin with."

The pair looked at each other before Hector smiled. "I guess in some ways we both jumped to conclusions," he said.

Returning the smile Robin nodded. "It tends to happen when two people are trying their best to protect those they care about," he agreed and offered his hand in hopes this was finished.

"Agreed," Hector said, taking it. "Now we have much to discuss," he said, putting his arm across Robin's shoulders as they exited his quarters.

"Like what?" Robin asked.

"Like the pilots briefing room where you and the rest of the squadron will be fully briefed on the mission we were just discussing," Hector answered, leading the way.

Brother vs Brother

AFTER THE MISSION briefing Robin found himself back in his fighter flying in formation with the rest of the fighters. While in the center of them, a few tugs flew under their cover carrying the cargo they had taken.

"Okay ladies," Roaran said and after making a few adjustments Robin looked over at his fighter as they exited the asteroid belt. "We have a job to do and Tortuga is counting on us. Let's get the job done. Active sensors and keep your eyes peeled and heads on a swivel. Remember, they may very well be on their way, and we want them to come right at us."

"So, we're flying around with big bullseyes on our backs," Willa said from her fighter. "Bring 'em on," she said, and smiling, Robin shook his head at the eagerness in her voice.

"Always eager for a fight," Robin murmured.

"Always," Willa replied.

For the next few minutes, they flew through space trying to detect any ship anywhere near them. Keeping one eye and ear on the sensor readouts while the other was on the area of space around them. Trying to find those who could be following the bacon before they found them.

"Okay everyone heads up," Much said, and Robin looked over at him as they were nearing a star with a single gas giant. "I got a couple of big ships trying to hide in that gas giant down there," he reported, and Robin focused his sensors down in that direction.

"Okay, any com traffic?" Roaran asked.

"None boss," one of the other pilots reported. "They must be observing radio silence except for short-range frequencies. But they have a massive electromagnetic signature that's consistent with Black Dragon naval ships."

Looking over, Robin saw Roaran nod as he absorbed the information. "Ladies," he started to say before he was interrupted.

"ABORT!" was shouted over the coms and Robin's head whipped around to stare at Tuck surprised at the outburst.

"Pilot, you may have just given away our position! And you have no authority over this mission or its personnel!" Roaran barked at him.

"Those are not combat ships. They're supply ships left behind by a battle group trying to draw us in," Tuck said.

Eyes going wide, Robin pressed a few buttons to make a deeper reading from his sensors. "He's right, lead," he confirmed. "If these ships were left behind then Tortuga could be in danger," he said, looking over at Roaran.

"Lead, think about it," Tuck continued. "If they were a combat unit why would they have full active sensors? They're drawing us in; they might even be drones with foot print magnification to look bigger than they actually are."

For a second Robin watched as Roaran thought about what they said. "And what if you're wrong?" he demanded.

"If we're wrong?" he demanded.

"If we're wrong, you'll deprive the Black Dragon of a few more supplies," Robin replied, "But if we're right and we really don't want to be, Tortuga could already be under attack."

"Remember the belt Tortuga is in is flooded with Gamma rays," one of the Dormeanian pilots said. "They couldn't call for help even if they wanted to."

Again, Robin looked back at Roaran.

Tortuga...

Chikako walked into the command room and eyed Hector as he stood by a view screen, hands clasped behind his back. As he eyed the screens covering the whole wall showing the asteroid field beyond. While around him people worked with patrolling fighters calling over the coms or people monitoring the sensors.

Walking forward she stopped right next to Hector. "Any word?" she asked.

"You ask that every time he flies out," Hector answered. "And each time I saw we won't know until he returns to the belt," he started to say.

Stopping and whipping around as a cry came over the coms and through the screen, Chikako saw a small explosion. "Look!" she barked pointing.

Turning Hector was just in time to see several small gunships and fighters emerge from the asteroids with a company of fighters. "Launch the remaining fighters!" Hector barked. "Shields up weapons engage!" He snapped out orders and people rushed to follow them.

She watched as fighters flew from the station to engage the fighters and gunships. Through the confusion of all the fighter pilots ringing through the coms as they fought to repeal the attacking force aided by the cannons firing from various points in the station. Then the gunship's torpedoes were launched.

"BRACE!" Chikako barked a second before they impacted the shields.

A few were knocked off their feet from the station reverberating from the explosive impact. With waves of fire racing up the shields.

"Return fire!" Hector barked, clinging to the console, keeping him upright.

At once from the main launcher under the station launched torpedoes and missiles on the gunships. As it moved to dodge the barrage it ended up being hit full on its side blowing it apart. As the debris of the fellow gun ship floated around them the remaining opened fire again and once more the station was rocked by the impacting torpedoes and missiles.

"Sir shields down by forty percent!" one of the technicians called out. "And we have fires sprouting up on decks two, four, and eight! Torpedo and missile room is reporting one as well!"

"Sir!" Hector looked over at one of the women manning a sensor readout. "I'm getting a dozen more ships coming from behind the gunships!"

"They're bringing reinforcements!" Hector growled.

"We should be flattered," Chikako growled back as he pressed a button on the console of the man who reported the fires.

"Report!" he roared

"The torpedo autoloader has been damaged!" came the report from the torpedo and missiles room. "It's going to take a few minutes to bypass!"

"You don't have a few minutes!" Hector barked.

"Sir!" the woman from before yelled, her head whipping around the look at Hector, "I'm getting a coded friend or foe signal from the incoming ships!"

Stunned by that, Hector murmured, "Roaran's squadron!" as he and Chikako looked back out the view screens.

Robin...

They raced back through the asteroid field and Tortuga being engaged by the gunships came into view. "Okay, everyone!" Roaran snapped and drew their attention back to him. "Everyone but Dragon's Fire and Silver Ape engage those fighters!"

"Be careful Erik!" Willa said over the coms.

"You watch your back, Allison!" he called back as she and the rest of the fighters banked away toward the fighters.

"Bombers follow me in! Dragon's Fire and Silver Ape escort!" Roaran barked and the pair shot forward as several fighters moved to intercept them.

Quickly getting a lock on one Robin fired a missile then rolled away as the fighter exploded on impact. To avoid clouding before firing the pulse cannons on another blowing that one out of the stars. While not far from him Tuck blew the two fighters coming at him.

"Okay, you two head for the remaining fighters!" Roaran ordered and they peeled off.

After shooting down another fighter, Robin's head whipped around in time under heavy flack the bombers launched. One taking a direct hit from the flack and exploding. Going after another fighter and firing a missile on it he was in time to see the torpedoes impact on a few of the gunship's engines blowing them apart.

"Tortuga, can you deal with the remaining gunships?" he heard Roaran call out.

"Torpedo and missile launcher still offline and shields are failing!" came the reply.

"Okay everyone engages those gunships! Shoot down any torpedo and missiles fired on Tortuga. I don't want a single one getting through!" Roaran ordered and his fighter banked hard toward the remaining gunships.

"Then let's do that little return to sender!" came Adam's voice.

Robin's eyes wide watched as the tug dragging the cargo containers flew right toward the gunships. "Adam! Back off! Wait for fighters to clear the area!"

"No time!" came Adam's reply and like a whip he veered up releasing the containers.

"All fighters clear the area! Repeat, get clear of the pulse wave!" Roaran turned and banked his fighter away as the container's magnetic clamps activated. Attaching themselves to the gunships. Before they exploded.

Robin watched in horror as the shock wave raced through space and collided with Willa's fighter.

"Allison!" Robin barked into his comms as her ship was rocked by the shock wave and began to tear it apart.

Just as it exploded into fragments, he saw the ejection pod break away from the main body of the fighter. Before the wave could tear it apart as well, it was suddenly jerked out of the way to safety. Looking up, he saw Adam's ship had it drawn close in a tractor beam.

At the sight of it, he let loose the pent-up breath he didn't know he had been holding. Before his blood began to boil with rage.

When he landed, he leapt out of his fighter, ripping his helmet from his head as he stalked toward where Adam was climbing out of the tug.

"Well, I'd say," he started to say looking at Robin as he slipped off his helmet.

But was silenced as the heel of Robin's palm plowed into his face, knocking him off his feet against the tug. Before he could recover, Robin was on him grabbing him by the jacket over his flight suit.

"If you ever endanger one of my friends again..." Robin growled through his teeth, his face less than an inch from his brother's face. "Brother or no brother, I'll kill you," and he shoved him against the ship before he turned to walk away.

Before got a few paces away when something hard hit him square in the back. Freezing in place he slowly turned to see Adam unzipping his jacket.

"Aren't we due for a sparring match?" he growled back, tossing it aside as people started gathering to watch the pair.

"I guess we can bump up the lesson time!" Robin returned, unzipping and tossing aside his jacket as well and they both assumed a stance.

Adam threw a punch and Robin blocked it. "Nice forearm block," he said, blocking Robin's counter. "And back fist," he said, a grin forming on his face. "Now what was that combination again?"

Robin threw a series of punches Adam blocked. Before grabbing Robin by the arm and the next thing Robin knew, he was thrown over Adam's shoulder coming down hard on the flight deck.

"I guess you're going to have to be faster," Adam said, circling him as Robin rolled to his feet. "But you are improving." After sending him a smirk, he charged him.

Countering him Robin kicked low at his legs catching him just under his knee. As Adam blocked his jab he was sent back as Robin's cross connected with his cheek.

"And you need to keep that left up!" Robin sent back as Adam turned, glaring at him.

Standing straight Adam threw a couple more punches which Robin easily knocked away. "That's it," Robin said, returning the grin. "Stay loose!" he jibed, ducking under a punch and nailed Adam with a punch to his side. "You're improving," said Robin as he weaved away on the balls of his feet.

Stepping back, he blocked a couple more pooches from Adam before catching and trapping one arm and kicking him across the gut. The next thing Adam knew he was flat on the ground his arm locked out at the shoulder.

"You keep watching my hands when you should be watching my eyes!" Robin hissed out before getting back up.

"Okay, brother!" Adam growled facing him.

"Bring it, little brother!" Robin replied, waving him forward.

Adam ducked under a hook blocking a roundhouse kick from Robin. Blocking a few more punches he trapped one of Robin's arms locking the arm out at the elbow and slamming Robin back first to the deck.

"Why won't you just let me do my job?" Adam demanded.

Before Adam could do more, Robin gripped his head between his thighs and pulled him off him. They were back on their feet facing each other.

"I have no problem with you doing your job!" Robin snapped. "As long as you listen when it comes to the safety of everyone here!"

"Are you sure this isn't about you being afraid of me replacing you?" Adam demanded.

"More like you just can't understand or stand that here you have to obey orders!" Robin snapped back, throwing a couple more punches.

Tapping an arm again Adam locked it out, drawing Robin's face close. "I have no problems taking orders!" he snapped. "After growing up with the Raiders I can handle just about anything!"

Spinning out of the lock, Robin delivered an elbow strike to Adam's back. Then a sidekick to his gut as the blow turned him to face him. "Then act like it!" Robin spat before leaping forward delivering a hard spin kick across Adam's face.

Panting, Robin glared down at him as the sounds of the cheering formed crowd met his ears. "Good sparring with you!" he snapped, then without another word, turned, grabbed his jacket and started to leave the hangar.

"ACE!"

Turning, Robin was in time to see Adam soar through the air and collided with his midriff, tackling him to the ground.

A Sister's Words

A SHORT WHILE later the pair stood in Hector's quarters as he glared at them from his seat, eyeing the fresh bruises forming on them and Adam's busted lip. "From what I was told you two put on quite a show in the hanger," he said slowly and dangerously, and they glanced at each other. "Needless to say, we're in a dangerous section of space," Hector said, climbing to his hooves. "We could face the collapse of this base at any moment... we constantly face the threat of attacks... enemies virtually everywhere we go," he counted off as he circled them.

Again, they glance at each other. "I would have thought the both of you would know. That the last thing we need is for its people to not regress to the level of five-year old's!" he barked, whipping around to look at them.

"Sir..." Robin started.

"DON'T TELL ME WHO STARTED IT!" Hector barked, silencing him under his glaring eyes. "Now, I don't know what the problem is between you two. And frankly I don't care. But I expect the pair of you to start acting like brothers and settle it right now!" he said, taking a few steps away before facing them again.

They stood there shooting glances at each other.

"SETTLE IT!" Hector shouted, stepping into Robin's face. "THAT'S AN ORDER!" He looked at Adam.

They shared one last hard glance. "Can't think of any problem," Robin said, looking forward again.

"It's settled, commander," Adam said.

Taking a deep breath Hector looked them over. "Report to medical," he said, turning away from them. "Then I want you back here, Ryuu. We have to decide what to do now," and he returned to his seat. "Now get out of here!" They turned and left.

Once they were in medical Robin headed straight for Freya while Adam paused before turning and heading in the other direction. "Let's see how much damage you idiots have done to each other," she hissed in frustration, running her hand down his side. At once he hissed as a sharp pain laced his side. "Looks like you may have a few cracked ribs..." She took his head between her palms to examine him before picking up a medical sensor and began running it over him. "A heck of a shiner coming in which you're lucky didn't detach your retina... and possibly a bruised kidney," she counted off before she laid her hand over his lower back, and he flinched again before raising up to his ribs again.

"If you got something to say, just say it," he said as a light glow formed under her hand and his ribs started feeling better.

"I think you have more to say than I do," she answered.

Sighing with a shake of his head, he looked over at Adam. "I don't see how he's our brother," he grunted as her hand moved over to examine his kidney again. "He's hot headed, arrogant..."

"He's you," she said, interrupting him and he blinked, looking at her.

"Not you're just insulting me," he said as her hands moved over his eye.

"Am I?" she replied. "He's also loyal, brave, willful, from what I've seen of him. He stands by and doesn't abandon those he cares about and do anything he has to, to do the right thing. And will gladly lay his life on the line for those friends and family he cares about." She started running her hands over his bruises and they started to fade away.

"Many of the same qualities you have that many admire. The only difference is..." she said as she finished looking at him, "unlike you who had some form of stability, he's had to fight every day for his life. So, he had to learn to do what he had to in order to survive even if it was dirty."

For a second, he just looked at her.

"So, where did this knowledge come from?" he finally asked.

She held his gaze. "When you spend most of your life as a slave," she said before turning away to put away the scanner. "You either learn to read people fast or you die." She walked away.

Assemble

AFTER ROBIN AND Adam had gotten clean bills of health, they grudgingly went their separate ways. Neither really saying anything to each other.

Before he reached his quarters, Robin met up with Willa. "Allison," he said and enveloped her in his arms. "You, okay?" he asked, stepping back hands on her shoulders.

"Well, considering how things could have been," she answered, taking a deep breath running her hand through her hair, her thoughts drifting back to the fact she'd almost been killed by Adam, "surprisingly well enough." She looked him over. "Though I wish you had left a piece of him for me," and she turned to look out a window into the field.

"Right now, I'm just happy you're okay," Robin said, stepping behind her. "If he had just waited. It wasn't like they could get a signal out through all the gamma rays."

"Maybe he was thinking whether or not this station could take a direct torpedo and missile assault," and they turned and watched the leader of the Elves walk toward them, his hands linked behind his back robes brushing the deck. "Though impulsive his heart was in the right place," and he looked at Robin. "Sorry to pull you away from your friend but Hector wishes to see us."

Nodding, Robin turned to Willa and after giving her another comforting hand on the shoulder. She gives him a nod he turned and left following the Elven leader.

"I don't think we have been formally introduced," the Elven leader said as they walked down the hall into a lift to get to another level. "I am Valarian of the ancient house of Silverstar."

Looking at him Robin nodded. "Nice to meet you," he replied.

"Certainly, in some ways, good to know some things don't change," Valarian murmured as the lift shot them up the decks.

Blinking Robin looked back up at him. "What do you mean?" he asked curiously.

"That your people still have a flare for both fiery tempers, moral codes, and sense of territoriality," he said in return.

Blinking Robin just looked at him. "What are you talking about?" he demanded, facing him fully.

Blinking, the elf looked down at him with a confused look on his face. "You don't know, do you?" he asked.

"Know what?" Robin demanded clarification.

Valarian just looked at him. "Then it is not my place to say," he finally said, turning back to face the closed lift doors.

Blinking Robin stared dumbfounded at him. "Wha... why?" he demanded.

"Because there are those who believe true knowledge can only be gained by taking the journey without any short cuts," he answered before the doors opened and walked out.

Leaving Robin rooted stunned and confused to the spot. He barely managed to reopen the doors before it was called to a different level and took off after him.

When he finally caught up to Valarian, he was already in the command section along with the rest of the leaders. All turned to watch as he entered, some even moving out of his way.

"Nice of you to join us," Hector said, and Robin looked at him as he moved to lean against one of the consoles. "As you all are aware the recent attack has made us even more vulnerable than we were before," he started pacing around the main display where a holographic image of the area floated above it. "Which means we have two options: either we find a way to deter whatever is coming next from coming," he turned to face them, "or we evacuate to a new location," and he leaned against the emitter.

"At least gunships were sent instead of the Scylla," Roaran said, and everyone looked at him from where he sat. "Let alone the Vancor brigade of the Black Dragon, which keeps growing and growing with each of the people they are sent to attack."

"Do we have a backup location?" Robin asked not wanting to think of the horror stories he's heard of the ship and brigade or that none survived an attack by them.

"No," Hector answered, and everyone looked at each other. "It was a security measure in case we had to evaluate so no one would know where we would be going."

Robin looked over as a rapid series of pops and clicks came from the Dormeanian from its rapid moving mandibles. "How long do we have?" came the translation.

"We will send out scouts immediately," Hector replied. "The first one or group to come back with either the deterrent or a place to go wins."

"Then maybe we can get lucky and this Robin Hood we keep hearing about will just swoop in and save us," one of the other human leaders said and a few chuckled at that. While Robin did his best not to react to it.

"Or maybe these rumors about the Knights return will come sweeping across the stars and wipe out everything in their path. And the mountain sized Gold Dragon will bring the Black Dragon to its knees," another said and more chuckled.

Again, Robin did his best not to react.

396

As Hector stood straight, silence fell, looking at them all as they eyed him. "Assemble teams and prepare to disembark!"

Nodding, the leaders turned and left with only one thought on Robin's mind. The map concealed in the armors. And what laid at the end.

Saying Good-Bye

LATER ROBIN WAS in his quarters packing a bag when the door hissed open. "So, you're leaving again," came his mother's voice.

"I have to," he replied, turning to face her slinging his pack over his shoulder after checking the pistol he had strapped to his thigh.

"Then who are you going to leave behind to look after things here?" she asked as they walked out of his quarters into the hall heading for the hangers. While people moved up and down it to wherever they were going.

"You and Tekmet," he said simply and after a few steps he paused, looking back at her where she had stopped in her tracks in surprise.

"You're not leaving one of the others here?" she hissed under her breath when he walked back to her.

"I can't!" he hissed back with a hand on her back, urging her forward again. "I need them all because it's the only way we can access the map hidden in the you know what," he continued on again.

"You could just make a copy?" she hissed back.

"I don't want a copy of that map to exist for anyone to find," he said as they rounded a corner. "And already we have a hard trip ahead of us."

"Finding the Knight that keeps attacking you?" she asked as they entered a lift going down. "What makes you so sure how to find her?"

"If we don't find her, we may never find whatever is at the end of this map," he argued back.

"You could just go out there trying to find a place for us to go or a better means to defend ourselves!" his mother pointed out. "Like everyone else is doing!"

"It could very well be a case of two birds with one stone," he defended. "This map was hidden so well, the only way to find it was if the new Knights worked together to find it. So more than likely whatever is at the end of it could very well help us!" and they entered the hangar which was full of activity as ships and crews readied to leave.

Eyeing the *Odysseus*, he saw Little John, Adam, Much, and Freya looking it over making sure everything was prepped. When they saw him, a couple paused in what they were doing watching him. Frowning, he wondered where Willa and Tuck were.

"So right now, I need you and Tekmet to look after things while I'm gone," he said and turned to head toward the *Odysseus* before he paused. "And make sure Dulglad doesn't cause trouble while we're gone," he added, looking at her.

Sighing, she nodded. "You just come back in one piece you hear," she said, worry lacing her voice.

Smiling, he stepped back toward her and fondly cupped her cheek. "I'll be back," he said, trying to reassure her before leaning down to kiss her brow before he turned and walked to the *Odysseus*.

Stopping near the ramp he let his pack slip from over his shoulder to his side. "Everyone ready?" he asked as everyone turned to him.

"At least this time I can make sure my ship comes back in one piece," Tuck said, coming down the ramp face hard as he looked at Robin and Freya. "Not like the last time you guys left with it."

"It was in one piece when we got back," Robin defended. "It just had a few dings you had to buff out," and he looked around for Willa.

"Not to mention the engine looked like someone was trying to mangle it," Tuck replied, shooting him and Freya hard looks.

Sighing, Robin shook his head as he glanced around. "Where's Allison?" he asked when he still didn't see her.

"She said..." Adam started then paused, standing straight from a container of supplies. "There she is."

Frowning, Robin turned looking in the direction he was looking. Then blinking did a double take. Along with virtually everyone else who caught sight of her, and more and more people turned in her direction.

Willa was walking into the hanger dressed in regular battle armor, her hair tied back in a braid with a pack slung over one shoulder.

Slung across the other was the strap of a very large blaster and gauss rifle with multiple barrels of various sizes; the main had six smaller ones mounted on an electric rotator. On each hip was a pair of pistols, along with a combat and grenade harness. Which made Robin think that at least one of those other barrels was a grenade launcher.

"Does she always go for overkill?" Adam said, a sly grin on his face.

After shooting him a look, Robin answered, "Let's just say that rifle..." Adam looked at him, "...is probably just her side arm," and he slapped his arm across his chest before walking into the *Odysseus*.

A List

IN THE ODYSSEUS once they had cleared the asteroid belt and had taken refuge in a system a good distance away. Hidden in the rings of a still developing planet.

"Okay so what's the plan?" Freya asked when they had all gathered at the table in the main room.

"Well, we're obviously gotta find this other Knight a new place to hide or a deterrent," Willa said leaning against the wall of one of the sleep slots, one hand resting on a drawn-up knee.

"Or we could do both," and everyone looked at Little John from where he sat at the collapsible table.

"He's right," and they glanced over at Erik. "Whatever is on the end of that map was so well hidden that only Knights could find it," he said and a few nodded in agreement. "Maybe it's something that could save Tortuga or a place for them to go to."

"Then the question is how the heck do we find her?" Much said walking across the floor, arms folded. "She just seems to show up everywhere, no way to know when or where."

"That's not completely true," and they all look at Robin. "There is one common factor," and he looked at them. "The people. Wherever she shows up the people are suffering..."

"You do realize this is the Black Dragon's Empire," and they all looked at Adam. "There's no shortage of that."

"...as well as desperate...

"Again, it doesn't exactly narrow it down."

"...not just desperate," Robin continued shooting Adam a look tiring of the interruptions. "These people would have to be at the end of the line... oppressed by not just the Black Dragon.... The worst off." And he looked at them all.

"Okay..." LJ said, rubbing his chin. "That could narrow it down a bit. So, we just have to find the system with the people that are suffering the most," and he sat back in his seat.

Robin moved forward and leaned against the table palms flat against the surface, his ponytail slipping down one shoulder. "That would be a very long list," he said before running one hand through his hair to rub the back of his neck.

"Maybe not," and they all looked at Adam. "I think I know someone who can help us," and he looked at each of them in turn.

A short while later they watched as he made adjustments at the comms. "Are you sure he can help us?"

"Remember what I told you at Bedie?" Adam asked, looking up at him. "Then remember what I said of him," he finished looking back forward at what he was doing. "And the Code says we are not to raid suffering people, but those who hurt them."

"Then what do you do?" Robin asked, leaning over his side hand resting on the back of the chair, eyes on the coms.

At his question, Adam paused before slowly, his head turned to face him. While Robin's eyes shifted to meet his.

"Am I interrupting something?" a voice said, and they looked forward again to the holographic head of the Ice Raider. "And which one of you two is Adam?" he asked slowly confused.

"Me, Pa," Adam said and the Talark smiled.

"Then it's good to see you, my boy, but I have to say..." he looked from Adam to Robin again. "I have to say it's virtually impossible to tell you two apart..."

"Well, if it helps, I'm the one who knows when to think," Robin said, and he heard Adam growl a bit and Talark blinked. "But right now, we need your help again," Robin continued. "Though I didn't catch your name last time."

"Talark," he answered after a couple seconds. "What could I do?" Talark said after a second of shifting his gaze from one to the other.

"We need a list of systems on your 'do not attack' list," Robin replied.

Head jerking back, he frowned. "What for?"

"Pa," and Talark looked at Adam. "This is important; we need this. And if it works out it could help in perhaps forging an alliance with Tortuga and its people."

Talark just looked at him. While Robin waited in silence looking from one to the other. Before he slowly gave them a half grin.

"Good argument but I was going to give it to you anyway," he said with a light chuckle. "Whatever you're up to Adam, I wish you luck," he said with a nod. "as well as the rest of you," and he looked at them all. "And be careful."

A short while later the group was pouring over the holographic list Talark had been sent to them, which slowly scrolled up the air. "Geez this is definitely not a short list," Much murmured.

"The question is where do we start, or do we split up?" Willa asked, looking at the group. "Cover more ground that way."

"Probably not the best idea," LJ said.

"But for where to start," Adam said, moving forward. "Best place to start is always at the one that is the worst off. Which is always..." and he wiped his fingers, sending it into a blur into a sudden stop. "At the top," and he turned to face them, crossing his arms, a small smile on his face.

Glancing at him Robin stepped forward eyeing him before looking at the name at the top of the list. "The Drago System," he murmured. "How appropriate..."

The Drago System

WITH A CLAP of thunder, they dropped out of hyperspace in a system that bore the scars of battle. Flying through it they eyed the fragments of old battleships and defenses.

"The site of one of the last stands from when the Black Dragon took over," Robin murmured as they maneuvered around a fragmented planetary defense mounted on an asteroid "right before she killed the last Gold Dragon..." then paused as a planet came into visual range and was zoomed in on with various storms moving through the atmosphere. "The planet Dagon... the world had been terraformed to be the homeworld to the dragons," he murmured as he eyed it with the deep scars marring the surface. "Scattering them to the wind and into hiding."

"While she hunts them down and kills all who won't join her," Willa said. "Those who remain here fight for life on a daily basis. And there is no system in the Empire's known galaxies that is probably patrolled more. Or scavengers hit more for any hidden riches left behind."

"What do you expect when she fears what could happen if the Dragons reorganize against her, especially with the other races with them?" Tuck said as he turned to Freya at the sensors. "Need help reading those?" he asked, and she slowly looked up at him, a deep frown on her face.

"If I am..." Freya said, turning back to it while Little John shot him a look. "We have scattered populations across the planet, I doubt any of them are very large. As virtually all from what I guess are the major cities are in ruins," and she turned facing him again.

"Any ships in orbit?" Robin asked, looking at LJ who was still shooting Tuck a hard look.

"There's so many things and ship fragments flying about in this system we could scan it for a month and probably wouldn't find anything intact."

"Then it's the perfect place to hide one," Robin said. "Friend or foe there may be more ships out there," and he scanned the area.

"Then we better get on the ground fast," Adam said. "May I suggest..." and Robin looked up at him. "That we set down in the grouped population... if the Knight is here and helping them, they might be able to help us."

For a couple seconds the pair just looked at each other. "Sounds like a good idea," Robin finally said. "Let's get her down," and he accelerated the ship.

When they landed on the outskirts of a small shanty and tent settlement. When they descended the ramp to the outside dressed in black tactical gear. Will's rifle slung over her shoulder across her back.

"By the gods," Robin muttered as the people started coming out of whatever dwelling they had managed to scrape together. All dirty in ragged hanging clothes and with desperate beaten looks in their eyes.

"Freya," Robin said, turning to look at her. "Go get as much food and clothing as we can spare," he said and nodding, she turned and went back inside with LJ. "Please we'll give you what we can..." he said, and the people started to gather around them moaning for help. "Please stay calm we'll give you what we can..." The people grew louder when the two reappeared and they started passing out food.

"But we need your help," and a few turned to look at Robin. "we're looking for someone. Someone who might have," he started, but paused when he saw a few go stiff, looking over his shoulder.

Frowning Robin turned to see what had grabbed their attention. And saw scout ships on the horizon.

"GET OUT OF HERE GO!" Robin barked and they shot back up the ramp as the people scattered.

"We gotta get them away from these people now!" Robin barked jumping into the cockpit seat and started powering up as everyone strapped in. "HANG ON!" he barked, and the ship shot forward and making a tight turn tore away. "They are following us?" he asked.

Before an answer could be said alarms blared and the ship shook from small impacts. "That answer your question?" Tuck snapped.

Drawing Fire

WEAVING THE ODYSSEUS left and right as the scout's ships continued to fire on them. "Rear shields are holding but unless you want that to change you better find cover fast!" Tuck snapped. I don't need anyone else putting dents in my baby!"

"Yeah, yeah," Robin moaned, rolling the ship. "Anything nearby?" he snapped, looking over at LJ.

"Little busy!" he snapped back.

"I may have something!" he heard Much say behind him. "There's a large crevasse to the east that might be large enough to take cover..."

"It will have to do... HOLD ON!" Robin barked and rolled and banked the ship in that direction.

With a crevasse in the surface appeared with a clap of thunder, Robin rolled into it surprised by the superstructures built in it. "What the heck is this?" he snapped aloud as he maneuvered around the various structures.

"I said it would be here!" Much said, while the scout ship kept firing on them some of their shots hitting parts of the structures, they streaked past. "Just didn't know anyone built anything here!"

"Well, a little more information would have been nice!" Robin barked back, rolling under a structure that stretched from one side of the crevasse to the next before the end of the crevasse caught his eye.

"Robin, what are you doing?" Tuck barked as the throttle opened more, then he looked at the view screen. "DON'T WE WON'T FIT!"

"WE'LL FIT!"

"NO, WE WON'T!"

"YES, WE WILL!" Robin snapped, rolling the ship onto its side and rocketed into the passageway between two buildings built into the end of the crevasse.

With cries of surprise from the people behind him, Robin did his best to keep the ship going in a straight line while dodging obstacles built into the sides. While, every now and then, he couldn't help but scrape the top and bottom with a shower of sparks. Before they burst through the other side into an unbelievably large structure which gave them plenty of room to move about despite parts of it having collapsed.

"Told you we'd fit," Robin moaned, half surprised they had before glancing back at Tuck, who just glowered at him, teeth bared. "Okay... let's find a place to set down and hide."

"Not sure yet," Much said, looking over his sensors.

"Same here," Little John said. "Which kinda worries me."

"Why?" Freya asked.

"Because it means the sensors were either damaged in those scrapes, we lost them..." Adam started to say but was interrupted by Robin jarring him, coming to a sudden hovering halt. Eyes on three other scout ships in front of them weapons pointed right at them.

"...or they're jamming us," Robin finished for him, looking at the rearview screen to see the other one come up behind them.

"Unknown transport! Land at once and surrender!" came a loud voice.

"Any ideas?" Robin asked.

"Here's a question: why aren't they shooting at us anymore?" Freya asked.

"Probably because we're in an armed transport and they think we're resistance fighters. And they want prisoners to capture, torture, and question us. Before they kill us," Adam answered.

"Unknown transport! Land at once and surrender!" the loud voice repeated.

"Tuck, can we get the top and bottom guns going?" Robin asked.

"Not from what I'm seeing here," he replied. "Those scrapes jammed them in place!"

"And if I use the forward weapons we'll be blown away," he said aloud.

"Unknown transport! Land at once and surrender!" came the voice again. "This is your last warning!"

"So, what do we do?" Freya asked.

"Obey for now," Robin said, and started to slowly drop the ship to the ground and lower the landing skids. "Then take them by surprise," as he watched one of the scout ships drop lower before lowering a group of sentinels to the ground.

Before another move could be made suddenly a series of blaster fire hit some of the sentinels knocking them to the ground in a series of sparks. Head whirling in surprise Robin saw a lone figure in a long coat obscuring its figure, its head covered as well. On a raised platform firing on them firing with a blaster in one hand and a small cannon in the other, which when fired sent one of the scout ships careening to the ground a large piece missing.

"Who the heck is that?" LJ demanded.

"I don't know but whoever it is may need help; let's move!" Robin ordered, tearing out of the cockpit, them all following. "No armors! We don't know who the heck it is!"

"Didn't look like it to me!" Willa said, grabbing her rifle as the ramp lowered.

Opening fire as they barreled outside as the remaining ships lowered more sentinels into the fight.

Drawing his plasma sabers into his hands, blades extended, Robin charged at the sentinels and before they could turn to face him. He leapt forward spinning, cutting two down before spinning back, decapitating one and running the blade of his other sword right through a second. Whirling reversing his grip on one around he kicked the head off another behind while impaling another.

As he kicked it off the blade, he saw LJ staff in hand spinning it in both as in a blur of motion. He blocked, deflected, and struck out at multiple opponents. Then in a flurry of movements he locked out the arm of one sentinel with its arm wrapped around the staff before shooting one on each side with both ends of the staff.

Then after ripping off the arm brought the staff down to sweep the legs out from under it. Shooting it before turning to face another, which he whacked across the head before knocking it to the ground with a strike to the back of the legs. He shot one in front of him before jabbing another end through the chest of the one on the ground.

Next to him Tuck's buster sabers converted to a tonfa form. After shooting a couple blades extended from the front and back with a series of movements to cut one down, before turning and cutting the head off another with the back blade. Then, altering his grip on one, he drove the handle, which sharpened to a point like a hammer. While in the rear of the other a hook blade emitted from the other end and dug into the chest of the sentinel behind him. Which he ripped apart by drawing the tonfa back and struck out with the elbow into the neck of another sentinel.

Not far from him, Much and Adam stood on the spot, shooting the sentinels around them. Before Much's plasma sabers extended and with rapid motions after deflecting and landing multiple strikes with the sticks to the side arm and finally to the head knocking it off. He turned and after deflecting the arm of a sentinel and wrapping one arm brought the staff behind the sentinel's head and using the mechanics brought the sentinel to the ground. Then reversing his grip on the other stick shot the sentinel on the ground before facing the next, which he leapt at with a cry.

While Adam barked, "Behind you!" and shot a couple of Sentinels coming up behind Willa. After she looked at their sparking bodies, which had collapsed to the ground before she looked over at him. After giving him a curt nod, which he returned, both jumped back into the fight.

While behind him, Freya wielding her sabers with a pair of dagger blades out of one end and after decapitating one turned and shot another. Before she dived toward another as it fired the shot impacting the ground where she had been. Rolling, she whipped around and slashed at the support for the ankle, and it collapsed to one knee before she drove both blades into both sides of the neck.

Robin fought next to Willa, her rifle firing with a whirl of the spinning barrels as she cut them down, light reflecting off her exposed ebony skin. They turned as she pumped the grip for the grenade launcher on the underside of the barrels. And they both shot a pair of sentinels at the ledge of the drop off. Sending them over the edge.

Darting forward, they looked down and watched them drop. "Mine hit first," she said when they impacted.

"Yours was fatter," he said, shooting her a look and glancing over their shoulders and they dove for cover.

He eyed the figure above as it spun left and right shooting down sentinels as they charged at it. A couple reached the platform, were knocked off their feet by the cannon as the figure spun and swung it and hit the back of their legs with it. Before it fired it again in their direction and Robin spun intime to see the arms and head only remains of the sentinel it hit crash to the ground along with the legs behind a stunned Freya.

Then turning again, it fired on another of the scout ships as it turned to face them, blasting it out of the sky and into another with part of the front section blown away. Where they both crashed to the ground in fiery wrecks which rolled across the ground.

Then with the scout ships taken out it dropped the cannon and leapt from the platform. Before it landed with a roll forty feet away it shot two more sentinels who crashed to the ground, one with a missing head, another with holes through the chest. At the end of the roll, its hand coming out from under the coat it hurled something at a sentinel which embedded into the chest before exploding.

Turning to another the figure threw its rifle whacking the raised arm of another sentinel away before its cannon could fire. Before drawing a pair of daggers from the small of its back and driving one into the base of the neck of the sentinel before it could recover. Then turning it slashed another sentinel across the abdomen with one before driving both into the sides of another.

Whipping back around, it kicked one across the face, sending it hurtling to the ground before hurling one dagger into its chest and the other into the back of the head of the last. Walking forward, it picked its rifle back up and started toward them. The barrel pointed toward the ground.

A Lone Guardian

WITH A CHARGING sound, Willa turned her weapon on the approaching figure. "Put that down little lady!" the figure snapped, and Robin blinked at the feminine note in the voice. "I think it's obvious if I wanted to kill you, I could have," the woman said, drawing back the hood, her long dark hair blowing in the wind before lowering the cloth covering the lower part of her face. "Or just let them kill you."

"Who are you?" Robin asked and she looked at him and he was taken aback by the depth in her violet eyes.

"A survivor just like you," she answered, slinging her rifle over one shoulder and she eyed them. "You scavengers?" she asked, voice going hard. "Come to steal hidden riches?"

"We're looking for someone," Robin answered, and she looked at him.

She just looked at him. "Those who come to the Drago system rarely want to be found," she said slowly.

"Well, we don't have a choice," Willa said, keeping her weapon still on the woman, who glanced at her.

"Well, it sounds like an interesting story I'd like to hear sometime," and she turned to look out an opening in the structure. "But it looks like a storm is coming. Best take shelter and stay here for the night," and she turned and started to walk away.

"We may not have that kind of time!" LJ snapped, stepping forward, and she paused.

For a second, she was silent. "From the looks of things, your ship needs repairs," she said, her back still to them. "I doubt you'd want to take off without it fully operational," and her head turned to glance at them over her shoulder. "How long would it take to fix?"

Frowning, Robin looked over at Tuck. "A day max," he answered the unasked question. "That is unless you want the top and bottom guns working," and with a hard look on his face he tilted his head as if daring Robin to argue.

Coming Together

HOURS LATER, TAKING a break from working on the repairs on the *Odysseus*, Robin wandered through the structure. Eyes wandering over the elaborate carvings on the walls which in some sections were carved out rock tunnels. Which still bore multiple carvings in various designs, and sizing some even looked like writing.

Pausing at one point to lightly brush his fingertips along a carving. Trying to shake or understand the sudden feeling of familiarity.

When he came out the other end he paused. Stunned by the sight before him.

The opening came out to an enclosed ledge. The view beyond showed the sun rising over the horizon with rays of light stretching across the barren landscape with the canyon ending a few miles away. With rolling and jutting rock formations darted throughout it where it met what looked like what once had been rolling plains. But it was now mostly cracked ground with patches of grass here and there. In the distance, he eyed mountains covered with dark spots, which he guessed were burnt out trees.

"Breathtaking, isn't it?"

Whirling at the sudden voice he spun around. To see the woman still in her long coat which he now saw she wore tactical gear under it sitting on a rock one leg resting on one knee. While she was looking over her rifle.

"Absolutely," Robin said looking back at the view. "Even if this is a sacred remnant of it," and sorrow laced his voice for what was lost.

"It was beautiful," she said behind him, and he heard her make adjustments to her rifle. "That used to be a vast plain of grass stretching to the horizon in one direction. To the edge of a desert in another. As well as those mountains in the distance. There used to be dense jungles, deep oceans..." she continued, and Robin heard the sadness of the loos in her voice, and he glanced over his shoulder and saw a tear roll down her cheek while the top of the rifle was exposed. "Then she came," she hissed, and she jammed the top back into place. "By the time she was done this planet could barely contain life!"

For a couple seconds he watched her as she jammed a power mag in and after she checked the readout on the side. Raise it to her shoulder so she could check the sights.

"You're a dragon?" he asked, and she paused slowly, her eyes turned to meet his. "Aren't you?"

For a couple seconds, she looked at him. Before without a word, she lowered and powered down her rifle with a whining hiss.

"Look, you jumped forty feet off that ledge like it was nothing. You swung the cannon like it weighed nothing," he counted off as she put away her maintenance gear before she climbed to her feet after tucking the now stored equipment in a pocket of her jacket. "Not to mention I fought a dragon before, so I know what I'm talking about," he continued, turning to face her as she started to go back down the passageway.

At his words, she paused. Slowly she turned to face him, a surprised look on her face. "You faced her?" she asked. "You faced the Black Dragon?"

Sighing, he looked away back to the scene. "And barely survived it..." he said softly, eyes roaming the landscape.

"That in itself is something to be praised," she said, and he looked back at her. "Very few can claim that."

"Are you one of them?" he asked, looking back at her.

417

For a second, she looked at him. "Mostly the aftermath," she said, stepping back to stand next to him.

As silence between them, his eyes turned to look at her out of the corner of her gaze. "Why are you here?" he asked, and she looked at him.

"Because I was born here," she said softly. "This is my home... I grew up here... I feel in love here..." and he looked at her frowning. "...the best and most noble man I ever knew..." she said in a soft, mournful voice. "But right now, it feels like I'm trapped in a nightmare... he's gone... my world is gone... my family..." and she turned away from him and he frowned as it seemed like she was trying to keep something locked in.

"Then why are you here?" Robin asked.

She looked out at the view again. "Because like I said," and she looked at him. "This is my home."

For a couple seconds they just looked at each other. Before they turned at the sound of footsteps. And watched as Adam and Freya stepped out of the gloom. Who paused at the sight of the pair.

"Everything okay?" Freya asked looking from one to the other then next to Adam who was partially in shadow.

"Yeah," the woman said before she could say anything, and Robin looked at her. "Everything is fine," and she looked at him before turning back to the two. "I'll leave you three alone," she said and started to walk away, and the pair moved to let her by before continuing forward.

When they stood by him Robin paused and glanced over his shoulder. And saw the woman had paused looking at the three of them. As soon as she saw he was looking at her she turned and walked away.

Frowning at the strange feeling he got from the look on her face. "It is weird being here," Freya said, and he looked at her where she sat on the ledge, one knee drawn close chin resting on the top of her hand's eyes scanning what was before here with her hair dancing lightly in the breeze. While next to her Adam arms crossed leaned his side against the frame as he looked out at the scene not looking at either of his siblings.

"I'll say," Robin said, turning back at the landscape. "Ever since we got here, I've been getting a weird sense of familiarity..."

"...and electrifying," Adam finished for him, and Robin glanced at him.

"Thanks," Robin said after a moment before turning his head back forward again. "Thanks for saving Willa during the fight."

For a moment silence rang between the two with only the wind making noise. "When I get a chance, I gotta mark this day on my calendar," and Robin looked at him out of the corner of his eye before looking away. "My super-sized big head big brother thanks me for saving his friend instead of punching me in the face for it," and Robin glanced at him as he rubbed his jaw and cheek where he had hit him.

Rolling his eyes, Robin looked away, shaking his head. "You earned that punch. You nearly got her and about a half a dozen other pilots killed with your impatience, glory-seeking and impulsive grand standing."

"I seem to remember you doing something similar to save me," Freya said before glancing up at him.

"That was different," Robin said, facing her his back and one leg drawn close to rest his foot on the wall. "I didn't put anyone's life but mine on the line."

"Not true," she said standing as he looked at her. "What about Hannah?" and she looked at him.

At once his face hardened as he straightened and faced the view, hands on his hips. "That's different," he growled looking at her.

"Why?" she asked. "Because your back was broken, and you could barely drag yourself, let alone fight anymore because you didn't know who you had been fighting?" and she turned back to the view, a tear running down her cheek for her friend. "But Hannah is still dead, and her daughter is an orphan. You could have just shot the crystals and gotten us out after the Knight you fought had run," and she looked back at him. "But you didn't, you stood your ground and fought. And frankly..." and she turned to look at Adam. "I don't think Adam would have done any different," as she looked from one to the other who blinked at her. "Neither one of you likes to run from a fight. So, whether you like it or not you two are more alike than you want or care to admit."

The two brothers just looked at their sister before their eyes drifted up to look at each other. Then without another word Freya turned on her heel and walked back down the tunnel. Leaving the two of them alone.

"Maybe she has a point," Robin admitted, and Adam looked at him.

"Maybe," Adam replied.

For a few minutes, they just look at each other. "Look..." Robin finally said after a moment. "We need to start working together and stop fighting each other. Because we are both fighting for the same thing."

"I can live with that," Adam said with a shrug. "As long as you stop treating me like I'm an idiot."

"I never thought you were an idiot," Robin said, and Adam arched an eyebrow in suspicion of those words. "I always thought you were brave and smart. Considering what you did with those kids from Bedie."

"I just wish you had remembered it before at Tortuga," Adam grumbled, rubbing his jaw where Robin had hit him before.

"Well, what did you expect would happen when you nearly got someone, I consider family killed. Especially when I already lost the only father I've ever known," Robin returned, not backing down from what he did. "I'm sure you would have done the same thing if the roles were reversed."

Adam just looked at him. "I guess you have a point there," he finally answered, looking out at the view. "Though I probably would have done worse," he admitted after a moment of thought. "I guess we both have a different way of doing things," and he looked back at Robin.

"But we'll always be on the same side in this fight," Robin finished, and Adam nodded in agreement. "But the question is can you follow my lead when the time comes?" he asked, crossing his arms.

"You know your friends better than I do. And they will always trust you over me," Adam answered. "If I try to lead them they will fight me on it because they don't trust me enough yet."

"Then why do you keep trying to..." Robin started then it just seemed to click, "...Willa," he said slowly. "You like Willa."

Adam's jaw set before he looked out at the land again.

"Is that why you've been acting like a jerk?" Robin demanded jabbing his thumb back down the passageway an exasperated look on his face.

"I have not been a jerk," Adam defended, standing straight.

"This coming from a guy who stuck a gun under my chin during training and nearly got her killed?" Robin pointed out a half grin on his face.

Adam's jaw set and his eyes sharpened. "Look I don't have to take this from a guy who keeps leaving his friends," Adam said standing straight and started toward the passageway.

Robin's face hardened at Adam's words. "No, I'm just the guy who grew up with her and knows her like a sister," Robin said, his gaze going to the ground. "And despite it being a split second decision, I always gave them a way and trusted them to find me. Because I know they will always have my back."

He heard Adam pause and glancing out of the corner of his eyes saw he had stopped just outside the entrance. Before he slowly turned to look at him. Hands on his hips, a neutral expression on his face.

"Okay," Adam said as he slowly turned to face him. "Say someone was interested in her," he started not quite looking at Robin, his hands going to his hips. "...what would you... as someone who knows her, suggest?"

Smiling Robin stood straight. "For starters..." he said, taking a few steps toward him until he was in front of him. "...stop acting like a jerk or a creep," and he shot Adam a broad grin. "She broke the finger of the last one who tied," and swatting the back of his hand across Adam's chest started back down the passageway.

421

Unexpected Help

LATER THE WHOLE sat around a makeshift fire while an animal the woman had managed to catch for them to eat before she cooked over it slowly turning on a spit. Every now and then, Robin would look at her as she turned the meat to cook it evenly. While around him, Willa was checking over her rifle Freya looked over some of their supplies with LJ while Much sat next to Robin and Adam also eyeing the woman as he rubbed his upper lip in thought. At the sound of approaching footsteps, they turned and saw Tuck approach as he wiped his hands on a rag.

"How's she looking?" Robin asked as he sat down next to Adam.

"Until I get her back to dock and with a proper maintenance team, she won't be pretty," Tuck replied, shooting him a glare. "But the turrets should deploy now."

"Well, that's something," Robin said, feeling a little uncomfortable under Tuck's hard glare. "So, what was this place?" he asked the woman as he looked around to change the subject.

Not pausing in what she was doing she looked up at him. "This was once the great council chamber," she said looking around. "Where the great dragon council used to meet."

Jaw dropping slightly Robin looked around as everyone went still at what she said. "That explains why this place is so big," he said as his head slowly turned as he tried to take everything in. "would have loved to have seen this place in all its glory…"

"People used to come from all corners of the known worlds to see it," the woman said as she tested the meat. "It was truly glorious, matched only by what was built on earth after the Knights were formed," and after she drew the meat from the spit and onto the makeshift platter and using a knife she drew from a sheath in her boot to cut portions for everyone. "It was one of the first places she got stuck when her forces got through the planetary defenses," and she looked around.

"Why didn't she blow up the planet like she did Amal?" Willa asked and the woman looked at her. "Why leave the planet in ruins?"

"Because it would hurt the Dragons the most," she answered as she started handing out the makeshift plates of food. "And a constant reminder to all who would resist she took down the most powerful of the magical races. And what she could do to them."

"I would have thought her killing the Knights of old would have been warning enough," LJ said before taking a bite.

"That only martyrized them, and it caused many to rally against her," she said as people ate some of their food. "Some even say it's how the resistance started."

"The way you fight you could have been in the resistance," Adam said.

She paused before glancing up at him. "Once upon a time," she said before she glanced down at Robin. "But that was a long time ago," she said as Robin opened his mouth to say something. "For now, I just have to survive."

"Until when?" Tuck asked.

"Well, it might be time if the stories I've been hearing are true," she said and took a bite from her plate.

"What rumors?" Robin asked, glancing around as everyone was acting like they were just hearing about this.

"That the next generation of Knights have been born," she said, and she slowly glanced at all of them. "But then they've been saying that for years. Especially when they're starting to say they've already struck blows against the Black Dragon herself."

Later, after they'd all eaten and were just getting ready to settle in for the night, Robin had the others gathered around him. "So, each of us will be lookouts in shifts," he started, looking at them all.

"Yes, Robin, we know the drill," Willa said, her rifle slung across her back.

"Except for those who don't," he said, and he looked over at Freya and Adam.

Adam let out a huff. "Like I really need a refresher course on how this works," he muttered.

"Repetition and knowing we're all on the same page," Robin said, shooting him a look, eyebrow arched. He fell silent. "Now I'll take first watch," he started, looking at them all.

Later Robin stood alone, eyes scanning the horizon for any sign of danger coming their way. He paused, head turning slightly to the side. "You can come out," he said openly to the darkness.

There was silence. Then with a crunch and shifting of stone and dirt, the woman stepped out of the darkness and into his line of sight.

"You on first watch?" she asked.

"I wouldn't be here otherwise," he answered again, scanning the horizon and the land in between.

"Mind if I join you?" she asked.

He patted the ground next to him. "More eyes the better," he answered, and she sat down next to him.

"So, why are you really here?" she asked after a moment of silence.

"I told you, we're looking for something," Robin answered, still scanning the area ahead of them.

"Then why come here?" she asked.

"She has a habit of showing up in places like this," he answered.

For a second, he felt her penetrating skeptical gaze on him. "For what reason?" she finally asked.

Frowning he slowly looked at her, a deep frown on his face. "Not to hurt her if that's what you're worried about," he defended in an insulted voice. "She just might have something we might need."

"What could she have?" she asked.

For a second Robin just looked at her, thinking fast on how much to reveal. Afraid if he revealed too much it might cause problems for them, some that might be fatal. But if he revealed too little it might spark her curiosity more.

"Something that may help find something lost," he finally said.

At his words, her eyes narrowed in thought as she kept her gaze on him. "Sounds more like you're on a treasure hunt," she said slowly.

Not looking at her, his mind raced again. "At the end of every journey there is usually a treasure," he finally said. "Isn't that the point of any journey?" he asked and looked at her.

For a second, she held his gaze before she nodded. "In that I would have to agree," she finally said looking back out at the landscape covered by the dark of the night. "Some might even argue the journey itself is the greatest treasure compared to what you may find at the end," she said.

"Which always begins with a single step," Robin said, and he also turned to look out at the night covered ground.

Again, silence fell between them for a few moments. "Then maybe a step you should take is to the west," she said, nodding in that direction. "Though most of the remaining scattered population is nomadic to avoid patrols. Every now and then they gather, and many are gathering in that direction," and she turned to look at him. "If this person is like you say, more than likely she will be there if she is here at all."

A Dark Past

THE NEXT DAY, Robin was awoken by a hand coming to rest on his shoulder and with a charging hum. He jerked the barrel of his plasma saber into his waker's face. Willa didn't even blink.

"What is it?" he asked, and he twisted his wrist, so the barrel was pointing off to the side of both of them.

"She's gone," Willa answered simply.

"What?" he barked, jumping out of his bunk and racing through the ship and down the ramp and started scanning the area. "When did this happen?" he said, and he turned to look at her again.

"No idea," Willa said, looking around with him.

"Did anyone hear or see anything while they were on watch last night?" he asked looking back at her.

She shook her head. "Nobody said anything."

"When did Freya come on shift?" he asked looking at her.

"She was the last one on and reported she was gone," Willa said, returning his gaze after scanning the area one last time.

"Thanks for your vote of confidence," Freya said, coming over from where she was helping LJ pack up the camp.

"Actually, out of all of us, I'd say you have some of the sharpest eyes," he answered, scanning the area again. "Usually, the first and last stages of the watch shifts are the most dangerous. As either the people are too tired or just waking and a little slow because of it," and he looked at her after scanning again. "But frankly I'm not surprised," he said with a sigh, "the way she just appeared and considering how long she's probably been on her own... who could have stopped her if she wanted to just leave," and he turned back to head back up the ramp and into the ship.

"Shame really," Willa said as she followed. "I wanted to know where she got the cannon," and Robin rolled his eyes.

Once they were all packed up, they took off exiting the building through a hole in the roof. Before Robin opened the throttle, he paused at a sudden feeling. Before he slowly turned his head and looked out the corner of the view screen. Where he saw the woman standing on the roof her coat billowing in the wind and the exhaust of the ship engines as she looked up at them with the dirt and dust dancing around her.

He just looked at her. Before he reached down and opened the throttle, shooting them forward.

"So, where are we going?" Adam asked.

"West," Robin said, turning the ship in the right direction. "Keep an eye on the sensors and let me know if we have large groups of people coming together," he said.

"Why west?"

He glanced over at LJ. "Let's just say I got a little advice," he answered.

"You think it's a good idea to take the advice?" Adam asked.

Robin glanced at him over his shoulder. "Right now, it's the only lead we got," he said before facing forward again. "That is unless you want to just fly aimlessly across the planet, hunting down each and every group and people trying to find her when we have no real way to know it's her," and he looked at him again.

For a second, they were all quiet as they looked at each other.

"I guess that's the best place to start," Adam relented. "But just in case," and he stood from his seat. "I'm manning one of the guns," and he walked out of the cockpit.

"Willa, you go with him," Robin said and, nodding, she climbed to her feet and followed out.

For the next half hour, they flew across the bleak barren landscape that stretched to the horizon. Searching for any large or gathered populations of people. With little to show for it.

"And ladies and gentlemen in this direction we have a whole lot of nothing and in that direction, we have a whole lot of nothing..." Much said from his station carelessly waving his hand in various directions. "And in that direction..." and he waved it again. "...more of a whole lot of nothing."

"Thanks for that inspiring tour my friend," LJ said as he sighed as they continued flying in the same direction. "Though it may be time to alter course, otherwise we'll just end up circling the globe," and he looked at Robin.

Sighing, Robin scanned the horizon as he opened his mouth to agree. They all jerked in surprise from a blipping alert from the sensors.

"Well, that damn near gave me a heart attack," Much said as he scanned the data as more reading started to show. "Looks like we got something on the ground a few clicks ahead of us... and a few ahead of that we got a large gathering."

"People?" Robin asked, looking over his shoulder at him.

"Not just people," Much answered, looking at him. "Looks like a good many animals as well."

"Pack animals," Robin murmured. "Looks like we found where the gathering is going to be. What is the object a distance from them all?" and he looked at Much again.

"Could be a small ship," he said looking back at Robin. "Could be her."

After a second of thought, he turned to Little John. "How about we set down a mile from them and huff it over?" he suggested.

"Not a bad idea," LJ agreed.

After they set down, landing in a cave for camouflage, they locked down the ship and headed out. Moving as quickly as they could toward what could be a small ship they had detected.

When they drew close, they slowed their pace to move more quietly. And from various hiding spots eyed the small transport in front of them. With people moving about on the ground or going into the ship.

"Raiders?" Robin asked, looking at Adam.

"Might be," he answered as he continued to eye the people below them.

"I thought you said the raiders don't hit places like this planet," Willa snapped looking at him.

"We don't!" he snapped back, looking at her. "They must have touched down for repairs or something like," he started then paused, going still with Willa, Tuck, Freya and Robin going still as well.

"What is," Much started.

But was interrupted by Robin whipping around and pointing his plasma saber at the people who had been sneaking up behind them heads covered by hoods and faces with environmental masks. Who at his sudden action and with a rapid series of charging hums turned their weapons on them. While around him all but Adam turned weapons on the group ready to fire.

As the group had moved up behind them gazed down at them, they froze as their covered heads turned toward Robin. "Well, it seems this planet has picked up a new level of degradation," one said, his or her voice masked.

Frowning, Robin blinked up at them. "And just what is that supposed to mean?" he demanded. "After all, you don't even know me. So, what gives you the right to judge me?"

For a second, they were still before the one who spoke reached up with one hand from his rifle and lowered his hood and mask. "As if you don't know!" he growled, glaring at Robin.

Blinking Robin's eyes darted to Adam, whose back was still to the group. "I think you have me confused with someone else," he said, looking at the man again.

This seemed to make the men even angrier. "Despite everything you've done you would do this to me, Adam!" he growled as his eyes narrowed, his grip on his weapon tightening. "You would play me for a fool!"

"He's not," Adam finally said and slowly turned onto his side to look at the man who blinked in shock. "Because until now my brother has never met you before," he continued as the man looked from Robin to Adam and back again. "But I have to say it's good to see you again, Venar; it's been a long time," Adam said with a nod.

Venar just looked at him. Then with a growl he lowered and powered down his weapon, his people quickly following suit. While Robin twisted his hand forward so his plasma saber, so it wasn't pointed at them.

Then without a word the group pushed through them all, giving Adam as much room as they could so they wouldn't have to touch him. Blinking at the coldness of them all Robin watched them go. Before he glanced back at Adam whose face grew harder and harder as he watched them go.

Then with no warning he leapt to his feet and followed them down. "You can go to hell!" he snapped after them as he charged down the hill. "You have no right to condemn me for what happened!"

"Then why follow us?" Venar asked, whipping around to face Adam.

"Because I did the right thing that day and you know it!" Adam barked back, jabbing his finger into the man's chest.

"What I know is you broke the code that united us!" Venar yelled at him as the others came to stand behind Adam watching as the Raiders stared Adam down. "Raiders don't leave their own behind!"

"I had no choice!" Adam defended face, growing harder stepping more into the man's face. "If I hadn't both ships would have been destroyed!"

"You let them die in an act of cowardice!" Venar snapped, shoving Adam back before grabbing him by the shoulders. "If you honestly think I enjoyed in any way supporting having you exiled... you're wrong," he said softly for the first time, with an equally soft look in his eye. "Fact is, you broke all our hearts," and he and his company turned and left back into their ship, each shooting Adam a glaring look.

After watching them go, Robin stepped forward until he was level with Adam. Before he slowly turned and looked at the look in his brothers' eye. And all the sorrow and longing that lay within its depths.

A Brother's Truth

LATER THE GROUP had set up camp outside the Odysseus with a fire made up on the ground and their daily rations. From where he sat, Robin looked up from his meal and eyed Adam as he sat off on his own. Elbows on his knees, head resting on the palms of his hands. Eyes locked on the night-covered scenery before him.

Sighing, Robin laid his food aside and climbed to his feet, walked over, and sat down next to him. "So, what happened?" he finally asked after a few minutes.

Adam's eyes shot a glance at him before shifting forward again. "Why don't you ask them?" he answered, nodding in the direction of the Raiders ship.

"I'm asking you," Robin replied, his voice hardening.

For a few seconds Adam was silent before, with a sigh Adam ran his fingers through his hair in frustration. "Remember when we first met?" he asked, looking at Robin, who nodded. "Remember what I said to you when you asked why I wasn't with the raiders?"

"They were taking a break from you," Robin answered. "They considered you their lucky charm."

"I also said 'not all luck is good,'" Adam continued before his face lowered to rub his forehead. "They considered me their bad luck charm or black cat as the saying goes. Because whenever I was a part of a plan it always seemed to go wrong one way or another despite whether we got what we came for. Though I never understood what was so bad about a black cat," and he fell silent.

"It was a year before I met you," he started, "We had attacked a supply ship. For a while, it seemed to be going just fine. Then there was a massive leak from the engine room. It spread fast. I was part of the group who went back into the ship to rescue people still there. When it went from bad to worse."

"How?" Robin asked.

"I was just bringing my latest person through the airlock," he continued, and Robin eyed a tear rolling down his cheek. "The second I walked through it one of the men's arms wrapped around my shoulders to keep him up. Which happened to be the man you met earlier. When the alarm that the engine reactor was going critical with vibrations that vibrated through our ship nearly knocking me to my feet. And the bridge crew was reporting a Black Dragon ship was coming out of hyperspace and heading toward us."

"What did you do?" Robin asked, encouraging him.

Sighing, he leaned back, eyes going to the stars above. "After depositing him against the corridor wall I returned to the hatch holding on to the frame to keep me on my feet through the vibrations. Yelling at people to move faster back onto the ship as bursts of fire issue from vents. One by one they came bringing people with them. Just as the final warning for the core rupturing the bridge reported the cruiser was closing. But there were still people on the ship..." he continued before falling silent as if he could still hear the cries of the people rushing to get back to the airlock and him yelling for them to hurry.

Robin just looked at him. "You sealed the airlock," he finished for him.

Adam nodded. "Some tried to stop me, but I sealed the airlock and separated the ship," he said. "I left four people to die on the ship, including my best friend, which we barely got clear as it exploded just as the cruiser met it, crippling it from following us into hyperspace. When he got back a tribunal was held, and I was exiled."

Robin looked away shaking his head at the conclusion of the story. "I take it the Ice Raider couldn't stop it?" he asked.

Adam shook his head. "No, otherwise he risked dividing the clans," and Robin nodded at that. "But he helps me when he can."

"Well, there's an old saying from Earth 'the best thing you can do is the right thing, the second best thing you can do is the wrong thing, the worst thing you could do is nothing at all,'" Robin said before looking back at Adam. "You certainly didn't do *nothing*. But you did the right thing," and Adam looked at him, a frown on his face. "If you hadn't done what you did both ships could have blown or the cruiser could have destroyed your ship," and he held Adam's gaze. "As far as I'm concerned, you're still a raider," he said firmly, putting a comforting hand on Adam's shoulder.

"That goes the same for us," and they turned to see the others watching the pair. "And if they stay stupid and not take you back," Willa said, sitting down next to Adam. "Then to hell with them, you got us now. And I, for one, would hope to have someone who would put the people first," and the others nodded in agreement.

"And besides," and Adam looked over at Little John. "you're a Knight now. Which means you'll always have us watching your back," he said formally.

"As long as you're not being an ass," Much put in and a few laughed as LJ smacked the back of his head.

When things quieted down a little, they all just sat there looking out at the landscape. "So, the better question, for now, is... how do we lure in this Dragon Knight who keeps attacking us?" Erik said.

"I think I have an idea," and they all looked at Adam.

Where I Hoped to Be

A FEW DAYS later, people watched in awe as the female Dragon Knight walked through the crowd with a couple of people walking behind her. Handing out supplies as they went. Around them were hordes of people all wearing dark, loose covers over their bodies. While some held the rains of various animals either being loaded or was being ridden in.

"We'll give what we can," she said as she turned from one group to another, patting one person on the shoulders as she passed. "Sorry it wasn't as much as last time," she continued before she turned and eyed another person hunched over and covered.

"Are you okay?" she asked, moving forward. "We got food if you need any."

"You do have something I need," the figure said in a rough voice.

"What?" the Knight asked, dropping down to one knee trying to look at his covered face and reach out to uncover it.

An armed hand shot out sizing her by the wrist. Before she could do anything, Robin shot up and had her face down on the ground arm locked out at the shoulder and elbow to keep her pinned. While he kept one knee at the small of her back and one foot on her other hand to keep it down and from her using her weapons.

"You!" he snapped as the people who came with her drew weapons from under their robes.

"DON'T MOVE!" LJ shouted as he and the others sprang to their feet, pointing weapons at them and they froze. Then with a jerk one tried to raise his weapon at once one of them shot him and he spun to the ground stunned.

"WE SAID DON'T MOVE!" Willa snapped and she pumped her rifle.

After the Knight's head turned to look at the man on the ground she growled at Robin. "That man had a wife and two children!" she growled with hatred up at Robin.

"Trust me, they won't miss him," he replied calmly.

"Face me with honor, you bastard!" she barked as she tried to arch her leg up to kick him off her.

"I would but you really haven't given me much choice," Robin replied, shifting to easily avoid it. "After all, every time we meet you just attack me for no reason!"

"Robin!" and he looked over at Adam as he and the others drew closer. "We got incoming," he nodded in the direction of several large clouds of dust moving fast in their direction.

"Then let's get what we came for," he barked, drawing her arm with her bracelet crystal up higher and she moaned.

Each of them linked up at the wrist. Robin used his free hand to close her fingers around the wrist of one of theirs. There was a multicolored flash from all the crystals and a holographic projection of the map appeared.

"Capture!" Robin barked and they each took a picture of the map with her piece in it.

Then without a word Robin rolled forward after releasing her arm and whipped around pointing his bow sight down the arrow at her. As she pointed one of her plasma sabers at him after springing to her feet.

"YOU AGAIN!" she shouted, eyeing them as they stood in their standoff. "How dare you use these people to trap me!"

"We did nothing of the kind!" Robin snapped back. "We just hazarded a guess you'd be here because how desperate these people are," and he slowly inched back until he was shoulder to shoulder with the others. "Besides, it's not like you're one we could walk up to and ask a favor," he continued as the remaining people that came with her edged up to her so both groups were facing off. "But now we have what we came for. And we're leaving."

"What makes you think you're going anywhere?" the knight in front of them said.

Before Robin could say anything, the sensors issued an alarm and after looking at it his head whipped around and saw several land vehicles coming right at them. "Any ideas?" Willa said in a private coms as Robin shuffled one leg back.

"Get back to the *Odysseus*," he said, eyes on the approaching vehicles.

"Duh," Much said. "And just how are we supposed to do that?"

"On my signal, we all take off in different directions..." Robin started.

"...and we'll meet up at the ship," LJ finished for him. "Not like they can't follow all of us!"

"I thought of that," Robin replied, "we'll just give them someone they'll want to chase," and he crouched low one hand on the ground.

"Robin... what are you..." Freya started but was interrupted as Robin launched himself at the other Knight, wings extending. Hitting her full in the chest, both pairs of her wings extended forward as his momentum carried them high into the air.

Struggling to keep a hold on her, he shot them through the air before leveling over the ground. And after plowing against a couple of rock formations one she managed to dig claw-tipped hands into stopping with a sudden jerk. The sudden movement dislodged his grip and she launched herself at him.

Ducking under the spinning kick he kicked her in the small of the back sending her hurtling her forward away from him. Launching himself after her and spinning around she ducked under the punch he followed up with.

Grabbing him as he spun back to face her again, she drove her knee into his gut.

Before he delivered a couple more punches before grabbing him again and spinning around hurled him against the ground. Landing hard rolling across the ground he came to a stop crouched low one leg extended and hand on the ground wings partially open eyes on her. Before he glanced over his shoulder and saw one of the land vehicles came to a skidding stop behind him.

Before the driver could react, he flipped over the vehicle. And, grabbing him, threw him out of it before leaping in himself.

"Always wanted to try out these old-fashioned things," he murmured before pressing his foot on one of the peddles and the engine roared. "Me likey," he said shifting the gear and with a cloud of dust from the spinning wheels shot away from them.

Driving fast through the wasteland every now and then he glanced back seeing the people still chasing him. After checking again, he brought it to a skidding side stop at the edge of a cliff. Leaping out of the vehicle, looking over the edge before whipping around as those chasing him surrounded him.

Then from the sky, the Knight came and after pulling up sharply and dropping down landing right in front of him down on one knee. "Did you really think you could escape us in one of those?" she asked, standing straight, drawing her plasma sabers into her hands.

For a second Robin was still before he shrugged arms spread wide. "Actually, I'm exactly where I hoped to be," and leaning back fell right over the cliff.

At once she rushed forward and looked over the edge but froze as the *Odysseus* rose above the edge of the cliff. With Robin standing on the ramp holding onto one of the frames. With a smirk behind his mask, he gave her a two-finger mock salute before the ship turned and flew away.

An Ancient Course

AFTER ROBIN RACED up the ramp and raised and sealed it alarms began to blare. "what's going on?" he demanded, racing into the cockpit.

"We got incoming!" Willa reported from his usual seat in the cockpit. "More scout ships coming in this direction."

"They must have detected us," Much said from where he sat. "They sure have picked up speed."

"Adam, with me!" Robin barked. "Willa circle around! We can't let them find that Knight!"

"Are you kidding?" Adam barked as Robin raced for the ladder for the top and bottom cannons. "You want to help the person who attacked you twice, including me and Freya? From what she said before."

"Maybe it will finally convince her we're on the same side," Robin snapped and started climbing the ladder. "Now stop talking and man the gun!"

Slipping into the pod and after strapping into the seat activating the screen took the controls. "You two strapped in?" Willa asked over the comms.

"Nice and tight!" Robin replied.

"Like a bug in a rug!" Adam reported.

"Then hang on! Swinging around!" and at once the ship went into a spinning loop before with a thunderclap from the engines raced back the way they came.

"Target acquired!" Robin snapped, swinging the cannons to bear. While seeing the forward weapons being uncovered. "And I have a feeling you are just loving this Willa," he sighed with a shake of his head.

"What can I say I got the big guns," she said, and he could hear the smile in her voice as the cockpit targeting system was linked.

"Then pick a target and take them out," he said as he turned to take aim. "We probably can only do one pass at this!" as they raced closer and closer.

"Light 'em up!" he called, pulling the trigger.

All weapons fired and in front of them, the scout ships heading in their direction exploded. As they'd started firing on something on the ground. Before they whipped back up into the air and back into space before making the jump out of the system.

Later the group sat in the main room eyeing each other, just sitting in silence. LJ sitting on the edge of the bench with Freya close by in the corner of it rubbing her top lip, elbow resting on her raised knee. Willa sat in one of the seats, a knife in hand bobbing up and down with her thoughts. Adam sat close by in another chair, turning it left and right lightly. Robin leaned against the entrance of the cockpit arms crossed with a distant look in his eye while Much laid in one of the sleep alcoves.

"So," Much finally said, breaking the silence, swinging his legs out of the alcove to sit up. "When are we going to see whether or not all we just went through was worth it?" Much finally asked after almost ten minutes.

All eyes turned to him, which he returned without flinching. Before a series of chuckles reverberated around the room.

"Might as well get it over with," LJ said with a sigh running his hand through his hair. "Let's just hope it was worth all the trouble."

440

"Time to whip off the band-aid," Much said as they all stood and moved closer. "Maybe it will be just as painless," and a few people rolled their eyes.

The images they captured were all displayed before them in midair with a series of beams of light. Slowly Robin shifted from the wall to his feet and began to slowly circle them, examining them closely.

"If we're all reading this right," Much said standing as well. "Looks like we got the very piece we needed," and he looked at that newly filled area. "The end piece."

"True but that doesn't exactly solve our biggest problem," Adam said standing eyeing the map up and down. "For starters the last jump point is set between two closely grouped mega stars, which makes the gravitational fields hard to navigate through. One wrong move or miscalculation with it and frankly we're toast," he said, looking at them all as they each shot him a side look. "Pun intended," he said, looking back at the map. "But if the stars don't get us this might," and he pointed to two black holes about half a light year from the stars. "Again, according to this map, we have to go straight between these as well. Hopefully, we have enough data on this map because otherwise..."

"...otherwise, we get sucked into oblivion one molecule at a time. Because as far as I know both places have claimed many ships who came too close," Robin finished for him. "Or if you believe the theory into another dimension," and he rubbed his jaw in thought on what they would have to do next. "But something tells me this is not what worries us," and he looked at his brother.

"Worries all of us," and they looked at Willa as she slipped her knife into her boot sheath as she stood. "It's this," and she pointed near the edge of the part of the map they had just collected. "I don't know about the rest of you," and she slowly turned to face everyone, locking eyes with each in turn. "But this takes us way too close to Centurium for my liking," she finished, crossing her arms.

"It's not just you, Willa," Robin said, running his fingers through his hair in frustration, his eyes going to the ceiling. "According to this map, we're going to have to fly right through it and their hyperspace sensors pick us up, they'll have whatever they got all over us in seconds to try to catch our wake and slip in behind us."

"And in hyperspace we won't be able to shake them unless we drop out," Tuck finished from where he sat rubbing his chin in thought.

"But," and they all looked at Little John, "if there is anything that could help us at the end of this map. Then we have to take the chance to find it."

After a second, Robin nodded in agreement before he looked back at Centurium on the map. "Tuck!" he snapped, looking at his friend still in his seat but sat up straighter at Robin addressing him. "I need you to get to the engines and get us as much speed and power as you can out of it. And when you're done with that, I need you to find some way to make our sensor signature as small as possible."

With nothing more than a curt nod, Tuck climbed to his feet without a word he walked toward the engines.

"Willa!" he snapped, looking at her, and she glanced at him out of the corner of her eye, arms still crossed. "I want you to go over weapons inventory and make sure they can all fire right, straight, true, and detonate. If we have to bring the pain, I want to either be able to turn them back or turn them to space dust."

Like her brother, she nodded before turning and after walking to it climbed the ladder to the top turret gun.

"Freya!" and he looked at his sister who climbed to her feet from where she had been sitting. "Go over the supplies we need to know how many medicines, how much food, water, whatever you can find. Count it down to the last spare part for repairs, then do it again," he instructed her.

She nodded then moved to get started at her task walking in the same direction Tuck went.

"Much!" and he faced him as Much turned to face him, hands going to rest on his hips. "You have to calibrate the sensors then calibrate them again. If someone on a ship so much as sneezes, we don't want to just feel the mist, we need to know about it before they're going to do it."

Like the others, Much nodded before setting out to complete his task.

"Adam, Little John," he said, facing them both. "The three of us are..."

"No," Adam said, crossing his arms as Robin blinked, frowning at him while Little John turned a deep frown as well on his face.

"What?" Robin asked.

"If you're going to ask me to contact the Raiders to send them on a suicide mission to give us a distraction, I won't do it," he said firmly, looking at each of them firmly with a determination that wouldn't back down.

For a couple seconds Robin and Little John just stared at him with the same looks on their faces after his declaration. Before then broke up into fits of laughter that had Robin doubling over. Leaving Adam to blink in confusion at them as they kept laughing, which rolled and echoed through the ship.

"Though it's good you stand up to defend the lives despite them kicking you out," Robin started when he was able to start to control himself. "But if you were going to take the time and listen," he continued as he straightened back up. "What we're going to do is go over the map and pan or program our route right down to the smallest detail," and he stepped forward and placed his arm across Adam's shoulders. "And hopefully you can help us with some Raider tricks which might help," he said as they started toward the cockpit with Little John right behind them. "Then I want you to see if you can help Tuck with either shrinking or obscuring our sensor signature."

The Race

FOR OVER A day, they worked completing their tasks with others who had finished early and helped those still working on theirs. Until long last, most sat in the cockpit with Robin making final adjustments to their course. Before the door hissed open and glanced over his shoulder and saw Adam and Tuck come in and take seats.

"We all set?" he asked as they were strapped in.

"Just finished with some last-minute things," Adam said, shooting him a cocky smirk before turning his attention to his station.

"Tuck?" Robin asked, looking at him.

"I've done my best I could in modifying the engines," he said as he activated the holographic read out on the engines. "Just be careful; I don't know how much strain it will put on it."

"Meaning...?" Willa asked, turning in her seat to look at her brother.

"Meaning..." he said looking at her over his shoulder, "be as sure and make the ride as gentle as possible. It could either give us the power we need to make it to the last section of the jump," he said, and Robin frowned.

"Or...?" he asked, feeling like there was something that Tuck wasn't telling them or was avoiding.

"Or... we blow up," Tuck finally said as all eyes turned on him.

After a moment of silence, Freya looked over at Robin from where she sat. "Does he give that outcome often?" she asked.

"No that's just often enough that's the worst-case scenario," Robin replied before glancing back at Tuck. "But it's good to go?" he asked.

Tuck nodded.

"Then engage," Robin said, turning. "Let us know exactly when we get close to Centurium," and Little John nodded, looking back to face the view screen and reaching forward pulled the lever and with a roaring clap of thunder. The ship shot forward jumping into hyperspace.

All eyes on their sensors as they raced through hyperspace and whatever lied before them on the path they had chosen. "Much," Robin said as he could feel the nerves grow tighter and tighter in the cockpit. "Let us know when we get close to Centurium," and Much nodded and made a few adjustments to the sensors.

"How long do you think we have until we get close?" Freya asked, glancing over at Robin from where she sat.

Robin glanced over his shoulder and started to answer before he was interrupted before he could say a word. By the blaring of the alarms.

"Does that answer your question," Little John said, pressing a few buttons.

"We got here faster than I thought!" Robin barked as he scanned the sensor readouts. "Looks like we got a couple who managed to get in our wake!" before he glanced over at Much. "Fighters?"

"It's hard to tell," Much answered. "But if we don 't lose them in the next few seconds we're going to lead them to wherever the hell we're going!"

"Adam! Tuck!" Robin barked, focused on going back to his controls again for what was to come.

"Jettisoning!" Adam said.

"WHAT?" Robin demanded head whipping around to look at him as he heard something being jettisoned. "What did you just jettison!"

"A few useless spare parts that are being put to good use," Tuck answered as an alert sounded from the computer.

"Alert! Proximity detonation in progress!"

"Much! Confirm!" Robin said.

"Confirmed!" he reported. "One of those ships must have plowed right into them! But there's still one left on our tail!"

"Deploying now!" Adam replied and Robin felt the Odysseus shift again.

"And what was that?" Robin heard Willa ask.

"Whatever it was, it dropped out of hyperspace with one ship dropping out with it," Much said from his post.

"An old Raiders trick to throw off pursuers," he answered. "A little drone with a footprint magnifier mimicking a little leak. Usually, it's meant to get them to drop out and allow us to escape, but..."

"...but instead of empty space... the ship just dropped out between the stars or the singularities," Robin said, closing his eyes.

"But we still got one on our tail!" Little John snapped.

"Robin!" Tuck barked and he whipped around to look at him. "We got a problem!" he snapped.

"What?" Robin shouted.

Before Tuck could reply the computer answered for him, "alert! Hyperdrive engine failing!"

"We must be caught in the singularity!" Robin shouted.

"If we don't shut them down the hyperdrive engines will blow!" Tuck shouted over the alarms.

"And if we drop out the singularities will kill us!" Little John shouted back.

"Well then, we gotta find a way to get more power because I don't think we got enough!" Much yelled.

"I'm open to suggestions!" Robin shouted back before a flashing of multicolored lights caught his eye. Turning he looked down at his bracelet as its crystal rapidly flashed before the armor began to expand up his arm. "What the—" he started as his head was encased and the screen flicked on.

Glancing over he saw all the others' armors had expanded as well. Then he saw tendrils extended from their bracelets and attached themselves to the consoles. As soon as they made contact images and a series of numbers flashed across Robin's screen. Then without warning the engines revved louder.

"Alert! Hyperdrive engines are now at two hundred and fifty percent!" the computer announced.

"Wha... how?" Robin muttered.

"I don't know, but whatever it was is allowing us to break free!" Tuck answered as they shot forward again. "Hang on! I think we're nearing the exit point and it's probably going to get rough!"

Then with a jerk and with rings of fire shooting out from around the *Odysseus* they exited into normal space. As they shot forward into whatever lay beyond them, they were all shaken about while the screen in front Robin's eyes flickered and died. Leaving Robin in complete darkness that his eyes could not penetrate.

When the screen flicked back on and the armor rebooted, he looked around to see the others as their armors came back online. Before retracting into their bracelets.

Robin looked over at Little John. "Have the breaking thrusters fired?" he asked in an exhausted voice as the adrenaline left him.

Little John nodded in a silent reply.

With a sigh of relief, Much slumped against his chair as his safety harness retracted. "Oh... have I ever told you how much I love you," he said, raising his bracelet to eye level.

Before he gave it a long loud smacking kiss while the others around him chuckled.

"And that goes double for me to you baby," Tuck said before he spread his arms across his console with the side of his head before he too kissed it lovingly. "I always knew you had it in you," he said lovingly caressing it.

"Should we leave the four of you alone?" Adam said to a few more chuckles. "Now the more immediate question is where the heck are we?"

After his seat drew back Robin climbed to his feet. "Much?" he asked, walking over behind his friend.

"I'm not exactly sure where," he said as he looked over his sensors and new star chart data. "But we seemed to have come out in an eight or nine planet system. Two are gas giants, one with a pretty set of rings. Two seemed to be life-bearing with moons while some of the moons of the gas giants seem to be life-bearing as well. But might have been terraformed long ago... there seems to be a few things in orbit around them. From the looks of it, they could be stations and shipyards along with what could be lunar colonies on each of those planets. But none appear to have any life signs from them. But from what I can tell they still have power but running on minimum...."

As he spoke Robin's eyes seemed to widen and the others around him slowly turned to look down at Much. All with the same stunned hardly daring to believe it looks on their faces. Before pausing, Much slowly looked up at Robin not sure to believe what the data was telling him.

"Bring up a holographic display of the system," Robin said in a quiet voice, hardly daring to believe where they could be.

After looking at him for a moment, Much slowly pressed a few buttons and turned to look for himself. And from the emitter on the ceiling a hologram of the system they had exited out into was displayed.

All they could do was stare at the rotating image. Then slowly with a tear in his eye Robin pressed his finger to the third planet from the sun. at once it was zoomed in on as it filled the room, a smile growing wide on Robin's face as he eyed the vast oceans and massive continents.

"We're here..." Freya said quietly tears running down her face before wiping them away. "I can't believe we're actually here... and all the stories about it are true. But they could never do it justice..."

Nodding, Robin unashamed of the tears of happiness and wonder running down his face. "Sol System..." he muttered. "We're in Sol System..." and he looked at his friends and family around him. "And for the first time in over a century, people have come back to it..." before he returned his gaze to the lost planet Earth still rotating before them.

The Oldest Temple

AS THEY FLEW through the system after detecting no other means of exiting the system through hyperspace but the way they came in. They marveled and gaped at the planets of the stories they grew up hearing about. From Neptune's deepest blue and its famous moon, Pluto's and Uranus's mix of colors with its thin rings of rock and radiation.

"She really does have a nice pair of rings," Much put in leaning over Robin and Little John's seat as they neared Saturn. "It's no wonder we used to worship them…"

At those words, Robin froze. "What did you say?" he demanded, head whipping around to look at him.

Blinking as everyone turned to look at him at the seriousness in his tone. "That we used to worship them in ancient times. Wh—" he started, but froze as Robin's seat shot back and he leapt from his seat and raced out of the cockpit.

After the group looked at each other in stunned silence in the wake of him leaving them. Before they all shot to their feet and followed him out.

"Robin, what are you…?" Little John started to demand when they met him in the main room.

Where he raced around not paying attention to their stunned gazes on him. "Could it really be that simple?" he asked himself under his breath. Before he turned to look at a holographic image of the solar system appeared before him. "The ancient temple of the gods," he said in barely more than a stunned whisper.

"What was that?" Adam asked, stepping up next to him.

"During the time I was captured and," he started before he glanced at them, a slight grimace on his face trying to find the right way to say it. "... well, owned..." he finally said. "I ran into this lady who was a street fortune teller..."

"Please tell me that we're not following the advice of a street con," Adam said in a moaning voice.

"It's not to say she doesn't have the gift," and everyone looked at Freya. "It's the rarest of magical gifts but there have been those who can foresee the future," and she held everyone's gaze one after another. "But I admit more than likely she's a fraud," and she crossed her arms and a couple nodded.

"Usually I don't go for that," Robin admitted. "But when she knew about you two before I even told anyone I had a brother," he said, waving a finger between Freya and Adam with her eyes narrowing and his rolling. "And she knew I was a Dragon Knight," and those words caught everyone's attention as they all looked at him in surprise and Adam blinked in surprise.

"How could she have known?" Little John demanded in surprised wonder.

"That is the interstellar question," Robin admitted. "But she also said part of what I seek will be found 'in the ancient temple of the gods,'" he said facing them and they glanced at each other.

"So, what we're looking for is on Earth," Tuck said, stepping forward. "Where the ancient temple could still be standing."

Bobbing an erect finger Robin shook his head looking back at the hologram. "I don't think she meant an actual building," he said slowly. "I think we're actually already standing in it," and he could practically hear the confusion emanating from them. "Much reminded me that we once worshiped the planets as gods. And temples besides a place of worship were once believed to house the gods on planets..."

"And what temple is more ancient than the solar system," Willa said in realization. "Mercury the Messenger God, Venus the Goddess of Love and Beauty, Mars the god of War, Jupiter the King of them all, Saturn his Queen and Goddess of Marriage, Uranus the God of the Earth, Neptune the God of the Sea, and Pluto the God of Death," she said pointing out each in turn. "But we already know the Knights of old hid this system away by cutting it off from hyperspace however they did. The only way in and out is the way we came in and we nearly died on the way in. we don't even know if we can get out."

"Remember the last bit," Robin said looking at them over his shoulder. "What Mr. Orleaus said at my birthday?"

For a second, they were silent as they thought over his question. Then all at once, all his old friends' eyes widened in realization.

"'Hidden within the eye of the god of gods,'" Little John murmured.

Smiling with a nod and pressing on the holographic image of the planet Jupiter, it filled the room, where it continued to rotate.

"So, what we're looking for is somewhere on Jupiter," Much said, stepping forward. "Question is where?"

"We already know," Willa said, walking forward and using both hands to rotate it, so the swirling storm was in the center. "What does it look like to you?" she said, jabbing her thumb at it.

Again, silence fell for a moment. "An eye..." Freya said in a slow whisper. "But what did they hide there?"

"That's the interstellar question," Robin said, turning back to the hologram. "But either way it's where we have to go to find it. And could it really be true?" he asked aloud and they all looked at him. "Could the rest of the story be true... could the Sherwood really be there?" and he took a couple steps close to the floating image of the planet. "And if she is.... could she hopefully still be intact."

Before another word could be said the alarms blared.

Eye of the Storm

THE GROUP RACED back into the cockpit and Robin looked over Little John's shoulder as sensor readouts appeared. "We got incoming and fast!" Much said when he saw something coming at them and Robin turned to look at the readout. "One of those ships must have followed us through."

"Which means by now they now know what system this is," Robin muttered his mind going a mile a minute.

"That means they're just as trapped here as we are," Willa said.

"But why come after us?" Freya asked openly. "Why not just turn around and head back through to Centurium?"

"They must want to make sure only the Black Dragon knows the location of Sol System," Adam answered before Robin could. "Imagine what could happen if we get back to Tortuga or the Resistance."

"The people could rally to them especially as they would have a safe home to go to," Robin said, mind still working. "They take us out, they give the Black Dragon the means to make an untouchable staging point or destroy everything here," and he looked at the people around him. "We gotta get to Jupiter before they do. If they find what the Knights of old hid and destroy it or get back to Centurium it's over."

"Robin, that storm is big enough to hide two or three planets the size of Earth. What was hidden there would be a speck of dust. And now we got this ship coming at us fast, hoping to turn us to space dust. How do you

454

expect us to find it with all this going on?" Tuck asked, eyes on his instruments.

"Whatever happens you can't let them get out of the system," he said before he turned and left the cockpit, his armor expanding.

***

For a couple seconds, the group continued what they were doing. "Did he just say, 'you can't?'" Little John suddenly asked.

Before another word could be spoken Tuck turned as he got an alert. "The inner airlock door was just opened!" Half a second later, they all leapt out of their seats and raced out of the cockpit.

***

He pressed the button to close the inner airlock door just as the others slammed against it. Stepping back, they crowded around the viewport to look at him.

"Robin! Robin!" they shouted, pounding their armored fists against the door.

"ROBIN! OPEN THIS DOOR!" Adam called out.

"ROBIN! DON'T DO THIS!" Willa cried, pounding her fists harder.

"I have to," he murmured in return.

"No, you don't!" Freya cried, pushing herself to the front of the crowd.

"Tuck, open this damn door!" Willa barked.

"I'm trying!" he snapped back. "He engaged the override! I'm trying to bypass it!"

Stepping forward, Robin pressed his palm against the force field. Locking eyes with him, Freya placed hers below his.

"Why does it have to be you?" she murmured.

With his free hand, he reached for the outer door release. "Because I already lost someone I love,"—he pressed the release, and the thirty-second

455

delay started — "and I'll be damned if I lose another one, especially if I can prevent it."

"Damn it!" Tuck barked, springing up. "He engaged the outer airlock! Nothing can open those doors now until it recompresses!"

Before they could protest any more, he turned his back to them and dropped to one knee while his wings extended from his back. With a snap, the outer door opened, and he was launched through the vast vacuum of space beyond towards the eye of the storm.

***

"What do we do now?" Freya asked as they watched him fly away in the direction of Jupiter's storm.

"We do what we have to give him time to find the ship," Little John said firmly, putting a comforting hand on her shoulder. Then turned as the alarm sounded again, reminding them of the other ship.

"These guys want trouble," Willa said. "Let's give it to them," and they rushed back to positions with Willa and Adam climbing and descending the ladder to the gun turrets while the others raced for the cockpit.

***

Racing through space Robin kept his eyes on the storm of the planet he was racing toward with the thrusters in his wings blazing. Taking a second, Robin rolled onto his back and looked back at the Odysseus as it peeled away back toward the incoming ship. Which he could barely make out as it headed toward them.

Hoping it wasn't the last time he saw them he rolled back around and locked eyes on the coming storm

.

What Was Lost

WITH LITTLE JOHN in the pilot seat, they rolled and swerved as the ship opened fire on them. "And this thing just had to have fighters attached to it!" he growled as he rolled the Odysseus to avoid more fire from the fighters. "it's not like this thing can move like a fighter!" and the ship vibrated from being hit by blaster fire from one of the fighters moving around them.

"And everything moving around doesn't exactly make things easy to get a clear shot!" Willa said over the coms.

"And they're blocking us from getting close enough to attack the ship!" Adam barked as they had to swerve away again. "If we can't get to the ship eventually, they'll get a lucky shot in on us!" as another missile or torpedo lock and they swerved away.

"Well, hopefully Robin will find that needle in that several planet sized haystacks!" Much said as he adjusted the shields as they took another hit from the fighters. "Though it would help if those fighters would stop herding us closer to the ship!"

***

Closer and closer Robin raced through the atmosphere of the planet into the storm. "Okay now how the heck do I find it now?" he asked openly as was brought to a stop and covered amid the storm with the winds roaring around him and he struggled to stay in one spot.

As if the suit was answered, one of the sensors on the screen moved to the center. It didn't seem like anything more than a direction indicator. When Robin turned away from it was indicating and it moved in the direction it was indicating like a compass pointing north.

"Well, that way is as good as any!" and turning, shot off in the direction that was indicated by the sensor.

***

Trying to buy time from the fighters, Little John shot towards the larger ship suddenly. Before they could get a lock on us, we were rolling over them as we shot past.

"How do you like it when someone can shoot back!" Willa barked, taking the opportunity to open fire on it.

"Missiles loose!" Much suddenly through the coms.

At once Willa spun her cannons around and opened fire on the missiles streaking at us. After shooting down one, she started to take aim at the other. Before she could squeeze the trigger, it was shot down by Adam on the bottom gun.

"Missiles dispatched!" Adam said through the coms.

"Well, I don't know how much longer we can keep this up!" Little John said as the fighters again started to swarm us keeping out of range of the forward weapons with Willa and Adam opening fire on them again.

***

Flying through the storm Robin doing his best to keep his course through the strong winds and near zero visibility. Guided only by the direction indicator. With no sign of how close Robin was to what he was being led to.

Suddenly he got a proximity warning, and it was closing fast. He barely managed to straighten out before what looked like a wall of metal appeared. And was slammed flat against it, arms and legs at awkward angles.

"Ow..." Robin moaned his cheek against the surface of whatever he had hit. "So that's what a fly on a windshield feels," he moaned before pushing off from what he'd hit, stopping to hover a few feet from the object.

In all directions, all he could see was metal of whatever he hit. Then the screen in front of him changed viewing modes and he gaped.

"Please let this be it..." he murmured as his gaze followed the shape of what he had hit. Before a wide grin spread across his face and he let loose a loud cheer. Then shot off in another direction with the metal to his side so as not to lose what he had found.

***

The fight had dragged closer to Jupiter and the fighters were still circling around them even though they'd managed to hit them a few times, not enough to penetrate their shields. Either drawing them in a direction or preventing them from getting into a good attack position on the larger ship.

"If we don't tag one of these fighters soon, they're going to nail us!" Much called.

"That doesn't matter," Little John said as they rolled again around a fighter. "All that matters is giving Robin enough time to find what was hidden out there! And pray the stories of what was are true..." and they looped back toward the larger ship.

"Then don't you think we should start fighting back for real?" Willa asked. "Before," she started when a lock on alarm sounded. Before they could do anything the ship trembled violently with an explosion that rocked it.

"Report?" Little John barked at Tuck.

"Engines down to sixty percent attempting to compensate! Shields are virtually gone!" he reported. "I don't know if we can take another hit!"

With a growl, Little John turned the ship back toward the attacking ship. "It's time to fight back!" he growled.

"LJ! On our six!" Adam warned and they looked at the rear-view sensor and the fighter seemed to slide into position.

Just as they got lock on warning the fighter suddenly exploded. "What the..." Much said then he saw. "There's another..." he barely managed to say before what shot down the fighter streaked past them.

Before the other fighter could recover Willa gave a cry over the comms as she blew it out of the stars.

Leaping from his seat Much watched as the small arrowhead shaped fighter with forward swept wings shot toward the larger ship. They watched as it rolled left and right before it opened fire on it first with Gatling blasters attached to the underside of the main body sticking out in the gap between the cockpit and the wings. Then with a missile attached under a wing that blew the shield generator.

Taking advantage of this Little John locked on and fired a barrage of weapons on it, blowing it to pieces. Before they could issue contact with the fighter it looped around and turned with it, they watched as it dropped down into the storm circling Jupiter. Not long after before they could wonder what happened they watched wide eyed as something else emerged from the storm.

Found

AGAIN, CHIKAKO WAS rocked as the ships fired on the station. "How many fighters left?" she barked at one of the people at her station.

"About a little more than half are left!" she reported, and Chikako looked back out the screen that stretched across the wall.

From it, she watched as the two ships continued their attack. Though bigger than the gun ships which had originally attacked. One was barely more than a stick like super structure with horizontal engines which had fighters attached which dropped from it not long after it appeared.

The second was a support craft, which was a little larger, which resembled an angled hollowed out half cylinder attached to a square like rear with a flat top almost with the front with open hole leading to main hanger while around the opening torpedo tubes were lined on either side. With main engines in the direct rear, with the command section rising above it, with two more angled down at the top end. The bottom right behind a pair, right behind a pair of trapezoid shaped wings with sensors attached to the bottom and top front.

When the larger ship fired more torpedoes at them. Again, what fighters they had intercepted and shot them down. While still fighting the fighters released from both ships.

"Sir, we got another coming in?" one of the people at a console called out.

"Friend or foe!" Hector barked, moving closer to the console.

"Unknown!" the tech replied.

"What do you know?" Chikako demanded.

"That it is big!" the tech answered, looking over his shoulder. "Enormous!"

Before another question could be asked their questions were answered. On the view screen, a large ship moved between the two attacking ships. From the angle they could see of it, which was cylindrical in shape with an angular edge coming to a straight point on the front. On top, a sensor array was situated with a pair of stubby wings on each side and were tipped with a pair of large engines.

"Tactical analysis?" Hector ordered in a stunned voice as he pointed at her, keeping his eyes on the new ship.

After the right person gave her herself a shake, she looked over her sensors. Then a holographic image of the ship appeared in the above main emitter. Seeing it from the side they saw it was a stretched-out ship with the blunt rounded arrow or egg shaped front end attached to the main superstructure slightly raised from the center. The back of the front section at sharp angles met the main body of the superstructure. Along the back were two raised structures, which were bridged by a suspended structure that flowed from the back of the forward section to the second raised section near the rear.

From the structure near the rear a second pair of curved sections created a half circle to sections of the superstructure that stretched out to meet them. With two more suspended structures stretched back to better secure the engines to the main body. Which curved back down into the main central section. As the holographic image rotated, they saw a large hollow section in front of the engine section curved down into it. Just below where the main engineering was attached the delta wings with the engines attached to the tips they saw earlier.

But aside from strategically placed double barreled pulse cannons it seemed almost harmless in its appearance.

"Fifty torpedo launchers on each side behind retractable armored covering. With four in front two in the rear. One hundred double barrel cannons throughout the surface. Eight pop-up missile launchers fore and aft with four retractable cannons two above and two below. Primary and secondary shield generators as well as long- and short-range sensors. And twenty total fighter launchers on the sides and a hanger entrance in the rear in front of the main engine pod," she reported, and with each of what she reported, people around the command center stared in stunned silence in horror.

"Friend or foe, she's a predator..." Hector muttered in the silence as he moved closer to the rotating image.

"Let's just hope whoever is in command of that ship is on our side," Chikako murmured before looking back at the giant view screen watching as the ship drew closer and closer to the station.

Slowly the large ship moved between the attacking ships. And Chikako felt she could cut the tension with a knife as the people in command watched the ship moving toward them. Every now and then she glanced over at the tactical waiting for them to report the ship was targeting them.

"What are they waiting for?" she murmured aloud.

"Probably toying with us," Hector replied, still eyeing the ship. "They know and we know they have the power to take us out."

For the next few minutes, the silence continued. Even the other attacking ships and their fighters waited for what this new ship would do.

Or allowing them the kill.

Then suddenly the armor cover on the side banks of torpedo batteries on the new ship shot up. And the ships fired a pair of broadsides on both ships on both sides of it. At the same time, its pulse cannons opened fire as well as the missile launchers popped up and opened fire on the fighters.

In stunned silence they watched, surprised by the sudden attack all ships were soon nothing more than wrecks floating in the depths of space. Then all at once, everyone in command leapt to their feet with cheers of jubilation. In the midst of high fives, hand grasping, and back slaps Chikako stood eyes locked on the ship still approaching.

"Robin..." she said in a low whisper as a smile spread across her face.

***

Aboard the Sherwood, Robin in his armor helmet retracted like everyone around stood on the bridge eyes on the wall screen.

"Well, that takes care of that," he said before glancing over at Willa at her seat at tactical.

"What?" she asked with a smile and shrug. "You said clear the magazines."

"Not complaining," he replied. "Just wanted to see the look on your face," he said with a smile and chuckled, which she returned.

"Robin," and he looked over at LJ and Much who sat at the helm. "They're hailing us," LJ said.

Robin still wasn't sure what to do. He slowly looked at the rest around him.

"This isn't just my decision," he said seriously.

For a second, they all looked at each other. Silent questions passing from one to the other. Each asking the same thing.

"What should we do?"

Sighing LJ turned his seat to look at them all the signal they were being hailed continued. "It's going to happen eventually," he said, and Robin looked at him. "I'd rather it be my choice."

"He's right," and Robin looked over at Tuck from his station at engineering.

"At least we'd be able to give them a place to go," Freya said as Robin turned to him.

"She's right," and Robin turned to Willa at tactical. "And we got one of the best ships in the known worlds. And Tortuga is no longer safe."

"I agree," and they looked at Adam. "And once word gets out the Sherwood has been found, it will be a rallying cry."

"But if the Black Dragon hears it has been, she's going to have her Navy out in force..." and Robin looked at Much. "But..." and he slowly turned to look at them. "We don't have to reveal everything..." he said, and Robin blinked.

After a second thought, he looked at each of them again. All nodded.

"Bring us alongside..." he said.

***

Chikako and Hector watched as the ship came alongside the station and the name printed on the side in bold letters came into view.

SHERWOOD

At once tears of joy began to fall as both her hands went up and covered her mouth as she let out a burst of happy laughter. While around her the people began to cheer after stunned silence at what they were seeing.

"I almost believed it was a myth..." Hector murmured in stunned awe.

"Commander," one of the people at her console said and they looked at her. "They're answering our hail... audio only."

"Open a channel," Hector said in a soft solemnly disbelieving voice.

The command turned silent as the cackle of the communication sounded.

"Tortuga!" came Robin's voice over the coms. "This is the Sherwood. Requesting permission to dock?"

People started cheering again as Hector replied, "permission granted."

Stay or Go

AT THE AIRLOCK, Chikako waited with Hector and the assembled crowd swarming around them. With more and more arriving each second.

Then with a hiss the lock opened. And Robin and the others walked into the station with most of his friends right behind him.

After his eyes scanned the gathered people around them Robin's gaze locked with the stunned Hector. "Team ten reporting may have found either a deterrent or new place to go sir!" he said.

Blinking Hector looked from him to the Sherwood which he could see through the nearest view port. "I'll say you did... the question on everyone's mind is how in the name of the Gods did you find it?"

"You'd be surprised what kinda leads you get on the Drago System," Robin answered, glancing at his mother as a wide-eyed, surprised look crossed her face before it quickly disappeared.

Again, Hector nodded looking back at them. "Are there any Knights aboard?" he asked, a hopeful tone in his voice.

After glancing at Chikako, Robin turned back to the airlock. Which hissed open again. And a string of gasps issued through the crowd.

As LJ in his armor stepped out and walked toward Hector. "I take it you're in charge here?" he asked in his altered voice.

Stunned and gaping Hector just stared at him for a second. Before he mutely nodded his head.

"Then I am Little John or LJ," LJ said, extending his hand and after a second stunned silence Hector took it. "On behalf of the new leader of the Dragon Knights, Robin Hood, I offer Tortuga either our protection or sanctuary for its occupants," and he glanced at the people around them. "If you have a council, I suggest you confide in it and decide on the matter fast. Because I don't know how long we can remain here for now."

Hector looked from him to the people around him and back. "Council meeting ten minutes ago!" he barked and with hooves clopping on metal he walked away down the hall.

Robin glanced at Little John then turned and followed Hector. As he did, he mouthed to her, "talk to the others. Vote leave or go" as he passed her.

Less than ten minutes later Robin once again sat with the leaders. As many debated on what to do next.

"...did," Roaran was saying from his position. "She may be old but she's still a testament to Dwarf engineering," and he looked at the men and women around him. "We all know Dwarfs not only build to last but to survive. So, I say we take the New Knights' offer of sanctuary," and he retook his seat.

"I agree," and Robin looked over at one of the human leaders. "For over a year my people were running and hiding through the stars until we found Tortuga. If we have to go on the run again, I'd be with the biggest and baddest ship out there."

"And with the biggest guns," another said in agreement.

"You've been awfully quiet, Ryuu," and Robin looked at Hector. "What are your thoughts? After all, you're the one who found them or they found you whichever it may be," Hector said, eyeing him.

Locking eyes with all. The last being the Elven leader and his cool steady gaze. Robin turned back to Hector.

"And maybe that's why I shouldn't cast a vote," he said, and they blinked at that. "We've all seen what the ship can do. And she's big enough to either house everyone or get us someplace safe. So, either way, whether we stay or go, it's up to the people on this base," and he pointed to the ground. "After this I plan to ask my people what they want to do. If they say go, we go, if stay we stay," and he sat back.

As silence rang after what he said the people in the room looked around at each other. "I agree," and everyone looked at the Elven leader who sat in his usual spot with the same calm demeanor. "This should be a decision for the people. Even when there was a King or Queen the people would still have a voice on issues like this."

For a moment Hector looked at each of the people around him. And standing he walked to the computer and pressed the button for the intercom.

"People of Tortuga!" he said, his voice booming over the intercoms. And Robin winced a little, rubbing his ear. "As you all know the Knights and the Sherwood have returned. And right now, we all have an important decision to make.

"The Knights have offered to either house us on the Sherwood. Or we can remain here, and they will protect us.

"So, the choice is all those who wish to leave on the Sherwood, pack your things and prepare to disembark. And be quick they may not be here that long until they leave," he announced.

Stand Together

AS ROBIN MOVED through the corridor nodding at a few people he knew as he passed them. Before he paused at a corner. His eyes meeting the Elven leader whose deep eyes were locked on him. For a couple seconds, the pair just looked at each other. The whole time Robin could see that despite nothing showing on the man's face. His mind was working with deep thoughts and Robin couldn't help but wonder what the man knew about him.

Then very slowly the man gave him a deep nod. Before he turned and walked away down the corridor.

Frowning after him Robin watched him go for a few seconds. Before he turned and walked down the corridor towards his quarters.

When he entered his mind was still on the look in the elf's eye. He paused when he saw his friends waiting for him in the room.

Blinking, he looked at them all. "Sit down, Robin," Willa said from her seat in one of the chairs which she had reversed with her arms resting on the back as she watched him.

Blinking at the seriousness in her tone he walked to the wall and pressed a button for a chair to come to and sat down. "What's going on?" he asked, looking at them all.

"We were just wondering something," Tuck said from beside his sister.

"What?" he asked, frowning as he continued to look at them all.

"When are you going to start trusting us again?" LJ said and Robin blinked at him as he leaned against a wall, arms crossed.

Stunned at that, he looked at them all. "What makes you think I don't trust you anymore?" he demanded, practically springing to his feet. "You were my first and only friends for years! You welcomed me before anyone else besides my parents!" and he looked at them all. "You all know I gladly trust you with my life!"

"Not from the way you've been acting lately," Much said from his seat on Robin's bed. "On Bazaar, Bedie, and recently, you just jump right in without consulting us or allowing us to be what we were on Amal," he said before sitting up. "A team."

"What makes you think we're still not a team?"

"Because of how you've been acting," Tuck said, and Robin looked at him.

"Robin," Little John said, stepping forward placing his hand on Robin's shoulder. "We know how much losing your father hit you," he started,

"If you know that," Robin said, interrupting him, "then you know how losing one of you, Adam, or Freya, or my mother would do to me," he said, voice hardening. "Don't you think I would do all that I can to make sure you all stay safe?"

"And what do you think it would do to us if we lost you? When we knew we could have saved you?" Willa demanded springing to her feet. "The Knights of old did what they did because they were a team. And right now, we pale in comparison because of your desire to protect us!

"When we could very well become better than they were and defeat the Black Dragon because we're more than a team! We're family!" she declared, and everyone nodded in agreement.

"She's right, Robin," Freya said, pushing off from the wall she'd been leaning against and took a step toward him. "We may have recently found each other again... but you're my brother and it would kill me to lose you!"

"Same here," Adam said, remaining against the wall.

Robin held her gaze before he lowered his in thought.

"Robin," and he looked back at Little John. "Everyone here feels the pain you still feel. We all lost someone we care about to the Black Dragon. And despite everything you can't face her alone," he said, and Robin held his gaze. "It would only get yourself killed... leaving us with nothing because we wouldn't have you."

Robin just looked at him before he turned, rubbing the back of his neck in thought.

"You're right," he finally said, turning to look at them. "We need to start being a team again..." and he looked at them all. "But I still can't bear the thought of losing any of you," he said.

"The thought is mutual," Willa said, stepping forward before placing her hand out, palm down.

For less than a second, they all looked at her. Before they moved forward and stacked their hands-on top of hers. Before Robin looked over at Adam and Freya and after a second, nodded them over.

They were still for seconds before stepping over and placing their hands-on top of his. "From now on," Robin said looking at all of them. "We do this together..." and they all nodded in agreement.

ABOUT THE AUTHOR

Andrew discovered that life outside of his head was strange and unpredictable, but in his imagination, he could be anyone he wanted to be. That discovery made the rural Sandwich, New Hampshire native actively seek out the good in life.

He has overcome many obstacles, but never let them strip him of his dreams to write stories readers will love and to try new things, no matter how difficult they were. His stories are his lifeline and his dearest friends.

If you want to learn more about Andrew and see where his imagination takes him.

Made in the USA
Middletown, DE
20 January 2026

26846338R00283